The Waterman

The

Waterman

A novel of the Chesapeake Bay

by **Tim Junkin**

Algonquin Books of Chapel Hill

1999

Published by
ALGONQUIN BOOKS OF CHAPEL HILL
Post Office Box 2225
Chapel Hill, North Carolina 27515-2225

a division of
Workman Publishing
708 Broadway
New York, New York 10003

This is a work of fiction. While, as in all fiction, the literary
perceptions and insights are based on experience, all names,
characters, places, and incidents are either products of the
author's imagination or are used fictitiously. No reference
to any real person is intended or should be inferred.

Library of Congress Cataloging-in-Publication Data
Junkin, Tim, 1951–
    The waterman : a novel of the Chesapeake Bay / by Tim Junkin.
        p.   cm.
    ISBN 1-56512-230-5
    I. Title.
    PS3560.U596W38   1999
    813'.54—dc21   99-23892
                                                          CIP

10 9 8 7 6 5 4 3 2 1
First Edition

In memory of my father,

George Junkin Jr.,

who brought us back,

and to Kristin

The Waterman

Remembrance

In his dream, ebbing from the darkness of sleep like a luminescent ribbon of tidal wash, a sleep born of the aching tiredness of dragging the river for his father's body, there is the mist above all. The mist and the quiet. They had stayed in a motel, he dreams. And then gotten up in the dark. And then driven the miles of country road in the quiet and in the dark to get to the mist.

He half wakes from the dream, and his conscious and unconscious seem to merge, and then he is remembering. That after the country roads there was a long dirt lane leading to what was once a grand house. He can see himself, as a boy, and his father, standing outside the car in the dark, feeling the looming silhouette of the house in the mist.

They removed their gear from the car, and he, the boy, followed his father down across a large lawn, into the trees, along a winding path, a long way, the boy thought, to the edge of the water. The boy carried with him his Browning twenty-gauge pump. It was clean and smelled of the gun oil and the polish he had used on the walnut stock.

He remembers the sound of their footsteps on the mud and grass and reeds. There was the lapping of the river and the occasional brush of swamp grass in the wind. But mostly there was the darkness and the mist and the quiet.

Following his father's direction, the boy found the rowboat and the stack of decoys, each wound in its own weight line. They filled the boat with the decoys, then pushed off, and as his father rowed out in front of the blind, the boy unwound the lines around the decoys and put them all in the water.

He was excited. He had been excited all night. And then he heard the whirring in the dark, in the distance first, then overhead. His father, in his oilskin coat, left open, and his heavy flannel shirt and Remington Arms camouflage cap, touched his shoulder. They heard the whistling pass again. Neither of them could see what made the sound. In the predawn mist they couldn't even see to the outside lay of their decoys. The father whispered, "Ducks . . . You hear their wings . . ."

The boy believed. Yet strain his eyes as he did, he could see nothing.

They were all around them that day. Often they heard them before they could see them—mallards, black ducks, canvasbacks, red-heads—behind them, over them, setting their wings, wheeling and tumbling over the decoys. And the Canada geese, larger, with their long necks out front, coming in wavering lines off the horizon. His father called to the birds. He was expert. He would call, and they would call back. The boy watched them turn, circle, whirl on the wind, and set, and when his father would say, ". . . Now," he'd stand up, aim, and shoot.

After the sun rose, it got noticeably colder. The wind picked up. His father divided the food his mother had packed for them—Maryland beaten biscuits, sausage and hard cheese, hot coffee mixed with milk in the thermos. And then his father excused himself, to pay his respects to the lady who lived in the house and had offered them the use of her land.

"You keep the goose call," he remembers being told. "We're near our limit on ducks, but I'd like to bring your mother home a Christ-

mas goose." The boy could tell his father didn't think he could hunt by himself.

He hadn't minded. He was happy to be alone in the blind on the river. He'd been pleased to be with his father too, but being alone there was different, special.

He studied and watched for a while, unmoving, until a small group of geese rose above the distant line of trees. He watched them and willed the birds toward him. They swung out wing on wing and gradually grew larger coming straight on. They honked to him and continued toward him, though high for a shot. His finger crept over the stock of the gun and felt the trigger and felt the safety he would need to release first. These geese came on and didn't flare off down the middle of the river as others had done all morning. These came, dipping, soaring, one fluid line, their long black necks visible, their silver chests almost overhead, filling his ears with their honking, and he rose and aimed, carefully down the sight and steadily as he had been taught, following and then leading his target, firing one time as they passed high overhead. One of the geese began to lose altitude.

It didn't drop as the ducks they had killed earlier that day had mostly dropped, but glided down at an angle, turning out into the river, crying and calling, and splashing as it hit. The boy could see it in the water, its neck and head held high above the moving river. It was wing shot and swimming toward the cove across the way.

He rushed to drag the rowboat out of the reeds and into the water, lay his shotgun in the bottom of the boat, and began to row with all his strength. His hands got wet and red and stung from the cold. The wind was sharper out on the open water and bit into his face and pushed him back. But he worked the oars, his own chest pounding. Each time he came within range and raised his gun, the bird would dive under the surface and reappear again just outside the distance the gun could shoot. He rowed harder. He placed the shotgun across his lap. The bird swam faster. He rowed and felt his arms ache and his back ache and his hands blistering. He saw the bird about to reach

3

the opposite shore. He was a good hundred yards away but rowed harder. He saw it reach the bar and run up on the beach. But there was a vertical embankment extending along and behind the beach, nearly ten feet high. As he came closer he could see the goose running up the beach looking for a way up the bank. It ran up the beach one way, crying out, honking, flapping its useless wing, and then it turned and ran the other way. And then the boy was there, not twenty yards from the beach, from the bird, watching it. The wounded bird had nowhere to go. Suddenly it turned toward the boy, the man remembers, and it spread its wide wings, baring its chest, and charged him, running and crying and trying to beat its broken wing on the one side as it beat its one good wing on the other. It came straight toward him as he raised his gun to his shoulder and shot it clean and without flinching.

When he picked the goose up, he felt its heaviness and warmth. The one wing was broken at the bone, and drops of blood and pieces of bone spattered the gray plumage. He sat there with his hands on it for what seemed like a long time. Then he put it in the boat and began the hard row back.

He remembers that he dragged the rowboat back onto the shore and covered it with the brush and then took the goose to the blind, wondering why his father was not back. His hands and face hurt from the cold and wet. He was shivering. He decided to walk to the house. He carried his Canada goose with him to show his father though it was heavy and got heavier on the long walk. He knocked on the back door, which swung open, so he walked in. He was in a kitchen, which was warm from a fire burning in a woodstove. He set the goose down and warmed his hands. He remembers the smell of cedar chips in a box near the stove. He called quietly for his father but heard nothing. So he took off his muddy boots and put them by the door. He walked into a hallway, with mirrors on the walls, that led to a living room, where he saw his father standing next to a couch, half dressed, with his undershirt in his hand. A woman was on the couch, trying to cover her nakedness with a blanket. The boy turned and ran out, with his father calling behind him.

Part One

Maryland

Light breaks where no sun shines;

Where no sea runs, the waters

of the heart

Push in their tides;

And, broken ghosts with glow-worms

in their heads,

The things of light

File through the flesh where no flesh

decks the bones.

—DYLAN THOMAS

I

When spring comes to the wide delta between the Atlantic Ocean and the Chesapeake Bay, the ice breaks off the rivers; the colors of the sky and water run sharp, chromatic, clear like crystal. The fields are brown and softer, patched with the melting, mottled snow. Young green shoots of winter wheat begin to fill some of the squares of tattered earth. Yet the flat terrain remains unbroken, the vistas absolute. From almost any vantage, specks of silver, miles away, reflect the sun beyond the fields, through the distant lines of trees, the incandescent bends in the river.

In that landscape, immersed in the rhythms of the tides, the young man, Clay Wakeman, having come back from college, spent day following day helping drag the river for his lost father. Days of solemnity and loss flashed with unexpected beauty. His senses heightened by his grief and regret, Clay's memories flooded, pressing his imagination toward revelation, toward a new purpose. It seemed it had been another life since he had spent successive days running the Bay—knowing the drift and flow beneath him, the reflecting surfaces of the coves and swashes, the firing of the light off the marsh, the pounding diesel of the workboat. These incantations of the Chesapeake renewed a reverence he had misplaced and thought he might have lost. Brought back home to recover some remnant of his father, he let go of a false resistance that had hovered inside him since the day his father had left him years before. In letting go, he knew it was time to be back on the water. With quiet certainty he strained over empty torn nets, until his stepmother, Bertha, called off the search and set the time for the memorial service at the old Pentecostal, in the town of St. Michaels.

Like the long days on the water before it, the funeral seemed dreamlike to Clay. He sat in the first pew until all the mourners had left, before finding the door at the back that led to the cemetery. Outside, he stood on the worn stone steps, looking into the morning light. The wind was damp, faintly brackish. He walked down and away from the small white clapboard building, out among the grave markers. The earth under his feet was soft. A stark line of trees, bone bare, bordered the site to the north. Easterly, flat open fields of green wheat ran down to the horizon. Under the March-gray ceiling, a red-tailed hawk banked off the breeze. But there was no view from the cemetery of the water that was the true resting place of his drowned father.

The granite headstone Bertha had chosen was inscribed GEORGE WAKEMAN 1924–1972 and was there to urge upon both of them a sense of finality. He ran his foot over the spaded earth at the stone's base and then bent over and gathered some of the dark soil in his hand, rubbing it between his fingers and into his palm, and stood there for a while longer. The wind came colder and caused him to shiver. He turned and walked back to the church.

Inside, the plank floors creaked under him. He could see Reverend Burns gathering the flower arrangements near the altar. His stepmother had invited everyone to come back to the house, and he had promised to be along shortly. He walked up the aisle. The single stained glass window set over the altar cast a shimmering prism of light over the pulpit. It depicted a young woman, Mary, holding her lifeless son in her arms. She seemed very beautiful, and she and Jesus looked to be the same age, as though they could have been lovers.

Reverend Burns heard him approach and turned. The two of them stood in the silence for a moment.

"Do you need any help with anything?" Clay finally asked.

"No, son. I'm fine, thanks."

"I appreciate the service."

"Of course."

"You going back to Oxford, Reverend? To Bertha's?"

"Yes."

"Well, I'll go on."

"Tell her I'll be along soon, if you don't mind."

"Sure." He stuck out his hand.

Reverend Burns looked at it, and then he took it to shake.

Clay turned and crossed in front of the altar and pushed against the metal bar to the side door of the chapel. He walked down the steps to the gravel parking area, where three people leaned against a pickup truck, talking quietly. Byron, his crew cut finally growing out, saw him first and stood erect as though coming to attention. Matty, next to him, wore a flannel suit, with three points of a white handkerchief showing at the breast pocket. He had a camera case strapped over his shoulder. Kate smoothed her dark pleated skirt. Her copper hair was tucked loosely under an embroidered linen scarf. She moved to him, took his hands, and pulled him toward her.

"I'm so sorry," she whispered, holding him tightly.

Matty put his hand on Clay's shoulder. Byron, standing somewhat stiffly still, reached out and squeezed his arm.

"You doing okay?" Byron asked.

Clay looked at him and nodded his head. Then he looked at Kate and Matty.

"It's good to see you."

"Likewise," Matty answered.

There was an awkward silence. "We should have come earlier. To help," Kate said. "We miss you. Everyone from school does. They all said to say hello. And how sorry . . ." She let her voice fall.

"You drive over from school this morning?"

Matty answered yes. "It wasn't bad at all, really," he continued. "Kate drove us over the Bay Bridge so I could shoot out the window. There was a huge tanker coming under."

"Nice threads," Clay said, trying to force a smile, nodding at Matty's suit. "You didn't trade in your Bolger blues, I hope," referring to a torn pair of jeans Matty had worn daily their second year of college and named for the Georgetown professor who had complained about them.

Matty ran his hand down the lapel. "Decided to go upscale. I needed a few suits for interviews. For summer internship."

Kate shrugged. "That one pair of jeans I finally threw out. When he wasn't looking."

Clay thought of the nights they would stay up at the town house they had shared, before he'd had to transfer away. How his mind and sense of the world had begun to open and how Matty first, and then Kate, had become his tutor after becoming his friend, had brought him to books and music in a way he had never before experienced. He thought how he missed all that, and then he focused past them, through the trees, and saw the traffic moving along the highway. He looked down and kicked at several stones with the tips of his shoes and noticed the dust rise up.

"We just wanted to come," Kate said. "I wish I could have come sooner." She reached for his hand again and held it.

"You will stay over?" Clay asked.

"We have to leave early, though," Matty explained. "It's spring break. We're taking a cruise." He put his hands in his pockets. "You're off too, aren't you?"

Clay considered. "I suppose," he then answered quietly. "I've already missed two weeks of school. Now class is out for Easter break. I may get used to this."

"We're catching a 7:30 flight to Miami," Matty continued. "Out of Baltimore. We're packed to the gills." He motioned toward his MG sports car, parked down the way, suitcases bulging out of the trunk.

Kate seemed embarrassed. "It's been planned for a long time," she offered, still holding his hand. She hesitated. "We saw some motels on the highway . . ."

Byron interrupted. "There's plenty of room at the farmhouse. Where I sleep and Clay's been stayin.'"

"Of course you'll stay with us," Clay finished. "We'll fix up a bed for you there."

He raised the back of his hand, the one she was holding, and passed it lightly against her cheek, then let her hand go. Looking up, he saw the red-tailed hawk just overhead and believed he felt the rush of air from its wings like a breath across his face. He looked at Byron, who had hardly stirred, but whose eyes also followed the hawk's flight. Despite his own demons, Byron had been with him there through the days of dragging the coves and the river. He wished for words to tell all three of them how he appreciated them, but he only shook his head. Kate started talking again and made it easier. Eventually he urged them to start back to his father's house, Bertha's now, in Oxford, while Kate announced that she wanted to ride with him in his rusty '66 Chevy wagon and climbed in. Clay shrugged at Matty, who just nodded and indicated that he would follow them.

Driving down Oxford Road, Kate had moved over next to Clay and taken his arm with her two hands and had leaned her head against his shoulder. Her scarf had fallen back and her hair was soft against his neck and he could smell her perfume. It was as if they had never been apart, this friend, who had always treated him like more, even from the first. It was as if she had recognized something in him and loved him for it in a different way from how she loved Matty. It was in a way just as real, yet constrained, of course, by custom and propriety. She began talking quietly as they drove. She told him how brave she thought he was, and then about how their house in Georgetown seemed so empty without him.

They crossed the bridge over Peachblossom Creek, and Clay pointed out Le Gates Cove and described how in winter everyone would gather there at night to ice-skate, and how the bonfire they would build with the old tires taken from Scully's Junkyard would light the shore and sometimes burn for days. His father had taught him to skate there, he told her, before his father had left.

Kate sat up, still close against him.

"I'm so glad I'm finally seeing all this," she said. "I knew it would be beautiful. From the way you've always described it."

When they crossed over Trippe Creek, he had her look out into the wider Tred Avon River and told the story of how, his last year of high school, before his mother died, the river had frozen solid, and the Downs boys had bet they could drive their car, "an old '59 red Stude," from the ferry dock across to Bellevue, and how they took her across and back, and the boys who had bet against her had run out on the ice and were climbing all over her on the way back, trying to make her heavier, with Billy Downs trying to shake them off, doing fishtails on the ice, and then Sheriff Clark came out after them, only on foot, because he wouldn't take his patrol car out on that ice, so Downs just turned upriver, and with the sheriff slipping and falling all over himself trying to give chase, he drove clear up to Easton.

Kate said she could picture it, and laughed as she spoke.

At Bertha's, the house was full of people. The dining room table overflowed with turkey and roast beef, ham, pastry dishes and desserts. Byron and Matty attached themselves to the adjoining bar. Both men were tall, over six feet, though Byron was broader in the shoulders and had a rougher face. Planted there, the two of them might have, in a different setting, been taken for bouncers.

Clay accepted the condolences from everyone as gracefully as he could but was uncomfortable with the mourners and the anecdotes about Pappy. Kate must have sensed this after a while because she asked if they could go back to the farmhouse. Clay spoke to Bertha, who understood but asked Clay if he would visit her soon for lunch. He agreed. Over Clay's objections, Bertha packed them up ham and turkey, oyster stew, and bottles of beer and whiskey.

They drove down Oxford Road, took the bypass toward Trappe, and turned off to Hogs Neck Landing, where Byron had been living since his discharge from the hospital and the navy. It was a white aluminum-sided two-story farmhouse that sat about a half mile down a dirt lane, surrounded by fields of soybeans and feed corn. The lane ran fifty yards past, ending at the headwaters of La Trappe Creek. Two brothers, Junior and Curtis Collison, owned the house and occupied the upstairs bedrooms. Junior was in the merchant marine and was gone much of the time. Curtis was a plumber by trade but mostly shot pool, played cards, collected the rent, and drew his unemployment. Byron lived in the attic, which had a potbellied stove in the corner and a narrow back stairwell to the first floor. There was also a small fourth bedroom off the kitchen, with a double bed, where Clay had been staying, and he directed Matty and Kate to put their things in there as he helped them unpack the car.

Kate changed into blue jeans and a T-shirt and came into the kitchen, where Clay had lit the stove, tucking her shirt deep into her jeans, and let her hair down while he watched. It fell in a wave of auburn along her white neck and rested on her shoulders as she threw it back, her eyes fastened on his, compassionate, uncompromising. He pulled his attention away from her to put the oyster stew on to warm and put the ham and turkey slices in the oven to heat. Byron had Patsy Cline playing on the phonograph. They gathered around the warped pine-top table in the center of the kitchen, feeling the heat from the stove. The breeze outside had picked up and was whispering through the siding into the walls. Byron opened more beers for everyone. He lit a cigarette, taking a long pull, then poured out shots of whiskey. He and Matty had been trying to match each other at Bertha's, and they were arguing over who was next to drink. The conversation turned toward the memorial service, which they all approved in turn.

After a while Matty started talking about the photographic exhibit he was working on—all sunsets. He described it in detail, then went to his car and brought in a portfolio of his pictures. He also brought in an Ansel Adams book, a collection of sweeping photographs of the West, and started comparing artistic styles. He went on until Kate took the Ansel Adams book from him gently and closed it, assuring him that his pictures, by themselves, were more interesting. He had some promising prospects for summer work, he told Clay. He'd been asked to submit some photographs to the Virginia Historical Society in Richmond, which had a quarterly magazine, and his father knew someone at Colonial Williamsburg who was going to interview him for a project they were doing on plantation restoration. As he spoke, Kate walked over to the stereo on the sideboard against the wall, where Patsy Cline had just clicked off. She put on George Harrison singing "My Sweet Lord" and began to sway with the music.

Byron seemed to hesitate over a question he had. He went on, though, and asked Clay if he'd learned whether anything was left from his father's bankruptcy.

Clay drew a breath, leaning back. "I finally spoke to Bertha about it this morning," he slowly answered. "I've got the bateau. Pappy apparently put it in my name some time ago." He turned his palms up. "Everything else's being sold to pay the debts. The wharf was mortgaged. The dredgers. Everything. Except the house. House is Bertha's. And some life insurance for her too."

Kate came over and put her hands on his shoulders.

Exhaling on his cigarette, Byron turned his face up toward the hanging ceiling lamp and into the glare and heat above. Then he turned back. "Why don't you ask Bertha to put up some of the money she's gettin'?" He spoke softly. "To help you through."

Clay shrugged. "Not her problem. And she needs the security."

Byron raised his shot glass and studied the amber liquid against the light, then drank it down. He waited, then looked at Matty for him to follow, but Matty put up his hand.

"In a minute," Matty said.

"Ask me, you're gettin' the piker's end there," Byron went on, speaking to Clay.

"No." Clay drank his shot of whiskey down and pushed his glass over toward Byron for another. "No. I don't see it that way." He gestured for him to pour. "Hell, I've got the workboat. That's something. For sure that's something."

Clay knew Byron wanted to ask him the question that was really on his mind. The question about what he had seen in Clay's face and eyes while out there together on the river, searching for Pappy. And now with the boat his. But as they watched each other, Byron recognized that Clay foresaw the question, and with that came an unspoken understanding. Clay would talk about it soon enough. Reaching for the bottle, Byron poured out more shots. He turned from Clay and leaned over and spoke to Matty, nodding at the whiskey in his glass. "Gonna leave you behind there, pal."

Matty winced.

"I'll try one. What the hell," Kate said.

Everyone looked at her, surprised. "Hold on," Matty muttered. He raised his shot glass and finished it. "Okay, pour out four. We'll see."

"Well, let's all raise a glass," Kate then said.

Matty now seemed amused. He poked Clay to watch.

"To the sons of sailors and seamen," she offered.

"To quellin' the parched thirst," Byron added.

"And to Pappy," Clay said, which they all echoed. Clay drank his whiskey and watched as Kate tasted hers with a grimace.

"Go on," Matty scolded, lifting his to his mouth.

She looked up, determined. Squinting, she gulped it down. Clay handed her a beer and told her to wash it through, which she did without complaint.

"Impressed," Matty said. "A new page in your book. Another?" He teased.

She was unrepentant, though her face was flushed. "I'll sip another," she whispered to Byron, though her eyes were on Clay's as she spoke.

The gurgling of the oyster stew caused Clay to turn and then rise from the table. He began to fix everyone a bowl. Kate, after him to sit down, got up and began to lay out the turkey and ham slices and biscuits. Byron opened a fresh round of beers.

After they ate, washing down their food with the beer, Kate tried carefully to ask about how the process worked, looking for a man lost overboard in the Bay. "It was actually in the Choptank River," Byron corrected her. As he began trying to explain more, Matty made the comment that he wished he could have photographed that operation. Clay got up, excusing himself, and started on the dishes.

Matty, noticing, pushed his chair away from the table and changed the subject. He began reciting for Clay and then imitated some student election speeches at school, trying to get Clay to laugh. Matty carried a southern gentility in his voice, which softened and helped mitigate the intensity stamped in his eyes. By now, though, his words had begun to run together. In a loud voice he announced that he wanted to walk down to the creek. He had to go to the car first and retrieve his equipment. He wanted to set up his tripod for a perfect sunset shot.

"It's only four-thirty, Matty," Kate chided. "Sunset's not for another hour or so."

"I need to find the right spot. The light, the sky. And setup takes time. To get it right. You want to come?"

"I'm warm and comfortable right here, thank you."

"I'll go," Byron offered. "Fresh air'll feel good." He picked up the bourbon bottle. "This'll keep us warm. Help that 'get it right' business."

"You two go," Kate said. "We'll be along in a while. Closer to sunset."

As they left, Kate started drying the dishes. She and Clay worked together, hearing the wind against the eaves. She tried to get him talking, but he had grown silent. She went to the sideboard after a while and started the other side of the Patsy Cline record. "I Fall to Pieces" was the first song. She came over and took his dish towel from him and dried his hands, and then she dropped the towel on the floor and put his hands around her waist and pressed herself against him, laying her forehead against his neck, and started swaying in his arms to the song. He felt the heat from her body, her breasts soft against him through her thin cotton shirt, and her lips brushing his neck.

"Kate," he whispered into her ear.

She put her finger up to his lips to quiet him. "I just want to help. If I can. Like this," she said. "Just hold me now and allow me to hold you for a time. Let's let it be some comfort. To each of us. Enough."

He thought he understood. With his mind. With his sense of the order of things. And so he danced with her there, alone, and held her as the dusk descended, and he accepted this just as she offered it, as some comfort, as enough. But none of this thinking, nor the numbing rush of the alcohol, nor other knowledge he possessed, could diminish what it was she made him feel and had always caused him to feel, more poignant for the separation, for a heart already rent and open from grief, holding her there, that lightning flash in his blood, Kate clinging equally to him, each with the other, song after song, as the shadows drew upon them. Walking with her toward the water, toward Matty and Byron, the horizon a darkening bruise of purple, his mind whirled in intoxications of confusion, of grief and loss, of new purpose, of longing and regret.

2

He slept fitfully that night on the back room couch, his dreams haunted by successive images: of Pappy, of his mother Sarah, of Kate, all merging in incongruous circumstances. Rising early, he helped his two friends repack their car to leave for the airport. Kate got out of the MG and came back to hug him one last time. Standing on the porch landing, he watched them drive down the dusty lane.

In the kitchen he fixed a pot of coffee and he poured himself a cup and sat at the table. He got up and took a plate of leftover ham out of the refrigerator. There were cold biscuits on the stove, and he made himself a ham biscuit to eat with his coffee. The house was still, but he could hear the murmur of the breeze as it came up off the Bay. After he had eaten, he stuffed a few more biscuits with ham and wrapped them in tinfoil and filled a thermos with the coffee. He put on his father's old oilskin coat, which he had been using, and put the biscuits in one of the pockets. The heater in his car didn't work, so he had to keep the window down to defrost the windshield as he drove past Easton to St. Michaels Road, over the Oak Creek Bridge to Pecks Point.

He found his father's workboat riding high in her slip. The key to the ignition was where his father had always kept it, under the rear port floorboard on a small hook. He had to turn it over a bit, with full choke, but within minutes he had her started and had cast off the lines and was heading down the Tred Avon toward the mouth of the Choptank, which opened to the Bay.

He ran the north shore of the river that he knew and had always known, through the mouth of Plaindealing Creek and past the ferry dock at Bellevue, around Cooper's Shoal, past Bachelor Point to the south and the Benoni Point lighthouse and into the wider Choptank, where you could see out into the Bay, the horizon an undulation of whitecaps. It was along the north shore of the Choptank, off the mouth of Broad Creek, that his father's dredger had been discovered, foundering in a drift on the neap tide, well after a storm, her skipper washed away. He traversed the drift line once again, scouring the steel-like surface of the shoreline, and then went on.

The wind out of the northwest had strengthened and was throwing spray over the bow. He stood in the open cockpit and could taste the salt, and after a time he rode the waves by instinct, knowing where he was. He followed the Choptank's north shore across the mouth of Irish Creek and pushed south to clear Tilghman Island's southernmost tip, Blackwalnut Point, feeling his aloneness on this great watery plain, which was his and belonged to him as he belonged to it. It had always been so, from his earliest memory, since he had first recognized it as a boy, taken by and surrendering to the miracle of such water and its unfathomable mystery. Blue and deep beyond imagining, it filled him with a familiar wonder, as he knew it must have filled those who had come before, who had suffered the blow and the churning, the whipping white and darkening browns, the ghosts of the watermen before him, the sailors and sea captains, knowing the calm as well, and the feasts of crab. And before them and after them—the single Susquehanna returning in his canoe, hugging the shore to avoid the tidal wash, his nets laden with shad and mano, and innocent of any knowledge of the end of his world that was to come. Clay drove the sharp bow of the workboat into the swells and thought of those of his father's generation who had known the Chesapeake pure and pristine, and of those who had known it first, known it perfect when it had no taint to its beauty nor limit to its abundance.

He rode the waves out into the Bay with no sense of time, immersing himself in the solitude. A squall blew by to the south, and after it passed, fields of mist lay over the water. Blanketed in the fog but still knowing where he was, he turned northeast and ran the tide up along the veiled shore. Just off the southern tip of Poplar Island the breeze freshened and the fog banks cleared, swirling away. The swells burst sharp against the bow. Flocks of black cormorants, startled at his approach, careened off the waves, and long-necked mergansers pitched over the shoreline against the moving sky. Far out in the shipping lane a single tug pushed a weighted barge northward toward Baltimore. He had long since eaten his biscuits and finished his thermos, and as he angled the boat—which his father had affectionately called the bateau— toward the shallow half-moon landing cut by the winds and tides along the northeast edge of the abandoned Poplar Island, what remained was the taste of the brine that had dried and caked against his face.

The tide was running and near high, and he figured he could get close to shore before grounding the bateau. He had prepared a forward and stern anchor and had sufficient stern line to play out. He checked the depth with the anchor. When he hit four feet, he gunned the engine to increase his forward momentum, then cut the propeller. He dropped the stern anchor and let the line play out as he coasted toward the black bank. With the engine off, he could hear the egrets and wrens crying from the trees. Scraping sand, he dropped the bow anchor and tied the boat secure.

He pulled the waders out of the cockpit and put them on. He dropped over the side and waded ashore to the island, thick with loblolly pine, vines, and undergrowth.

His father had built a cabin on Poplar Island, and two duck blinds along its northeast shore. Pappy had hunted the island for years and used the cabin as a sanctuary. He had brought Clay along many times to share its perfect isolation with him. That was years before. But Clay remembered the promises his father had made to him, and, of course, the buried ammunition box. He knew that it would be there for him if the time ever came.

He climbed the sandbank, which crumbled under his weight, and stepped into the soggy undergrowth. He walked between the knobby pines, avoiding the thick clumps of leafless thorn, and after fifty yards or so saw the ruined shack ahead. It was a crude, one-room shelter, built of logs cut on the island with a hand ax, with a stone hearth and short chimney on the north end layered with cinder block. The logs were joined with pitch. Gaps in the roof spilled the late afternoon light. The door was gone. The spoor of racoon and fox lay on the floor.

The cabin seemed smaller than it had been in his mind. And then he measured twelve steps from its front door due south toward the Dorchester marsh, and then six steps near due west toward the sun. Breaking a thick branch off one of the pines, he began to dig into the damp ground. He dug about a foot deep and began to widen the circle. After a while he struck something hard. He dug around it and knocked away the soil. It was the old steel box, sealed with a frozen combination padlock. Working it out of the earth, he set it aside and filled the hole with loose dirt and leaves. He then carried the box back to the beach and out into the river, hoisting it over the side of the boat. Once on board, he stashed the box in the cabin and got under way. The current ran swift in the cut between the island and the Eastern Shore.

It was late afternoon when he pulled into his shortcut home, the channel at Knapps Narrows that separated Tilghman from the broader delta above. He tied up at Morrison's, went inside, and sat at the bar to order fried clams and beer. Afterward the waitress refilled his thermos with hot coffee. He went to pay his bill. Behind the register stood Buddy Morrison, the proprietor.

"You're George Wakeman's son, Clay."

"Yessir."

"Sorry about his disappearance, son. He was good company."

Clay thanked him and waited for his change.

"Hard on the family. For a good waterman to lose himself awash like that. And then not be found."

"Yessir."

Morrison counted out the bills. "She takes some slow and some sudden, but she takes all who give themselves over, don't she?"

Clay nodded and accepted the money.

"He may wash up soon. Most do. But I am sorry, son. Truly am."

Outside, the air had stilled and the sky was clear. Clay breathed in deeply. Angling southeast, the bateau pierced the mirrored surface. Off the mouth of Broad Creek, he cut the motor and coasted into the current. He used the crowbar from the engine locker on the metal box. The lock held, but he was able to pry open the steel top, bending it back. Inside lay his father's Navy Cross, wrapped in stained brown paper. There was a photograph also, of his father and him, and his mother, Sarah. Pappy was seated on a chair and Sarah was kneeling next to him, her arm around their young son. He turned it over. There was no inscription. In a brittle envelope there was money—five hundred dollars—and folded up behind the bills, the chart his father had made and showed him, years before. Pappy had marked the chart where he had found the wreck while tonging for oysters, where he'd pulled up the antique battle-ax. Clay remembered the books Pappy brought home from the library in Washington, convinced they proved the wreck was a Spanish frigate. Pappy had written its name and the date it was lost on the chart. "The *Buena Ventura,* 1688." The ax had disappeared en route to New York for study by the Peabody Institute, an offense that Pappy had often recounted and never forgave. Still, Pappy had kept the chart, and when the mood struck him he would spread it across the dining room table, swearing to find and salvage the sunken ship. But the Bay had not provided for that.

Clay folded the chart back up, returned all of the contents to the box, and stored it above the cabin berth. It wasn't the chart he'd been after. That had been Pappy's pipe dream, or one of them, though it was a pleasant enough fancy. Rather than the chart, rather than the money, he had hoped for a letter. From his father to him. Or even a note.

3

"I'm thinking about going on the river," Clay said. He sat holding his beer, looking back at his friend.

Byron shook his head. "I was worried you were leanin' that way." His tone was unsympathetic.

"Refurbish the bateau. Now that she's mine. She's solid enough. Good for potting. If the summer works, then I might try to oyster this winter. Maybe even take out some fishing parties."

It was Tuesday. Clay's father had kept a spare set of oyster tongs in the garage in Oxford, and Clay and Byron had taken them out and tied them to Byron's pickup and driven down to the workboat. Off Cook Point there was a bar Clay had fished with his father, and he and Byron had ridden out to it on flat water. The late afternoon sky was clear, and way south they could see the twin white rotundas of the Calvert Cliffs nuclear plant on the far shore of the Bay. Anchoring in about twelve feet of water, Byron had worked the tongs for a while. The rakes brought up dozens of mud-caked oysters. Then Clay had taken a turn. Standing on the rail, he worked the long wooden stiltlike tongs down to the river bottom. The muscles in his shoulders and arms had gotten soft at college and then sore over the days of dragging, and he had felt them strain as he worked the rakes through the mud of the oyster bed. He filled the rest of the bushel, though. Using a canvas bucket on a line, they had washed the oysters down and then cleaned the rakes. A range of purple cloud stretched across the western sky.

"I thought you had brains, man," Byron said. Byron had brought his navy corpsman's knife, clipped to his belt. He pulled it out and flipped open an oyster, severing the muscle that attached it to the shell, and offered it to Clay. It sat fat and floating on its juices. Clay took it and tasted it with the tip of his tongue. Then he sucked the oyster down.

Byron waited.

"Fresh enough."

"Salty?"

"Not bad."

Byron opened one for himself. "Good for the pecker," he mumbled, drinking it down. "Could use some horseradish."

"I think I can make it work," Clay continued. "With a good season I could build a second boat. I'd like to start on that. Eventually maybe I could try to buy back the wholesale operation."

"Big thinkin'."

"It's been done before. Look at Pappy. It's called horizontal monopoly. I've studied it."

"Times change. The life's gotten harder. Just go down to Tilghman and listen to the oystermen for a while. Better yet, just look at 'em."

"I've seen them. Plenty."

Byron gestured with his arms, opening them wide toward the open water. "Bay ain't what she used to be."

"The Bay needs managing. Needs people on her who understand that."

"May not be enough left to manage. Or time left."

After a while Byron wiped the blade of his knife across his pants leg. He turned it, watching it flash the fading light, then sheathed it. It was one of the few things he had brought back from Vietnam. "Bones of the deep," Byron muttered. "To all the bones in hell . . ." Raising his beer, he crumpled the empty can in his fist and threw it into the oyster bushel. "Could use some good dope right now."

Clay sat on the rail, quiet, sensing the turn in Byron's mood. "You think about it too much, don't you?" Clay said after a while.

Byron hesitated. He wiped his forehead with his sleeve. "Nope. Not at all. I don't think about it at all." He paused. It was not something he had been able or willing to speak about. "It's just there, though," he continued, "like something stuck in my gut. Attached. But I try not to notice it. In fact, I think mostly about trying to think about other things."

Both of them listened for a moment to the silence. The sun started to dip below the horizon, and spires of violet fire radiated up into the round of darkening space. The bateau, motionless on the still water, seemed suspended in a perfect element, suspended in silent time.

Byron opened another oyster for Clay, then one for himself. "I think about that afternoon, for instance, when you and me went fishing. When we were kids. That time in that rickety goddamn rowboat." He paused and reached into his jacket for his cigarettes. "And we hit into them stripers off Castle Haven."

Clay leaned back against the cabin and stretched his legs down the rail. He watched the water, still as death.

"Caught a boatful. Before that diddly engine quit. They bit off all our tackle and you wouldn't stop. Remember? You tore up your shirt and put a piece on the hook and caught that one."

Byron flicked a white-tipped wooden match against the gunnel and it flared. He lit a cigarette, taking a long, deep drag, and exhaled slowly. "The sunset over the churning water turned it all red, and I thought it was blood everywhere and got scared."

"Well, we weren't more than ten."

"God. Remember how we got blowed out in the channel and then couldn't make any headway and then dark coming on and with no lights?"

He leaned and spat a piece of tobacco over the side. "And how we saw this figure comin' at us, above the mist, like Jesus on the water, from out of the dusk? I was glad to see your pappy and then this here boat under him, I'll say that. And then I thought he was gonna kill us. But he surprised me."

"He was full of those."

"What's that?"

"Surprises."

Byron dragged on his cigarette. "You were hotter than he was."

"I lost track of my way. On the water."

"Well, what'd you just say? We weren't more'n ten."

Clay smiled. "Still."

"How about that time before? Might've been that same spring. When Pappy first let you take the rowboat. And we went chicken-neckin' in the creek." Byron chuckled to himself. "Remember? Neither of us had shoes on, and one small bushel basket, overflowin'. Crabs everywhere. The whole bottom of the boat full of 'em tryin' to pinch us. So we jumped over and swam to shore and had to go lookin' for some shoes." Byron pulled on his smoke. "He saw the boat out there floatin' and thought we'd both drowned. Shit."

Clay studied his friend, there doing as he had over the past two weeks or so, trying to make him feel better about Pappy. He reached his elbows back to stretch his shoulders. From high overhead came a clamor, and he looked up and watched the contours of two migrating flocks of Canada geese converge, blending into a single focus northward.

Byron changed subjects. "That Matty is a piece of work, ain't he?"

Clay didn't respond.

"Some guys are just born with it, I guess." He shook his head.

"What's that?"

"You know. Looks. Money. Chicks."

"Think so, huh?"

"Yeah."

Clay sniffed at a stir of breeze and watched a cat's-paw scuttle across the coppery surface. "There's a price everyone pays for what they have."

"You suppose?"

"Matty's got a generous side. The way he took me in right off. He and Kate. I told you. But he's kind of adrift, a little bit. Got no need to be otherwise, maybe."

"What's his family got? Like a city block they own in Richmond?"

"Something like that."

"Where did he go to high school again?"

"Near Charlottesville. Woodbury-Forest. He boarded from like tenth grade. Didn't like it, though."

Another pocket of rolling breeze lazily rippled the water, quiet like the rustling of a skirt. Both young men paused to listen and feel the imperceptible motion of the boat.

"That Kate's a looker," Byron continued.

"Yeah."

"She's got her eye on you."

Clay shrugged. "It's a friendship."

"Uh-huh."

"She's just like that."

"With you, maybe."

"You shouldn't be commenting on what you don't know."

"I know what I see."

"She was just trying to offer some comfort. In her way. Just like you do in yours." Clay watched Byron shift his position. "She's with Matty. Our feelings for each other are different. Anyway, you know how I feel about that."

"Well, I'm sure you're gettin' your mind off her, then."

"Right."

"You need to find some new dolly bird anyway."

"You think I wouldn't like to?"

"What?"

"Find one."

Byron grinned. "Yeah. Tell me about it." He held up the ash of his cigarette, burning down. "Why is it that all we think about is women."

Clay grunted his assent.

"Makes me kinda mad."

"No sense being mad at them. They're as lost as us."

"I've seen Laura-Dez a few times," Byron offered. "Saw her last weekend."

It always struck Clay funny how Byron pronounced his girl-friend's name, which was Lourdes. Her father was a dentist who had emigrated from Cuba. But Byron had called her Laura-Dez from their first date in high school, and she had somehow taken to it.

"She still sweet as ever?"

"She had some great pot. Took me to the drive-in in her VW van. We watched the *Culpepper Cattle Company*. We laid in the back. She let me strip her right there." He paused. "Her skin is the smoothest. Pure. But she won't come near my scar. Won't touch it even. She's scared of me now. Something. Distant."

"Doesn't sound too distant."

"We can't talk. Like there's nothin' to say."

"She'll come around. She probably needs you to talk."

Byron paused. "Well, talk is cheap."

"Not all talk."

"Maybe not all talk."

Another flush of breeze rippled the surface of the river. It carried off the last orange flecks of ash from Byron's cigarette just as he flicked its stub into the water, and they both watched it sizzle and die in an instant.

"You know, you might as well finish school anyway. You've got this far."

Clay folded his arms. "I've been hearing that advice enough. Like an echo."

"Don't sound from your tone like you got sense enough to follow it." Byron grabbed two more beers from the cooler. He threw one to Clay.

"Probably not."

"I was watchin' you out there. Searchin' the creeks. I saw your face. I saw it comin'."

Tapping the aluminum top with his finger, Clay opened his beer and took a drink. "I don't particularly like where I'm heading now," he said. "I don't want to go to the city. I don't want to sell stocks. Or insurance."

"Bay's hurt. Gettin' sicker. You know those fellas in the statehouse don't give a good goddamn."

Clay sat fingering his Adam's apple. "Well, least it's honest work."

"That's why it don't pay. Don't they teach you nothin' in college?"

"Anyway, I've mostly made up my mind."

"Mostly, huh?"

"Yeah." Clay turned back to the water and studied the jagged moon hovering just under the surface. "Yeah, mostly." Then, turning, he added, "You know, you could use a job yourself."

Byron seemed to ponder this for a while. "I hear Mac Longley just bought hisself a new Grady White. Like a two hundred on the back. Cuddy cabin."

"She's a waxing gibbous moon," Clay said, transfixed by the water.

Byron gulped down the rest of his beer. "Right nice. Really. I mean the Grady White." He waited and then went on. "Heard he's also buyin' one of the cottages down Town Creek."

Clay pulled his gaze up from the river. "Yeah? Well, crabbing must be good." He nodded distractedly.

"It ain't crabs, Clayton. He ain't waterin' serious at all anymore."

"No?" Clay blinked, and his eyes seemed to focus. "Then what?"

"He was clammin' mostly and crabbin' some. Got beat bad, what with that clam moratorium two years back. They shut 'em down. Remember? The bacteria. All the nitrogen from the farm runoff. So they say. And overfishin'. Then after, they cut the boat limit back from sixty to fifteen bushels. Bank nearly took him down, heard tell. Hurt Pappy too, I'm sure. Anyway, word is he's runnin' dope. Part of some network, I heard. Smooth operation. People can't get enough."

Clay was silent. He waited for Byron to continue.

"Started with his Bay-built. At first. Expandin' now, I suppose." Byron grinned. "New opportunities for the enterprisin' water-man."

Rising up, Clay frowned.

"Money's good, I hear. Real good." Byron paused. "Gettin' rich gettin' folks high. Not bad."

Each quietly eyed the other.

"It's a thought," Byron said absently.

"Not for you." Clay spoke in almost a whisper. He coughed, like something was caught in his throat.

"Just a thought, man."

"A bad one. It's a wrong turn. I know that. You know it too." Clay took a long breath. "Wrong for you. That's for sure."

Byron looked away. "Figured you'd probably say that." He tried to change tacks. "It's just marijuana anyway. Ain't no harm in it. Hell, I like it. You do too."

"Byron."

"Well, is there?"

34

"What?"

"Harm in it?"

"Smoking a joint and selling dope is different."

"How's that? You're on weak ground there, pal."

Clay pursed his brow. "I sure can't recall one drug dealer I care for. Or ever have. Mac Longley included."

"So?"

"It's not a right direction. That's all. It's trouble."

"Life is trouble."

Clay watched, uncertain of what to say, as his friend opened another beer and took a long drink.

"Forget it." Byron waved him off. "I'm just kickin' it around. Tryin' to sort shit out." He drank again. "Really. That's him. I ain't sure it's me."

"No. It's not you."

"Yeah. Well, when you aimin' to start on your foolishness?"

Clay looked out, scanning the darkening streaks of colored light firing the dusk. "Soon enough," he answered. "Spring coming, anyway."

"Don't cut your anchor line, you know. You may want to go back."

Clay made a pretense of accepting the advice. "Good thinking."

"Yeah. Well, there may be a shortage of that around here lately."

"I can drink to that," Clay retorted.

"I'll drink to anything," Byron answered, raising his can.

They stood there facing each other and then were quiet, together taking in the peace of dusk out on the water. And after a time Clay nodded and moved over to the center console and started up the bateau.

Riding back, he had Byron take the tiller and walked up front to the bow and sat leaning back on the cabin window, watching the sky turn to mauve and the river to mauve dark. It disturbed him, what Byron had said. Clay wouldn't have expected him to consider selling dope. Even as hurt as he was. He sat and thought about it, leaning back against the glass, and thought about his own decision and what was ahead. As the boat cut through the dark water, as night settled overhead, he studied the canopy of the universe, tracking the glimmering polestar as though he were a soothsayer searching the mystery for a clue, and knowing only that he was alone and making decisions now, traveling in life.

4

Pappy won his first skipjack in a poker game. It wasn't two weeks after he had gotten home from the war. Some eighty percent of his original squadron had been shot down over the Pacific, but he'd made it home with just a small sliver of anti-aircraft shrapnel lodged in his knee. The way he'd told it to Clay, it was mid-June when he got home, with the river warming but the jellyfish rare. In shorts and a T-shirt he would swim across the Tred Avon to the Dutch Inn Hunt Club, where he kept a locker. He'd change clothes, drink Jack Daniel's, and play poker all night. He always took Gus, his Chesapeake Bay retriever, with him. The night he won the skipjack, he'd bet his veterans disability with a queen under and two showing. He was dealt a pair of deuces on top of the queens and beat three aces. Afterward he was too drunk to swim but went in the river anyway. He grabbed hold of Gus's collar and Gus swam him clear across. The next morning, Sarah Rush found him unconscious, sprawled over the stone bulkhead that runs along the Strand, reeking of whiskey and muck and smeared with seaweed. She took him in and nursed him, and he took her heart for her trouble.

Sarah was the daughter of Dr. Samuel Rush, and according to her, her fine Baltimore family's trepidations at the announcement of her engagement were blown aside by the whirlwind that was Pappy, the son of a turkey farmer from off the Miles River who had made it through one year of college, flight school, a naval aviator's commission at age nineteen, and war heroics fighting from Midway to the Battle of Leyte Gulf. With some help from Dr. Rush, but mostly through hard work, timing, and a willingness to risk, that one skipjack became a fleet of oyster dredgers and workboats and a small seafood wholesale and packing company.

In the 1950s, Pappy took a chance on Fletcher Hanks's newly designed clam dredger. He borrowed from the bank and put three of the pump-belt dredgers to work, refitting a part of his packing plant to handle the softer and more brittle shells. The river bottom was an unplowed cornucopia for Pappy and the other dredgers, and they reaped the harvest, changing the contours of the Bay's bottom in the process. And during Pappy's mad acquisition, after two miscarriages, Sarah gave birth on a raw Saint Patrick's Day, 1951, at Easton Memorial Hospital, to Clayton Rush Wakeman. The birth was difficult, spanning a day and two nights, and Sarah was a long time recuperating. Afterward she was told that she should have no more children.

Despite his alcohol and gambling binges, and despite his wildness, Sarah adored Pappy, even after he started buying refrigerator trucks and adding new docks to the wharf, and even after the clamming dried up, and the oyster beds were depleted, and the money became scarce. Sarah adored Pappy and lived to please him until the day he left her for Bertha Wilkes, the young actress who played Tennessee Williams's Maggie in summer stock at the Cambridge Theater. That was the year Clay turned sixteen and pretty much the last year he saw his father until his mother's funeral, and he saw him little after that. Sarah died of a massive heart attack, in her own car, having picked Clay up on the last day of his senior year in high school, the last day of her life. Clay was in the car with her, there to hold her, feel her hand on his face and then gripping his arm, hear her gasping for breath, pleading with him to stay with her as the car swerved into a ditch. Clay believed he knew why she died and why he could never understand or forgive his father.

It was midweek, midday, when Clay opened the front door to Bertha's dress shop, on the sidewalk off Harrison Street in Easton, Maryland. A pewter bell attached to the top of the door jingled. The inside of the glass door was draped in lace. Mildred, Bertha's black seamstress, who'd spoken to Clay at the funeral, stuck her head around the corner into the carpeted foyer, where he stood.

"Hello, Mr. Clay," she said. "How you doin', chile?" She was thin and gray haired, and her eyes were gentle.

"Hello, Mildred." Clay shrugged. "I'm holding up, thank you."

"You have a seat now, Clay. Miss Bertha is expecting you and will be right out."

"Thank you."

Clay looked at the love seat against the wall where Mildred had nodded he should sit. It was covered in a floral upholstery. Mildred hadn't turned away but stayed watching him.

"Clay, honey, you sit there now," she urged. She smiled. "Could I get you a Coke?"

Then Bertha came gliding down the staircase, interrupting them.

"That's just fine, Mildred, thank you, but we'll be leaving," she said. Bertha spoke with a rich Carolina accent. She hailed from Charleston.

"Hey, Clay," she went on, leaning over and brushing his cheek with hers.

Outside, a fine mist hovered over the street. Clay took Bertha's red umbrella and opened it for her. He held it to shield her as they walked down Harrison to where it met Dover Street. A black man in denim overalls stood balanced on an aluminum ladder in the light rain, replacing the letters on the movie theater marquee with the name of the new film, *The Last Picture Show*. Clay'd heard it was worth seeing. At the entrance to the Tidewater Inn, Clay closed the umbrella, shook it dry, and placed it in the rack against the brick facade.

Inside the dining room, red embers glowed in the stone hearth. A waiter came by, bringing firewood. A girl Clay had known in high school—he remembered her name, Paula Firth—showed them to a table in the corner and gave them each a lunch menu. She was pretty, with short blond hair and long legs. She asked Clay how he'd been, flirted with him some, and told him it was nice to see him and that she'd bring some water. The restaurant tables were about half full, mostly businessmen in suits. Clay caught several of them staring at Bertha, who didn't seem to notice.

After they had sat down, Bertha looked at her menu for a moment and then set it aside.

"Thank you for joining me today, Clay," she said.

"You're welcome."

Bertha smiled but seemed embarrassed.

"My sisters are leaving this week. I'm a little afraid."

He thought her face was thinner than he had remembered. Her tinted hair was pulled tight under a round blue brimmed hat. Her eyes looked flat.

"What do you plan to do?"

"I don't know. What is there to do? Keep on, I guess."

"You're afraid of being alone." It was a statement.

"And I'm afraid of not being alone."

Paula came over and poured their water. She asked them if they were ready to order. Bertha asked for a salad, and Clay, a crab cake sandwich.

Bertha remarked about the memorial service and how amazed she was at all the people who came. After a while she turned the conversation. "I always admired you, Clay. The way you handled it all."

He didn't reply. He was aware of the clinking of dishes from the kitchen and the background hum of conversation.

"I never really knew what I did until it was too late."

Clay fidgeted. "There's no need," he said.

"No. I want, this once, to tell you. I should have said this to you long before now. The time just never seemed right."

"If there ever was a right time, I'm not sure it hasn't passed."

"Clay."

He picked up his spoon and turned it until it caught the reflection of the fire.

Bertha leaned her head back. "I was in trouble. I was twenty-six. I thought I was running out of time." Bertha paused for a moment. She sighed. "The details aren't important. But love was what I believed in. Your father was taken with that show. He was there nearly every night. It just happened. And it was like God had put me on this earth to love him. Nothing else mattered. It was as if there were no choice to be made."

Clay was staring into his water. He picked up the glass and sipped it and set it down.

"I don't blame you, Bertha. Not mostly, anyway."

"I'm blameworthy. But I believed it was true and right, and I didn't know what a family was that could be broken like that."

Paula came toward them with their lunch plates, and Bertha stopped. The food was set before them. Clay poked at his crab cake.

"I don't know what went wrong between your mother and Pappy. But he was already distant. He was there with the same need I had. I didn't think I caused it."

She stopped talking. They both were silent. Then she went on.

"He wanted more children. You might not know. He said he wanted you to have brothers and sisters. I wanted to wait, while your mother was alive. And then it just never worked. I thought we'd have more time. I'm sorry."

Paula brought over a pepper grinder and asked Bertha if she wanted some pepper on her salad, and Bertha said yes, thank you. After Paula finished, Bertha picked up her fork and mixed her salad, then put her fork back down.

"Clay, I'll always love your pappy. But you and I . . ." She lingered over her thought. "We both have a good measure of life left."

Clay acknowledged this. "I know that, Bertha." He watched her. "Strange, but you're the closest thing to kin I got left."

Bertha reached over and put her hand atop Clay's hand on the table.

Clay felt awkward but kept still.

Bertha gently pressed Clay's hand and then released it.

"I have more than enough with the house and money and my shop. You see, after a few years being married to Pappy, I realized I should never count on anyone else taking care of me but myself. That's why I started the shop. It brings me a small but steady income. Plenty people think your pappy took care of me, but in the end it was the other way around."

"He worked hard, you know that."

"That is true. Pappy worked hard and he played hard and he spent hard. And he grieved hard too."

Bertha looked up at the ceiling.

"He loved me, Clay, and there was fire between us. But he was hurt from what he did. It ate at him. I believe truly he would have undone it if he could."

She looked down and picked up her fork.

"Food's getting cold." She motioned.

Clay ate a few bites from his crab cake.

"You going to keep the house?" he asked.

Bertha waited. She finished her bite of salad and wiped her mouth with her napkin.

"Yes. For now at least. One day at a time." She took a sip from her water glass.

Clay thought of Pecks Wharf, the marina, the boats, all mortgaged, all being sold.

"Clay, will you do something for me? Will you go back to school and finish? That's what Pappy wanted."

"Pappy's gone now."

"Yes. Well, I'd like you to finish. It's the smart thing to do. If you'd let me, I'd like to lend you what you may need to finish, to get your degree."

Clay reflected on this. "I appreciate the offer, Bertha."

"Well?"

"I'll think it over. I've got a few hundred left in the bank. I expect that will see me through for a while. I haven't decided about next fall yet. But I appreciate the offer."

"What about the summer?"

"I'll be around. I'm planning to rent a room at the farmhouse, where I've been staying with Byron. I'm going to work the river some. I'll come by. Anything you need done around the house, you let me know."

"Clay, does it have to be the river? So soon?"

He looked away. "It's what I want now. Hard to explain. Even to myself. But I feel it. And the summer's mostly calm. I'll be careful."

She slowly sighed. "Of course."

He didn't answer.

"Thank you, Clay," she said then.

He turned.

"I mean thank you for everything."

5

It rained in sheets all that Thursday. Clay had slept late. In the afternoon the telephone rang, and Byron answered it. It was Barker Cull. Barker needed help with his pound nets down off Ragged Island. They could make good money for the day, though it would be blowing right rough and stormy. Byron was heading out for the evening with Laura-Dez, so they agreed, in case he didn't make it home, to meet at the wharf at five the next morning. It rained all night.

It was still dark when Clay pulled into the lot at Pecks. The oyster shell surface crackled under his tires. Through the beams of his headlights, the raindrops seemed to float to the earth. Occasional gusts would send the swarming droplets curling across the light. With the engine off he sat watching the rain swish sideways and listened to the whine of the wind over the water.

He got out and walked past the boathouse and restaurant. Out on the dock he passed the sailing yachts, tied tight in their slips, their halyards snapping in the wind and clanging against their aluminum masts like so many bells in a churchyard. The largest, a Swan 50, he believed, its teak deck shining under the wharf lights, was named *Mood Indigo,* out of Wilmington, Delaware. He had never seen it before. He had sailed since he was a young boy, and in his teens he'd moved some nice boats for his father, before the break, but nothing so luxurious. He looked at her and wondered about the runs she had made and the people who owned her. The wharf had always caused him to dream.

Looking back, he saw the lights from what looked like Byron's pickup pull into the lot. He walked out to the end of the dock. The waves were pounding the pilings, and the river was high. Byron came out walking wobbly. His eyes were swollen and bloodshot.

"Didn't make it to bed last night," he mumbled. "Had Laura-Dez drop me off at the pool hall. Card game."

Clay frowned. The Bay would be rough. At least the air wasn't too cold.

The two of them untied Clay's workboat and were out in the Choptank by seven and running with the wind behind them. Clay periodically checked his compass and his watch and after a while told Byron he figured they were nearing Ragged Island, where Barker Cull was supposed to be. They couldn't see more than about fifty yards through the rain, which splashed and streamed off the cabin windows. Both had full slickers on. Clay had tied down everything aboard that could move. The boat pitched like a bronco. Inside the cabin, Clay sipped coffee from a thermos, while Byron held on to the stanchion.

"Barker said his poles were off the southwest point in thirty foot of water," Byron said. He looked pale as a gutted fish.

Clay opened the chart and studied it for a moment. He angled southward to avoid the broadside swells. After a while he turned east.

The rain came in vertical walls, intermittently pounding across the windshield and then relenting, as if resting for the next on-slaught.

"Gonna be tricky out here."

"Was waves like this sank the Sloat boys," Byron mumbled. "A wave over the stern. Just before I got shipped out."

Clay squinted into the rain. "I remember hearing something about that."

"Was cold though. That's what kilt them. The cold water. Ice everywhere. They were winter draggin' for rock. Two boys, not even twenty. And their father and uncle, Seth. Seth Sloat. It was his boat."

Clay turned to hear better.

"The boat was weighed down with the ice. It had caked around it. Like a skin. And fish in the hold and in the net too. They say one of them was probably on the rail, trying to knock the ice off, and slipped and went over. Seth tried to back up and took a wave over the stern, which was already way low. From all the weight. They radioed for help. Two other boats had just left 'em and weren't more'n ten minutes away. But she sank fast. They found the boat under water to its canopy top. And they was all froze. The two brothers were floating right there, arms wrapped tight around each other. Found the father, miles away down water, locked onto an ice pack. Never did find Seth."

Clay took a breath.

"Yeah," Byron answered it.

"Remind me never to go ice trawling."

"I will."

"Keep your eyes sharp now."

"I'm lookin' for 'em. If they even came out here, that is," Byron answered. "Hell, we could ride around all morning and never find 'em in this shitstorm, even if they are here."

Clay checked his depth finder and studied the chart again. He moved the bow around farther to the east. The bateau felt solid still, even in the chop. They plowed forward.

"Keep looking," Clay said. "I figure we're getting close."

The rain and sea spray swept laterally across their bow. Moments later they seemed to cross through a fog bank into a clearing. Through the clearing and into the wall of mist on the other side appeared the shape of another, bigger boat.

"There they are!" Bryon said. "You found 'em!"

Ahead, Clay made out the haul boat and gradually recognized Barker Cull and three others slicked up in foul-weather gear. Behind Barker's boat he just made out the tips of the pound stakes, stripped pine trees that had been driven deep into the river bottom, running along in a linear hedge for several hundred yards, perpendicular to the prevailing current, and supporting the net. The schooling fish, following the current, would be intercepted by the net, turn away from shore, and follow the net into a circular enclosure, or pound, that funnels them into the trap net, from which few fish escape. Clay pulled up alongside Barker, close enough to shout but not so close as to get wave slammed.

"You fella's half crazy comin' out here in this blow," Barker bellowed. He seemed to be smiling despite the rainwater and spray spewing across his face. "Earl didn't believe you'd come, Clay. Or even that you'd find us out here below the bar. I figured different."

"What's your trouble?" Clay shouted. "Looks right friendly out here to me." He smiled in turn.

Barker was a big man, about six three and maybe 240 pounds. He had played fullback and linebacker for Easton High and taken them to the state championship some years back. Had a scholarship to Towson State but had only lasted one year and then got drafted. He had been home a year or so. Clay felt a bond with Barker. After Clay's father had left him, Barker had taken Clay on as crew occasionally on his workboat and on his log canoe, which he raced, and Clay had always been grateful. Barker was able on the water. Clay admired what he did. There weren't many pound netters left.

"Beely had his appendix out," Barker shouted. "Won't let anyone run his boat. Pa can't help 'cause his back went out Tuesday. We been waiting too long to pull already. Moon's full and there's been a good run of fish. And I can't get no help now. Not in this kinda shit. Traps are full and the fish are smotherin'. Nets are gonna tear if I don't haul. Particular in this blow."

Barker reached into the cabin of his haul boat and grabbed a towel and wiped his face.

"Y'know my little brother, Earl," he shouted. "This here's Roy Martin and Pal Tyler. Clay Wakeman and Byron Steele."

Everyone nodded.

"Trap's a mite large, there," Byron commented.

"Yeah. We got a bit greedy, there," Barker answered. "Now we're paying the price. Use your boat as my trap skiff, Clay. It'll be awkward big, but it's too rough for a smaller boat out here. Take Earl and Roy with you. We're shorthanded, boys. Net's overfull. Got to give extra today."

Barker threw Byron a line, and they pulled the boats close enough together so that the two men could leap from their top rail over to Clay's boat. Byron gave them each a hand, pulling Earl clear just as a wave pushed the boats apart.

"Hey, I appreciate you boys helpin' out," Barker shouted as he backed his boat away. "No shit."

Clay followed the line of stakes that ran neatly across the current line, and he could see the funnel nets leading into the trap he was heading for, some thirty-odd poles curving around in a tight circle. It would take some skill to haul in this weather, he thought.

As he neared the trap pocket, he could see the net was full. Even in the gray chop, silver fingers flickered under the surface. The menhaden, known as alewives in the Bay, catapulted over themselves, cartwheeling across the slate troughs. Definitely some big-eyed herring down there and maybe a shad underneath, Clay thought.

Barker tried to maneuver his haul boat up tight against the southwest edge of the pocket, but a large swell pushed him off.

Only after his second attempt were he and Pal Tyler able to tie it fore and aft to the downwind stakes. Once Clay's crew released the trap net from the upwind stakes and, by heaving and bunching it, worked the bottom of the net toward the surface, concentrating the fish, Barker and Pal would work the motorized brailing net and dip the fish into their hold.

Clay began to work his bateau around the trap net as his crew looped lines to the stakes to hold fast long enough to release the top sections of the net and shake the shimmering fish into a tighter bunch toward the haul boat, gathering and tying hunks of the net inside the bateau in the process. At the same time, they had to keep the bateau from being washed into the pound. The rain made everything more treacherous. They worked slowly as Clay guided the boat down along the trap. With the crew leaning out and into the stakes, a rogue wave could crush an arm, or worse. The men yelled to heave in unison as Clay steadied the tiller. They snapped and bunched the net, concentrating the fish into the decreasing net area, and pushed off as Clay moved slowly along its windward edge. He backed and centered, working the throttle and tiller, anticipating the swells and breaks, sensing the pull of the current. "Wave!" he yelled when he knew he couldn't keep his position, and the boat was thrown into the stakes, bending the poles and straining the lines, and the men had to give back some slack in the net. If pushed too far, the men would have to let go, and the fish could all be lost.

He worked his crew around the pocket slowly. They regained much of the lost slack. But their progress gradually slowed and seemed to stop. Earl began cursing, then yelling. Clay hardly heard anything except the whine of the wind on the water, but he knew that the net was heavy. They couldn't move the fish any farther. The haul boat was still too far away and had to stay downwind of the pound. He knew they would never be able to reset the net. Byron suddenly slipped on the wet deck and crashed down, cursing, losing his share of the net. Roy swiped for it, catching an edge in his fingers. Barker was yelling then too from the haul boat and gesturing, and then Clay saw him suddenly in and under the water, fighting his way to the boiling surface and swimming around the net and for the bateau. Clay knew how cold the water was. A wave broke over Barker, burying him in foam, but he came up spitting and cursing and with several powerful strokes reached one of the stakes against the bateau and somehow grappled his way on board, then immediately began hollering and heaving at the nets with Byron, Earl, and Roy. "Heave!" he yelled, and again "Heave!" They all yelled and pulled in unison, again, and then again, and Clay felt the give and with it fought around farther to the back as the men bunched more of the net together, pulling it inside the boat. He got nearer to the haul boat, near enough, he thought, and then he heard its dip net engine crank. Barker yelled "Hold!" and was over the side again, and Clay saw him in the water and then clambering over the gunnel of the haul boat. Clay worked to steady the boat and net and thought, Come on, boys, tie her right, and saw Byron and Earl lashing the pound net secure. The fish were thick in the water. He heard the dip net engine strain and crank, strain and crank, and letting his eyes leave the water, he saw Barker guiding the brailing handle of the large dip net as Pal Tyler tended the windlass and purse line. The net scooped down and, bulging with fish, came up and over the hold as Pal Tyler snapped the purse line, bright twisting alewives raining everywhere, two hundred pounds easy, Clay figured. Clay gave a sigh of relief. He watched them dip again and again until Barker, knee-deep in fish, was satisfied. On his signal, Earl quickly tied the bunched top net to the aft stake.

"We're done," Earl shouted, pushing off from the pole. "Thank God. We'll reset it when she calms a bit."

Clay backed the bateau off. He looked at Barker Cull, who returned the stare. Barker was breathing hard and his face was flushed. His eyes were riveted. River water and rain streamed over him.

"Appreciate it, Clay," he said in earnest, raising his arm.

And then Barker started to shiver.

"Better get dried off," Clay hollered back.

Barker waved them off, though he headed into his cabin. Then he poked his head out again.

"Washington Street Pub," he shouted. "'Bout seven. On old Barker." And then he disappeared.

Once back at the farmhouse, Clay stood under the hot shower for what must have been half an hour, letting the jets breathe new warmth into his body. He toweled himself dry, threw on his jeans and sweatshirt, and walked down into the kitchen, where he heated a bowl of leftover oyster stew. Afterward he fell asleep on the couch and dreamed of being deep in the river, emerald dark and clear, and he could breathe its oxygen and flash through its liquid universe without fear. He saw Pappy floundering above him in the tumult near the riotous surface, and he couldn't get the attention of the strange faces on the boat above to help his father, so he sounded an alarm, a bell, and rang it and rang it until he awoke to the ringing of the telephone on the table in the hall.

He let it ring and it stopped. It was already dark through the living room windows. On the side table the clock's fluorescent dials showed it was after seven. He was surprised Byron had not returned. He got up and turned on some lights. He splashed some cold water on his face, brushed his teeth, and changed. From the refrigerator he grabbed a beer for the road.

Outside, the night air was sharp and clean. The front had moved through. As he drove toward town, the moon followed him over the fields. He rolled the window down to feel the cold air and his own blood in the rush of the wind. He rode and felt alive. He thought of Kate, her hair damp against his face, her lips brushing his neck, her body against his, dancing in the darkness as the light receded over the fields. He tried to push the image away, making a motion to turn on the radio, oblivious to the station, his face half out the window in the cold rush of the wind. Pulling back inside, he caught the end of the news. Something about another offensive in the Quang Tri area. Thirty-one marines killed. He pushed in the eight-track sitting in the player under his seat to listen. The cut was "Gangster of Love." The highway rolled by. He sat back, trying to relax, and listened and smiled as Stevie "Guitar" Miller sang, "and I said yes sir brother sheriff . . . and that's your wife on the back of my horse . . ."

Inside, the pub was already filling up. Clay said hello to Clem Saunders, who sat at the bar watching two middleweights fight on the overhead television. Clem was about ten years older than Clay. He had been a waterman once. Now he worked for the local Sea-gram's distributor as a salesman. As Clay walked toward the back room of the long, rectangular structure, he heard John Prine whining off the jukebox, "There's a hole in daddy's arm where all the money goes . . ." In the back, in a booth, sat Barker, Byron, and Pal Tyler. They had finished plates in front of them, and long-necked Budweiser bottles were scattered over the table. Byron had by far the most bottles in front of him. He had come straight from the river, he announced. Because he was thirsty. His clothes were streaked with dried salt.

Barker, when he saw Clay, stood and bear-hugged him, slap-ping him on the back and praising their day's work. Byron started to rise but lost his balance and sat back down as Barker spoke.

"Damn if we didn't shine out there, boys. Goddamn! Close one though. Near foolish, I must say."

"We were lucky," Pal said.

"Luck? Shit, Pal! That was sheer miracle, boy!"

"I still can't believe you jumped in."

"I sure as hell didn't plan to, but I figured you boys had some muscle. Might as well have brought Missy over there as you boys."

Barker grinned and called to Missy to come over.

"Yes, honey?" she mocked.

"Come here, girl."

She sauntered over and, pausing, cracked a bubble from the gum she was chewing.

"You want another round, boys?" she said, ignoring Barker.

"Missy, these boys want to feel your muscles."

"Right." She turned to go.

"Missy darling." Barker's tone apologized. "Hold on a minute. Just kidding." He put his arm around her. She made a pretense of shrugging it off but let him keep it there.

"We do want another round. And I want dinner for my friend here. He's an artist."

"Yeah?"

"Truly. What you want, Clay?"

"I'll take a cheeseburger. Make it two. Fries, apple pie. Bud. No salad. Thanks."

"Burgers for my friend, Missy. And let me tell you something." Barker leaned into Missy's ear in a conspiratorial way, winking at Clay. "You know they say boats are like women? Well, you oughtta see this boy work a boat."

This time she was successful in throwing his arm off her shoulders.

"I'm putting you on probation if you don't watch it, Barker."

People began drifting in, filling up the aisle of the back room, which ran long and narrow to an oval dance floor, where a disc jockey was setting up his records. The back bar was built along one side, and across the aisle were the booths that ran along the other. The booth seats were a red Naugahyde patterned with cigarette burns. Byron and Pal between them knew half the people who ambled by. Pal tried to talk to every female; Byron would just raise his hand in a silent salute. Clay's food arrived with a smile from Missy. More beers were ordered. Byron ordered shots of Jack Daniel's. The disc jockey started turning records. Laura-Dez showed up and said hello to everyone. She saw Byron and his condition and declined to sit, but with Clay's help she coaxed Byron up and out while he could still walk.

In the din, after beers and tequila shooters bought by Barker, Clay ended up talking and laughing and finally dancing a slow dance with Paula Firth, the waitress from his lunch with Bertha. He bought her several rum drinks and danced with her again. Her voice was deep as she talked in his ear, and with her arms around his waist, she began to move against him to the music. He smelled her sweat, her earthy scent, and felt her sigh deeply, her body gradually surrendering against his. They danced, finished dancing, waited for the music, and danced again. He bought her another drink and told her she smelled delicious and that her crab cake had been good too. He asked her if she would like to leave with him and she said yes. They drove together out to the old ferry dock and parked and began to kiss. Clay studied her face, which seemed to capture all of the light in the half-moon sky, and kissed her again. Paula let him unbutton her cowboy shirt slowly and part it, and she looked at him and never said a word. She held his head in her hands as he kissed her breasts and belly and then unzipped and pulled off her skirt. Clay took off all of her clothes and then his as well because he wanted to feel her completely against and around him and was lost with her and afraid only that she would tell him to stop. When they were finished, they lay tangled together for a long while, listening to the radio play country songs. Clay felt grateful. He wasn't quite sure how it happened or even who this was that he was with. He asked her if she might like to go to the truck stop and have breakfast, but she said that she had to work in the morning and needed to get home. She kissed him on the cheek and started looking for her clothes. They helped each other dress, and then he started the engine and drove her back to her car. Before she left, Clay thanked her, and she looked at him as though he were strange. He then told her that he had to go back to college for a week or two, to arrange some things, but would like to see her again when he got home. She said sure, to call her if he felt like it. Then she told him he was sweet, and she got out.

Clay watched her until she had started her car and was pulling out of the lot. Then he turned and headed down the highway for the farmhouse.

The next day, Saturday, he tried to call Paula but got no answer. Byron was nowhere around, either, so he left him a note. He drove to town and went by the restaurant where Paula worked but was told she was off. It had started to rain.

He stopped off at Bertha's to say good-bye. She started to cry. He held her hands and talked to her for a while. He fixed her a cup of tea. She told him she wanted him to go but that for her his departure seemed a breaking off. He told her that it seemed that way for him as well.

They sat in silence for a while, listening to the rain against the windows. Finally, when it felt right, he kissed her on the cheek and left. In the rain and fog he drove down Route 50 toward the Chesapeake Bay Bridge, alone, watching the corroded wipers on his windshield smear the water back and forth.

6

The place where he slept, near the University of Maryland campus in Baltimore, was next to the railroad track. Though it came by several times a day, he had already stopped hearing the train sometime before. He subleased a small back room from a graduate student who was constantly stoned and who kept his rent money and seldom paid the landlord. Every week or so the landlord would come by and beat on the door, hollering, and the graduate student would haul out the back window and down the fire escape.

It was a five-minute drive to class, but he could never find a place to park, so he usually walked. He cut through a maze of fast-food parking lots, then walked adjacent to the boulevard and by the time he got to class felt stained from the smell of grease and the soot and smoke of the traffic. Before the news of his father, he had worked three afternoons a week at a checkout counter at Safeway. At night he would study. Sometimes after studying he would go to the corner diner and order the ham and cheese omelette with coffee. From the diner he could hear the music from the strip of bars, and after eating he would walk by them and sometimes go inside and stand by himself amid the jostling crowds, pulsing beat, and drugs and beer to watch the girls dancing.

Adjusting to college in Washington, D.C., had been difficult the first time. But at Georgetown he had found Matty and Kate, or they had found him. Making other friends followed, and he had gradually begun to enjoy the city. When the bank first garnisheed Pappy's accounts, he had transferred to the less expensive state college in Baltimore, and there he'd found things harder. After class he would sometimes cross the parking lots behind the mall and walk into the strip of trees, sit on the pine needles with his back against the resined bark, and study the light in the leaves. He would close his eyes to shut out the congestion he felt around him. Sometimes he'd sit through the receding of the light from dusk to dark.

He spoke regularly with Kate on the telephone though, and Matty also, and their kindness helped sustain him. Kate was from the Washington suburbs and had all the latest gossip, news on the school, their classmates, on the city, anything. Sometimes she sent Clay records of a particular piano recording she had discovered and wanted him to hear. Even though she knew why Clay had needed to transfer, Kate liked to try to cajole him into coming back. She even offered to lend him the money, laughing, as though it were a trifle. She told Clay jokes over the phone and would laugh at her own stories. Occasionally she would put the phone on the piano top and play for him. The pieces she chose were always lyrical, adagio: Prokofiev, Chopin.

He had returned to campus to salvage the winter semester, which ended the first week of April because the school was experimenting with a new five-week spring minisession. Though exams had never been difficult for him, the classes he had missed required some effort to make up, and his decision had left him distracted and with little motivation for studying. Still, he finished his tests, then went to the registrar's office and signed the necessary papers for his leave of absence. Back at his room by the railroad tracks, his few belongings were already packed—clothes mostly, some record albums, and a secondhand stereo. Now, for some reason, he heard the train. One last time, he thought. He picked up the phone and called Matty and told him his decision and plan. Matty didn't seem to approve. They had a long discussion. Kate got on the phone after. She listened without saying anything as he told her he needed to make this change. She said she wanted him to do it too. She told him that she was learning that people needed to follow what they felt in their bones.

Leaving the campus, he drove out of the city to the beltway and around toward Annapolis. There was little traffic. He turned on the radio and listened to the news for a while. President Nixon was returning from California. McGovern and Humphrey were battling it out in the Democratic primaries. The Paris peace talks had stalled again. The negotiators were at odds over the shape of the bargaining table. He changed the channel and listened to Country Joe and the Fish singing "one, two, three, what are we fighting for . . ." The news came back on and he turned off the radio and started thinking about all he had to do to get ready. The day was cold and clear. Driving over the Bay Bridge, he could see south past Thomas Point to the West River, and north past the Magothy to Gibson Island and beyond, where the horizon met the sky in a thin stream of silver vapor. A single oyster dredger moved under sail plowing the banks below Rock Hall. She was running with the wind, and her sails were spread wing on wing; she looked like a huge white seabird puffed out proud and steady against the moving blue of the Bay.

Before Clay had left the farmhouse near Trappe to return to school, Curtis Collison had agreed to rent him the small bedroom for $120 a month. Curtis was there when he arrived and watched him and Byron unload his belongings. Afterward, Clay and Byron hung out in the kitchen. Byron had put some water on the stove.

"You want it black?"

"Yeah." Clay sat resting at the table.

"Be sure when Curtis gets drunk to leave him alone," Byron mentioned. "When he drinks, he gets ugly. He likes to fight."

"How often is that?" Clay asked.

"Not too often," Byron returned. "Not as often as me." He didn't smile when he said this.

Byron poured out two cups of instant coffee and brought them to the table. They each sipped at the hot liquid. A clock radio on the counter was on, and the disc jockey was counting down the top ten country tunes.

"So what's your plan?"

Clay stirred his coffee with a finger. "I told you before. I'm going on the river."

Byron shook his head. "I hoped you might come to your senses."

"There's a pull to it. I feel it, that's all."

Byron leaned away, tilting his chair. "You know, I was thinkin' back. There used to be shad in the Bay. Tons of 'em. And sturgeon. Oyster beds like natural reefs, big enough to give names to. Clams. Shit."

Clay nodded. "I know. The whole world's that way. Changing."

"Yeah. But making a living on the water . . . Ain't so easy no more."

"She's still got life, Byron. She's changed. But she's still brimming."

Clay heard a commotion outside and stood and walked to the kitchen door. Opening it, he looked through the screen to the southern cornfield. It was full of snow geese, and so was the air above it. He stepped out on the porch, and their barking filled his ears as hundreds of them dropped like leaves from the sky, floating the last few feet to the ground, where others snorted through the stalks, feeding on the kernels left by the husking machines.

Byron had joined him on the porch. "Never seen so many snow geese as the last few years," he said.

"Yeah."

"Different cycles seem to play their way out, I guess."

"There's a cause."

"Sure there is. Those guys on the moon. Upset the balance of gravity."

"Right."

"I'm serious. Think about it."

Clay gave him a playful shove with his shoulder. "How about all those jets landing at Friendship Airport every day. Suppose they knock the earth off kilter?"

Byron frowned. "Moon's different. Smaller. Virgin."

"Sure."

"Well, no one really knows, do they?"

"The Bay has her cycles too. And the crabs are strong as ever. If I can just make one or two good seasons, I believe it will work. I could build a business. That's what I plan to do. I figure I'll give it a year or two. Build up my pots. Then reassess." Clay turned toward Byron. "I'm going to be needing a culler. At first. Then a partner for the second boat, I figure. Eventually."

"I doubt it."

"Got any ideas?"

Byron backed up, shaking his head. "You're doing too much dreamin'."

"What are you living on now, anyway?"

Byron thought for a moment. "I really don't want to know."

"One day you got to make a move. Put something in front."

"Maybe." Byron walked down the steps and opened the door to his pickup. From under the front seat he pulled an opened bottle of Calvert whiskey and returned with it to the stoop.

"Living off the water, you live free," Clay said.

"To be free, you got to be free in your mind." Byron took a drink from the bottle and offered it to Clay, who took a drink himself and passed it back.

"Bay air might help some with that."

"I think maybe you've gotten too much air."

Clay kicked a stone off the porch. "We'd make good partners."

"You got a college education. Think with all that learning you'd know enough not to throw it away."

"I want to be outdoors. I don't like working inside."

Byron took another drink. "Yeah, I know."

"What do you got to lose?" Clay asked. "Could be like when we were kids."

Byron raised the whiskey bottle and held it up to the light. "Not much left. There or here, right now."

"Well?"

"I ain't really right, now, Clay. And I ain't sure I want to be. I just don't know."

"Well, will you think on it?"

Byron gulped down the remaining whiskey. "Sure," he said. "Course I will. I'll think on it. But don't hold your breath, now."

Clay, satisfied, turned to watch the snow geese swirling over the amber land. White petals free-falling, awhirl in a vortex.

7

The Bay-built workboat rested on crosses of seasoned hardwood, having been hoisted and wheeled in the day before. The barn was womblike, dark, warmed by a torpedo space heater that glowed red-hot in the shadows. Shrouds of tobacco leaves hung drying from the rafters above, emitting a sweet, torpid aroma that mixed with the creosote and varnish used on the boats, the smells of river decay, brine, flesh, urine, and sweat. The power spray had knocked loose the bone and barnacle fragments grafted to the bateau's hull, along with the slime and matted cockle hair. The lead copper underpaint was gone in places. Even the color of the wood had been leached away by time and salt, leaving scoured streaks smooth as oil.

Clay had been sanding since morning. He put his hand on the transom of the bateau and began to walk her line. Built on Tilghman Island for his father when Clay was a boy, she was solid mahogany, ran thirty-six feet to her bow, and needed three feet of water for her keel and single propeller to clear bottom. Driven by an oversize 280-horsepower GM gas engine set just aft of center and enclosed in a large engine box, she had speed greater than most workboats of her size, the majority of which used diesel power. A canopy top running from midship forward offered ample headroom above the cockpit, which stepped down into the fully enclosed bow cabin, with icebox, bunk, and marine toilet and sink. A marine radio, depth finder, and compass were set in the cabin, above the wheel. The boat could be run from inside the cabin or from the open cockpit at midship, where a full set of engine controls and a tiller post were fixed to the port side, adjacent to the engine box. For one man to run pots or a trotline by himself, he had to be able to maneuver the boat from midship, where he dipped the crabs or pulled the pots.

He walked outside and sat dangling his legs from the wharf his father had once owned and lost. Shafts of sunlight streamed through the porous clouds, creating halos that shimmered across the cold, clear skin of the river. The watery breeze cooled his face, sweaty from his work. He shaded his eyes from the wind and the shifting light.

He tried to remember Paula Firth and how she looked in his car that night, so smooth and bare. It was Friday. He had finally reached her, and she had told him to meet her later at a party down Wye Neck. He realized he hardly knew her and wondered where they would go from where they had been.

Another day of sanding, he figured, and he could begin to patch and paint the bottom. Then he would work on the sides and rails. He planned to spend some time on Saturday in Cambridge looking for used pots and a bait supplier. He figured he could bend a few pots himself as well. He also had to find a hydraulic pot puller and attach it to his port rail. That would cost him and would be done last, after the pots were ready, if he could find a way to pay for it.

"You lay your bait pots when the first dogwood buds swell open." That's what Pappy always said. He figured on about two weeks till then, which fit well, as it would take two weeks to get ready. He got up and went back inside the boat barn, back to work. He picked up the electric sander, put the gauze mask on over his nose and mouth, and ducked back under the hull. Within moments the taste of the lead from the paint dust was again in the back of his throat.

He had offered to pick Paula up, but she had told him that she was going to dinner with some girlfriends and would meet him at the party. She gave him the address and directions. He was on Wye Neck Road looking for a sign that said FERRY BRIDGE FARM. He found it and turned onto a long, poplar-lined driveway. There were cars lined up along the drive, and he could see people in blue jeans milling around in the front yard.

He parked and walked up to the columned front porch. A few people he knew were on the portico, holding beers or drinks. Two girls in sweaters sat sharing a porch swing and a joint. They offered him some as he passed, and he declined politely. Sounds of laughter and conversation mixing with the beat of Eric Clapton filtered outside.

Seeing a crowd in the entranceway, Clay backed down the stairs. He walked along the front of the house, landscaped with symmetrically trimmed boxwood, and past the red brick two-story extension, which ran east and ended at a stone path leading to a pool house. He turned off the path and walked around the house to the back and out onto a sweeping lawn that sloped down to the Miles River. He walked down away from the house. The air was turning cold and he could see his breath. The river was still, lapping gently against the riprap bulkhead. Overhead the sky was dark and starless. There were no lights on the pier, which ran about a hundred feet out into the river. He turned and watched the figures in the windows and the light that filled the windows and flooded through. He saw girls silhouetted in the light, laughing. He watched them move and bend, and while he watched, he felt the breath and pulse of the river, measured, steady, faithful. He thought about himself and his own fevered stalking and wondered how the sanctuary of the river—for all its beauty and power— could be insufficient, and how his own longing and loneliness remained.

Inside, the house was crowded and filled with smoke, music, and movement. He found the keg in the kitchen and helped himself to a cup of beer. He knew a few people but didn't see Paula. He worked his way into the living room, where in one corner three girls in cowboy boots danced to Van Morrison singing "Brown Eyed Girl."

Downstairs he found Barker Cull at a pool table, playing dollar eight ball. Clay watched as Barker cracked the cue off the break, sinking the five, and then dropped three more before catching the corner of the side pocket on a bank shot.

"You whore, you."

Barker took a deep draw from a joint and held it out to Clay. "Some monkey weed there, Captain?"

Clay took a hit.

Barker looked at a skinny blond leaning against the wall with two friends. "Shirley, darling, run get us a few more beers out of the keg, will ya?"

Shirley reached for the joint and sucked at it between her red fingernails, blowing him a smoky slipstream kiss as she exhaled. Then she passed the joint to her friends and turned up the stairs.

"How's the pot-bendin' business?" Barker said, reaching for a half-full bottle of tequila.

Clay shrugged.

"Might try talkin' to Dell Swann down at Pier Street for extra pots. He's sellin' 'em. Most are usable. Another season or two anyway."

"Yeah?"

"I got a good trade for alewives. Had a fair sale to the feed plant.

Froze a bunch too. The rest salted up nice. Just let me know when you're ready, and I'll fill a barrel or two for you. Get you started anyway. Part of your payment for savin' my pound haul."

"Thanks."

"Where you gonna sell?"

Clay watched Barker's opponent bank the six off the side into the corner.

"Not sure. Probably stick close to home. Jed Sparks. He's running Pappy's wholesale operation now. You know, for the bank."

"Let me know his prices. I might have a deal on a refrigerator truck. Ship to D.C."

"Appreciate it," Clay said.

He wandered up the stairs to the second-story hallway, which was lined with people he didn't know. He walked its length, and as he turned back he glanced in one of the bedrooms and saw Mac Longley sitting cross-legged on the floor with his back against the bed. A round mirror was on the rug in front of him, holding lines of white powder. To his left sat Teresa Bonner, who had gone to Easton High School with them, and to his right, Paula. She wore a sailor's cap and held a rolled-up dollar bill in her hand. She waved to him.

He stepped into the room.

"Clay Wakeman. Goddamn. How ya been? Wanna try a sheep's leg?" Longley asked, grinning. "Take the edge off."

"Sit down, Clay." Paula gestured generously with her arm, sweeping it before her as though offering him the field. Her silver bracelets jingled with the motion. "Get high." She reached for her beer, and Clay saw her breasts move under her blouse.

Clay stood, wrapping his arms about him. "I think I'll hold off for now," he said.

Mac licked the tip of his finger and ran it over the mirror, gathering some powder on it, and then put it in Paula's mouth and pressed it over the front of her gums. "Like a freight train."

"Been here long, Clay?" Teresa asked.

"Watched Barker Cull shoot some pool."

"Nice party." Paula laughed.

"Heard you're going on the water," Longley remarked.

"Yeah," Clay answered.

"Fool's life, there." Longley pointed to the lines of coke. "Better off getting high." He sniffed. "Bay's going sour, you know." He squinted up at Clay. "It's the government dumping that's doing it."

Clay was suddenly impatient. "How about a dance?" he said to Paula.

Paula looked quizzical. "Now? I'm sorry, Clay, but not now." She reached across the mirror and squeezed Longley on the thigh. "I can't leave in the middle of dessert, now can I, Mac?" The two of them laughed. She looked up at Clay, pouting. "But we'll share with you."

Clay studied her for a moment. "You go ahead," he finally said. His voice seemed to him to come from a far-off place. Longley offered the mirror to Teresa, who bent over it and snorted. Clay felt tired. He studied his hands, which were bruised and stained from the day's work, and then he saw himself for a moment, earlier, beneath the underside of his bateau, smelling the lead from the sanding, his fingers feeling those places that were so smooth, the mottled streaks, shell gray, almost like driftwood. He heard Paula saying something but had lost his sense of the present. He tried to focus. There was some commotion behind him, and someone lurched in carrying two beers and handed one to Longley, nearly falling over. It was Byron, and as he started to slide down the wall, Clay took his arm and held him up. Paula was talking about the band that was supposed to be playing at Kent Island on Saturday and how she knew the lead singer. Longley began to lay out some more cocaine. Clay told Byron he needed to talk to him about something.

"Leave him be, Clay. Let him party," Longley said. "He's grown."

Byron started to shake his head, but Clay held him and asked him again, telling him he needed his company, and then Clay had him going, down the hallway and the stairs and out the front door. Clay sat them down on the porch steps and breathed. He could feel the low, moist cloud front across the sky.

"I appreciate your company right now," Clay repeated. "That's all."

He got Byron back up and walked him to his Chevy wagon. When he drove Byron back down the lane, he saw couples in some of the cars, embracing.

Back at the farmhouse, Clay made coffee. The telephone rang. It was Byron's mother, Blackie, and Clay talked to her.

"What's up?" Byron slurred through half-shut eyes.

"Blackie called. Your father's been picked up again."

"Where?" Byron tried to speak more clearly.

"VFW."

"I mean, where's he at?"

"Town jail."

"I got to go." Byron started to try to rise.

"You can't go anywhere. I'm going."

"Like hell. I do this one."

"Not tonight you're not. They'd take one look at you and lock you up with him."

"Got to, though."

"Tonight, I'll help," Clay said, and talked to Byron until he came around. "Come on, then," Clay finished. "I'll drive. We'll go together."

Clay fixed more coffee for Byron, for the road. At the jail, he made Byron wait in the car.

Once inside the jail, it took about twenty minutes of paperwork to get Byron's father, Mason, released. As Clay knew, he was a frequent Saturday night visitor. He was brought out into the office by one of the deputies, who held on to his arm as he staggered.

Mason was red faced and walked bent over. He looked at Clay and then slowly around the room and then at the deputy, as though he had just noticed him and just noticed where he was. Then he pulled a red handkerchief out of his back pocket and threw it at the floor, imitating a referee in a football game, and shouted, "Flag on the play! Flag on the play! " and then doubled up laughing with a whiskey wheeze. Clay had to grab him to keep him from falling.

Clay put him in the back of the station wagon and drove into town to Grady's Diner and took Mason and Byron in and made them both order coffee and breakfast. He wasn't particularly hungry, but he ordered a scrapple sandwich.

Byron made a face at Clay. "How you eat that shit?" he said, shaking his head.

"What?"

"It's pig peter, you know."

"Bull."

"No. Not bull peter. It's pig peter."

Mason started laughing again, like he had in the jail.

Clay held on to Mason so he wouldn't fall off the stool. He looked at Byron. "How would you know? You ever tasted pig peter?"

"I ain't neither, and I don't aim to."

Clay didn't answer.

"It's bad enough watching you eat it, though," Byron went on, trying to wink at his father.

It was after midnight when Clay drove them down to Planters Wharf, figuring some fresh cold air might help. Byron was sobering up some. The three sat shivering on the dock, and Mason babbled for a while about the waitresses at the VFW. Two half-tame mallards swam up toward them out of the dark, looking for bread. Mason cursed them away.

"Goddamn scavenger house pets," he shouted. "Where is your

wildness gone to?" He began coughing and Byron patted his back. "Where have they gone to, boys?" he implored. "There used to be millions of 'em. Millions! And they didn't beg for bread, neither. Not a one, damn it." He let out a wheeze. "When I was a youngster, my daddy would take me up off the Susquehanna Flats. Cans and reds would just smoke up the sky, there were so many. They would blot out the sun. They'd be everywhere. I'm sorry you boys never saw that.

"Go on, get away," he shouted at the mallards, and then he started coughing again, coughing and wheezing.

"They tore up all the grass and seedbeds dredging, I suppose." Clay spoke softly, patting the older man's back. "The wild celery's mostly gone. Eelgrass is scarce. Lack of food."

"It's just like Joe DiMaggio, selling Mr. Coffee machines on the TV. It's shit," Mason hacked out. "The man was a hero. Now he's selling goddamn Mr. Coffee machines like who gives a good goddamn."

The boys looked at each other at that. "I see there's a link there, Mase," Byron finally said. He hiccuped at Clay. "Somewheres."

They all sat silent for a while and listened to the quiet stirring of the river and the rustling of the boats in their slips. And then Mason started talking again and gradually got around to talking about what he always talked about when he got that way, about being on the sea at night in the war against the Germans, and how the sea had a soul that wrapped the earth and contained all life, and that the men who were lost on the sea were contained in her soul, and how it felt to wait for the submarines to attack, to wait for death on the sea at night, in the silence, night after night, listening for the torpedoes that they knew would come. Byron listened and didn't speak, but his face betrayed the images of his own war branded in him.

Traveling back to Blackie's, Mason fell asleep between them in the front seat. It had begun to drizzle and then the rain changed to snow, a light April snow, just dusting the earth, muffling the night. On Oxford Road, Clay slowed and then came to a stop and turned off the engine and the car lights, and the two young men, with one of their fathers asleep between them, watched the translucent flakes float to the ground in the luminous spring snow in the soundless night.

8

Outside the boat barn, a rusted conveyor belt lay disintegrating in a field of weeds and trumpet vines. In better times it had been used to unload the bountiful oysters. Clay walked past it and past a graveyard of beached dredgers, abandoned years before, most with their sides staved in. A field mouse scampered over a rotting timber, split from the belly of the *Tessie May,* the name still faintly readable across the gutted transom. A gray gull, perched on the broken masthead, surveyed the swollen river. Clay liked the stiff breeze and the sound of the sailboat halyards ringing.

Like a branching oak tree, the wharf at Pecks Point sprawled into Plaindealing Creek and faced out into the Tred Avon River. South of the loading platform, a new dock of unweathered pine ran into the creek, where a few luxury slips had been built to handle pleasure yachts. The new wood seemed out of place among the older structures and the rusting husks from another time. For two hundred years the wharf had been home to boatbuilders and watermen. In colonial times, when the town of Oxford was competing with Baltimore to become the leading port of the upper Bay, the wharf was first an unloading station for shad and oyster and then served the herring trade and, still later, the crabbers. Built originally on hard-packed sediment, the wharf area had grown with the commercial dredging for oysters by sail-driven skipjacks, expanding into the creek on its accumulated oyster shell base, the refuse and legacy of generations of watermen, watermen's wives, and the Negro women shuckers who used to fill the warehouse.

Clay knew the history of this place. He had learned it from his father and read about it as well. But he had also come to know it just by being on the river, by learning the slow track of the musk-rat in the eerie backwaters of the Dorchester marsh and learning when and where to set the traps, and what the traps did to the an-imals, and how to finish them. And by finding home through the spartina with the bow of his skiff laden with muskrat pelts and rounding Pecks Point and catching the thousand eyes of the sun on the Bay.

That was before Bertha had played Maggie at the Cambridge Theater and Pappy had stopped coming home. Before his mother had stopped caring. Before she had moved him over near Denton, and for her, and for himself and his own hurt as well, he had not come back to Pappy, not once until well after she died, and then only to visit, and it had never been the same. Now he kicked at an oyster shell and pushed away these thoughts so the pain wouldn't be quite as sharp. He shook his head, wondering how a person could be so interfered with, as Pappy had been by Bertha, how a man could turn on or away from his family, how people who cared for each other could break each other like that. He stopped and breathed and made himself think of the morning and what he needed from it and from the day. He watched the water. The waves frothed forward and combed back upon themselves, blue-green in the sun. The northeaster had followed the lunar pull and pushed in the flood tide, but it had peaked and was starting to settle. Tough on the crabbers, he thought. Knock the pots around. He heard a diesel approach from the east, but his view was blocked, and he heard the engine reverse and then quit.

Approaching the old dock, he turned and walked in front of the second warehouse, known as the picking shack, though crab pickers could no longer compete with the machine-operated seafood plants, and this building was mostly used for storage. Behind it ran the rows of molt tanks, big wooden crab boxes filled with river water and irrigated by overhead spigots. The live peeler crabs were kept there, studied daily, and moved to successive tanks as they got closer to their molt, the shedding crabs in the last tank, picked out by hand, soft as wet clay, ready for the markets across the Bay Bridge on the western shore.

Just beyond, on the loading platform, stood Jed Sparks. The platform jutted out over the wooden bulkhead and was plastered with old tractor tires on the water side and cluttered with cleats, hoses, bushel baskets, and barrels on the landing. One workboat was tied alongside, and an older man with a grizzled stubble was unloading bushel baskets from his boat onto the wharf where Jed Sparks stood watching nonchalantly, his hands in his khaki trouser pockets, black suspenders holding them high and running up over a dirty sweatshirt. Seven bushel baskets were heaved up on the dock, each about half full with crabs. The older man looked over the remainder of the baskets in his boat, but they were all empty.

"Jimmies still right sluggish." He looked up at Sparks. "More each day, though."

Sparks eyed the baskets half full of crabs. He kicked one of the baskets, watching as the crabs inside scrambled around. "Shit, Chester, you ain't doin' no worse than the rest. No more'n a few bushels, all told, though. I figure one and a half a number ones, two bushels a twos, and a half a liver-bellies and sooks." He turned toward the door to the office behind him. Two men were lounging in chairs under the entrance roof. "Billy, pick 'em up," he hollered.

Turning back to the waterman, he continued. "Payin' twenty, twelve, and eight today. Premium price as they're still right rare. Comes to sixty." He reached in his pocket and pulled out a thick roll of bills. Peeling back several hundreds, he found the twenties and pulled three out. He handed them down to the man in the boat.

"Yeah," the waterman grunted, accepting the money. "Be better tomorrow. Going deeper. Catch 'em crawlin' up the bank, out of the mud."

"Tomorrow, Chester." Sparks turned away and saw Clay leaning against one of the tanks.

"Cap'n Clay," he yawped, sauntering over. "How's the work comin'?"

Clay held out his hand and Jed took it to shake. "I'm making progress, Mr. Jed. Been bending pots all week."

"How many so far?"

"About a hundred, I'd say."

"Need more."

"I know. And I need to find a hauler. And a cheap one. I'm about tapped out."

Jed Sparks squinted against the sunlight on the water. He had worked for Pappy running the wharf for as long as Clay could remember. Now he was tending things here for the bank.

"I ain't for sure, but Lester Quill's been workin' on some pot boats down in Tilghman. He might have an old hauler to sell."

Clay thought but couldn't recall the name.

"He's got a work shed right next to Morrison's."

Clay nodded. "Thanks. I'll drive down there."

"We'll stick her in your ole slip when she's ready. I told the bank that I was trying to rent it but I ain't had much luck." Sparks grinned. "You might as well keep on using it for the time being."

"Appreciate it. Once I get some crabs to sell, I'll make it good."

"Nothin' to make good, as far as I see it. You got a line on your bait?"

"Barker Cull might spot me for a while. I need to scrounge up some more pots, though. Or raise some cash to buy 'em."

"Course you do."

"When you figure they'll start comin' in full?"

Jed thrust out his jaw in a way that he had. "I 'spect another two to three weeks." He looked at Clay. "'Bout when the dogwood buds swell open." He chuckled and Clay smiled. "You should hit 'em just about prime."

They both heard another diesel coming down the channel and looked.

"Appears Buddy Claggett's had his fill," Jed stated.

"So it does," Clay agreed. "Well, I'll get back to it. Thanks for your help."

"Sure."

Clay turned to go.

"Hey, Clay." Clay turned back. "You seen that center-cockpit beauty, blue hull, named *Mood Indigo,* out in the new wharf?"

"Hard to miss."

"The owner's looking for a cap'n to run some weekend charters. Seems pretty free with his cash. Paid six months' slip rental in advance. In hundreds. Probably pay good for a cap'n. Name's Brigman. Claims he's from Delaware. Jersey accent. Seems a bit slick, but you might try him."

Clay thought for a second and then nodded his head. "Yeah. Right. That might work. I could use the money right now. Thanks, Jed." He started to walk back past the peeler tanks and then changed his mind and turned to go out on the new wharf. He went out on the dock, past the smaller flat-bottom and centerboard boats, toward the larger slips. Underneath the dock the water was spring clear, and through the ripples he could see the eelgrass growing on the bottom, four to five feet down. He walked out to where the *Mood Indigo* was riding high in her slip. She was tied too loose for the flood tide, and her bow was nearly scraping against the pier. He quickly pulled her in and stepped aboard and tightened her cross lines, reining her back safe in the slip. He walked along her varnished teak deck. She was a beauty. He thought about sailing her. He wasn't keen on chartering for weekenders, but the boat would be a fine run. It had been a while since he'd sailed anything. Maybe weekends for a few months anyway. Money for more crab pots and bait. He turned and stepped off her and went back to work.

That night, Byron wasn't around when he got home. After showering and changing, he drove into Oxford and ordered some fried clams from the carryout. He ate them and stopped off at Pope's Tavern for a beer. The place was quiet. He drove into Easton and then to St. Michaels, but the Crab Claw was closing and the restaurant empty except for two buses of seniors from Baltimore. He wasn't ready for sleep yet, but went back anyway and sat in the quiet.

The phone rang and he picked it up. It was Kate. She started talking. She was lonely, she said, because Matty was away on an interview in Williamsburg for his summer internship about a plantation restoration. The others in their group house were off studying. When was he coming to visit? she wanted to know. What was he doing? She hesitated. Then she said that wasn't the only reason she was lonely.

"How long has Matty been gone?" he asked.

"Just tonight."

"Have you talked to him?"

"No."

"He'll call soon."

"Probably. But I wanted to hear your voice."

"Yours sounds good too," he answered.

Kate was silent. Clay could hear her breathing. "I don't know, but I felt I needed to call," she offered. "I miss you. I know that." She paused. "Tell me about your boat, Clay."

He thought about the past days and began to explain his prepa-
rations, the hauling of the bateau, and the sanding. The painting.
He told her about the traps he was building. He even described the
Mood Indigo and told her his thoughts about that.

"If you captain it, I'll come charter it," she said. "You know, I've
never known anyone from a place like you come from," she went
on.

"How do you mean?" he asked.

"Like, from the earth."

"Come on, Kate."

"No, really. All the guys I knew from Woodbury, at all the
schools actually, till I met Matty, you know, they were all so . . ."
She waited before completing her thought. "I don't know, urban.
Of course the girls at St. Theresa's weren't much different. And
here in the city now. Well, I've never known any watermen, that's
for sure." She finally laughed, and Clay told her it sounded good.
To hear her laughter.

"You know what you're doing," she added then. It was a statement. "And what you're doing now—I think there's a dignity
about it."

Clay thought about this. "I'm not sure about that. But thank
you," he said after a while. "It's just plain work, though. The kind'll
tire you out. And risk. I'm not sure it's as idyllic as you think."

"I guess I'll have to come see for myself."

"Yes, you will."

"Can I?"

"Whenever you want, you're invited. You know that. Soon, I
hope."

He listened, but she didn't speak.

"Talk to Matty, and the two of you come soon."

"Oh, Clay," she said.

He heard the sadness in her voice. And the rain starting outside
the farmhouse.

"What?"

"I don't know," she answered. "It's just that I've always felt you were such a special friend. You know?"

He held back. But the silence didn't help. "I know it too, Kate," he finally said. "You know I do."

"Why is it?" she asked.

"I don't know any more than you." His words echoed back to him, hollow.

"It just is, isn't it?"

"I suppose."

He heard her sigh. "Yes. I suppose." And then she said she *would* come soon and thanked him for cheering her up, though he didn't believe he had. She asked him if before she hung up she could read him a poem, and she read the last few stanzas from T. S. Eliot's "The Love Song of J. Alfred Prufrock." Her voice, when she read, stayed silky and soft. She was unrelenting with him; he knew that much. Or with herself. It was hard to fathom. While she read, he watched the black rain run down over the windows, and the sound of her voice took him back again to dancing with her that evening after Pappy's funeral. Then he thought of her and Matty and Byron, and knew they were really the only family he had left, and vowed again to look elsewhere to quench that place in himself, so parched, so dry-docked.

Over the next few days, Clay continued his work on the bateau and on bending wire. By making the pots himself, each cost about half the ten dollars charged at Wilkerson and Cromwell, the local wholesaler. He wore heavy gloves and worked with cutters and pliers from a roll of eighteen-gauge steel wire treated with zinc. This wire was sturdy enough to last several seasons, but thin enough to give the crabs a good view of the tunnels leading to the bait. The zinc retarded corrosion. Despite the gloves, his hands were swollen and blistered from the work.

Each crab pot, when finished, looked like a square cage about two feet across. Steel rods were attached along the bottom of the cage to act as sinkers. Conical funnels were cut and bent on two opposite sides, leading into the lower half of the trap. A mesh cylinder was fitted into the center of the trap for the bait, and the crabs, smelling the bait fish in the cylinder, would find their way through the narrowing funnels into the lower portion of the trap. A wire shelf divided the lower half from the upper half, with funnels leading from the lower section into the upper, and the crabs, looking to escape, would quickly work upward into the top section, where they would be caught. Each pot was attached by a nylon line or warp to a pot buoy of cork the size of a football. Clay painted all of his buoys half orange and half yellow, easy to identify and easy to see on the water. The ones he had finished were stacked against the barn wall. He figured he needed at least another fifty to start and hoped to have two hundred by midsummer.

On Friday he drove down to Tilghman and located a used hydraulic hauler that would fit fine. His problem was money. He could only make a down payment on the hauler, and Lester Quill agreed to let him pay it off by the week, but he still had little left. He also needed money for bait and bait barrels, for fuel, and money just to live.

Jed Sparks had told him that Hugo Brigman usually came over on Saturdays to sail his yacht, so early Saturday morning, Clay was there waiting. He sat on the front ledge, just outside the shed Jed used for an office, and watched the river, which had calmed, and the workboats moving in and out of the creek. The sun was straight away, about even with his face. He savored the warmth on his face and against his chest. Here, finally, was one of the first of the warm days, and he sat and soaked it in. He sat and enjoyed being there for a long time until he began to feel hungry and impatient with the time passing. He noticed a car coming too fast up the wharf drive, sending dust everywhere. As it pulled into the parking lot, he saw it was a red Porsche, and an attractive woman, not much older than him, got out first and headed for the new dock. The driver remained in the car, reading a newspaper.

Jed had been in his office but poked his head out.

"That's the girlfriend, I believe. Amanda, I think her name is." He grinned. "Forgot to mention her, I guess."

She wore new jeans that looked like they pinched when she moved. Above the jeans she wore a leather flight jacket over a T-shirt that had a picture of Janis Joplin on the front. Clay got up and started to follow her out toward the yacht. She walked fast despite her high heels. When she heard him behind her, she turned around, tipping her gold-framed sunglasses down off her eyes, then turned as though she hadn't seen him and continued toward the *Mood Indigo*.

Clay slowly approached.

"Excuse me," he said.

She was searching through a small duffel bag she had set on the dock.

"Damn," she said. She turned her head to face him. "Yes?"

Clay introduced himself and told her he had heard that the owner might be looking for a weekend charter captain.

She stood up straight. "So?"

"Well, I wanted to apply for the job."

She studied him for a second. "This is a hundred-and-fifty-thousand-dollar boat, pal."

Clay looked out at the river, which had begun to stir under a feathery breeze. Out across from Valiant's Gas and Marine some gulls were swarming, and he watched them circle and dive, too far away to be heard. He bet there were some chopper blues underneath the bait fish, and he wished he were there. He looked back and saw Jed Sparks and another man walking out on the dock toward them. The man with Jed carried a newspaper and had a pair of binoculars hanging around his neck. The binoculars clinked against the gold chains that fell into his half-open shirt. He was tanned and muscular and appeared to be in his late thirties.

"Here comes Hugo, anyway," she said. "Talk to him, if you want."

Clay waited for the two men. They arrived and Jed introduced Clay to Mr. Brigman. Amanda had removed her heels and had already climbed aboard and was unlocking the cabin. She climbed down inside. Brigman invited Clay on board, and Clay followed him down inside the yacht. Jed hollered, "So long," and left.

"You met Amanda?" Brigman asked. "Amanda, lovey, this is Clay Wakeman."

"We met, Hugo," she said, looking at Clay. "I'm going to change now." She ducked into the aft cabin and shut the door.

In the center of the main cabin was a table of polished teak, where Brigman motioned for Clay to sit. Brigman took two cups and a jar of instant coffee from a cabinet in the galley. He filled a pot with water and put it on the propane-fueled range, and the burner lit automatically when he turned the knob. On the table lay the newspaper, folded to the racing page, and Clay could see the schedule of starts at Pimlico, with several horses' names circled. He could hear Amanda behind him, changing her clothes.

Brigman leaned against the galley. His eyes had a way of darting around.

"Jed Sparks says you're an experienced sailor."

"I've been around boats some. Yes, sir."

"He says you could handle being a charter captain for my *Mood Indigo*. That you're real qualified."

"I could sail her."

"What do you think of her?"

Clay heard the cabin locker open behind him. Amanda brushed by, wearing a white bikini and holding a towel and a tube of suntan cream in one hand and her small duffel bag in the other. She got to the ladder and twisted around toward the two of them.

"She's beautiful."

"I got her name from a jazz song. '*Mood Indigo.*'" Brigman seemed pleased with himself. "You know it?"

"It's Hugo's theme song," Amanda added with a smirk.

"Fits nice," Clay responded.

"Yeah, well." Brigman paused. "Clay Wakeman, huh. I was thinking of somebody older. More experienced, maybe. Weren't you, sweetie?"

Amanda yawned, then turned and climbed out of the cabin.

The water started to hiss. Brigman put the coffee into the cups and poured in the hot water. He came over and sat down and handed Clay one of the cups.

"Do you have a charter captain's license?"

"Don't believe I'd need one for inland water, sir."

"Well, do you have one?"

"No, sir."

"How about those Coast Guard courses? Ever had any of them?"

"I'm not sure what courses those are."

Brigman sipped his coffee. "But you grew up around here? On the water?"

"Yes. Mostly."

Brigman half closed his eyes. "Why do you want the job?"

"I'm refitting a workboat. A crabbing boat, mainly. For pots. Though it could be used for trotlining or oystering." Clay paused. "So I'm starting up my own business. But I could use some extra income for expenses. Jed said you just wanted someone for weekends."

"Maybe not every weekend," Brigman interjected. "Two a month or so. I've got friends, clients, whatever. Want to sail the whole Chesapeake. Maybe take her down to the Norfolk area, like the York River. Take her down one weekend. Bring her back a week later. I'd cover your land transportation."

"You have dockage down there?"

Brigman ignored the question. "So what exactly is your experience?"

Clay watched the shadow lines made by the halyards across the beams of light that came slanting through the starboard portals. He looked up and saw Amanda's legs as she stepped across the hatch. He looked back at Brigman. "I grew up sailing. Moved some bigger boats for the wharf here a few years back. When I was in high school. When owners needed it."

"High school?" Brigman sounded skeptical. "Offshore?"

"In the Bay. I've crewed offshore. When I was younger."

Brigman swatted at a fly in his face. It kept coming back. "So you know this part of the Bay well?"

"Yes, sir."

"How far south have you been?"

Clay took a sip of his coffee. It was weak and he set the cup down.

"I've been south past the Hooper Islands, through the strait, and below Smith and Tangier Islands on the east. My father took me down there quite a bit. We used to crab and fish around Smith and Tangier. He liked it down there. We sometimes stayed over on Tangier. On the west side I've sailed to the Potomac and up to Cobb Island, and along the southern shore of the mouth looking for shelter."

"And north?"

"I've sailed the Susquehanna, and I've been through the canal and down the Delaware Bay and through the cut at Cape May once, which is enough times for any man. The Delaware Bay is no place to sail."

"This is a Swan Fifty."

"Yes."

"You know this boat?"

"I sailed a Dickerson Fifty once. Built here in Trappe. Never a Swan."

"Do you have a résumé or anything like that that you could leave with me?"

"Not really, sir. I suppose I could make one up."

Brigman sighed. "What's the biggest boat you've handled?"

Clay thought for a minute. "Probably the Dickerson. Sailed a big Gulfstar once."

"And how long ago?"

Clay shrugged. "It's been a few years."

Brigman leaned back. "Uh-huh. I see. Any questions you have?"

Clay thought. "What kind of business are you in, sir?"

Brigman paused. "Varied interests. Seafood. Real estate development. Complicated." He reached for a dish towel and snapped it, killing the fly on the table. He got up and put his cup in the sink. He turned to Clay. "Nice of you to come by. I'm not so sure this is the job for you, though. I wanted someone who knows Virginia waters better. Maryland *and* Virginia. I'll leave word with Sparks, okay?"

Clay got up and shook Brigman's hand.

"Yes, sir," he answered. He didn't feel disappointed, for some reason. He wasn't really surprised. He was just glad to be leaving. He turned and climbed up the ladder. As he stepped into the cockpit, he was almost on top of Amanda, who lay on her stomach on a blanket on one of the cockpit seats, out of the breeze, her top unsnapped and her tan legs oiled and shiny in the sun. She wore earphones attached to a radio. Clay softly said good-bye to her as he stepped over her, though he knew she wouldn't hear him.

9

They sat in Byron's room, the farmhouse attic, Clay leaning back against the frayed blue corduroy couch pushed under the eaves, and Byron on a low rocker, a half-full fifth of Jim Beam between his thighs. Smoke still hung in the air from the joint that smoldered in the ashtray. They each held a bottle of Budweiser and were listening to Van Morrison sing "Tupelo Honey." The song ended and the turntable clicked off.

Byron shook his head back and forth. "Curtis Collison grew this pot in his garden." He took a gulp of beer. "Fuckin' guy is into everything."

Clay sat back up. "Not bad for homegrown."

It was late, and the deep calm of the night wrapped around the farmhouse. Clay had left the wharf in the afternoon, and coming through town, he'd seen Byron's truck parked outside the pool hall. Byron was inside the door arguing with Clifton Dodd. There were nearly a dozen empty beer bottles at Byron's table, and Clifton was insisting he leave, so Clay had driven him home and was making him tea when he passed out. Clay found two goose breasts in the freezer and took them out to defrost. Later, he broiled them in the oven, and made a rich currant gravy as well. When he went to rouse him, Byron was already awake, sitting in his room with the bottle of Jim Beam. They ate the goose breasts with the gravy and some canned yams that Clay found in the pantry and then drove back into town for more beer and to retrieve the pickup. The night was cool. Once back home, Byron started a fire in the black cast-iron stove in the corner. They watched it light up and then gradually burn down to a fine, hot pitch.

"I've been bringing old Mase home from the VFW since I was about ten"—Byron tilted the Jim Beam—"which you well know. You'd think I'd've learned something."

Clay considered. "You have, I'm sure."

"I'm worse. And worse than that, I don't give a fuck."

Byron turned the label of the whiskey bottle to face him and studied it.

"Give it some time. Yourself. You're deserving of some patience. From your own self."

Byron rocked for a while.

"I feel like I'm going in circles. Can't see nothin' ahead. I remind myself of that story about poor Johnnydog."

"About who?"

"Johnnydog Cooper."

"What?"

"You never heard? Don't guess you knew him. Terrible, really. From Cambridge. Drowned hisself last fall. Young waterman. Strong swimmer, everyone said."

Clay shifted.

"Was out trotlining, late season. Near dark. His engine quit. Story is he figured he'd anchor and swim to shore. Apparently swam into a swarm of nettles with his face down and his eyes open. Blinded him. Couldn't see the shore. His boat. Nothin'. Swam in circles till he drowned."

"Jesus."

"Yeah."

"Christ, Byron."

"I know. They found him with his lids swollen shut. His eyes were burnt blind."

"Damn." Clay shivered and took a drink. "You do hear the stories, don't you?"

"It was all over the county. In the papers, even. You were at school."

Clay watched his friend as Byron rose and walked across the low-lit room to the stove. He had to duck to avoid the slanting roof. With the black apron of the iron stove already open, he threw in some pieces of split oak taken from the stack next to the wall. The two of them gazed into the orange center of the fire, crackling blue and violet, and let the fire burn away the image of Johnnydog, out there swimming to nowhere, unable to see.

"You still being courted by Mac Longley?" Clay asked after a while.

Byron frowned. "He does go on with me. Told me the other night his quote *operation,* unquote, runs the whole length of the Bay. Delaware to Norfolk. Said his people—the ones he works for, I guess—used to smuggle shit in from South America by using carriers pretending to be tourists. They'd swallow the coke packed into condoms before flying home. Said one girl's broke on the airplane. She didn't make it. So they had to find a better way. I know he's at least half full of bullshit. But apparently they have."

"What's that?"

"Found another way."

"What?"

"I don't know what. I guess it involves him. That's all I know."

"Nice folks," Clay added. "Cocaine inside condoms."

"Yeah."

Clay asked Byron to wait a minute and got up and went to his room. He came back with the corroded green ammunition box, opened it, and carefully unfolded Pappy's creased and dried-out chart of the location of the wreck of the Spanish frigate, just above the Virginia line, above Smith Island. Clay showed the chart to Byron and told him the story. "That steel was so perfect," he finished, "Pappy said that six weeks out of the water there wasn't even any oxidation. I'd like to find somebody today who could forge steel like that."

Byron held the chart down at his side, looking queerly at Clay, his eyebrows knotted.

"We're talking the sixteen hundreds." Clay took a drink. "Once we raise enough money crabbing," he went on, "I figure we can go on a treasure hunt."

Byron got off his chair and sat on the floor, placing the chart in front of him so that the firelight fell across it. He traced the coordinates with his finger. With eyes gleaming and new images in his mind, he laughed and sat back up on the rocker. "Your father," he said. "What a fuckin' pisser. Smith Island. Wide as an ocean down there. Right above the Virginia line. You think this is the real thing?"

Clay shrugged. "Pappy found the wreck. And the ax. He was convinced."

"Well, goddamn. Why don't we just go scuba down there?"

Clay shook his head. "Pappy went back. He tried. A bunch of times. Said it needed a proper salvage boat. Sonar, metal detectors, vacuums. The bottom's too shifty down there. The silt covers everything." Clay reached for the chart. "This stays private now, Buck."

Byron handed it to him. "Whatever."

"It's a dream anyway. But for me I want it to stay private. Between us and Pappy."

"Pappy ain't gonna say anything."

Clay gave Byron a look, folded up the chart, and put it back in the metal box. He got up and took the box back to his room, came back, and worked the fire, stirring the red ash.

"Sorry," Byron said.

Clay took another drink of whiskey. "Hell. You're right, I'm sure. He's gone. But what do you think?"

Byron was quiet for a minute. Then he got up and walked over to his bureau. He opened a drawer and pulled a photograph out. He handed it to Clay. The picture showed three guys in army fatigues. Byron was in the center. All three had their arms around one another's shoulders and were smiling. The one on the left was a black man. None of them looked to be over twenty.

"They were the ones that helped me. Saved my life. But I couldn't get them out."

Clay studied the picture for a long while, then stood up and returned the picture to the drawer. After he shut the drawer, he sat on the couch, his arms on his knees. "I'm sorry."

Byron took a deep breath.

Clay was silent.

"You know, it never bothered me. What you did. Protestin' about the war and all."

Clay watched Byron squat down and take another turn poking the fire.

"It was more avoiding than protesting."

"Well, whatever. Being a pacifist or whatever."

Clay thought of Byron that summer after high school. Getting ready for boot camp. Driving around with a near arsenal in the back of his pickup. Talking the talk.

"It seemed to make sense at the time." Clay reached over and took a swig from the bottle of Jim Beam.

"You were smart. To avoid it."

Clay put the bottle down. "I don't know. Maybe. It was the easy way to go. I jumped on the easy train, really."

"Safe is smart. Trust me."

Clay mulled this over. "I'm not proud about it. Not sorry or anything either. I was just lucky, maybe. I mean, peace sounded right. But I was just taken up. Going along. Taken up by events, the same as you. Most everyone I knew in school was the same. It was just easy. We weren't thinking enough about you guys. We pretended we were, but we weren't."

Byron closed the cast-iron hatch and sat back down on the rocker. He looked at Clay.

"You were there at the hospital."

"Yeah. Well, of course I was. "

Clay was surprised that Byron was speaking about this and waited for him to continue. But Byron stopped.

"We just didn't think enough about finding a way to object and still show support for the boys getting the worst of it."

Clay halted, then tried again. "I know it was bad over there."

Byron didn't respond. The only sound was the crackling and hissing of the wood from the squat black stove. Finally, Byron changed the subject back.

"I suppose I could get a job with the pool service. If I wanted a job, that is."

"Sure."

"I'd probably do better on the water. Cleaner. Less like doing somebody else's shitwork."

"You got that right."

"Not that I think it's such a good idea for you. I already told you that."

"You did, in fact."

The two friends watched each other.

"Better than drug running," Clay commented. "Whatever Mac Longley's doing."

Byron took another swallow of bourbon. "I suppose. Course, now you got a treasure to find. That's something different. Something worth considerin'." He rocked back. "I ain't gonna make it for long like this, just sittin' around, am I?"

"I'd say you're a goner if you don't find something to put yourself back into."

"If the crabs get us goin', I reckon we could do some oysterin' in the winter."

"Yeah. Maybe run some fishing parties too."

"I'd like to see the rock come back."

"Blues are good fishing. And they're catching some big drum down south a bit. Least that's what I've heard."

"That would all be to supplement, though."

"That's right. But with a good season we could start on another boat over the winter. With you helping, we could probably build it before spring. With two boats next year, hell, we'd have ourselves the start of a business."

Byron seemed amused at all this. "How many more pots you need to get started?"

"Maybe another fifty. To get a decent lay. Then we could add to them."

"About five hundred bucks?"

"Less if we bend them."

"Barker'll front us some bait, I'm sure."

"He's already offered. He's got frozen and salted."

"Five hundred, huh. I probably got that much. In the bank." Byron considered. "Ain't that convenient?"

"Convenient. That's the word for it."

Byron stretched his arms over his head, then winced, bringing his hand down to his side, the side where the ragged scar ran across his skin above his hip. He put his hand under his shirt, touching it, while Clay watched. Byron seemed to relax. "Okay," he said. "I'll give it a try. That's all I can say. If you're sure you want me."

Clay broke into a grin.

Byron shook his head again. "Maybe you're goin' brain-dead, though. Talking me into this shit. Brain-dead." Byron reached for the remainder of the joint. He found a match and struck it on the floor. The match fired into blue flame. Clay thought back to the hospital in Bethesda where Byron was laid up, and he thought of the other boys there and how they were hurt. He had stayed for days with Byron and his mother, Blackie. Mason was there too, but Mason couldn't visit without crying. Clay thought of the hospital, and then he thought of Pappy floating on the river somewhere. He pushed both thoughts aside and saw an ancient frigate, rusted and mysterious, in the silt under the dim water. He pushed that thought away too and saw his workboat sitting quiet and polished in the boat barn, silent in the night, waiting for her launch, and as he breathed in the marijuana, he saw the river, its surface shimmering in the light, and felt eager to start.

They were ready by Monday, the fifteenth of May. Clay noted the date. He heard Byron wrestling on his clothes in the attic. It had taken them longer than he had expected to finish bending the pots, install the hauler, and complete the engine work. He had hoped to have been ready earlier. But over the past week, Byron had worked with him nearly every day, and he felt pleased about that, though Byron drank while he worked and was mostly useless by late afternoon. The bateau had been launched on Saturday, and the pots and the bait barrels loaded the day after. Before the launch he had renamed the bateau the *Miss Sarah*, for his mother. Byron got Laura-Dez, who was studying art at Chesapeake College, to paint the name nicely on the stern. She wouldn't take any pay for it.

Clay heard Byron come noisily down the stairs. In the kitchen they drank coffee. Byron went back up the stairs and came down with a pint of Calvert whiskey, mixing some in his cup.

"I'm thirsty. Dry as the desert."

Clay shrugged.

"Sorry," he said. "Up all night." And he took a long drink.

"Don't bother me. Long as you do your share. And you always have."

"Just a couple to dry the sweats." He took a drink directly from the bottle.

"You want some toast?"

"Nah."

"I've made us some beef sandwiches. We'll get hungry."

"Good."

Byron brought the bottle but let it lie on the seat between them as they drove through the predawn mist down St. Michaels Road, the canopy of oaks along the Bellevue stretch looming like overseers above them in the hush of the dark country morning. They drove without talking and parked in the wharf lot, the oyster shells crunching under the tires of the pickup.

The air was still as they walked past the picking shack and onto the dock toward the *Miss Sarah*. Low across the eastern sky, a mantle of crimson tinged the horizon and began changing texture as they watched, the faint light ascending in miniature spires to violet and expanding to spheres of blue. In her slip the *Miss Sarah* looked overladen with the pots, which were stacked and lashed high on the deck and on the canopy above, but she rode serenely on the water. The two of them looked at her for a minute and then climbed aboard. Clay primed and fired the engine, which started smooth and idled steady. Byron released the lines. Clay put her in gear, and moments later they were clear of the slip and moving slowly past the wharf and out into the creek.

Without hurry, the *Miss Sarah* cut across the Tred Avon. The light from the rising sun reflected off the Oxford water tower, and Clay noticed the crew of the Oxford-Bellevue ferry doing their morning chores. The air was soft and the water mirrored the sky, flashing the rising sun's sharpness. They traveled along the bar off Benoni Point, the sandy beach edging steadily past, a lone blue heron standing on one leg in the shallows, unmoving, eyes scanning the bottom for food. Clear of the bar, they slanted southwest, aiming for Cook Point, the southernmost tip of the Choptank, easily identified by the stands of loblolly pine that seemed to extend from the watery horizon, like a cluster of ships' masts in the distance. A swarm of gulls chased the bait fish across the way down near Cambridge. A few flocks of geese were moving just above the tree line from Blackwalnut Point below Tilghman over toward Dun Cove. The air was balmy and fresh and tasted of brine, and the sky was clear, as the newly painted bow of the *Miss Sarah* sliced through the flat silver surface, her white wake foaming behind.

Clay ran the tiller from midship. After a few minutes he angled further southward. Byron noted the change and ducked in the cabin, took a drink of whiskey, and lit a cigarette. He came out and sat on the starboard rail, slowly exhaling and looking around him and over the Dorchester marsh.

"Pretty, ain't she."

Clay looked at him. He seemed better. "You ready to work?"

Byron tapped his forehead. "Born ready. You give up on heading for Hills Point Neck?"

Clay studied the water. For the past few days they had been discussing where to lay the pots first. Clay wanted to find some fresh ground that hadn't been claimed by another potter. Hills Point Neck would be lonely enough, they had agreed, and the bar had a nice slant, but it was below the Choptank and a far run.

"You know that little half-moon swash, runs just outside of Cook Point?" Clay said.

Byron thought. "Yeah. Kinda shallow, ain't it?"

"Well, the bar runs out a bit, that's true. But there used to be a nice, gradual drop, well before the channel. And there's no harbor close around it at all. I thought we might check it out and see if there are any pots around."

Byron went in the cabin, found the chart, and brought it out.

"Chart says, though, that it drops quick from about four to twenty plus."

"Chart was wrong last time I was here too. There was a sweet little shelf, runs southeast about ten to twelve. If we're right, it should be perfect."

Byron dragged on his cigarette, then exhaled. He threw the cigarette overboard, climbed onto the rail, and started untying the ropes that lashed some of the pots to the canopy.

Cook Point jutted northward off the Dorchester peninsula and extended to the place where the southern flood of the Choptank met the Bay. The land lay low and marshy, and as they cut across the channel, heading toward the southern shore and then around the point, Clay could see the spartina spreading south across the landscape, gleaming under the rising sun. He checked the depth gauge and watched as the numbers gave the distance between his keel, which sat about three feet under the surface, and the river bottom. As the numbers dropped from the twenties to fifteen to twelve, he slowed the *Miss Sarah* to a crawl. The numbers read ten feet, nine, and then ten again.

"We're on the slope now," he barked to Byron. "Let me coast her length."

Byron pulled a pot down from above and unwound the line that was wrapped around it and attached to the orange-and-yellow cork buoy. "Looks right lonesome," he remarked.

Clay continued southeast, studying his depth. Satisfied, he reversed the engine for a moment and then put it into neutral. He looked around him, studying the near shore. He turned and took his bearings off Cook Point and then across the mouth of the wide Choptank, marking Blackwalnut Point.

"Okay then. Tide's running and should take us back up the shelf nice for a while. Let's work fast before the slack."

Byron unwound the line of each pot, clearing any tangles, and handed the pot to Clay, who dipped into the barrel of alewives and stuffed the bait cylinder with the fish, thawing in salt. He closed the bait latch, made from a square of sheet metal he had cut, pulled tight by an elastic hook, and heaved the pot overboard, watching the attached buoy angle off the tide, judging its depth from the slack, and noting the buoy's location in his head. With the drift of the boat, each pot was about thirty yards from the next. They worked silently together, and Clay was pleased with the feel of the bait in his hands and the smell of the alewives and the water, with the notion of the pots' being made and placed right, and with working the river together with Byron this way. He felt the wire of each pot he had made and saw the crabs it would catch and how it would look filled with fat jimmies, and imagined a boat full of bushel baskets stuffed with crabs. They worked slowly but hard and his sweat soaked his shirt. After a while Clay looked back at the string of buoys extending nearly parallel with the shoreline. About fifty pots were overboard, he figured, laid out true along the shoal, where the crabs would crawl up from the channel foraging for food. He threw another pot overboard and watched as the line played out.

"Getting too shallow," he said. "Let's move."

Clay started the engine, and they worked farther north, back toward the point, where they baited and dropped another fifty or so pots. After that they took a breather and Clay brought out the beef sandwiches. Byron was hungry and ate with Clay. Past noon, with the sun passing over to the western half of the Bay and a light breeze rippling the Choptank, they finished setting out the last of their pots, along the bar in the neck under Cook Point, in twelve feet of water, cool and emerald green under the slanting sun.

Clay gave Byron the tiller for the journey home and sat down on the cot with the chart and marked the areas of his first three lays. He looked behind him. Byron sat on the engine cover, guiding the tiller post with his foot, a cigarette in his hand, the bottle of whiskey nestled in the crook of his arm. Beyond him the river ran to the low shoreline, the marsh perfect in its solitude. Clay's father had loved the marsh. The salty spartina, half river, half land. Its isolation and emptiness had pleased him. Clay studied it and saw a group of buffleheads flying above its surface. They flew low across the flats, nearly brushing the tips of the marsh spikes, the marsh a dance of light and shadow, rippling like music. He forced himself to turn back to the chart. As he studied it, thinking of the marsh and then of the crabs already moving toward his pots, the *Miss Sarah* traveled across the Choptank, steadily, with the breeze off her stern, into the Tred Avon, heading home.

Clay was dozing when Byron rounded the port channel buoy off Bellevue too fast, just as the *Miss Sarah* hit the wake of a large cabin cruiser. As the boat rocked with the wake, Clay opened his eyes. Byron slowed her, which caught the bateau in its own backwash, but it didn't really faze her. The wake passed. She was sturdy, Clay thought, and fast for a workboat. And then for some reason he thought of his mother, and that she would have been pleased. Pappy had always had one of his boats named for her. There was a dredger he had named the *Sarah W,* and before that, a fishing boat Pappy had christened *Sassy,* which he used to call her sometimes. Clay had thought it was because Sarah would now and then throw Pappy's sayings right back at him. "Nothing ever happens to a river man as long as he stays on the river, where he belongs," she liked to echo him. To his mother it had been inconceivable that Pappy could love another woman, let alone betray himself and his family so. When he did leave her, the shock never left her face, never for a day until she died, never left her eyes, which grew more and more hollow, never left her heart, never left her lips. Only once did she speak to Clay about it, and then not in terms of herself so much, but rather to ensure that Clay knew a wrong had been done, but that the wrong had not been directed at him or in any way caused by him or because of him, as if she wanted to help Clay leave an open place in his heart for his father, a hope, though she herself had abandoned all hope. He had tried to turn her back to her old self, to love her enough, but she hadn't let him find the way to do that. Later he had stopped thinking about it so much. It was no help thinking about it. But he was pleased with the bateau, and with her name on it. Pleased with everything about it. Pappy, when he first had this boat built, had named it *Seahatch*. Afterwards, he had always referred to it as the bateau because it was the smallest boat in his fleet. Some said it was bad luck to change a boat's name. But Clay didn't think so. Or didn't care. He was pleased that the first boat in the fleet he would build was named for his mother. Now he was ready to get on with catching crabs and building something from the river.

10

That night he was supposed to eat with Bertha at her house. She had called him a number of times, and finally he had promised. He was late and drove fast down Oxford Road.

Once in town, Clay slowed his station wagon to a crawl. His car window was down. Turning along the Strand, he drove very slowly and listened to the lapping of the river on the stone bulkhead and the beach. Looking across the Tred Avon toward Pecks Point, he could see the lights that fixed the end of the wharf. Out in the channel were the markers, the five-second red and, farther out, the three-second green, isolated colored beacons blinking. In front of Bertha's he pulled over to the side and stopped the car. He got out and approached the house. The brass handle on the door to the screened porch was cool to the touch. He opened the door and went inside the porch. He saw her shadow cross the light under the front door as she came to open it. He had a vague longing, almost like a pain, and wished he were somewhere else, wished he were about to see a woman for a different purpose.

He spent a quiet evening with her, trying not to think of his mother.

The next morning Clay was up early. He looked out the window in the dark of the morning to see if Byron's pickup was there. It had not been when Clay got home from Bertha's. The shadow of the pickup was visible, and next to it was another car, just a shape, really. Clay was relieved. He got dressed and went into the kitchen, where Byron was sitting, already dressed and drinking coffee with whiskey chasers. An ashtray with a dozen or so butts sat on the table in front of him.

"Hey, Cap," Byron volunteered.

"Morning."

"Didn't sleep much. Fact, not at all." Byron tilted his head in the direction of the stairs, grinning. "Got Laura-Dez up there."

Clay looked toward the stairs.

"Why aren't you up there with her?"

Byron smiled. "'Cause we got work to do, Cap. And we don't want to burn no daylight this mornin.'"

Clay didn't have to look at Byron. He knew Byron was riding a wave, and he knew he would have to crash sometime.

"C'mon," Byron beckoned. "Let's have at it."

They reached Pecks by five-thirty. By quarter to six they were on the river, which was like pitch in the moonless dark, and as they churned into the Choptank, they watched the first sluice of light invade the distant horizon. The breeze from the Bay was moderate. Sipping from the thermos of coffee and whiskey he had mixed, Byron worked the upright tiller post while Clay put on his oilskin apron, which had been Pappy's. Gradually the sky uncovered itself, and the silver water glimmered pastels. They changed places again, and Byron put on his smock and the thick rubber gloves he would use to cull the crabs. They reached their first buoy at about half past six, and when Clay got close enough, he grabbed the six-foot gaff off the washboard. In one motion he hooked the buoy and brought it over the hydraulic puller, setting the line in the brass wheels of the puller, which brought the pot up from the river bot-

tom and alongside, where he set it on the rail. The pot was streaming with eelgrass and mud and inside were at least eighteen or
twenty medium- and large-size Chesapeake Bay blue crabs. Byron
let out a whoop at their first catch, and they both took a moment
to look at the crabs scrambling about in the upper section of the
trap.

"Right fair, for spring," Byron commented. "Right fair catch on
the first try."

Clay opened the top side of the trap, which was fastened by a
stretched piece of surgical tubing with hooks at each end, and
emptied the crabs into the crab box. He stuffed a handful of menhaden into the bait cylinder, sent the pot back overboard, and
started toward the next buoy. Byron started culling the crabs. The
large males, or jimmies, went into one basket, and the mediums
into another. The females, or sooks, and the recently molted crabs
that hadn't filled out their new, larger shells, known as liver-bellies,
went into a third.

"Big crab, yessir," Byron said, tossing a large yellow-bellied jim-
mie into the basket. "Fatter'n a rich man." He had a cull stick to
measure the males, point to point if necessary. The minimum size
for a keeper was five and a half inches. Anything smaller was
thrown back. There were only two small crabs in this first bunch.
He finished just as Clay was guiding the next buoy line into the
pulley. Seconds later the trap came up with even more crabs, and
Clay said, "Damn!" and then Byron said, "Damn! I think they like
your pots there, Clay."

Clay swung the trap onto the rail. "You mean *our* pots."

"Well, they do appear to fancy 'em."

Clay grinned. "It's these sweet alewives that Barker saved for us,
probably."

"Whatever works."

"Yeah, Buck."

Clay emptied the crabs out, rebaited, and reset the pot, moving down the line, as Byron culled. They worked their first lay and then the others, and by midday two full bushels of large, fat blue crabs, four and a half bushels of mediums, and several bushels of sooks sat in the sun. Clay looked at the crabs in the boat, then studied their line of pots running southeast in the swash along the extended spit of land. His hands were swollen and sore and his arms ached. He looked at Byron, who was wobbling a little.

"You ain't tired, now, are you?"

Byron spit over the rail. "I don't know nothin' about tired."

He kicked the bushel baskets. "But I'm done cullin' and I got no whiskey left to celebrate."

Clay took a jab. "Just suck on your own breath for a while."

Byron snorted and, trying to take off his apron, nearly fell and had to grab the rail for support. Then he tottered his way to the cabin.

"Maybe I'll hit the cot for a few minutes while you take us home."

"Don't miss the payout, now."

"Just hold my share, partner," Byron said as he ducked into the cabin. "And wake me when the party starts."

At the dock, Jed Sparks eyed the crabs. "Right handy catch," he commented as Clay lifted the bushels up on the loading dock. "Still paying high, though catches like these'll move the price." He counted out six twenties and two one-dollar bills and handed the money down to Clay. "Prices'll probably drop after Memorial Day, anyway."

Clay received the money. "Appreciate it."

"Thank *you.*"

"It's a start."

"Good start. Where's Byron?"

Clay motioned forward. "Snoozin' in the cot."

"There's a girl came by for him. Said she'd come back later. Laura somebody."

"Thanks."

"Sorry about Brigman," Jed offered.

Clay was untying the stern line from the loading dock cleat. "Yeah," he muttered.

"Figure'd he'd take my advice." He shook his head. "Apparently he's got his own agenda." Jed paused. "I heard yesterday he's gone to the bank with an offer."

Clay stopped what he was doing.

Jed's face was lashed with salt and rigor tough. Still, Clay could see the wince. "It's a ways off. May not happen. Course, some-body's gonna buy this place." Jed spat, away from Clay. He turned back. "I hear he wants to keep the restaurant and marina. And for some reason the seafood wholesale operation. Wants to tear the rest down, though. Build condos. It'd require all kinda permits and state approvals."

Clay felt a surge of weakness well up, an incapacity, like vertigo. He realized he should have been ready for this, but he wasn't. He sat down, holding on to the rail.

"I'm sorry, Clay. I think the same as you."

Clay nodded.

"Strange combination. Condos. Crab and oyster wholesalin'. He likes cash, though. Crabs are an all-cash operation. But still . . ."

Clay tried to focus. He looked down the dock, but the *Mood In-digo* wasn't there.

"Boat's been gone a week. Must be nice," Jed added.

"Whose her captain?" Clay mumbled.

"Don't know. Him, I suppose."

Clay pressed his temples.

"We'll talk later," Jed finished. "I'll keep you posted."

"Yeah," Clay mumbled again. He sat for a while, just breathing. He brought his chapped hands up to his face and cupped his eyes, shielding them from the light, searching the docks, the decrepit buildings, searching out the fabric of his past. The image of Poplar

Island, once grand, now mostly washed away by the Bay's tides, slid into his thoughts. He struggled for balance. Slowly he rose, trying to center on the tasks before him. He restarted the engine, backed the *Miss Sarah* away from the dock, and took her into her slip, trying to stay with the present and the things he needed to do. He washed down the boat. When he finished, he checked his bait barrel. The brine covered his diminishing supply of menhaden. On Wednesday he would make another run to Barker. He had money in his pocket. That was something new. A good thought. But everything seemed obscured by what Jed had told him.

He checked the lines once more and then checked on Byron, who was lying mostly on his back, one leg hanging off the cot, snoring sporadically. Clay took the army blanket that was stowed in the forward hatch and arranged it lightly over Byron. He turned on the small chart light on the captain's table and wrote a note to Byron, telling him about Laura-Dez and to call him when he woke up, and then Clay left two dimes for phone calls on top of the note.

He walked around to Jed's office to cut through to the parking lot, and standing there, leaning against the side of the building and looking out over the creek with a vacant stare, was Amanda. Her hair was pulled back and braided, and she wore a halter top over faded cutoffs, her bare legs crossed over each other. He muttered hello to her and she looked at him as though she didn't recognize him. He stopped next to her without thinking and then had no idea what to say.

"Waiting for someone?" he blurted out.

She turned and then went back to looking at the creek. "Maybe."

There was so much about this place that she and Brigman needed to understand. He had no idea even how to begin, and he also knew that any words from him would be wasted. He stepped back and moved off across the landing, then got into Byron's pickup and left.

When he got back to the farmhouse, the telephone was ringing. He was surprised because he thought Byron would be asleep longer than this, but it was Matty calling from Washington with news. He had gotten the summer internship working for Colonial Williamsburg. He would be taking photographs of the restoration process at a plantation house in Gloucester. Kate had decided she wanted to spend the summer on the water, and a real estate agent they had called had found a cottage for them to rent in a waterfront town called Gwynn's Island, just up from Gloucester. They were moving there after classes were over. He and Kate were celebrating and they wanted to see Clay soon. He asked when they could come.

Clay didn't mention the wharf. He didn't want to blunt Matty's enthusiasm. He did tell him about the crabs he had caught, and Matty said he wanted to photograph the whole crabbing operation. Clay thought for a moment and then mentioned that the first summer regatta would be held over the weekend of June 14, in celebration of Flag Day, and he invited them to come for that. He told Matty that they could certainly stay with Bertha. Matty said it sounded fine and then Kate got on the phone. She told him that her trip over the Peachblossom Creek with him, after Pappy's funeral, was what made her want to live on the water. She got Clay to repeat everything about the crabs that day. She had their calendar and said she really didn't want to wait a month to come see him, but she would, and that the weekend of the fourteenth would be perfect, and they'd try to come Thursday or at least very early Friday. Later he couldn't remember much else of what she had said, just that they were coming in a few weeks. Clay had visited Matty a few times, at his father's big house in Richmond. He had even been to Kate's parents' once, in Potomac, Maryland, a suburb of Washington. But except for Pappy's funeral, neither Matty nor Kate had ever seen his world. He was pleased they were coming. Especially for the first summer regatta.

11

Clay ran the bateau out with the fifty new pots they had just bought. They'd had four good weeks and he felt prosperous. In addition to the pots, he had purchased more bait, paid rent, and still had money in his pocket. He had also gone to see his father's banker, Frank Dawson, who had been an old friend of Pappy's and who spoke courteously with him. Hugo Brigman's proposal was contingent on a "due diligence study." Rezoning would be required and the process would not be a fast one. Other alternatives were still being explored. Clay had felt better after learning this. With the warm air at his back, he arranged the new pots along a zigzag course running southerly from the others. He worked more slowly harvesting the crabs without Byron, who was nowhere to be found that morning.

Clay culled the crabs and rebaited, but he was impatient. The June sun climbed high, and the river seemed swollen as it rose and fell, as though it were breathing heavily in the heat of the day. A girl water-skied past, pulled behind a twenty-two-foot Whaler with a Johnson 150 on the back. She waved as she cut the water on one ski, sending a rooster tail his way that left rainbow droplets hanging in the air. He edged back the throttle and watched her slice through her own wake. She had long legs and looked beautiful on the slalom, sliding side to side on the spread of silver wave. She looked almost familiar.

He worked through lunch and finished up in the afternoon. The river turned flat and the sky high and pure as he crossed the Choptank. A little breeze for the weekend, and the weather will be perfect, he thought.

Docking alongside the landing at Pecks, he saw Jed Sparks on the office porch, leaning back in a rocker with a Budweiser in his hand. Clay threw two half hitches over the piling to his stern and jumped out with the painter, which he quickly notched around a cleat on the landing.

"Good catch?" Jed asked.

"Average." Clay looked around, not seeing any of Jed's men.

"Let the boys go early, what with the races startin' tomorrow." Jed reached back into a cooler and pulled out a beer. "Here," he said. "You crewin'?"

"Might," Clay said, taking the beer. "Thanks." He popped it and drank half of it as he walked back to the *Miss Sarah* and started loading bushels onto the landing. "Barker Cull's asked. He's sailing *Misty*," Clay hollered back. He threw onto the landing a bushel of number one jimmies with no lid, the top crabs hissing and scrapping with their pinchers. Jed got up and walked over.

"*Misty*'s right smart. Clacky Wheeler's sailin' *Flying Cloud*, though. Be tough to beat."

"But I've got some friends coming up tonight for the weekend," Clay went on. "I've got to see if I can work it."

"Lady friends?" Jed's face turned conspiratorial.

Clay heaved the last bushel up, ten in all. "One's a lady all right. But she's with the other, whose not, I'm afraid."

Jed Sparks winked. "You need some polshky, boy." Clay looked at Jed, who was grinning like a sheepshead, and figured he must have had a few. "Personally, I'd like to frig with that Amanda there."

Clay shook his head. "Right. She's a friendly one."

"She does have her nose stuck in the air." Sparks chuckled. "That ain't all that's stuck up there, though. And she's the kind that needs it—and would do it too, if she thought she could get away with it."

Clay smiled at the way he was carrying on. Jed was trying to wink again, but he looked more like he had a facial tic.

Clay pointed. "That bushel with no top, I'd like to stash in your cooler. I need to take about eighteen jumbos home for soup. If you can find me a paper bag. The rest in the bushel are for a crab feast tomorrow night down at Bertha's. Come on by if you feel like it. These other bushels, I'd like to sell. That is, if you're not too busy thinking about other things."

Jed Sparks eyed the full baskets and took out a wad of bills and paid Clay. He picked up one of the baskets. "Help me carry these inside, will you. Truck'll be by soon to get 'em." He started walking, then stopped and turned to Clay. "Thanks for the invite. I'll probably be drunk with Clacky." He laughed to himself as he walked inside.

Clay stopped at the grocery and then went home to start cooking the crab soup. He straightened the house and swept the walkway outside. After a while he lay down and fell asleep in the hammock that hung underneath the twin silver oaks. When he woke up, Byron and Laura-Dez were sitting out in front of the house on the picnic table, drinking gin and tonics. He rubbed his eyes and sat up. It took a minute for him to get his bearings. He studied the sky. The lawn and trees were tinted with amber. Down the lane the creek shore seemed to burn with small fires. Byron went in and brought him out a drink. Laura-Dez was rolling a joint when the car came bouncing up the drive.

Matty was the first out of the car, with his camera in his hand, shouting for no one to move as he angled to capture the scene in the fusion of light and color. But Kate came bounding around the car with a champagne bottle in her hand, jumping to embrace Clay, who, trying to get up, fell out of the hammock. She helped him up, laughing. Then she wrapped her arms around Byron's neck and sat on his lap. Laura-Dez frowned, and Kate, seeing, composed herself, rising and apologizing as they were introduced.

At the picnic table, Matty popped the champagne. They drank it out of plastic cups and then continued sipping the gin as they watched the light recede and dusk take over. Matty and Kate had just moved into the cottage on Gwynn's Island, and Kate described it to them, calling it country charming. Matty mumbled something about small-town nostalgia, then said the cottage ought to be at least charming after all the moving he'd done. "Damn piano almost killed me," he finished. Kate was disappointed with the real estate agent, though, because it really wasn't right on the Bay, but you could see the Bay across the road as well as from behind the cottage, through a row of houses. Still, it at least had the feel of the water about it, she concluded. Matty passed around his first set of plantation house pictures and began talking about his newest project, which was to collect enough photographs of disappearing Eastern Shore "relics"—that was the word he used—to compose a coffee-table book.

Clay started to say something about the wharf and then changed his mind.

"I'd like to get some shots of you doing your crab pots. And maybe shoot you working those oyster tongs you've told me about," Matty continued.

Clay wondered if he qualified as a relic.

Byron had come out, carrying the pot of steaming crab soup. "Oysterin' season's over, Matty," he said. "Gotta wait till September." Clay was looking in the pot, surprised. "Laura-Dez and I picked a few of the biggest ones while you were sleeping," Byron continued. "We broke up a few and left them in for character."

"Damn." Matty said. "Couldn't you act like you were tonging?"

Byron snorted. He took a long drink, finishing his gin, then seemed to examine the sky. "Full moon's gonna rise, though, Clay. New summer slough. I could unravel the seine."

They all started eating.

"What's that—the seine?" Kate asked. "And a slough?"

"The old seine. She still in one piece?" Clay asked Byron.

"Sewed her over the winter."

Clay swallowed a mouthful. "Soft crabbing," he answered Kate. "You want to see it the old way, Matty? We got to get up early. It's a real throwback."

"Make for a tasty breakfast too," Byron added.

"Sounds reliclike," Matty said. "How early?"

"About six, I'd say. We'll use the pickup and stop by your daddy's to get the seine?" he said to Byron, who nodded. "Be in the water by seven."

"I'm going," said Kate.

"I think I'll sleep in," said Laura-Dez.

"Did you say in the river?" Matty asked.

"Up to about your waist," Clay replied, "though you can take pictures from shore. We'll have to scrounge up some old tennis shoes for you each to wear."

"Do you think we'll get some?" Kate asked. Her face was rapt with fascination. "I mean, for real?"

"Slight chance," Byron said. He winked at Laura-Dez.

"Seining is almost a lost art," Clay said. "And if you want, I'll take you later to the boatyard. Rusted-out dredgers, clam conveyors. Even the picking house is antique."

"Cool," Matty said. "Right on."

"And I got another one for you, Matty," Clay added. He paused a moment. "The Chesapeake Bay log canoes are racing tomorrow and Saturday. Saturday, Byron and I are crewing on a friend's boat, and you're invited too. Nice canoe. She's called *Misty.*"

"Sailing a canoe?"

"No camera though. These things go over right easy."

"Matty, my sailor boy." Kate's inflection was maternal.

"Depending on the course they set, Kate might get a chance to see us pass close to the ferry dock, and she could take a picture or two if you want."

"I don't know that much about sailing, though."

"Don't need much know-how," Byron said pouring three fingers of gin into his glass. He made a motion with his arms, like throwing a potato sack. "Just how to heave those springboards, climb out on 'em, and hang on. Don't get your fingers pinched, and move quick when the skipper yells."

"The springboards are just loose planks," Clay said. "Like two-by-twelves. About fourteen feet long. You've seen 'em. At least in pictures. The boat carries too much sail, so as she heels over, we throw these long boards—three of them—out the windward side, and the crew climbs out on them to balance the boat. Two men can climb out on each board."

Matty looked bemused.

"Don't worry. I'll explain it all to you. And Barker Cull, our captain, 'll give us a few practice runs before the race starts."

"Uh-huh."

"But we all best pace ourselves," Clay said, looking at Byron. "We got a full weekend ahead. Crabs tomorrow night at Bertha's. Saturday night, the dance."

After the soup, Laura-Dez brought out a hot apple pie, and Byron uncovered a bottle of brandy. Clay had changed his mind and began explaining about the wharf and the bank and Hugo Brigman. "Best get all the photos you can now," he said to Matty. "They might be all we'll have left."

Kate saw how Clay was feeling about this and hooked her arm

into his, scooting up against him. "What would it take to buy it back?" she asked.

Clay rubbed his eyes. "I don't know, exactly. Hundreds of thousands, for sure."

"Is it a good investment? I mean, without tearing it down?"

"I believe it could make money," he said. "Probably make more, though, as real estate."

"I wonder if we could talk to your father, Matty," said Kate.

Matty yawned. "My old man is impossible. You know that. It's bottom line. All he ever cares about. Cap rates and such."

"Well, maybe we could talk to him about it?"

"Sure."

"That's not necessary," Clay interjected.

"Well, would you?" she pressed.

Matty forced an interest. "For Clay, of course."

They finished off the pie, and then Matty rose and took a glass of brandy and moved to the hammock. Byron and Laura-Dez got up and walked down the lane toward the creek and disappeared into the shadow. Kate helped Clay take some dishes in, then they sat back down at the picnic table. As the night enveloped them, Kate made him tell her about his boat and the pots and how he knew where to put them. With the settling darkness, the fireflies had begun to flash and the cicadas in the trees filled the silence. Clay and Kate, and Matty in the hammock, were there together, not speaking, just listening and watching the fireflies flash their mating lights, flickering, flickering. The night air was awash with the smell of the honeysuckle that grew wild against the house's southern side. Just as Byron had said it would, the moon of the first summer slough, round and golden, crept up over the trees in the east.

After a while Matty called for Kate. She whispered to Clay to excuse her, and went and lay with Matty in the hammock. Clay sat and watched the moon rise until it was well clear of the treetops. Then he got up and finished taking the dishes inside.

In the morning, Clay woke up first, before dawn. He dressed and went to the kitchen to put water on the stove for coffee. As before, he had given Matty and Kate his room and slept on the couch. In the kitchen the only light was from the gas fire pitching out from under the kettle. He sensed a presence behind him, and before he could turn, a slender arm encircled his waist, and Kate was behind and up against him. Her soft body was against his back, and her breath upon his neck. He turned slowly. She looked up at him and put her hand on his cheek.

"I want you to know," she said, "that I think what you're doing here is . . ." She paused as though searching for a word. "Is perfect." She reached up on tiptoe and kissed him on the cheek and on the corner of his lips. "I'll get Matty up," she said, and she turned and walked out through the door.

The four of them headed out in Byron's pickup. At Mason's, Byron and Clay tried to be as quiet as possible as they retrieved the seine from the garage. They got it into the back of the pickup, and Byron went in the house and found some old beat-up tennis shoes of Blackie's for Kate to wear and some torn Top-Siders for Matty.

Clay suggested they try the bar off Bruff's Island, so they rode down the back roads through Tunis Mills to the Wye River. They parked the pickup near the Hooper farm, and the four walked across the flat fields of new corn.

Matty said he wanted to stay on the bar with his camera and take pictures, so he made himself a seat on an old oak stump, setting his tripod before him. Clay stepped into the cool water and helped Kate in and told her to stay close. He took one pole of the seine, and Byron the other, and they began backing away from each other, unraveling it as they went. The seine was about the size of a tennis net, with weights sewn along the bottom, cork sewn into the top, and each end attached to a pole. Once it was unraveled, Clay pointed to where he wanted to run the net, in three to four feet of water, along the edge of the bar. He and Kate swung out into the river together, and she held the back waist of his jeans with both hands. As they walked, feeling the silty bottom, little eddies swirled around them. The water came up over Kate's stomach. Clay held one pole. Byron carried the other one. Once out where he wanted to be, Clay nodded to Byron and they began walking a parallel course, dragging the net along the bottom. It was easy at first, but the net got heavier as they dragged their catch with it. After they had worked it about forty paces, Clay swung his end in near to shore and worked the net up onto the shallows of the bar. Minnows flickered and danced along the net, and sunfish darted everywhere, escaping where the net went slack. In the bottom, though, Clay showed Kate the first softy, pushed over on its back trying to right itself, a medium-size female. He picked it up and handed it to Kate, careful not to let its claws flop, as they could tear.

She took it in her hand, touching it with her fingers. "It's so soft."

Matty shouted, "Bravo!"

Clay pointed to another, a large male hidden under a clump of kelp. He picked it up. Byron felt around in the matted grass and found another soft crab. He said, "Hard crabs'll outrun us, but the softies can't move well enough."

Matty had been taking pictures the whole time and came over for close shots of the crab and net, snapping his camera's shutter. Clay pulled a small plastic garbage bag out of his pocket, and they carefully laid the soft crabs inside it and placed it on the sand.

"You ready to take the pole this time?" he said, handing it to Kate.

"Oh, I don't think so."

"I'll be with you. Go on. Just let the net do the work."

Together they held the pole and waded in for another drag. When the net got heavy Clay helped her more and they pulled it around to the shallows. They found two more softies. They ran the seine upriver and in two drags got six more soft crabs. Each run offered up crabs.

"The slough is a fat one, ain't she," Byron said. "Crabs'll be all over this river soon. And in our pots, I bet."

"It does look rich," Clay returned. "You want to try, Matty?" Clay asked.

He retreated to his tripod. "Oh, I think it's too early to get wet. I'm content here," he answered. "Hell, *National Geographic* might put this on its cover."

Clay took the pole from Byron, and he and Kate walked the shoreline south, working the bottom carefully and smoothly with the net. He had tied the bag of crabs to one of his belt loops, and it floated when he walked in the river. A white egret stood statue-still on a fallen tree and waited until they were almost on it before fanning out its wings and gliding away. They brought the net in twice more, and onshore he untied the bag from his belt. They had seventeen softies, enough for any breakfast feast, he concluded. "You stay there," he said to Kate. He backed away from her, stretching the net taut, and then he slowly waded toward her, rolling the seine carefully around his pole, until he was upon her. Her hair was damp and ruby red against her flushed face, and her blouse soaked and transparent. She wore no bra. He looked at her, and she watched him, expressionless. Then she smoothed her blouse tight against her skin, looking down at how she had revealed herself. She looked back at him, tilting her head. "I guess I should have worn something underneath."

Clay nodded.

"Sorry."

"It's okay. I mean, I don't mind. Who would mind?"

She laughed. "I shouldn't go back like this."

Clay took his shirt off. Then he helped her put it over her shoulders, and she buttoned it. She held his arm in hers as they walked upstream.

Back at the cottage they showered and changed while Laura-Dez sautéed the crabs whole, in butter. She had made pancakes and fried potatoes and they ate it all, wiping their plates clean.

Afterward Clay rode with Matty and Kate to the wharf. They walked in the high grass among the rusting hulks in the back field. Matty took photographs of the dredgers and machinery. An old skipjack with half a mast leaning crossways against the grain of the warehouse in the distance caught his fancy, and he went back to the car for his tripod and another lens. Clay watched him walk back. The summer grass was up to his thighs and blew in the morning breeze.

"Look," Kate said as she grabbed Clay's arm and turned him around to face the river. "Is that a log canoe?"

Clay watched and saw *Flying Cloud* looking like a white bird tipping to leeward, with her kite raised, running the tide, her springboards fully manned.

They pointed for Matty, who watched with them as *Flying Cloud* sailed past the point and around into the cove and out of sight. Clay tried to explain the kind of balance and feel it took to hold a log canoe in the wind.

They spent a couple of hours at the wharf. For a while Clay and Kate tried to help Matty with his choice of photographs. He went from the boat graveyard to the picking shack, and then started shooting the soft crab molt tanks, full of peelers and sooks, and moved on to the workboats in their slips. After a while, Clay took Kate over and showed her his bateau. She wanted to go on board, so he helped her onto the rail, then took her by the waist and lifted her down into the cockpit. He showed her how the tiller was worked from the center cockpit, and opened the bait barrel for her to smell. She didn't make a face. She dipped her finger in the brine and held it up to her nose to smell and then touched her finger to her lips. Then she touched his nose with her finger, and then his lips with her finger.

"Strong," he said.

"Yes. Salty. Like you." She laughed.

"I smell like fish, huh?"

"No. Not fish."

Clay looked at her. He shook his head.

"What?" she asked.

Clay wasn't sure how to respond.

She watched him for a few moments. Then she took his hand. "C'mon," she said. "Let's find Matty and go on to that picnic that Byron invited us to. I'm getting hungry again. How can that be?"

"Must be the salt air."

She cocked her head. "I suppose. Now, where was it? The picnic?"

"At the boathouse."

"Yes."

"The old Walker Boathouse."

"Help me up?" And Clay took her hand as she stepped up on the rail and balanced herself. He pulled the bateau close to the dock, using the stern line, and she stepped off, and he followed.

They found Matty lying over one of the shed boxes, staring through his lens into the water, trying to capture a crab in the exhausting act of trying to disengage its limp, molluscan body from its hard outgrown shell. After some coaxing they finally got Matty to stop clicking his camera. They headed down to Bellevue and took the ferry across the Tred Avon to Oxford. Kate stood against the wooden rail, and Matty came up behind her and wrapped his arms around her. The river was a kaleidoscope, glistening like sapphire in the sun.

The regatta had begun earlier that morning, miles away across the Chesapeake, with a 10:00 gun starting the Annapolis-Oxford race. The starting line stretched across the mouth of the Severn River, adjacent to the Naval Academy. A hundred or so sloops would be racing. They would sail all day and finish in Oxford, between the red spar off the yacht club and the yellow balloon the club had set out across the river. The leaders were probably somewhere off Poplar Island, Clay thought, still heading for Blackwalnut Point. He drove off the ferry, down Oxford Road, past Goose Neck, to a gatepost marking a dirt drive that led to the boathouse.

Clay got out of the car, and Matty and Kate followed him down toward the river's edge. They heard guitar music and singing as they walked through the trees and down the riverbank, and then saw the blankets and people, young women mostly, with a few children. They found Laura-Dez and joined her on a horse blanket. She pointed to the long dock that led out into the mouth of Island Creek fifty yards or so. At the end of the dock sat a two-story red boathouse supported by pilings, with a ladder that ran up its side to a slatted cedar-shake roof. Standing at the edge of the roof, the young men were lined up, high above the river. Shoulder to shoulder, they were all naked. The roof was a good forty feet above the surface of the river, a long way up, Clay thought. He saw Byron in the center of the group. There were at least ten in the line.

"Jesus," said Matty.

The guys in the line on the rooftop stood still. Most of them had long hair, some even shoulder length. Byron was the exception. They all appeared muscular, and their muscles were flexed and ready. They were taking deep breaths, their chests expanding and contracting slowly, and in unison. They all seemed to be concentrating. Everyone was watching them. The one closest to the side of the boathouse raised his arms straight up, and the rest followed. They brought their arms down slowly, and then they all dove out, in unison, out far away from the boathouse, far into the sky, arms reaching, out over the river, suspended for a moment, and then falling in a dive, together, toward the water, and they seemed gone. And then they were up, splashing, shouting, and laughing, and the girls on the blankets were cheering.

"Wow," said Kate. "Why haven't we been here before? I've been missing this?"

Clay counted heads in the water.

Matty said, "What a picture that would make. I have to get my camera."

"I think that was their only dive," Laura-Dez said. "They were just jumping before. At least it better be."

"Now, that should be in *National Geographic!*" Kate exclaimed, laughing. "Endangered creatures of the Chesapeake, or something."

"Give her some binoculars," Matty quipped. He stood up.

"It's not like that," she said. "And sit down, why don't you? You've taken enough pictures. Enjoy the day." She reached up for his hand, but he ignored her.

The divers had begun to climb the ladder to the dock on which the first landing of the boathouse sat. One of them pushed another off the ladder. Another jumped up on the handrail and dove back into the water. One was shouting for his girlfriend to strip and come in swimming, but she pretended not to hear. Byron had climbed out and was walking along the shore toward them, dripping wet. His right hand covered the purplish scar that ran across his side above his hip. Laura-Dez threw him a towel.

"Sorry," he said, grabbing it and covering himself.

"You're cute, but not that cute."

"That was such a rush. But my head's still ringing." He shook the water from his hair and then wrapped the towel around his waist. "How'd we look?"

"Like a bunch of naked boys showing off," Laura-Dez said, feigning disinterest.

"I thought you all were amazing," Kate said. She spoke carefully. "I will remember you like that. In the air. So beautiful."

Byron seemed to appreciate her for the remark. "Yeah. It felt very cool," he responded. "Wild."

The rest of the afternoon unwound itself at a languorous pace, a picnic on the river. People moved from blanket to blanket, sharing food and wine and an occasional joint. Children ran through the picnic baskets. A few splashed in the shallows. Byron had brought his guitar and played it with some others. It was about four o' clock when Clay, out on the dock, saw the first spinnaker running up the Choptank, billowing like a golden cloud. Soon after, through the distant sheen of river air, he could make out the figure of a red serpent emblazoned across the sail, wavering like a mirage. The *Scarlet Dragon*. He knew the boat, one of Annapolis's premier racing sloops, and was not surprised she was first. Behind her he saw a second sail, pale with rose stripes, and then a third spinnaker, riffling crimson, as the racers raised their headsails after coming around the mark off the tip of Tilghman Island.

"Look!" someone shouted from the bank. And soon there was a crowd with Clay, watching the distant colored sails, puffed out like red-and-gold roosters, approaching as though in slow motion through the thin and sparkling haze of the Choptank in the summer sun. Clay was watching when Kate came up and put her hand on his shoulder. Then she took his arm, nestling close.

Clay looked at her. Her fine hair blew around her forehead. He looked back at the river. "Where's Matty?" Clay said.

"He ran to get his camera. He couldn't miss this sight."

"He's already missing it, if he's worrying about his camera."

Kate gazed out at the wide river adorned with the gilded spinnakers. "But we're seeing it," she answered.

12

Barker Cull didn't waste any time the next morning. They were rigged and on the river by eight, and only *Flying Cloud* was out before them.

Including Barker, and his nephew, Lex, who was ten and was the bailer, there were twelve on *Misty*. Barker showed each crew member his place in the boat. He gave Clay the foresail sheet, and his brother, Earl, the main. Pal Tyler had the kite. Byron was to work the jib sheet and direct Matty on the springboard until he learned to balance with the other crew members. Two crew members would climb out on each board. Like parallel seesaws, angled high, they would counterbalance the effort of the wind to push over the streamlined sail-heavy racer.

The wind was out of the south and brisk at twelve to fifteen knots. "A good spike of a breeze," Barker called it. The sky was deep blue with an occasional cotton fluff trailing like a banner. The river gushed up green and foamy along the gunnels of the boat and stirred silver out to the horizon. At anchor were the hundred or so sailing yachts that had come up the day before from Annapolis, all tied alongside each other in rafts of eight or ten boats along the shore near Oxford. Teenagers worked Boston Whalers as ferries, taking the sailboat crews to and from the yacht club for showers or breakfast. A flotilla of party boats and cruisers milled about, waiting for the race to get started. The log canoes would sail in the morning, and the afternoon was set aside for the smaller Penguin, Flying Dutchman, and Star one-designs to race.

Barker pinched up close on a starboard tack and let his crew work the boards for a while and feel the sway of the wind and water. He took her downstream and then came about and traversed the channel. During the first few tacks, Matty was slow and clumsy compared to the others, but he soon got the idea. He started out second man on his board, but he had bulk, and once Barker saw he could move, he put him first on the middle board.

The race started at half past nine, and at the ten-minute gun Clay looked up and saw the river full of white sails moving across one another and surfing the blue swells in a dreamlike minuet. *Misty* carried two stepped masts, raked aft, holding their massive leg-of-mutton sails, and a boom-fitted jib—three large sails of canvas spreading from bowsprit to stern—and then a kite rising above the head of the foresail, all powering a narrow dugout hull with a deep centerboard. Barker began talking to Clay, Earl, Pal, and Byron in a steady chatter about strategy. At the five-minute gun, Barker was abreast of *Flying Cloud,* and he and its captain were shouting at each other.

"Looks right sharp for an old gal gone in the beam," the other man hollered. "Hope she likes tastin' my stale air."

"Keep to your point there, Clacky," Barker hollered back. "You don't want your crew to be swimmin' too soon, now!"

Clay motioned to Jed Sparks, who was handling *Flying Cloud*'s main, and Jed saluted in return.

Barker called out, announcing three minutes to the start. At one minute he started cussing. "We're too fast, boys," he shouted. "Too goddamn fast." *Misty* was rapidly approaching the starting line but couldn't cross it before the starting gun or she would have to come round about and recross the line. Clay eased off the foresail sheet, and Earl and Byron both let out sail, and they slowed some. "Thirty seconds. Men, drag off the boards," Barker bellowed. Even with the loosened sails, *Misty* was flying from the momentum. "It's gonna be close—get into the goddamn water!" he screamed. Matty looked and saw the other crew members hanging on to the boards with their hands and lowering their bodies into the river, dragging their mass through the swiftly passing water, trying to slow the boat.

"Matty, goddamn it, get into the water!" It was Byron echoing Barker, and Matty slowly lowered his legs into the water, holding on to the board, but went no further.

"Five seconds!" Barker shouted. The nose of the boat was even with the line between the two orange buoys. *Bang!* The gun went off. "We made it! Get your lazy asses out of the water! Out now! Up! Up, boys! Move it, goddamn your lazy souls!" Matty was quick, up first as the rest hauled themselves back onto the boards, drenched. Clay had tightened up on his sheet, as Earl and Byron had on theirs, and *Misty* was surfing through the spray, boats on either side of her, boats moving faster because they had not had to slow their momentum for the start.

"Tighten that main. Pull in on the kite." *Misty* accelerated, rushing through the foam. Matty, out on the tip of his board, could almost have reached and touched the boom of the boat next to them, except that he was holding on for dear life. "Come down, Matty," he heard Byron say quietly, and he inched down the board. The foam rushed and seethed below him. "Steady there, boy. Feel it. Pay attention. Feel that blow now."

As they sailed past the Town Dock, Clay looked and saw Kate standing out on the end, waving a red scarf. Matty, balancing on the springboard, had his back to her and couldn't see. The wind, Clay could sense, was strengthening in incremental gusts.

A smaller canoe, one that had taken an early lead on the first leg and was down the channel, was the first to go over. Clay saw it lurch and swamp but wasn't sure which boat it was.

"That's *Island Bird*," Barker yelled. "Built in 1882. She's done. Her sister *Island Blossom*'s up ahead. Built in 1892." He grinned. "Gettin' blustery now, boys," he continued. "She won't be the last. Be ready now! You, Lex, work that bail." Lex was in the center of the boat, with a halved Clorox bottle in his hand. His job was to constantly scoop up and throw overboard the water that came in over the side and sloshed around the bottom of the canoe.

Clay felt the line and the pull and give needed to keep the sheet full and right with the wind. No winches. Only block and tackle. It took strong arms to man the sheets.

The boat flew off its port tack and seemed to speed-glide through the element as though it were almost airborne—heeled over, perfectly balanced with weight and wind, its sails redundant. The green froth flew by the gunnel in a rush of sound and foam. *Misty* was faster than the smaller canoes and was able to pass them before the first mark. Clay saw that they were gradually gaining on the two larger boats ahead, but there was still considerable distance to make up.

He watched Matty, who was moving a few inches at a time, up and then down his board, watching the sails and the masts intently. Clay called to him. They locked eyes for a moment. Matty nodded and smiled, and then shifted his stare back to the sails.

After a few minutes, Clay could make out the windward mark, a yellow inflated buoy out past Bachelor Point. He watched it get closer as he worked the sheet, keeping track of the pressure of the wind in and around the sail.

"That's *Flying Cloud* and *Jaydee* ahead," Barker shouted. "Watch 'em close as they round the mark, and be ready to come about. Wind's getting swirly. I'll count down from 'five' to 'go' and then I'll swing. On 'go' you boys throw the boards, and be quick about it."

As they approached, they could see *Jaydee* reach the mark first and turn into the wind, the crew heaving the boards across to the opposite gunnel. *Flying Cloud* turned right behind her and slightly to her leeward. As *Jaydee*'s sails took, though, she seemed to go over too much, and then, in an overcorrection on the sheets, she bounced back too far. As though in slow motion she listed and fell on her side, over further and further, not righting herself, her skipper cursing and the crew shouting, as her sails settled into the river. *Flying Cloud* had to take evasive action and ease off the wind, losing some ground. Barker continued shouting through all the excitement and turmoil, shouting at *Jaydee*'s skipper and crew as he approached, laughing and shouting at the wind itself.

"We got a break there, boys," he continued. "Let's make the most of it." He started yelling the countdown, "Five, four, three, two, one, go!" as he swung the tiller hard to port. "Go, goddamn you lazy suckers, go! Bail there, Lex. Bail! Go, boys—run those boards across there! Now set them things and climb boys, yes, climb!" Clay released the port foresail sheet and simultaneously hauled in the starboard sheet, pulling it through the blocks and tightening with his arms and shoulders. Out of the corner of his eye, he watched Matty, who followed the others. He swung down off the board, grabbed his end, and in unison with a mate pulled out the board and stepped it across, then slid it out over the opposite side rail and fixed its edge beneath the leeward washboard before shinnying out to balance. The sails filled and the canoe surged forward, making new spray in the sun. She was balanced and never lost momentum. Barker cut just inside the floating *Jaydee* and, grinning widely, tipped his hat to the captain and crew as he glided by. *Flying Cloud* had moved back in, but since she had lost ground she was only two boat lengths ahead. The three other boats remaining in the race, smaller and not as fast, had yet to round the first mark and were well behind.

Over the first half of the next leg, *Misty* and *Flying Cloud* ran even, the spray flying and the wind strong, coming more from the southwest. *Flying Cloud* was outside, to windward, and began to move closer to *Misty*.

"She's tryin' to steal our wind, goddamn it," Barker shouted. "Pinch those sheets. Make some magic, boys. I want to cut out where she won't follow!" Clay started to pull his line tighter, but *Misty*'s sails began to luff as *Flying Cloud* took her wind and forged ahead. Barker cursed. They watched as she opened up her lead. Clay adjusted his sheet as did the others and they regained their momentum.

Flying Cloud jibed around the Ferry Neck mark and ran down-wind. *Misty* followed, remaining just behind throughout the third leg of the race. The two boats matched each other in speed and balance, their outstretched sails full as they surfed the waves. Clay, leaning back to hold his sheet tight, began to study the river's mouth out past Bachelor Point, where the Choptank opened from the south and the waves ran rougher. The Town Creek mark was getting closer. The last leg of the race, the longest, was a tack out past Bachelor Point to the Benoni light. He scanned the shoreline and felt the change coming. "Barker," he shouted, "after we round the mark, take us in toward shore. We'll run the shoreline."

Barker looked at him as though he were crazy. Byron seemed confused as well, but then turned and said something to Barker. Then gradually a smile crossed Barker's face. "We'll lose minutes moving in that far," he replied.

Clay shrugged.

Barker gave a thumbs-up. "Okay, Clay. You got that sixth sense workin', I can tell."

They watched *Flying Cloud* round the Town Creek mark with-out a hitch and head straight out the channel. A minute later they reached the buoy. The other boats were not in contention. Barker guided her around the mark smoothly.

"Let her fly," Barker yelled. "We're heading for the shore."

Misty raced, angling for the shore, seemingly off course and losing precious distance to *Flying Cloud,* which ran out the river's middle straight for the finish. After several minutes, Barker gave the command and they veered toward the finish also, but they continued to hug the shoreline. "Tighten the sail, boys," he yelled. "Bail, Lex, bail your heart out, boy." The wind was still stiff, but the river here was calmer, and *Misty* seemed to pick up speed. They watched *Flying Cloud.* She had begun to pitch in the channel waves and stronger current. With each heave she lost wind from her sails. "The tide's changin', boys, and the wind and tide are at odds," Barker hollered. "Out there in the channel it's much worse than in here. And they'll fight that tide the whole way. Goddamn you, Clay, boy," he went on. "Goddamn, you can be right smart at times."

Sailing smoothly now and balanced, *Misty* was gaining steadily. It looked like they were abreast of the other boat and then past her. But they still needed a fast tack back out to the finish line, and Clay wondered if they would build enough of a lead to win. They started angling back out. Barker was screaming a steady stream of epithets at his crew and at the wind, which was heeling them over. Then Clay noticed Matty pointing at him and gesturing, then starting to shout, his face changing complexion. It was at that moment that the Chris-Craft churned past them, coming from their rear, with no regard for the race or their delicate balance. Neither Clay nor Barker saw it coming, and its wake rocked them before they could prepare. The first wave nearly jolted Barker off the windward washboard and sent the bow angling around away from the wind. Clay let his sheet go, but Earl had wrapped his around a cleat for purchase and couldn't loosen it fast enough, and it held as the wind knocked the boat over. It all happened in a moment. She was on her side and they were all in the water spitting and cursing.

Clay quickly found Lex and made sure he was fine, and then he found Matty.

"What the hell?" Matty came up sputtering. "Jesus Christ!" he bawled, slapping the water.

Clay took hold of him, pushing him against the floating boom for support. "We capsized. Happens occasionally." Clay spat out a stream of water and grinned. Matty, who had taken his shirt off, looked for it now around the boat. Clay told him, "It's probably too early for nettles, but if there are any, they'll be out here, moving off the current. If you see any, just push 'em away with your hand. And just hold on to *Misty*'s side. She'll float. They'll come get us soon and tow her in. If you want, you can help make sure we find all the boards. Swim them over here and keep hold of them. I'm gonna help pull the sails."

They cursed the cabin cruiser as they worked on the sails and lines. Barker was muttering to himself while he worked. "Did anybody get the name of that filthy fucker?" he finally asked.

"Probably a charter," Clay said. "No goddamn sense."

"Bullshit to that. Sucker needs a punishin'."

"I was trying to point you to it," Matty said to Clay, "to warn you."

Clay explained how he'd missed it. It just happened too fast. And no one could have heard much above Barker's shouting, the wind, the rush of the river and spray. Matty seemed to agree.

In the water, they all continued working until the *Miss Beatrice* arrived. Ronald Price, Barker's cousin, skippered her, and he offered his condolences for what happened.

"We were out yonder at the finish and didn't really see her till you were over," he apologized. "By then she had throttled down and was out passing the lighthouse."

"Fucker ran us down without a twitch," Barker snarled. He continued yanking down the main.

"Was a good race, though," Ronald said. "Would've been a close'un."

Ronald's wife, Molly, big as a bait barrel, rose out of her deck chair. "I believe you had'em, Barker," she called.

Barker looked at them and then grinned. "Goddamn, I thought we had 'em," he said. "These boys made her fly. Yessir. Just made her fly."

Clay helped Lex up into the *Miss Beatrice*.

"Do you think we had her?" Lex asked after he was in.

Barker answered. "We did indeed, son. And you were a fine bailer. Hell, we were skipping along on the edge of magical. It was a thrill, it was. But it's a damn fine edge,that is. Hard to balance on that edge too long. It's fine enough just to be there."

They took a while longer to finish taking the sails off. Everyone pitched in and they handed them up. Clay, Barker, Byron, and Earl worked the masts loose, pulled them out, and tied them. Then they started bailing. While they worked, they watched *Flying Cloud* glide across the finish line well in front of the other two ca-noes that were still sailing. "She ran a good race and deserved to win," Barker said. "'Gainst everyone but us." After enough of the water was out, they hooked up the towline. Several more of the crew climbed into the *Miss Beatrice*. Matty declined and elected to stay with Clay. Molly took cold beers out of a cooler on the deck of the *Miss Beatrice* and passed them around. Barker grabbed two for each of them. Apparently taking Barker's lead, everyone's mood had improved. Barker, Clay, Matty, and Byron took their beers and then found seats in the river-swamped *Misty*. They began toasting one another. Clay smiled. He sipped his beer, leaned back, and re-laxed as the tow slowly brought them in.

Laura-Dez was waiting for Byron and took him with her. Clay took Matty and Kate to the farmhouse to change and pack, since they planned to stay that night at Bertha's to be nearer to the dance. Then they drove back down to Pecks. Clay needed to take the *Miss Sarah* out into the Choptank to empty and rebait his pots, and they both wanted to come. Clay told them they could cull for him and explained how to tell the sooks from the males, and the larger number ones from the number twos.

Churning downriver into the afternoon sun in the middle of the regatta, they could see the Penguins racing across from Bachelor Point, forty or more boats jockeying around the channel marker and turning toward Benoni Point light. They followed the sails out into the broad expanse of the Choptank. Turning southeast, Clay pointed out the landmark for his pot lay and readied the boat to pull. Beyond the shore lay the marsh, weaving with the tidal wash in the sunlight.

The pots were heavy with crabs. Clay gave Kate the rubber gloves and showed her how to avoid the pinchers. He was able to do most of the culling between pots, but she tried hard and helped some. Mostly, though, she studied him. Intent as he was, Clay couldn't fail to notice how she watched him at work on the water.

Matty, at first busy taking several rolls of film, eventually began to help with rebaiting the cylinders, though it was clear he didn't take to having his hands in fish brine. Clay had nearly filled all his baskets when he pulled the last pot. He whistled over his catch. He had eight bushels of ones, twelve bushels of twos, and seven bushels of sooks. The crabs were fat and heavy.

On the way back the sun was dropping behind them, and the river had turned the color of a copper cauldron. The sailors were finished and the big boats had all rafted inside the half-moon bay. The sound of horns calling came from every direction, and the ferries were busy. Clay let Matty and Kate off at the yacht club dock among the sailors and party-goers. From there they could walk down the street to Bertha's to shower and dress. He planned to meet them later. Before she got out, Kate made him promise her a dance, and from the dock she blew him a kiss.

Clay took the *Miss Sarah* slowly back across the Tred Avon to

Pecks. He was trying to get his thoughts in order, but they flew around in a confusion. Finally he just settled on watching the flaming river in the twilight.

When he got to the wharf, Jed had closed up. Clay had to unload the crabs himself into the walk-in cooler. He stood looking at the catch. He figured he'd caught over three hundred dollars' worth. He felt rich. He drove home, grabbed a beer from the refrigerator, and drank it while he showered and changed, then grabbed another for the road, suddenly wanting to hurry. Despite the long day and the sun, and the tiredness from being on the water in the heat, he was impatient. On the way to Oxford, the night air rushing through his car windows was like an intoxicant. Clay stepped on the accelerator.

At Bertha's, Kate came down the stairs wearing a short cotton dress that left her shoulders bare and brushed against her thighs when she moved. She leaned over to kiss Clay and he breathed the perfume in her hair. She took Clay's and Matty's arms, and they walked together along the Strand toward the yacht club. The moon shone over the harbor and gleamed off the many masts. As they neared the yacht club, they could hear the Dixieland band.

They looked around for Byron but didn't see him, so they found a table, and Clay brought over plates of food and a plastic pitcher of beer. Matty was retelling his sailing adventure and got Kate laughing at everything. Before he knew it, Clay was inside with them, standing at the bar and telling Kate that he would not dance with Matty and her in a threesome. She finally gave up and went off with Matty. Clay watched her moving in her summer dress. The dance hall was packed with partyers. There were young men in tuxedos and barefoot girls in cutoff jeans, and everyone was dancing side by side and together. Clay stood and watched. He saw Paula Firth and Mac Longley sitting at a table. She waved to him and he gestured back but did not go over to speak. He was thinking of going back outside when Byron grabbed him from behind in a hug.

"How you be there, pardner? How'd we do?"

Clay turned around. Byron's face was flushed, and he carried a bottle of applejack in his hand. Laura-Dez came up behind Byron and began dancing in place. She wore a black miniskirt and black cowgirl boots with silver buckles. "You wouldn't believe the crabs we potted today," Clay replied.

"Well, damn."

Clay looked past Byron and saw Kate. She began to move her hips and crooked her finger at him to come dance. He turned back to Byron. "We caught a boatful. Crabs are running. Should have some cash coming our way."

Matty brought Kate over and ordered a wine for her and a Jack and 7 for himself.

"How'd you like it, Matty?" Byron asked.

Matty drank half his glass down and then handed the wine to Kate. "It was like a dream. A watery dream, and we had speed and wings, and just before we flew we just lay down in the cool water."

"I mean about the crabbin'."

"Oh. Great operation. Slick as an alewife, I guess." He winked.

The band began playing "Mack the Knife," and Matty reached over and took Laura-Dez by the hand. "What you say there, beautiful?" She followed him onto the dance floor.

Kate poked Clay on the chest with her finger. "I culled his crabs today, but he won't dance a lick." She took Byron's hand. "Hardly seems right, does it?" She pulled Byron toward the dance floor. He resisted, but she kept pulling him till he gave. "You should talk to that partner of yours, Byron," she said as she led him off. "Try to get him squared away."

Clay saw Barker Cull and Jed Sparks in the corner, bought three beers, and took them over. Barker put his arm around him and bragged on the race for a while. Jed admitted it might have been close "had her skipper not tipped her over that baby ripple." They watched the dancers and talked about the races set for Sunday. After a while Jed went to the bar and came back with another round of beers in mugs with a shot glass full of whiskey sunk to the bottom of each. "Boilermakers, boys." He raised his glass. "To the hardworking people."

"And it's gettin' harder ever year," Barker grumbled. "First good season of crabs in a coon's age."

"Crabs're fat early, this slough," Jed agreed. "Maybe it's a turn-around cycle."

"I'll lift to that," Barker offered, again holding his glass high.

Clay walked by the back bar and around to the dance floor, where the band had been slowing things down. Matty was still dancing with Laura-Dez. He watched them and looked for Kate. Then he felt her. She had his hands and then she had him on the dance floor and was holding him close. "If dancing one dance with me in public is too much culture for you, Clay Wakeman, just take deep breaths, close your eyes, and it will be over soon." He took her advice. And then they danced again to "Moon River." When the band struck up "When the Saints Go Marching In," he took her back to the bar.

Matty and Laura-Dez came over and stood with Byron. Kate said thank you to Clay, who excused himself. He walked out onto the large screened porch, which ran the length of the hall, and then down the steps and out onto the sandy beach. The dark water lapped against the sterns of the day-sailers pulled up on the shore. The moon wavered just under the water, a beacon to be embraced by a drowning man, he thought. He heard some commotion and giggling out on the pier and saw a woman with her skirt up pushing away a man in a blue tuxedo. As he focused, he noticed it was Amanda and Hugo Brigman, and sitting on the dock piling next to Brigman was Mac Longley. Clay walked back in the opposite direction and ran into Laura-Dez, Matty, and Byron coming down the steps. "C'mon," they said, walking between some of the boats. Matty reached in his pocket and took out a joint. "Acapulco gold," he said. "Smell." He handed it to Laura-Dez. He lit it while she took a pull. Matty then took a deep drag and passed it to Byron, who took a toke. "We've had enough of the crowds," Byron said. He passed it to Clay. It tasted light and smooth. "Matthew here wants to take a drive out to the point."

"Yeah, let's," said Laura-Dez.

"Where's Kate?"

Matty answered, "Here she comes."

"I'll drive the truck," Byron said. "You all pile in the back and enjoy the evening." Laura-Dez and Matty started walking.

"Where we going?" Kate asked.

"Just some fresh air, Kate."

They got in the back of the truck, and Byron drove slowly out of town. Laura-Dez sat next to Matty, and Kate was half on Clay's lap. He could feel the whiskey and pot. The houses and trees whirred past. His head felt hot. Kate leaned her bare back and shoulder against his arm. Byron kept straight past Pope's Tavern and drove down the Wilgus's moonlit lane, past the stand of pines where the doves all roosted, and on out to Bachelor Point and parked. They all got out, and Byron put in an eight-track tape of José Feliciano singing "Light My Fire" and turned up the sound. Byron had a blanket in the truck, so they walked out on the point and then sat on the blanket in the sand, looking out over the river. Farther out they could see the beacon from the lighthouse circling around. Matty relit the joint. Everyone took a hit, and they sat and talked in whispers and listened. Clay lay back and tried to focus on the night sky. A barn owl periodically hooted from off in the pines, a soothing, ghostlike sound that carried out over the water. He tried to listen hard for the return call of its mate.

It was some time later that Laura-Dez whispered that they

should go swimming. Clay sat up, and his head spun. Byron and then Matty happily agreed to her suggestion. And then there she was taking off first her boots, then her halter top and skirt. Matty and Byron were up and with her, and they were both trying to help her and laughing and stripping as well. And then they both pulled up Kate, who was protesting.

"No. No." She shook her head.

Matty, wired, said, "Come on, Kate."

And Laura-Dez, nearly naked, said Kate had to.

"Should I really?" Kate whispered, as though she needed permission but wasn't sure who to ask. Matty had gotten behind Laura-Dez and was fidgeting with her bra. And then Kate just shrugged and turned to Clay. She bent and took the bottom of her shift and lifted it slowly over her head and then stood there. "Well?" she said, watching him, a fierceness charging her eyes. She continued to stand there, uncovered, her hair falling and shining over her breasts. And then she pointed at him. "Well?" she asked. He looked at her. Laura-Dez was naked and laughing and helping Matty pull off his trousers. Clay stood before Kate. He began to unbutton his shirt. Byron was naked, and he and Laura-Dez and Matty waved at them to follow and then linked arms and started wading into the water. Clay looked at Kate, and at them all. His eyes had adjusted to the night and traced the glow the moon bestowed on Kate's skin. He watched Kate step out of her panties and hold her hand out for him, her eyes never leaving his. Her hair fell like a red flame against her. He went into the water with her. The river was bath warm. He heard the owl calling to them from the pines. He was in a dream. The water was black and still, and she swam around and against him and they could hear the others splashing and frolicking in the water. Then they were apart from the others, waist deep, on firm sand, and she put her mouth against his, there in the moon-spun water, warm and still, and his hands were all over her, and all restraint was washed away, in the sweet breach of deceit, in the crook and anguish of a love that he knew wasn't his to take.

In the morning when he finally woke, he wasn't sure how he had gotten to where he was, there on a cot in Bertha's basement. He felt like a diesel was working inside his skull. And everybody was gone. They had left a note on the dining room table saying good-bye and thanking him. It was in Kate's handwriting. She had drawn the outline of a heart on the side. He put it in the wastebasket and looked around for Byron. No one was home. Bertha must be in church, he thought. Trying to put himself to rights, he ate some cold crab cakes. He drank warmed-up coffee that tasted like gunmetal. After a while he went out onto the front porch and found the Sunday *Baltimore Sun*. He tried to read it, but his eyes burned and ran. He put the paper down. Later he tried again but only scanned the headlines. He never got to the small column inside where the weather was reported. The article made mention of a storm developing in the Gulf, a tropical storm, early for the season, now somewhere southeast of the Yucatán. It had already been given a name: Agnes.

13

The following day, Monday, was the nineteenth of June. Byron mentioned this to Clay as they motored east along the southern shore of the Choptank. White streamers crisscrossed the blue sky. The water chopped as the morning tide ran against the wind.

"It's Mason and Blackie's anniversary."

Clay took this in. He felt weak still, anemic. "Mason and Blackie," he repeated. "Well, God bless them."

"I figured I'd take 'em a bushel of jumbos if you don't mind. Come on over, if you like."

"These crabs are half yours to do with what you want. Without you asking. You know that. You pick out the fattest crabs this river'll grow, and give Mase and Blackie my very best, Byron. From both of us. But I don't want to come anywhere near a drink for a while. I need a dry spell."

Byron lit a cigarette, striking the match off his boot. "Dry spell, hell. You're just a piker."

"How many years it been, Byron?"

Byron scratched his chin. "One more'n me, I guess. Really six months." He grinned. "Twenty-two years, I suppose."

Clay eased down on the throttle. Ahead the crab pot buoys were strung out southeasterly along the bank below Cook Point. They both saw the first one riding the chop like a fish bobber.

"Twenty-two years. That's a bite of time."

"Yes, sir, it is that."

"You think they still fire each other up?"

Byron took several deep drags on his cigarette and threw it overboard, readying himself to heave the first pot onto the hauler. "I ain't sure. I've heard 'em doin' something, though." He thrust his hips out. "Now and then. I mean Mason's no slacker. But mostly I think they just look after one another."

Clay eased up to the buoy, bringing the bateau alongside. Byron pulled the pot onto the hauler, and moments later it came up and was on the gunnel, full of scrapping crabs and eelgrass and slimed with a jellyfish caught in the mesh. He dumped the crabs into the cull basin.

"Smart catch here, Cap'n. Right full. Bait's light, though. A few look papery. Molt's just done, I guess." He began to fill the bait cylinder with the alewives from the barrel.

"I was in a rush on Saturday. Didn't have time to bait up right with Kate and Matty on board."

"They had fun, it seemed?"

"I hope so."

"Showed Matty plenty of Eastern Shore for his pictures."

"We did that."

"She's a dolly bird, that one."

Clay didn't answer.

"Hard to keep my eyes to myself, on the beach there."

Clay turned his face to the wind, breathing deep for ballast. "Tell me something I don't know."

Byron reached for another bait fish and stuffed it in the cage. "Course, Matty seemed to enjoy the show too. He was all over Laura-Dez—not that she seemed to mind. He's no shy one."

"He's always attracted women. Like a magnet," Clay answered distractedly.

"Well, I told you before, she fancies you, that Kate."

Clay held the bateau in neutral. "Yeah. And I told you, it's just her way." He ignored a wave of nausea.

"More'n that, from what's obvious to see."

He shifted, unsteady. "We all got carried away. We were drunk. Stoned. It's in her blood, anyway. She just loves people."

"Maybe. If you say so. But it's more'n that, where you're concerned."

"You going to finish with that pot or what?" Clay answered impatiently.

Byron didn't budge.

Clay sagged back against the stanchion, letting the boat idle. "It was a night, all right." His eyes strained. "Hell, I don't know. Of course there is something between us. But she and Matty have been together forever. Since high school. From the same world. Meant for each other. You just learn there are certain boundaries you can't cross. They're my friends. Like family."

Byron stayed quiet. Clay could feel it inside himself, and knew his eyes reflected it—the stamp and stain of his past.

"There are lines you don't cross, Byron. Pappy crossed them and broke my mother. I've learned."

Byron swallowed.

"What?"

"Nothin'. Not my business. It can all be hard to figure, though."

"There's no other way to see it."

Byron hooked the bait cap closed. "I won't argue. When you put it that way, Cap."

Clay straightened and put his hand on the throttle. "Are you finished yet?"

"Well, with all these jimmies on the bank, I stuffed her full," Byron commented, easing the pot back off the side. He watched it sink three or four feet as it disappeared into the sediment-dark flood.

Clay backed off and moved toward the next pot as Byron began culling the crabs, throwing them into the bushel baskets. He knew he should talk to Kate but didn't know what he would say. He felt frozen. Uncertain of what to do, except to work. To keep at his work.

They ran the line, harvesting the crabs steadily as the sun moved up over the white towers of Calvert Cliffs across the Bay and on up into the sky, which had turned milky with the day. They emptied and baited, culled, and worked their boat along the lines of pots as though they were connected by some invisible tether to each place they needed to be. They seldom spoke, both aware of the bounty of their catch and occupied with the steady harvest of the produce from the invisible bottom. They finished an hour before noon and turned northeast to run across the Choptank. The breeze brushed them from the south as they lazily crossed the river. They had on board their largest catch of the summer.

Byron broke open a can of beer from the cooler. After a while he spoke. "We ought to buy more pots," he said.

Clay agreed. "We'll stop in Easton this afternoon."

Clay steered past Bachelor Point and studied the beach where they had all gone swimming. He looked at the bushels of crabs all over the belly of the bateau and all full. He felt the breeze and the hot sun over his head, and a certainty that at least he was able to do this work well and proper.

They unloaded the crabs at Pecks, and Byron took one bushel of jumbos and put it in the back of his pickup for Mason and Blackie. Then they drove to Easton and bought all the traps the hardware store had on hand, twenty-three factory-made galvanized crab pots. Byron bought a six-pack of National Bohemian, and they drove back to Pecks and loaded the pots onto the roof of the bateau and tied them down. He drank while they worked, and when they were finished he left to go find Laura-Dez.

Clay stayed to wash down the workboat. There were bits of crab and bait stuck to the floorboards and gunnels, and he enjoyed washing her down to her white coat in the sun. There wasn't much traffic at Pecks. He stowed all the gear and took the key. Walking along the pier, he noticed *Mood Indigo* sliding out of her slip and coasting past the wharf toward the red channel marker. He saw Amanda up on the bow, sunning herself, and Hugo at the wheel wearing a blue captain's hat. Another man and a young woman were in the cockpit drinking beer and talking loudly. The boat was long. Her blue hull rode high in the water and her inboard purred with a perfect rhythm. Clay watched her round the buoy and continue to motor out into the channel, steady and certain in the flood tide.

Still tired from the weekend, he went back to the farmhouse and fixed himself an early dinner of fried rice and cornbread. He had been reading *Islands in the Stream,* and after dinner he lay on the couch with the screen door open and read as the light faded and the dark crept over the house and he shut his eyes. When he opened them, it was the dark before dawn, and Byron had not arrived.

In the morning, at Pecks, just as Clay was about to cast off, Byron showed up, wasted. He was wearing the same clothes he'd had on the day before and he staggered when he walked. Clay put him in the forward cabin and then started out for his pots.

Before the sun rose, the horizon exploded in a bright orange fan of color that filled the entire eastern sky. The Bay was rough. Clay studied his surroundings. He sensed a strangeness in the air.

North of his pot lay he found a stretch of deeper water where he decided to set his new traps. He untied them, filled each of them with bait, attached the buoys and buoy lines, and dropped them in the river. He worked easterly, laying the new traps in a line, perpendicular to the others, but in about eighteen to twenty feet of water. As he worked, the wind held heavy out of the northwest. Once they were all in the water, he checked the lay against the shore and in relation to his other pots. Satisfied, he moved to his old pot lay and began to work the line. The going was slower because of the wind and his working alone. He was nearly finished when Byron came out of the cabin, holding his head and moaning.

"Thermos of coffee's in the cockpit. Help yourself."

Byron found it and filled its upturned cap. He took a long drink.

Clay watched him. "You gotta get out of this rut. It's a dead end."

Byron hiccuped. "Bein' sober's for those who can't handle liquor."

Clay put the bateau into neutral and let her drift. He looked out at the Bay. Whitecaps were combing the mouth of the Choptank. The clouds in the eastern sky had been building and now looked like a vertical steel wall approaching in the distance.

"I don't like this weather, Byron."

Clay pointed eastward. Byron brushed his hand away. "Looks like a summer front. Blow over tomorrow."

"From the southeast? Not typical."

Clay went into the cabin and turned on the shortwave. The reception was broken up by static. He turned to the Bay weather channel. Byron came over, and they listened.

"Chance of storm warnings for the evening and morning depending on the course of Agnes. Still two hundred miles southeast of Cape Hatteras. Expected to veer out to sea. Moving at ten miles per hour in a northerly direction."

Clay turned off the radio. "I'm thinking we should pull the pots."

Byron eyeballed him, frowning. "Pull the pots? Fuckin' no way, man. You just put the new ones down. We'll lose two days of crabs. Fuckin' break our asses too. That storm's not comin' this way. There're a ton of 'em every year and they all go out. We're fine, for Christ sakes. It'll bounce off the jet stream like a beach ball."

"It's a hurricane, Byron. It could scatter the pots everywhere. Blow the buoys loose. Water could rise and snap the lines. We should pull."

"Here, have some coffee." Byron refilled the thermos cap and gave it to Clay. "Sober up. You heard the radio. Fuckin' storm's two hundred miles from Hatteras. Relax. Even if it were to come in this direction, it would take days to get here. Christ, Clay."

Clay's expression was unchanged.

"Look, Clay," Byron implored, "let's at least wait until tomorrow. The pots are fully baited and catching crabs faster'n a . . . a grunt on shore leave. If the storm gets closer, we'll consider pulling tomorrow. I'll help. Okay?"

Clay swept the sky with his eyes. "Tomorrow. I suppose. But I feel something coming."

Byron nodded. "It'll be fine. Let's finish gettin' our crabs for today and head in. We can watch the weather on the TV."

Clay shifted the throttle into gear. "I hope I'm wrong, Byron." He accelerated in the direction of the remaining pots, watching the easterly wall of cloud, which seemed to be holding in place. It started in the upper sky and rose like a cliff face, disappearing into a gray darkness across and over the delta.

In fact, Hurricane Agnes veered westerly overnight, picked up speed and force, and by Wednesday morning was threatening to hit the North Carolina coast. She boasted winds of over 150 miles per hour. Clay had listened to the reports all evening. He took a short nap after midnight but rose early to check the news. No change. Outside in the dark morning, the screen door was banging, and it had started to rain. He waited anxiously for a while and then decided to go after his pots. He dialed Laura-Dez's house, trying to find Byron, but got no answer. He called Mason's. Blackie answered the phone half asleep. Byron was not there either. Clay went outside several times and finally decided he wouldn't wait. It was just after four when he left for Pecks.

The morning was coal black, and the rain streamed through the headlights of his Chevrolet as he drove the back roads, bumping over the potholes in his hurry. As he traveled down the oyster shell drive, he noticed that cars were parked askew. The lights from the wharf were on, and the floodlights lit the dock and spotlighted several men working the boat lift. Jed Sparks was hollering to a man on a pleasure yacht to back out of the way. There were four or five boats, lights ablaze, backed up in a line in the creek, and general commotion everywhere.

Clay patted him on the shoulder. "Can you save me a spot for a lift about midday?" He had to speak loudly over the din.

Jed regarded him for a moment. "I dunno, Clay. I got forty-some pulls promised already. All good winter customers. Never make that, probably. I've turned down as many. Maybe the storm'll turn."

Clay understood. It would take as long to pull his three-thousand-dollar boat as it would to pull the thirty-thousand-dollar yachts already in line, and there wasn't time enough for everyone. The yard was already crowded and the confusion increasing.

"We get hit direct, this wharf gonna look like a junkyard anyway." Jed shrugged. "We only got so much cable." He looked at the sky and the water. "The river'll take what she wants. You know that better'n most." He eyed Clay. "Don't forget your daddy's diesel mooring."

Clay patted him once again on the back. "Don't worry. But if you see Byron, tell him I'll be unloading pots at Boone's Landing. Tell him to get his pickup there."

Jed grabbed his hand. "Careful out there. And good luck."

"Yes, sir. To you too." Clay turned and walked down to the *Miss Sarah*. He climbed aboard and felt her sturdiness. She started up on the first turn. He untied all of her lines from the pilings and stowed them aboard and eased out of the slip. He passed by the yachts, all backing and churning, trying to maintain their positions in the creek, and was out in the open river, aimed at the Benoni light, which marked the distant black horizon with the four-second beacon he knew so well.

In the streaming rain and with the steady drum of his engine, he worked his way out of the river, the wind sharp across his bow, the waves rough and rolling. He passed Benoni Point, and as the lighthouse receded behind him, he made out the first streaks of grayish light spearing the horizon, and underneath them gradually spread a haze of granite and brass. He angled south along the dim shoreline, found his pot lay, and began to work, pulling and then yanking open each pot, emptying the crabs into the river and the bait into the bait barrel. He wound the warp line and buoy around the pot, securing the buoy underneath the last coil, set the pot on the floor, and moved to the next. He worked with utmost concentration and was only peripherally aware of the awakening day. After he had coiled about fifteen pots, he stacked them and lashed them tight using a line running to the canopy top. Stepping down off the rail he slipped and caught himself on the stanchion. He realized he had almost gone over. The bateau was tossing more in the waves, which had been building with the wind. The color of the day was slate from river to sky, and the Bay was beginning to whip with whitecaps. He was soaked. He found a towel in the cabin and dried his face, then moved on to the next pot. He worked until the aft deck was stacked high and full.

He had not brought a watch, but he figured it was late morning when he turned the bow east for Boone's Landing. The wind, though uneven, was averaging about twenty-five knots, he figured, and out of the southeast. The rain had eased. Pointing east he advanced through the waves, which pitched against his starboard bow. He was carrying not quite half of his pots and believed he could complete another run if the weather held steady. He turned on the radio. The news was unchanged. Agnes was moving in. Hurricane warnings stretched from the Carolinas to New York. The storm was predicted to make landfall somewhere along the coast after dark.

Boone's Landing was a small, neglected public dock, next to a ramp used occasionally by the locals to launch boats from trailers. The dock was unprotected, jutting out from the northern shore of the Choptank, near the mouth of the Tred Avon. It was buckled from past ice floes. The water was deep enough for the *Miss Sarah*, though, and adjacent to the landing were some thick woods. As he approached, Clay looked for Byron's truck, but the dirt lot was empty. The waves were pounding the pilings and the shore, and Clay had to dock her with the propellers in reverse to counteract the violent thrusts of water. Once she was tied, he looked back out toward the Bay, which heaved in the braying wind. Unleashing the pots, he was able to carry four at a time onto the shore and into the thrashing woods, then partly up a bank to higher ground, where he found a place to stack and tie them, binding them together with their own warp lines and securing them to a stand of young poplars surrounded by other larger trees. He worked fast. His arms and legs ached from the effort, and his hands were raw. With each trip back to the boat, he felt the wind was strengthening, and he noticed the shearing of the tops of the whitecaps offshore.

When the last pots were set in the woods, he returned to the bateau and took her two Danforth anchors out of the forward locker. He brought them and a third anchor, which he had taken from Pecks, to the bow and coiled the lines for each so they would be ready. Casting off, he backed away from the dock in full reverse throttle with the spray battering the stern. Turning west, he ran the wind and waves with a slow lurch and bucking of the bow. Salty foam whipped across the water. The rain had started again and flew laterally across and against the bateau. From underneath the cabin bunk he retrieved his rain slicker and put it on, then took a dry towel and wrapped it around his neck. The Choptank had turned dark, and visibility was minimal. A steady whine filled the amphitheater of the river, overlaying the crashing of the waves as they toppled over themselves. Rising over each crest, the bow dropped into the next trough and rose again, waves threatening from behind, the progress forward wet and slow. Seeking any changes in the storm's course he turned on the radio and, finding static, moved through the channels. As he did so, he could hear "Mayday, Mayday."

Though it was breaking up, the message still came through over the static on the shortwave. It was the *Mood Indigo*. She was caught aground off Benoni Point, her mainsail shredded. Clay listened and cursed to himself. He needed to get his pots. He listened for a rescue response, perhaps from the marine police. Nothing. He heard "Mayday" again. He continued his forward course. Someone else would have to hear it and come to their aid. Then he heard it once more, a cry of fear and panic over the radio. Still there was no reply. He wavered. Then he turned the wheel and changed course moving northeast toward the foundering boat.

Rain and wind now came from out front, the wind having veered easterly. Angling off the waves, he was able to increase his speed as he broke across the channel rip of the river. Locking the wheel in position he went forward and gathered the dock lines from the bow. He attached them each to the other and tied one end to the aft port cleat. If she was stuck off Benoni Point, he'd have to work the east wind without being pushed farther into the bar. Returning to the cabin he tried to peer into the slate fury of the storm: nothing but wind and pellets of hard rain slashing across his view, melding into a gray, cascading tumult only yards ahead of the bow. The tips of the waves were shearing. Pushing forward across the running storm tide, estimating his position, counteracting the side drag, he saw in his mind's eye the sailboat aground. A pealing bell off to his starboard told him he was nearing the lighthouse, though it was not visible through the rain. He angled farther to port. The shore seemed too close when he saw it, and then, like a ghost ship silhouetted in the storm, the sailboat appeared, just as he had seen it in his mind. She was jerking spasmodically between the waves and the river bottom, and her crew was huddled in the cockpit, though Brigman stood and started waving his arms when he saw the bateau. He wore green waders that came up to his chest, with suspenders running over his shoulders. Fall overboard, they'll fill with water and take him down, Clay thought. A good way to drown.

The boat was heeled over away from the wind, her mainsail shredded and snapping above the boom, which groaned with the wrenching of the keel against the bar, the storm jib bunched and tied at the bow. From the starboard winch, an anchor line went out, but it was not far enough out to allow any purchase. Clay came around to her leeward side, surveying the emerging catastrophe.

Brigman was shouting, "You can pull us off with your diesel. Take Amanda and Joanna aboard first. Then pull us off. Use your diesel, for God's sake."

Clay knew she was deep into the bar, and to pull the keel through it would be impossible.

"What do you draw?" Clay shouted.

"Just throw me a line," Brigman pleaded.

"Goddamn it, what do you draw?" Clay shouted back.

The other man had gotten up and stood next to Brigman. "Almost six feet," Brigman shouted.

"Six feet," the other one screamed.

A surge knocked Clay off balance. Grabbing the stanchion, he regained his footing, reversed his propeller, churned back, and then idled in closer. The rain, coming flat across the water, bit into his eyes. Clay cupped one hand to the side of his mouth, shielding his voice from the wind. "There ain't no time," he hollered back, "so you do what I say, and maybe I can get you off."

"Just get us out of here, will you?" Brigman pleaded. "Take us off?"

"Do what I say, and maybe I can clear you off the bar. If it doesn't work, you'll have to leave the boat. Understand?"

Both men motioned that they understood.

Clay cupped his hand to his mouth again. "Okay. Start your engine and leave her in neutral."

Brigman bent over the controls of the lurching yacht. Clay heard the inboard motor turn over and start.

"You"—Clay pointed at the second man on board— "take that halyard that runs to the top of the mast and slip it on the end of your boat hook, and pass it over to me." Clay had to point to the line and repeat his command. The man nodded, and Brigman helped the man attach the halyard to the boat hook.

Clay worked the bateau, which was pitching like a bronco, as close as he dared. Using his own boat hook, he managed to snag the halyard as Brigman extended it. He quickly tied a bowline to attach the mast's halyard to the tow line he had secured to the stern of the bateau.

"You be ready to raise the jib as much as you can," Clay yelled to the man. "When I give the word. And keep her tight on your port side. It'll help blow her over."

The man started to work his way forward.

"Everyone to port with all your weight," Clay shouted. "This tow'll pull her from the top of the mast, bringing her over. The keel should loosen, come up out of the sand sideways. The boat will be heaved over on her side, and you put her in gear then and grind her out of there, Brigman. You got it?"

Brigman nodded.

Clay wasn't sure. "You're in five feet of water," he screamed. "We got to get that keel up by bringing her over onto her side. She'll want to fall back, but if the mast holds, I'll keep her over. Then you go. Got it?"

Brigman shouted yes.

"Watch the mast. If she starts to bend, get the hell out of the way. I'll pick you off." Clay wiped the rain from his face. "Ready?" he hollered. He didn't wait. "Get the jib up!" Clay screamed. He began to work away from the yacht. He knew the slack line was most dangerous as it came taut: the bateau's momentum, combined with a surging wave, might overtighten the tow and snap the mast. He edged away from the yacht, watching the line whip in the wind and begin to tighten. The whitecaps came over the line, burying it in the foam, and then it was up again, almost tight. He needed enough throttle to stay perpendicular to the sailboat. He felt the line like a fisherman feeling his rod for the subtle pull. He eased up, went into neutral as a wave carried him forward, felt the line tighten, started to fall back but instantly was into gear with a quick rev, felt it tight again, the strain a matter of feel, more strain, the groan of the sailboat, more throttle, steadily more, a crunching sound increasing in intensity to a wail against the wind. She was going to crack, he feared, and then he felt the gradual give and he had her over, he felt this and saw this, she was pulled onto her side, wallowing against the forces about her, and then she was moving, tentatively, like a wounded mammal, and he, keeping the line taut, turned to move with her. He saw them hanging on to the side, Amanda holding on with both arms to a stanchion, half over the deck, two others with their arms around the halyards and braced against the lifelines. The rain streamed down over his eyes, and he wiped them with his sleeve. He felt for the tension, for the speed and spread, and he stayed with them, slow going, inching their way across the bar, his left hand on the tiller, his right on the throttle and gear, faster now, he felt, one wave at a time, and he kept with them, perfect motion, timing, perfect pull on the line, he knew the waves, he had measured the distance, and his confidence grew and he knew he had it, and he felt it and kept them over, a bit farther, another wave or two, until the place he had marked approached, and then he was sure they were over, and he moved toward them and saw the boat right herself, and she was up and she was free.

Clay steered in close, the line falling slack behind him into the water, and then, setting his tiller, he pulled in the tow line until he could free the halyard. As he did this, the two boats moved side by side out to the open, thrashing river. Clay finished and looked up at the ragged group standing stunned in the cockpit, ashen faced and ripped by the storm.

"You stay in the channel," he shouted at Brigman. "There's plenty of time for you to get to Pecks." Brigman nodded. "If he can't pull you, there's a black-painted buoy up the cove just past Pecks, off the starboard side of the channel. You with me?" Brigman nodded again. Clay continued shouting: "It's a mooring chained to an old engine block my father sunk years ago, and it won't budge. Tie two strong bowlines to the chain on the buoy, and give her room to swing."

Brigman didn't seem to move. He didn't say anything. He nodded almost imperceptibly. The other man shouted a thank-you.

"You all right? You can make it?" Clay shouted again.

Brigman this time raised his hand.

Clay looked at them watching him. Then he turned the bateau away, easterly, pointing the bow to head across the mouth of the river. The rain began stinging his face, and he shivered and felt the cold for the first time. He slid down into a trough and the spiking crests were over his head, the spindrift streaking dense and white across the waves. He thought of his pots and knew better than to head out again. The Tred Avon was starting to rage. The open Choptank would be impassable.

Inside the cabin, he turned on the radio again. He heard no more calls for help, and the news of the storm was steady. The eye was coming up the gullet of the Bay.

Clay traversed the mouth of the Tred Avon, the rain now ripping across in horizontal fusillades from the northeast. Visibility was minimal, holding at twenty yards or less. He passed near the lighthouse and heard her bell but could not see her. He took dead aim in his mind for Bachelor Point, across the way, and held a steady course, as the water was deep to the shore. He plowed ahead, running the hurtling waves, and when he sensed he was close, he angled to starboard until he found the point and worked his way down the shore to the mouth of Island Creek, the water boiling off the northern shoal marking the entrance. He ran up the creek slowly, the waves slamming his bow, the water sloshing over the floorboards of the bateau. Hugging the bank, he searched through the blinding rain and thought he saw a light, and then he saw it again, and he said a prayer, for it seemed to be a safety beacon reaching toward him, and then he knew it was the dock lights at the end of the Lawlors' wharf, and he thought it was a miracle that they were on. The storm was lashing at the dock, the flood tide pouring over the boards like ocean waves, and the wind whipped the rain laterally across the pilings, blurring the lights. He gave safe distance to the dock, slowly working his way around it, his bow pitching violently, to where he could approach the shore and then see where the creek cut out a half-moon bay. Moving in toward shore, he saw the narrow cut that opened into the pond on the Lawlor property. He slid into the neck, lined on either side with widgeon grass that was blown back as though trampled down. The waves rushed to his stern, the wind whined above him, and the rain was relentless, but inside the cut, the water calmed as he glided through, into a deep water pocket, protected on all sides by banked woods except for the narrow channel that opened to the river. There were no other boats. Clay set to work in the stripping rain.

Pappy had once taught him the three-anchor mooring, bridled 120 degrees apart. "For a hurricane," he remembered being told, "or a permanent mooring where there is none." And so he set it out, one anchor out front with a double-long rode, the other two nearly midships on either side. Hurricane winds can come from opposite directions, first from the counterclockwise direction of the storm's cyclonic circle, and then, as the center passes by, from the opposite course. Clay thought of this as he worked, that with this anchorage, regardless of how the wind shifts, the bateau would swing in a very small circle, and there would always be one or two anchors to windward. The greater the load, he thought, the deeper the Danforths will bury. He worked with the storm about him, and the same thoughts cursed through his effort—that half his pots were still out there, half his business busting in the storm. Using the extra lines he had brought, he lashed closed the cabin doors and tied the hatches tight. He rechecked the anchors and anchor lines. He removed the foul-weather slicker he had on, stashed it in the engine box, and clamped down the lid. He looked at everything he owned. Then he swung himself over the side, swam about thirty yards, until he could stand in the sand, and waded ashore. On the riverbank he looked back and studied the *Miss Sarah*, certain that it would take a tidal wave to move her. Then he turned and started walking through the woods and up the hill toward the Lawlor house, seeing in his mind the buoys he had left bobbing in the furious storm.

14

When Clay reached the top of the hill and emerged from the woods, he saw a man he made out to be Jim Lawlor running from the front door of his house to his Jeep Wagoneer. Stumbling down to the edge of the driveway, Clay managed to place himself in the beams of its headlights as the Jeep started to swing around the drive toward the lane. Lawlor's eyes widened in disbelief. He opened the door and Clay climbed in.

"My God, son, you look like a drowned ghost. How the hell'd you get here, and what the hell are you doing out in this?"

"Trying to save my pots, sir. And my boat."

"Your boat! Jesus! You were out there?"

"Yes, sir. I got delayed some. Figured you got one of the best hurricane holes around."

Jim Lawlor owned several farms in the county, and acres of riverfront property. He had been a hunting partner of Pappy's. He told Clay that he had already moved his family into his cousin's house in town and was heading there himself. "Just in case," he explained. He asked Clay about his boat and how he had secured it and nodded thoughtfully on hearing the explanation. He asked about the river and kept shaking his head as Clay described it. "Of course I will take you home with me," he insisted. "You need some dry clothes, son. Don't say a word. Don't try to argue. Don't even mention it."

The brunt of Agnes hit that night. Winds in Easton were clocked at near a hundred miles per hour, shredding foliage and knocking over trees, but it was the rain that was like never before, flying laterally in sheets for hours in the howling dark, battering the Lawlors' frame house, pounding the windows, and sending flash floods cascading down the street. Clay, having showered and changed into some clothes the Lawlors had found for him, sat in the kitchen drinking coffee, watching the windows, and listening to the sounds of the storm for most of the night. The phones were down, so he couldn't call Bertha or Byron. Jim Lawlor had made a bed for him on the sofa, but it wasn't until first light that he lay down and fell asleep.

As Clay slept, Hurricane Agnes continued to rampage across the Mid-Atlantic seaboard before veering northeast, pouring more rain into the Susquehanna and the other tributaries of the Bay than ever before in recorded history, and causing the worst flooding in its huge watershed in two centuries. Some five inches of rain fell over the watershed in just four hours, the news reported. The Bay's saline levels would become inverted. South of the raging Susquehanna, the floodwaters, of the Sassafras, the Gunpowder, the Patapsco, the Chester, the West, the South, the Severn, the Choptank, the Patuxent, and the Potomac had begun their carnage, carrying mud, silt, topsoil, fertilizers, pesticides, and debris from the Blue Ridge to the Bay and wreaking environmental havoc throughout the huge estuary.

Clay didn't wake up until late Friday morning. By then the storm had tapered off to a steady rain, but the flood crests were still building. Clay mostly paced until the phone service was restored. He talked to Bertha first and made sure she was safe and then called Byron and told him where he was. Byron was pale and shaking when he came to pick Clay up. He stammered that he had looked for Clay everywhere, riding back and forth between Pecks and the house. The one person he had not spoken to was Jed Sparks, who had been more than preoccupied.

Clay told Byron what happened and to forget it. It was he, Clay, who had left for the river early. Byron was upset and then sullen. He cursed the *Mood Indigo*.

They drove down to Island Creek. On the way, Byron mentioned that Matty had called from Richmond. He and Kate had been worried. They had driven to Richmond to be safe. "Matty said to tell you that they talked about the wharf idea to his father," Byron continued. "Said he'd agreed to look at the papers. You know, the numbers. If we could get 'em from the bank."

Along Oxford Road there were trees down and debris everywhere. The lane to the Lawlors' was under several inches of water, and the culverts on either side were like rushing creeks. Proceeding slowly, the pickup worked its way down the lane to the house. From the Lawlors' yard, Island Creek was unrecognizable. The south bank had disappeared under water, which lay over much of the southern landscape. The rising tide had covered the Lawlors' dock, and the high brown water had flooded half the yard. A low, slate-colored cloud ceiling seethed overhead, though the air in the dissipating drizzle felt balmy and strangely calm. After moving carefully through the woods and sliding down the bank, they emerged at the pond's edge and saw the bateau, riding low and fouled with water but steady on her lines and unharmed. The pond water was muddied with thick sediment. They spent the morning bailing out the *Miss Sarah* and cleaning her, till she rode fair and light on the high and rising tide. At Boone's Landing they found the pots Clay had lashed to the trees. They untied and loaded the pots into the back of the pickup. Once home, they stacked them behind the garage.

After warm showers and a change of clothes, Byron and Clay pulled their hip waders on, put some tools in the truck, and started for Pecks Wharf. They had to park and walk down the drive. The water was nearly a foot deep over the lane and deeper over the ground. The first boats they saw were in the woods several hundred yards from the dock, twisted among the broken trees.

Those that had been hydraulically lifted before the storm and secured were untouched, and those properly moored with a safe swing were undamaged and floating in the harbor. Looking up the cove, Clay saw that *Mood Indigo* was one of these, swinging on Pappy's black-painted buoy. But dock lines tied too tight had snapped on some, and anchor lines, on others. There were dozens of boats washed up on their sides in the yard, and too many to count half submerged along the wooded shore. A small cabin cruiser had been lifted and smashed into the side of the picking shack. The yard was a confusion of destruction. Clay and Byron found Jed talking on the phone. They offered their services, and Jed put them to work.

Inside the Washington Street Pub the next evening, Clay sat drinking beer with Barker, Byron, and Mason. They sat and watched the old-time watermen passing by, who just shook their heads. "Never heard or seen anything like it" was the common refrain. "Gonna have to go beggin' to the government for help," Clay overheard. "This here killed the watermen," said another. "Kilt us all." Clay knew the answer to his question, about the crabs, before he asked it. And the answer was in Barker's face if Clay needed proof.

"You hearin' anything on the radio?" Byron asked his father after a while. "We've been in the muck since daybreak."

"News ain't good," Mason reported. "Terrible, really. Experts're all sayin' Bay's goin' into shock."

"Don't need no radio to know that," Barker interrupted. "Don't need no experts neither."

"More freshwater and pollution than she can handle, they're sayin'. Killed the salinity. And with all the runoff—the fertilizers and pesticides. Shit. I feel bad for you boys." He raised his beer and took a drink. "But you're young. Good thing."

"Bay's resilient," Clay answered. "Always has been. It's early yet to tell, anyway."

"Years." Mason eyed him squinting. "That's what they said today on the TV. Maybe several."

No one spoke for a while. They sat and drank and listened to similar talk coming from other booths in the pub.

"That's why I quit," Mason finally said. "State Roads pays me regular. It ain't the water, but it's regular." He finished his beer and raised his hand in the air until Missy, their waitress, saw him and waved for him to put it down.

"Your daddy was a crabber," Barker said. "Just like mine. Like Clay's."

"An oysterman too," Mason added. "And fisherman." He seemed to reflect for a moment. "Hell, he used to talk about the shad runs," Mason went on. "More fish than you could ever imagine, Daddy said. Claimed you could walk on 'em, they were so thick in the water. Walk on 'em." He chuckled. "Now, when's the last time you even heard of any shad being caught up here. Not in any quantity, noways."

He looked around for effect.

"He did some ocean trawlin' too. Off the Labrador coast." Mason paused, studying first Clay and then Byron. "Crabbin's done for this year, son. Crabs'll either die or migrate. They need the salt and cleaner water. Salt mix's changed for this year. That's what they're sayin' on the news. I'm sorry to say it to you. I know it's true, though. I figure you know it too." He crossed his arms in front of him. No one spoke for a while. Then he continued. "It's the waterman's way. My daddy, he'd come home and tell me over and over. It was one thing or another. This calamity or that. 'Get away,' he'd say. 'You get away, young Mase. Far from the shore. Get yerself somewheres else and get the salt outta your veins and give yerself a chance. Go where no sea runs,' he'd say." Mason shook his head. "'Where no sea runs and a chance for a decent life.' Course he never meant a lick of it. He was as salty as they come."

Missy came over with a round of beers, which she set on the table. She picked up the empties. "I'm sorry, boys," she said. "Damn shame, it is. Damn shame." Barker patted her arm as she left.

"And then I ended up on the ocean," Mason finished. "In the war. On the ocean in the night."

Byron raised his glass to toast, trying to change the subject. "To all our daddies," he offered.

They all nodded approval and clinked their bottles together and then drank together.

"I can't imagine," Barker said then, quietly staring at the table. "What?"

"Livin' landlocked. Not knowin' the water." He looked up. "Can you, Clay?"

Clay sat silent for a while. "What are you going to do?" He answered Barker with a question.

Barker drummed his fingers on the table. "I'll try and sell my alewives in Virginia. Or maybe North Carolina. I suspect the lower Bay may be all right. Up here, though . . ." He shook his head. "But then, I don't know. Maybe I'll ask Mase here for work."

"We like to hire vets," Mason stated. He looked at Byron.

Byron reached in his pocket and found a cigarette. He lit it slowly and carefully. "Aw, Mase," he said exhaling. "Me and Clay got to figure this one out first." He took another drag. "Don't we, Clay?"

Clay took a breath. "We lost half of what we built already." He looked around at the faces in the bar, faces chiseled dry and hard by the salt and wind. Most looked old for their age. He saw Byron watching him, trying to read his thoughts. Thoughts of a roiling Bay. Of torn, drifting pots below. Of sunken treasure ships. Clay's thoughts whirled with these and other images of the days past and ahead, but one thought remained constant: he had no intention of giving up. That was the thought he figured Byron was looking for and would see on his face and in his eyes.

Over the following days the swollen rivers crested their banks and the Bay water was opaque with mud and debris and reportedly unsafe for boaters as far south as the Virginia line. Marine wreckage was everywhere. Clay and Byron checked on the bateau every day, and every day she rode her lines steady. They recharged the battery and tested the engine, which started after a prime. The rest of the time they spent working at Pecks, helping out with the cleanup and salvage. Jed Sparks promised them good wages once insurance payments started coming in, but Clay figured he'd have been there anyway. He was needed there, and there was nowhere else to go. He knew he had lost half his pots, but he still wanted to go look for them. "But what good are pots," Byron kept reminding him. "What good are pots, when there ain't gonna be no crabs? Not this year, anyway."

During this time, Clay neither saw nor heard from Brigman. The *Mood Indigo*, seemingly unattended, road smartly up the cove, swinging on its borrowed mooring.

A week later, Clay ventured out into the Tred Avon and from the Tred Avon to the Choptank. The water was still high and the color of compost. Uprooted trees, sides of houses, wooden trailer frames, and creosote-covered pilings all floated in the muck trailing along the river surface. Large, dark areas of reddish foam stretched along the current. A wooden mast floated by, its torn sail tangled around it like a shroud. He rode slowly out in the direction of Cook Point, watching for underwater debris. The marsh grass to the south had disappeared underwater. Familiar landmarks were hidden under the tide. There was no sight of any of his crab pots. The sky was stained brown. The reports were coming in. The crabs were gone.

PART TWO

Virginia

*D*awn breaks behind the eyes;
From poles of skull and toe the windy blood
Slides like a sea.

—DYLAN THOMAS

15

It was Jed Sparks who reinforced the idea. The thought had been planted in the Washington Street Pub that night after the hurricane. During the weeks that followed, Clay had been turning it over in his mind. He had discussed it with Barker and then with Byron. Tentatively, carefully. To salvage some of the season, to try to save what he had left—what other choice was there, except to give up? It made sense. Go south. To Virginia. Work the southern flute of the Bay, the mouth of the Rappahannock or lower. South, farther below the salt line, where the salinity was said to be still potent enough and the water, filtered by the Atlantic's tides, still clean and alive with crabs. Ocean crabs were never as sweet, but the prices would be high. Work the crabs through the season, till October, maybe, and build his stash of pots back up. Then come north for the oyster. If the oyster had survived.

Money was the biggest problem. Or the lack of it. The insurance payments that the bank had been expecting had been delayed, so it had paid only minimum wage for the salvage work. And there were also concerns about intruding on the territory of the Virginia crabbers, though the Bay was wide down there. And then where exactly to go. How to start. And during this time, Clay found himself undecided, afflicted with hesitation, unlike himself, ignoring the obvious way to begin, until Byron called him into the kitchen one morning and handed him the phone. It was Matty. Byron had called to tell Matty that he and Clay needed to come down and check things out. Matty was insistent. Of course they should come, he told Clay. Immediately. He and Kate wanted to see him. They had just one guest bedroom, but one of them could sleep on the couch. "Plus . . ." Matty hesitated, his voice faltering. "It's a secret. You'll have to keep this quiet until graduation next spring . . ."

"What?" Clay asked.

"We got engaged. Kate and I." Matty halted. Clay could hear him breathing. Or was it his own breath, or his own pulse, that seemed to mark the space and silence between them? "Last weekend," Matty finally continued. "Her parents can't know until we finish school. After that, we'll announce it. We'll have a big party."

Clay reached out for a chair and sat, looking away from Byron. He knew his own face was a betrayal.

"It was kind of sudden," Matty went on. "We'd fought. We were both feeling—I don't know—like we needed to. Like it was time. We went to Williamsburg. I bought her a ring. It was a good way to make up."

Clay sat and listened as Matty described more of the details. Matty's tone became more natural and animated as he went on. Byron whispered, "What? What is it?" Clay struggled for composure. He made the necessary effort to talk, to ask Matty the right questions, to congratulate him. He managed to get these questions out and repeated his congratulations several times before finally handing the phone back to Byron, who knew what had happened from hearing Clay but received the news as though with surprise, congratulating Matty in his turn. Byron finished the call by making the arrangements for their visit. Clay heard him confirm and then promise that they would drive the truck down the next week for a look.

Later, as the news settled in, as Byron shared his whiskey, a vague sense of relief seeped into Clay's mind. He decided, that night, to raise a few extra glasses. For his friends, he told himself. He closed the pub down. Byron, for a change, had to help him get home.

It was the following Wednesday when Clay and Byron climbed into the truck. Clay had been anxious about the trip, raising objections, but Byron was set and unrelenting. Only after finding the highway, with the wind whirring through the open windows, did Clay begin to relax. Byron started telling navy jokes and Clay appreciated his friend beside him. He also appreciated having a direction, the delusion of travel as progress.

They started after lunch and drove Route 50 down the Eastern Shore, across the Choptank River and through Cambridge, slanting down the delta across the Nanticoke. At the Highway Inn, where Byron had once been in a fight, they stopped and Byron bought a six-pack of malt liquor. They slid around Salisbury, touching the Wicomico, down Route 13, through Princess Anne, over the Pocomoke River and through Pocomoke City, and down into the narrow marshy neck of Virginia's eastern peninsula. Clay studied the flat, unending fields and glittering marsh beyond and took in the vistas of the flatlands around him, land that you could see about you and believe in, and this too steadied him. As they passed these places, he found himself reciting the names that had been given to the land and the waters: Hooper Neck, Hurlock, Galestown, Shad Point, Bivalve, Onancock, Wachapreague, Honga River, Terrapin Sand Spit, Assawoman Inlet, Hog Island Bay, and on and on, down toward Cape Charles and the mouth of the Chesapeake. It was a fine summer afternoon, the water sparkling, and it was still light when they crossed the Chesapeake Bay Bridge

Tunnel, some twenty-six miles long. As they glided along the narrow ramp, to their right, northward, lay the great Bay, the basin for hundreds of rivers, inlets, and tributaries, cutting through four states, mixing the seas with the continental freshwater flows. To the south, to their left, lay the Atlantic, running a tide from the shores of Africa, Europe, the Arctic, carrying its store of life and history. Crossing here, over this mix of the world's currents, Clay felt a flush of gratitude, almost as though he were on the water again.

They got lost in Hampton because Byron wanted more beer, and Clay decided to find and inspect the old crab docks at the end of King Street, where the winter dredgers laid up. Winding through a maze of urban sprawl, they passed a series of commercial shipbuilding yards, the gantry cranes standing like giant sentinels above the clamor of iron and industry. Clay had Byron drive over the James River Bridge and back so he could look at the freighters and cargo ships lined up in the mouth of the harbor. Towering smokestacks billowed black smoke over Portsmouth and Newport News; tankers, pulled and pushed by tugs, worked in close to the loading docks; horns blasted the air; blocks of dilapidated housing, water towers, and gray storage tanks ran away in the distance. Following their instincts, the two of them wound their way east until they eventually found Queen Street and then the old district in Hampton, and slowly cruised along King Street to its end and the city dock, studying the ocean crab dredgers, some sixty feet or more in length, although they appeared small and anachronistic in their surroundings. Byron stopped and turned off the engine.

"That's what they use for winter dredging," Clay remarked.

"Uh-huh. They're taking all sooks."

Clay spat out the window.

"Cocksuckers."

"I'd heard they were big workboats."

"Livin' in all this shit these watermen musta lost their bearings."

"There's a dredger on the dock." Clay motioned at a contraption that looked like a steel plow with teeth and a chain net, sitting on the wharf. "Scoops them right out of the mud."

"Damn Orientals are buying all the sooks. They eat the eggs."

"Yeah, I heard that. Not right. That's for certain."

"Think the government would stop it."

"Too much money in it."

"Supposed to be a delicacy over there. You wanna get out and walk?" Byron asked.

"Not really. Seen what I wanted to. You?"

"I've had enough of the confusion round here."

"Yeah."

Byron turned on the engine and backed the truck out. They worked their way back until they found Route 17 to Gwynn's Island. The citylike surroundings lasted until they crossed the bridge over the York River and, after a few miles, hit the farmlands of southeastern Virginia. They drove through Gloucester and then up Route 14 as the sun began to fall behind the tips of the trees edging the fields of tobacco that receded in the distance, and the light passing through the trees slanted in muted layers. Driving between miles of cornfields, the corn stalks close to a man's height, they reached the turnoff to Gwynn's Island, crossed the bridge, and by driving along several of the back streets, finally found Kate and Matty's address.

Kate came to the door.

She was wearing faded blue jeans, an oversize green sweatshirt, white tennis shoes, and a Baltimore Orioles baseball cap. Her red hair fell in waves out the back of the cap and curled down the nape of her neck. At first she seemed exasperated, as though she were bothered by the knock on the door. When she saw Clay, she was startled. She caught herself, then smiled and drifted into his arms, murmuring his name. After a few seconds she stepped back and then gave Byron an embrace. She took their hands and pulled them inside.

"What a shock, you two," she said with an effort, as though out of breath.

"Didn't Matty tell you we were coming?" Clay asked.

She let go of Byron, shooing away the question. "He doesn't tell me anything anymore. You're staying the night?" She seemed to plead and then she answered herself. "Of course you are staying the night. Or maybe several?"

"We came to look around a little," Clay answered. "We're thinking of bringing our boat somewhere down here. Crabbing till the fall, maybe south of the Rappahannock."

"There ain't no crabs left in the upper Bay now. Not after the hurricane," Byron added.

Clay let her hand drop. "Byron called Matty, and he said you wouldn't mind putting us up for a night. We need to find a boat slip, and somewhere to sell our catch. I'm sorry you weren't asked. I hope you don't mind."

Kate took this in. "Mind?" she repeated, turning her head sideways. "I'm sorry about the storm, Clay. But if it brings you down here . . . well, of course I don't mind." She reached for Clay's arm. "Where are your bags? Do you have any? Let's go get them. We will just have to celebrate your arrival, now. Come on—"

"Congratulations," Clay stammered.

She stopped.

"On your engagement."

"Yeah," Byron added. "Likewise."

Kate looked at one, then the other. "Matty told you?" she said to Clay, studying his face. "He said he'd let me." She started to say something else but held back. "Oh," she answered in almost a whisper. "Well. Thank you." Her eyes dropped down to the floor, then lifted as she held out her hand, showing them her ring. "Nice, huh? Matty's very generous." She seemed unsure of what else to say. She moved forward and gave them each a little hug. "I've been so emotional lately." She paused. "I guess we're growing up. Or trying to." Then she turned abuptly, as if from shyness, and motioned for them to follow her to their car.

Back inside, Kate picked up the phone to call Matty. "Hello. Yes, is Matty there?" She saw them standing by their bags. She cupped her hand over the receiver. "Clay, I'm sorry. The guest room is at the end of the hall upstairs. Leave your stuff up there if you want. One of you can sleep there, and I'll make up the couch in the living room." She nodded her head toward the stairs. Clay and Byron walked down the hallway.

A fluted banister ran along the stairway from the hall to the second floor. The walls of the hallway and stairwell were covered with framed photographs. Sunsets and rainstorms, black-and-white shots of watermen and their boats, waterfowl, pictures of bridges and mountains.

"All Matty's work?" Byron asked.

"Appears to be."

At the top of the landing were more photographs, but these were mostly of Kate, some posing and some with family. Clay found himself talking, explaining to Byron the photograph of Kate and her mother standing on either side of a large chestnut mare. Kate's father, astride the horse, was decked out in formal foxhunting attire, derby and all. "Her father hosts a fox hunt every year. It's a big deal." Clay pointed to another photograph, taken at a debutante ball of some kind, in which Kate stood with ten or so other young women in a semicircle, all of them dressed in long white gowns.

"She hardly looks any older now," Byron said. There was one more of Kate, playing the piano in a concert or recital. In it her eyes were closed.

The only family picture of Matty was part of a wedding portrait, "his older sister's," Clay guessed out loud. In the photograph, sepia toned, Kate stood between Matty and Matty's father. The resemblance between father and son was remarkable. The three of them were on a staircase looking down at the bride and groom.

"Where's his mother?" Byron asked.

"She was killed. Car accident. Before Matty started high school. Something we've had in common."

Byron took this in. Then he whistled. "I see where he got his looks."

"He used to do his own developing. I assume he still does. Some of these are pretty nice, you've got to admit," Clay answered.

"Get's around a bit, I'll say that."

Clay led the way to a small bedroom at the end of the hall. "You might as well sleep here," Clay said. "I'll take the couch."

They dropped their overnight bags against the radiator.

"Good plan there, Cap."

Clay caught the drift. "Forget whatever it is you're thinking."

"What?"

"You know what. And not a word. I'll be glad to sleep here, if you prefer the couch."

"Whew. Whoa, now. I ain't said a thing. And I don't plan to, neither." Byron took out his wallet and set it and his keys on the dresser. "This here's fine. Of course, now that you mention it, it did seem sudden. I mean, I know you're fixed about what you've said. I know that. I don't know what *they're* up to, though. I hope she's in on the program. That's all. Those boundaries, like you talked about."

"You're thinking cockeyed stupid, Byron. Jesus." Clay tried to check himself. "Of course she is. She's just sensitive now. She just got engaged."

"Probably am. Thinking cockeyed again. Won't be the first time. Definitely not the last. You yourself now, I believe you could use a college course on women. Maybe if you'd've finished you'd've gotten one. Anyway, I do know one thing for sure: that you ain't made of stone. She neither."

"Byron, I wouldn't've come down here if this were even an issue. You might know that."

"Well, where is Matty, anyway?"

"He'll be here. Meantime, you get your thinking straight."

"Yeah. Okay, forget it. I won't say another word."

"Yeah. Don't think it, either."

"It ain't easy to stop thinking about something you don't wanna be thinking about in the first place."

"Try harder," Clay said.

"Yeah."

Back downstairs, the living room was heavily curtained, dark and soft. The floor was covered with worn, overlapping braided rugs. Against one wall stood an old red velvet sofa framed in sweeping black mahogany, with a white lace antimacassar spread across the back. The unused fireplace had three chairs gathered around it—a pine rocker, and two armchairs in corduroy upholstery.

"Matty is on his way," Kate said. "We found some of this at auction, down here. It's like playing house."

"Well, I thought Byron and I might go out and pick up a couple of pizzas or find some Chinese or something," Clay said.

"Nonsense," Kate answered. "We'll rustle something up. You're such a good cook, you can help me." Byron rolled his eyes. "Only we're out of beer. But we do have some wine," she offered.

"Good," Byron said. "And I have just a nip of whiskey in my bag." He rose to get it.

Kate took Clay's two hands and pulled him with her, saying, "Come on, let's see what we can find." Holding his hand, she walked him into the kitchen. She pulled a bottle of Beaujolais from the pantry and handed it to Clay. "I've wanted so much to talk to you," she said. "I wish you'd called." Her eyes were uncertain.

Clay glanced down at the bottle, then looked back at Kate. He tried to read her face. "I didn't know whether I should. I wish you'd told me, though. I mean, I'd have wanted to celebrate for you both."

"It happened so fast, Clay. Of course, it was something we've both taken for granted since . . . since forever, really. Since we were in high school. Matty's been so jumpy. Preoccupied. I don't know. Not himself. And he needed to, he said. He needed to . . . And I guess I did too."

Clay stayed quiet for a moment before speaking. "Well, I know he's very happy now. He sounded like he was."

Kate turned and pulled down some glasses from the shelf. She polished one, holding it up to the light from the window, and then looked through it, squinting.

"He's seeing life through rose-colored glasses," she answered. "Or maybe I should say through Rosa-colored glasses. And a Polaroid. He's already found a fast crowd down here."

Clay wondered at this, but they heard Byron returning. He found a corkscrew and opened the wine.

"That's a sound I like," said Byron, walking in with a bourbon bottle, half full, in his hand. He took a glass from Kate and poured three fingers, then clinked his glass against the wine bottle. "And that one too," he continued. He raised his arm high. "To beautiful young women," he offered, and swallowed his drink down.

"Pour some for us, Clay," Kate asked. She tilted her head at Byron. "And I'll drink to naked men diving off boathouses." She lowered her eyes. "And to swimming in the moonlight."

"And to you and Matty," Clay added. "To your engagement."

They found pasta, olive oil, and garlic, and Kate and Clay cooked while Byron, and soon Matty, who had come home, sat at the kitchen table sipping whiskey. Matty pulled out the contact sheets of the photographs from the regatta and passed them around. He promised them prints. Byron started telling them about how Agnes hit them, and they wanted to know all about Clay's being on the water in the storm. Matty opened a window, and the salty night air, warm from the summer sun and the sea, washed through the house and over the conversation.

Next morning, Clay and Byron were up and out early. They had a chart of the lower Bay with several of the dock areas circled. They drove through the small watermen towns along the western shore and down the coast, trying first Hudgins, then New Point and Mobjack, and finally Bavon, jutting out on the westernmost edge of the Gloucester peninsula at New Point Comfort and just inside Mobjack Bay. Bavon was just a smattering of white and ocher-colored houses, a public town dock and parking lot, and wharfs and dock slips for watermen and small pleasure boats, which ringed the head of Davis Creek, horseshoe fashion. On one of the wharfs skirting the town dock, which was laid out down a long, bottleneck crushed-gravel drive, stood a gray two-story building with a blistered white railed porch and a sign reading THE WATERMAN'S HOLE. A marine supplies store was on the first floor, and the second housed a small bar and restaurant, which opened early but closed at nine, according to the sign on the wall. Adjacent to this building was a loading dock. The loading dock, they discovered, was operated by a white-haired man who introduced himself as Calvin. Calvin bought crabs from the watermen and trucked them daily to Richmond. From the dock, the view south was down Davis Creek, bordered on both sides by wide swaths of sharp-bladed spartina and bog, and out toward the wide water of Mobjack Bay. Clay studied the chart. He liked the remoteness of the place and being surrounded by so much water. Calvin had a slip available and offered it to Clay for eighty dollars a month. "I'll take your crabs," Calvin said. "All you can catch. At a fair price. And you can get your alewives here too. I keep 'em boxed and frozen in my cooler." Calvin chewed tobacco and gave off a brown glob of spit as he pointed to a refrigerator unit inside a shed on the loading dock. "Yeah, and don't fret the channel there. She got ten foot all the way out."

"How many crabbers pot around here?"

Calvin pondered this. "We got quite a few. Lay around the inside of Mobjack. Not as many as there was, of course. Fore the oil spill year before last. Put a damper on it. Put a stain there. There's several buyers still. But I'll welcome your crabs."

Clay accepted and gave him a twenty-dollar down payment to hold it. He didn't have many twenties left.

"Hell," Calvin said. "Most are leavin' the trade. You're the first new one I seen in a time."

Clay thanked him and they drove back to Matty and Kate's to tell them the news. Clay then got on the phone and started making calls to find out how to get their Virginia commercial-crabbing license while Byron sat in the kitchen talking to Matty and Kate. It took Clay several calls and he was put on hold at one point, but he got the information before hanging up.

"I need a resident address to get a license," Clay told everyone, returning to the kitchen. "We'll need to find a place to rent."

"Not necessary." Matty said. "This will be your resident address."

"It's the least you can do for us, your friends, Clay Wakeman," Kate admonished him. "We want to board a waterman." She crossed her arms. "Don't you say a word, now. It's all settled. Just feed us that crab soup. Now and then."

"I'll fix up the cabin on the bateau and sleep there," Byron said. "You know it's not big enough for two, but it's perfect for me. And I like my privacy."

Clay protested. "It's very generous, but—"

"Where else we gonna stay, Clay? And how we gonna jack it?"

"Clay, of course you're staying with us," Matty finished. "End of discussion."

"Really," Kate said, as if exasperated. She walked over to Matty and put her hand in his hair. "We both insist."

Clay looked at Byron.

"We're good to go, ain't we, Cap?"

"Well?" Matty said. "When?"

"Today's Thursday," Byron went on. "We do need to figure a way to replace some pots."

"Need money for that," Clay mumbled.

"Need crabs to make money."

"Weather holds, we could run down Monday, I suppose. If we stop today for our license." Clay's voice cracked, still unsure.

"Beautiful."

"Monday, Monday."

"Well, goddamn."

"Matty, tell Clay about your father," Kate urged.

Matty stood. "You know it's a long shot, Clay. I wouldn't get hopeful. He did say he'd look at the financials, though. On the wharf. Mostly because he likes Kate, I think."

"We brought a copy with us," Byron volunteered. "Clay got it from the bank."

"I did do that," Clay said. "The banker told me there's not much here, though. Pappy didn't keep his records so good. Cash business and all." He shrugged. "There is an appraisal, though. I suppose there's no harm in your father looking at it. I certainly appreciate you all asking him. And him taking the time. Please tell him for me."

On their way out, Clay retrieved the packet of information from the glove compartment and gave it to Matty. "Tell him thanks again," Clay said.

16

Friday evening Laura-Dez came by and picked Byron up. She was taking him out for a farewell dinner, and they were going to spend the weekend together. They left Clay the pickup for hauling. On Saturday, around midday, she called Clay.

"I'm just worried, that's all. He started last night. He sat at the kitchen table with a whiskey bottle and drank it and wouldn't come to bed. Twice he woke me screaming from the kitchen. I finally got him on the couch, but when I woke up this morning, he was back at the table with a bottle of Seagram's he found God knows where. I know you all are going. He made that plain. It's not that."

"What's he doing now?"

"I take care of him, Clay. But who's going to in Virginia? Sometimes he's not right."

"Is he there?"

"He's watching the Orioles and cussing like a Cubano."

"Just stay with him, Laura-Dez. Put him to bed when you can. I'll pick him up Monday, early in the morning."

"You're not hearing me, Clay."

"I'll look after him, Laura-Dez. We won't be there but a few months or so. You come down as much as you can. But the work is good for him, I think."

"You don't sleep with him. I see it in his face at night. I feel it when his body starts shaking. It's not over for him. Whatever happened to him. It's still happening."

"I know what you're saying."

Laura-Dez didn't respond.

"I'm not sure what else there is to do right now. I'll be with him. You come visit often."

"Damn it, Clay."

"I know. I'll pack up his stuff and pick him up Monday. And thanks for the call."

That afternoon the wind died. The air seemed to grow warmer with the dusk, and a fine mist crept up from the creek, like the river's breath, wet and quiet, stealing over the fields. Clay went out and sat on the picnic table, smelling and feeling the air.

He tried to call Laura-Dez back but got no answer.

He had ridden the bateau that morning around to Barker's and filled two barrels with salted menhaden.

"Can't in good faith charge you," Barker had said. "Ain't no need for crab bait round here."

Clay thanked him. "I'm good for it. Check'll be in the mail," he said smiling.

"You're good all right there, Hoss. Just remember your manners down there. And by the way, Jed Sparks is lookin' for you, down at Pecks." Clay thanked him again, pleased that he had enough bait to get started.

Back at Pecks he had found Jed Sparks. Jed had given him an envelope.

"What's this?"

"Open it, Clay."

Clay tore apart the top. He counted out three hundred dollars in twenties. He held it out. "What?"

"Hugo Brigman. Me and Barker had a talk with him. About your pots. He's all glad-handin' and nothin' underneath, that one. Eyes of an eel. Made a contribution, though. You know Barker. Hard to refuse. Nowheres near enough. But something."

Clay started to hand it back.

"Save it. I ain't takin' it back. You earned it. Something else too." Jed motioned for Clay to follow and led him around and inside the boat barn. A stack of crab pots rested against the wall. "There's forty there, Clay. We can't use 'em here. Take 'em. Consider it a bonus for your help."

"Jed. No way," Clay protested.

Jed held out his hand to stop Clay. "Clay. We'll square up when you're rollin' again. And you will be."

Clay again started to speak, but Jed interrupted. "You need to learn to accept help, Clay. Not just give it."

He didn't know what to answer.

"Be careful down there, son." Jed turned. As he was walking away, he turned back. "Be smart and come back with money for the next round, now."

Clay spent the better part of the evening on the *Miss Sarah*, loading the additional pots, checking the engine and instruments, stowing his and Byron's gear, which he had packed, and rechecking the stacked and tied crab pots he had moved that afternoon from the garage. About half of those he had stored in the boat. The others were stacked and tied in the back of the pickup.

He had packed a cooler with beer, Maryland biscuits, and sausages, and stowed it in Jed's refrigerator for Monday morning. He wondered at himself preparing everything so far in advance. Walking out to the dock, he patted his pocket and the folded twenty-dollar bills inside. He noticed the *Mood Indigo* was not in her slip. She was gone from the black buoy as well. Good riddance, he thought. He climbed aboard the *Miss Sarah,* a Budweiser in his hand. Turning on the marine radio, he found the weather channel. The report was for several calm though overcast days. He found a channel being used by some boats down south, out night-fishing for shark. The reception was unusually clear. One of them was jamming about having caught a five-foot hammerhead off Hooper Island. "Got it to the side," the fisherman went on, "and we was scared shitless. Had to shoot four times into its brain with a nine-millimeter Beretta to calm the fish down."

Clay turned off the radio, thinking about the thrashing hammer-head. He wondered what lay in store that far below the salt line. He felt uneasy about moving a water operation into strange grounds. But he saw no other choice. Except to give in. Give up. His sense of the water would not desert him, he knew. He had an instinct there. It was a different state though, and it was the people he wasn't sure he knew. Watermen had particular ways and could be hasty to judge. And there was Kate. And with her, a foreboding. An inability to be honest with himself. He tried not to think about her but had not been able to help it. He stretched out on the cot in the cabin of the bateau. Without undressing, he fell asleep. He dreamed again of living and breathing beneath the surface, floating in the element of a sun-graced aquamarine universe.

He had agreed to have lunch with Bertha on Sunday. But Laura-Dez called around noon, upset. Byron hadn't quit, and he'd broken loose and was heading up Front Street to the pool hall.

Clay called Bertha and explained the situation. He took the pickup into Easton. The entrance to the pool hall was a side door, unlit and umarked by any sign. A regular crew was sitting at the bar. Clay knew their faces and a few names. Men who were un-shaven, eyes empty. He ordered a beer.

The building was an old bowling alley, long and narrow, built when boys were needed to set up the bowling pins after each throw. It had been converted into a pool hall and bar. Successive tables receded into the dimness at the rear of the rectangular structure. Each table was lit by an overhead lamp hanging on a cord. A few shadowed figures were sitting on the old church pews that lined the wall, grim and silent like paid mourners at a funeral. In the back were stairs leading to the second floor, where card games would be going on. A cracked jukebox was playing Hank Williams.

"Your boy Byron's upstairs," the bartender, Clifton Dodd, mentioned. "He's a mess again."

"I heard," Clay said.

"Mac Longley just lent him another fifty to play. Made him promise his guitar as collateral."

"Shit," Clay said. "His Martin?"

"Yeah. Made him write it down."

Upstairs there was a pile of money in the center of the table. "Ten to you," Longley said to Byron. Two others were in the hand.

"I'll see you all, goddamn it," Byron answered, slurring his words and fishing in his pocket as he leaned his chair back. He unfolded several crumpled bills. His hands shook. He saw Clay. "Yo!" he called, losing his balance, his chair nearly tipping over.

"Real charity," Clay said to Longley.

"Man's been down on his luck lately." Longley fingered the deck in his palm. "Few pearls in hard crabs these days. You learnin' that yet? Hell, you should have taken that job with Mr. Brigman."

Clay glanced at Byron, puzzled.

Byron held up his hands, turning them as he shrugged his shoulders.

Longley dealt out another card to each of the players. He sat back smugly. "I make it my business to know what's going on."

Byron unsteadily placed his new card under the others he had stacked. Then he picked them up and looked at them, cupped in his hand, one at a time. The man to his left said, "I'll go five."

"And five more," Longley said.

The third man cussed and met the raise, calling.

Byron uncrumpled three more dollars. "I'll call you boys," Byron mumbled. "Got to go light seven, though."

"Sorry." Longley put his hand out to stop him. "On the table or out. House rules."

"Jesus, Mac," Byron said. "Fifty's gone. You know I'm good for it."

Clay reached into his pocket and from his wallet pulled out seven. "You got a winner, Byron?"

Byron closed his eyes and bobbed his head up and down. As though it were obvious.

Clay set the money down on the table.

"Bullshit," said Longley. "Man plays with what he brings to the table. Piss off, Clay."

"Wrong," Clay countered. "He's staked by me. Money on the table. House rules."

"Money's money," the third player said. "Show the cards."

Longley hesitated. "Three queens," he finally announced, turning up his hand.

"Shit," the third player answered, throwing down his.

"Aces and eights," Byron slurred out. "Dead man's hand. But not exactly." He belched for emphasis. "'Cause I got three a these eights, makin' a full boat."

"Goddamn you," Longley muttered under his breath. He started to say something else.

"Pay the man his fifty, Byron." Clay's voice was flat.

Byron acknowledged him, bobbing his head again. Then he clumsily counted out the money.

"Debt's paid," Clay said.

"Here's your seven back too," Byron offered. "With interest . . ."

"Interest is coming with me, Byron. We got some things to do."

Clay helped him up from the table and then down the stairs. "I'm taking you back to Laura-Dez. She wants to be with you before we leave. You can sleep it off there." He got no protest and took Byron back to Laura-Dez, who never said a word but helped him inside.

Once back at the farmhouse, Clay called Bertha to say goodbye. While he was on the phone, Curtis Collison and his girlfriend came home. An argument turned into a fight. Having heard enough, Clay left and drove back to Pecks. He slept again in the cabin of the *Miss Sarah*. It felt right.

With the dawn, he drove back to Easton and knocked on the front door of the town house where Laura-Dez lived. Byron was up and answered the door. He stumbled as Clay followed him down the hall.

"Whoa there, now," Byron whispered to himself. "Don't go woozy on me."

They stood in the kitchen. Byron's eyes were still bloodshot.

Clay turned and heard Byron retching in the bathroom behind him. Byron emerged, wiping his face with a towel. He went over to the sink and rinsed his mouth out with water cupped in his hand. "I have a surprise for you, Cap." He spoke in a hoarse wheeze.

"What's that?" Clay responded.

"I'm riding with you in the *Miss Sarah*."

Clay looked puzzled. He poured and sipped some coffee. It was lukewarm. "How's that? You got to drive the truck."

"Laura-Dez is going to drive the pickup, and her sister Carmen is going to follow her down in her car and bring her back. I gave them directions. They'll meet us at Bavon. Is it pronounced *Ba*von or Bay*vonne*?"

Clay watched his friend.

"It ain't French down there. I know that." Byron pulled a cigarette out of a pack in his shirt pocket. He pulled open a kitchen drawer, found a match, and struck it. His hand shook as he got it to light his smoke. "Had a few too many snorts yesterday," he said indignantly. "Did get my mind up there. Higher'n a wedding prick. Thanks for gettin' me. Anyway, they'll drop off the truck and go on. They're going to stay a night at Virginia Beach."

Clay nodded. "Nice work, Buck."

Byron emptied the rest of the coffee into a cup and guzzled it down.

"She riding with us to the wharf?"

Byron took a long last drag, exhaling slowly. He flicked his ash into the sink. "Nah, man. We can go. They'll swing by and pick up the truck on their way."

Clay finished his coffee, set his cup down, and looked at Byron. "You up for this trip, man?"

Byron gently smacked him on the shoulder. "I'm fuckin' psyched."

"Let's roll."

17

The mist was beginning to lift as the bateau pulled out from the mouth of the Tred Avon and entered the Choptank. The river was placid, white, mournful in the morning stillness. Neither had said much to the other, but they had a six-hour boat trip ahead of them. Six hours at about twelve knots, if the Bay stayed calm and the wind didn't rise against them.

The engine pounded out a clear drumlike rhythm, firm and sure and without hesitation. It pushed the bateau smartly through the glassy water, sending out its foaming wake, parallel patterns running to wash the shore. The tide was out. As they rounded Cook Point, fields of flattened eelgrass, browned and bent from the storm, appeared through the mist, overshadowing an abundant spread of new green shoots, whose tiny points could be seen emerging from the dark root of the riverbed, like a false spring.

The morning bleached out as the mist dissipated. The sky was white paste from horizon to zenith, without any distinguishable differentiations of shadow or light, without even visible separations of cloud. And the still water was a flat, undisturbed reflection of the sky. Just off James Island and running south, they were not able to discern the line marking the horizon. All around them they could see nothing but white, as though they were proceeding into an immaculate white space.

The view was almost surreal. Passing Taylors Island, Clay and Byron were able to see down and across the Bay to the shoreline above Point Lookout, guarding the wide mouth of the Potomac. Distant vistas looked close enough to touch. Clay blinked in the eerie brightness and saw against his eyelids the image of a freighter beyond the horizon and then realized he had experienced second sight. He had seen over or through the horizon, through some unexplained telepathy—a reflection in the sky, some claimed. Clay blinked again, unsure of what he had seen, and again, but could not conjure up the image a second time. He gazed at the strange apparition of white that was the sky and then far into the distance toward their destination, looking for what lay beyond and wondering about his second sight and had he seized it more clearly, what else it might have revealed.

The freighter soon came into actual view. It came out of the south and gained in size and shape as it steamed up the Bay, passing eventually to the west, its screws churning a huge wake. Arabic letters were written across the stern, and Clay assumed they named her and gave her home port. A few pleasure yachts plied the channel, and an occasional sailboat passed by under power, there being so little breeze. Sometime around midmorning they passed the point off Hooper Island lighthouse, and Clay adjusted course to pass west of Smith Island and begin to cross the Bay for the western shore of Virginia. The day didn't change, though out in the expanse of the southern Bay soft, rolling swells began to build, running from the southeast. After a while they lost sight of land altogether, and the white sheet of the world enveloped them completely.

Byron disappeared into the cabin and fell asleep. Clay opened a beer and sat back, content, steering the *Miss Sarah* with his foot on the tiller, his thoughts melting into the white universe around him.

The *Miss Sarah* held steady and sliced up and over the barrels of swells, mile after mile. At first it was just Smith Point that came into view, a distant mirage of trees, like an island in a white ocean, and then gradually other parts of the Virginia shore appeared, like separate islands, clumps of trees, south of the mouth of the Potomac. The lone workboat traversed the narrowed entrance of the Great Wicomico and angled to clear the shoal off Windmill Point. A breeze began to blow out of the southeast, and only then did Clay first notice a streak of blue sky above. Slowly making headway, crossing adjacent to Windmill Point, he surveyed the opening of the Rappahannock, a wide stretch of river running a strong incoming tide. The saltiness of the air was strong. The swells grew and sent spray off the sides of the bateau. Gwynn's Island was just a glitter to the southwest, and he gave a wide berth to the land, studying the charts for the best approach into Mobjack Bay.

Byron slept for two hours before he came out of the cabin rubbing his eyes. Clay asked him to hold the tiller and went into the cabin to get the biscuits and sausage he had wrapped for lunch. He put them out on a plastic tray and cracked two beers, and they ate their meal.

Byron took the empty tray into the cabin and came back with two more beers. He sat on the rail across from Clay, who held the tiller. They were unfamiliar with the shoreline this far south in the Bay, and the distant trees, lee shore, and glassy horizon merged and unmerged in a mirage as the *Miss Sarah* traversed the swells and ran her course down toward her destination and new berth.

"I had this buddy," Byron started. "He kinda reminded me of you." He took some swallows from his beer. "His name was Peters. He was black. He helped me." Byron took out a cigarette, walked back to the cabin to light it, and returned. He inhaled deeply, held it, then exhaled. "I remember the first night we were fired on. I had spent only two days in Danang, when we were sent to a forward area called Dong Ha. It was an airstrip, the largest that far north. The marines had complete control of what they called the I Corps Area, the northern part of Vietnam from the Demilitarized Zone to Danang. At least they did at that time. Dong Ha was the main source of supply for that area. It was an ammo dump and an airstrip and could land Phantoms and C-130 transports. It was supposed to be secure."

Clay sat listening.

"My first night in, we all went to see dirty movies. The Marine Corps had bunkers where they would show skin flicks. After the movies, we all went back to our tent, and I fell asleep. I awoke about three in the morning from the sound of explosions. Everybody else, it seemed, had just jumped up and gone. They ran across my bed and knocked me over and knocked my medical pack over. I didn't know what was happening. I couldn't find my boots or anything. Well, Peters was sitting there watching me. The whole place was deserted but for him and me. And he was very calm. He said, 'Look, there's incoming, let's get in the trenches.' I didn't even know what 'incoming' was. I told him I was trying to find my boots, but he said not to worry about the boots, to just come on and get in the trenches. He helped me pick up my medical pack and led me to the trench. It was rockets they were firing on us, and as we shoved our way into the trench, one blew up our tent, where we had just been. I guess that's when I started shakin'. They hit us all night. I think this was the first time I remember being totally afraid, Clay. I was panicked. In the bunker, there were maybe forty men, and we were all pressed in. Peters and I were the last two to get in, so we were damn near outside the door. The explosions would light up the night. You could see the company area and all the tents that were burning. Some men were screaming. They blew up the mess hall, they blew up the supply tent, and I wanted to run. I was trembling. But Peters held me and talked to me. He was talking in my ear. We were so close together, I guess he could feel me trembling. He had his arms around me tight, and he told me just to wait, wait and we'd be all right. And I was crying, sobbing. And he held me like that all night. At dawn the Phantoms came. They chased the gooks back."

Byron stopped. He drank his beer, then studied the top of the can, as if it were a strange sight, one he had never seen before. After a while he continued. "Peters didn't hardly know me. But that was just the first night. It went on. It was night after night. And I didn't get much better. He stuck with me, though." Byron paused. "Figures, he wouldn't make it. Right in front of me. His rifle jammed. Up near a river called the Ben Hai. Some kind of experimental model M16, which had a flash compressor that worked the valves open, with three prongs on it. Peters thought it was defective. He'd already turned one back. He complained about the bolt action on the second one, and the major kept telling him to clean it. It wouldn't eject the rounds. 'Clean it, mister,' the major would say. 'Learn how to use your weapon, goddamn it.' Peters knew more about weapons than that fuckhead will ever know." Byron looked at Clay. "I was in trouble, pinned down, tryin' to wrap the guts back inside a kid, and he was coming to get me. It was an ambush. A setup. And it jammed. And this gook just took his time. Firing into him. Firing and firing. Until Joe Armstrong came over and killed the bastard. I was supposed to be the corpsman, the medic. I couldn't do nothin'. We carried Peters back in my poncho. His blood was sloshing over the sides."

Byron's cigarette had burned down. He flicked it overboard and, taking his time, walked back into the cabin and lit another. He came back out, took another long draw, and held it in his lungs before exhaling. "But I never got over being afraid. That was just the way it was. Funny thing. I wasn't much more than a scared kid out there. And what they did to the men. Men I was supposed to help. Their bodies torn apart. And usually I was useless. And always scared. A waste. I mean, the whole thing was a waste, but I was a waste within a waste. And it got worse. Joe Armstrong, there"—he waved his hand—"he was the third one in the picture. The one that I showed you? He helped me after Peters. Helped me so often. Like he was my bodyguard. He would kneel over me when I'd try to stop some poor boy from bleeding his life out. And I know he saved me in the end. When I was shot. It was kind of a relief, really, as I lay there. That it would be over, one way or another. I didn't know it was such a clean shot, through the flesh. But I remember him there, crouched over me, my protector, firing, until I went out. When I awoke, they told me."

Byron put his head in his hands. When he looked up, his face was damp. "There were too many of 'em gettin' split apart. And somewhere in there, I think I began to stop liking life, liking myself. And I still haven't stopped. Being afraid too, that is . . ." Byron paused again.

They sat there for a while, silent. The water rolled past, smooth waves of reflection, the cool, blue-green deeper element below. Sea ducks, roused by the intruder boat, whirled off the surface and skimmed about. Gulls cried to the sky in circles over the water in the distance. There were no other boats in sight.

"You did what men do in war, Byron. You did right. You were a hero. And you ain't no more or less afraid than the rest of us now. You just got enough guts to admit it."

Byron squeezed his empty beer can and slowly mashed it against the wooden coaming. "Don't see you that way. Afraid, I mean."

Clay hesitated. "Then look closer. I know I couldn't've of done any more than you. Or done it any better."

Byron shrugged.

"In my eyes you stand taller than most." Clay motioned at the beer cans. "You're strung tight right now. All this probably's not helping so much," he said quietly. "But I wouldn't want anyone else for my partner." He studied the water. "Time'll help, Buck. Just give yourself some."

Byron swept his gaze about them. "Well, time and space is what we got down here, don't we?"

Clay didn't answer. The two just stood side by side, staring trancelike at the shorelines appearing and disappearing beyond the running swells of the Bay, the steadily increasing breeze blowing the clouds apart and dissipating the aura of white that had girdled the day. The seascape was changing color, as though all along it had been viewed through a camera with a soft white filter over the lens, and that filter had just been removed.

"This here is what'll renew. Feeling it. Breathing it. Always has. Just take some time. Let it open you up again to all that strength you got inside there."

Byron wiped his brow and face on his sleeve. "That's what I'm trying to be here for. I'm feelin' it and I'm waiting. But I'm having a hard time moving forward. Like old Johnnydog. Like a deer in the headlights. Hoping I make it." He kicked at a bushel basket.

"You'll make it, Byron. You're healing already." Clay tilted his chin at the stacked wire cages. "And maybe you'll pull in some crabs while you're at it."

They breathed the saltier air and pushed the bateau on, continuing until Gwynn's Island was west of them and then nearly off their stern. They pushed on toward their point of destination. Passing the Milford Haven Spit, Clay angled the *Miss Sarah* due south, and after a while they both could make out the red buoy marked #4 on the chart off the island New Point Comfort and the stone lighthouse standing as a sentry marking the shoal. From there Clay set a northwesterly course for the entrance to Davis Creek, noting his direction as 342 degrees by the compass and realizing that they were entering Mobjack Bay.

It was even larger than they had expected. On the chart it resembled a giant hand stamped into the land, with the several rivers protruding into the western shore as the fingers. Davis Creek, their destination, was the first inlet on the northern side of Mobjack Bay, and the smallest providing safe harbor. It ran closely parallel to its longer but less hospitable neighbor, Pepper Creek, which was shallow at its entrance and, according to what Calvin had told them, required local knowledge to navigate. Well past Pepper Creek, and going around the bay, the larger tributaries of the East, North, Ware, and Severn Rivers, opened in a circle, the mouths of the latter two being across Mobjack Bay and indistinguishable in the afternoon haze, at a distance of about three miles, Clay guessed.

"What do you think?" Clay said.

"This here pond's right broad in the beam, ain't she?" Byron smiled.

Clay pointed forward to a black buoy in the distance. "That's the entrance to the creek," he said. "Easy enough to spot. Least on a day like this." He pulled back on the tiller post, sending the bow of the *Miss Sarah* hard to starboard. "Plenty a daylight left. Let's have a look around for a good spot to lay. What do you say?"

Byron pursed his lips, then nodded. "Shit. We got half the pots here. Let's put 'em out."

Reversing course, they headed back out, angling closer to the peninsula, a near perfect triangle jutting out into the Chesapeake. According to the chart, the bottom gently sloped from the edge of the sandy shoal to a wide channel. They were surprised that they saw no sign of crab pots or fishing nets. Continuing southeast, just adjacent to New Point Comfort, where the water deepened into the Bay's channel, they saw a line of black-and-red pot buoys bobbing on the surface.

Clay ran along the pot line. "Laying kind of far down, I'd say," he remarked. "Awfully deep."

"Virginia crabs ain't Maryland crabs," Byron responded. "Don't taste the same. Maybe don't act the same."

Clay rounded New Point Comfort and they pushed along the western edge of the shore, running north toward Horn Harbor. Several different pot lays were bunched along the shore in about fifteen to twenty feet of water, one red and white, another red and silver, and a third, orange and white.

"These make more sense, don't they," Byron said.

They turned around just south of Winter Harbor and retraced their course down the shoreline, around the island's tip, and back inside Mobjack Bay, and then ran past the mouth of Davis Creek and then Pepper Creek, nearing the mouth of the East River. One lay of about two hundred pots was set out between Pepper Creek and the East River, the buoys tinted a faded yellow.

Clay again swung the bow of the *Miss Sarah* around.

"You thinkin' what I'm thinkin'?" Byron asked.

"Seems to be plenty of room between Davis Creek and the point, doesn't there?"

"Like somebody made room for us right off our slip."

They cruised back to the half-moon shoal and began reviewing various depths on the depth finder. They found the slope off the bank Clay was looking for and dropped the anchor several times to see what kind of sand-and-mud mixture lay on the bottom. They cruised the area once more, looking for pots, but there were none.

Clay then began to wander some in the general area, watching the water and tide, checking the depths, and feeling for what he wanted. After a while he seemed ready and brought the *Miss Sarah* to the outermost point where he wanted to start the pot lay, perhaps a quarter mile or so off the beach of New Point Comfort, out of sight of any other pots and in a position to work with the tide.

"About fourteen feet, here," he said studying the water's surface. "Let's work 'em down toward the black buoy."

But he needn't have said anything, as Byron had already untied and unwrapped the pots and filled the cylinders on several with bait and was heaving the first one over the side.

They worked together for about an hour or so, carefully positioning their sixty-odd pots along the bank. As they were finishing, another workboat approached out of the east, the lighthouse on New Point Comfort looming behind it. The boat was slightly bigger, had a high, sharp bow, and was running fast, cutting a large wake and heading directly at the *Miss Sarah*. Clay and Byron watched as it approached without lessening its speed. Just before reaching them, not fifty feet away, it swerved parallel to them, turning back out in the direction of Pepper Creek. A barrel-built man was alone on deck. He seemed to be observing them closely. He wore jean overalls. A shaggy beard covered most of his face. Byron raised his hand. The man did not flinch or move but only watched them as he passed, never slowing, and rocking them with his wake. Clay tried to read the name of the boat, written across the stern, but it was half covered in sludge and he wasn't sure he got it right. He thought he made out the word *Vera*, though the rest was obscured.

"Friendly," Clay commented under his breath.

"He's a potter, all right," Byron said. "Got to be. You see that pulley rig he had? Not bad."

"Heavy duty," Clay responded, watching the workboat's stern fly away from them. Without slowing, it cut across and past the mouth of Davis Creek. After a few minutes it began to turn into Pepper Creek, where for a few seconds more they could see the upper half of the workboat and its solitary captain moving above the tidal flats.

"Our turn, now," said Clay. "Let's take her in to her new home. Hope she finds it tidy."

Clay centered the *Miss Sarah* in the opening to Davis Creek. The channel entrance was marked by a black spar, followed by two reds leading down the main cut. The channel was narrow and serpentine. Clay noticed some shoaling on the west edge. Expanding marsh bordered both sides of the creek, which he ran at half speed until they saw the town dock and, beyond, the slips near the Waterman's Hole. They located the one that Calvin had shown them, and Clay backed the *Miss Sarah* in without brushing the creosote-covered piling. Securing her, they took time in preparing her permanent lines. It was just past four. In the parking lot of the wharf sat Byron's pickup, loaded down with the rest of the pots. Laura-Dez had left a note on it. She and her sister had decided not to wait, but to push on to Virginia Beach. Written at the bottom was the name and address of the hotel where they planned to stay.

Byron backed the rusty green truck around so that the truck bed was nearest to the slip pier. Then they unlashed the ropes tying down the wire pots and carried them onto the *Miss Sarah*. When they were finished, Clay grabbed his duffel bag from the boat's cabin and threw it in the back of the truck.

"Long day," said Byron.

"Good day," answered Clay.

Byron told Clay that he was thinking he might want to find Laura-Dez in Virginia Beach. The note was a hint, he figured. Her way of inviting him.

"I think you got that right," Clay agreed.

Byron drove Clay over to Matty and Kate's. "I'll meet you before sunup," Byron offered.

"Like hell. No way. You enjoy yourself and stay with her all day tomorrow. You know how women are about their men loving and leaving."

Byron hesitated.

Clay continued. "I could use a day off myself sometime, so we'll swap. You'll owe me one."

Byron licked his dry lips. "How you gonna get to the boat?"

"I'll manage. They got two cars."

"Right. But okay," Byron stammered. "I'll see how it's going.

Maybe I'll be here." He grinned. "But don't wait for me if I'm not."

Clay patted Byron on the shoulder, opened the door, and got out of the truck. He grabbed his duffel bag from the back. "Tell her thanks again, for bringing our pots down." He gave Byron a look. "Show her a waterman's appreciation, now."

Byron reared back, and the tires of the pickup skidded as he put it in gear. Clay watched as he drove down the street and turned on the road leading to the highway to Virginia Beach.

18

Kate opened the door before he could knock. She had two glasses of wine in her hand and gave one to Clay, raising hers in welcome.

"How was your trip?" She kissed his shoulder as she spoke. She grabbed his duffel and led him inside. "I want to hear every detail. I'm so glad you're here. I'm making a gazpacho with herbs from the garden. You've never seen such a garden as this place has . . ."

Matty stepped into the hall from the kitchen. "And I'm marinating a butterfly leg of lamb to grill," he said. He seemed to peer forward. "Where is Byron?"

Kate looked out over Clay's shoulder. "And your truck? We were expecting you both."

"Laura-Dez drove half our crab pots down. She wanted him to be with her in Virginia Beach. Byron said to thank you and to tell you he was sorry to miss dinner. He took the truck. I hate to ask, but I might need to borrow a ride to the wharf in the morning. Maybe I could use your car, and Matty could take you to it after you all get up?"

"Clay, of course. Don't worry about it. You must be exhausted.

Don't you want a shower?" Kate lifted herself on tiptoe. "You do smell a little like seaweed, or crab. It's that salty smell again. Come on." And she began to climb the stairs, but the duffel was heavy for her. Clay took it. He followed her up and into the guest room. She had set a vase of fresh white irises by the bed, which was turned down. She squeezed his hand before she left.

Clay let a hard shower run until the hot water started to turn. He shaved and put on jeans and a T-shirt. When he entered the kitchen, Matty was calling from the basement for him to come down.

Spread out over the basement floor were large black-and-white photographs, all pictures of an attractive young woman Clay had never seen.

"What do you make of these?" Matty asked, surveying the lot. "They're for a portfolio I'm doing for a local model. She's hot. In the Miss Virginia competition."

Clay walked around the photographs, some of which were upside down.

"I need to pick three for her to use."

Kate called from upstairs. "Are you showing him those modeling pictures, Matthew?" They could hear her walking out, the screen door slamming behind her.

"She's been in a mood lately," Matty said. "She's getting a thing about this. Which do you think?"

Clay took his time picking out the three he liked. Matty seemed to approve. "She is hot, isn't she?" he said, then motioned for Clay to follow him.

Army blankets had been hung from ceiling to floor on a clothesline to block off one corner of the basement. "It's my darkroom," Matty explained, holding a blanket aside for Clay to enter. "I've been waiting for you for this." He opened a drawer in the table that sat along the wall and took out a small plastic bag and unrolled it. A portion of white powder was visible inside it. "Super coke," Matty whispered. "It's available down here. Lot of 'artists' in Gloucester." He winked. "Not even that expensive." With the handle of a spoon, he dipped some of the powder out onto a small oval of cut glass on the table, mashing and chopping the powder fine.

"I don't really think that's for me," Clay said, watching.

"Oh, just try some, Clay. Just a nose hit."

Matty had rolled up a dollar bill and snorted a bit into each nostril. "Whew." He took a breath. "Fine." He whistled. He handed the bill to Clay. "Have a taste. But don't say anything to Kate. She doesn't approve. It scares her, I think."

"How long have you been into this?" Clay asked.

"Now and then this past year at school. Easier to get down here." Matty smiled. "Small-town bennies."

"Where you getting it?"

"One of the carpenters I met on the plantation job. His roommate. Drives for a seafood plant. Smells like fish. But he has access to a boatload of it. Good blow."

Clay wavered, biting his lip. "I appreciate it, Matty. But not now. Another time. I'm just trying to stay focused down here. Tomorrow's a big day."

"Whatever," Matty said. "No problem." He took the dollar back from Clay. "For me," he said, clearing his nostrils and motioning at the glass. "You go on up and appease Kate. I'll be right along."

"Go easy, now." Clay measured his tone as he pulled aside the blanket.

"Oh, I do. Just special occasions."

Kate was standing on the back landing, just outside the porch door, a bunch of fresh-cut rosemary in one hand and purple leaf cuttings in the other. She called to him. "Here, smell," she said to Clay as he came out, and she pinched a purple leaf in her hand and held it under his nose. "Sage. My landlady keeps an herb garden." She gestured toward Matty. "He's into this modeling thing, now," she said. She laid the herbs down on the grill top. "If you will kindly come with me, though . . ." She took his hand. "I want to show you the view."

She led him off to the side of the cottage, and down a slate walkway that wound through a garden of azalea bushes and daylilies, and into a stand of weeping willows bordering a narrow creek. Between two trees was a stone bench. She hooked her arm in his, walked him to the bench, and sat him down, then pointed out between the houses, where the Bay arched away in the distance. Then she gestured to a deep pool in the creek at their feet. Under the surface, mottled tadpoles hovered in the nearly still water.

"I come here to calm myself down," she said. "To breathe in this tranquillity." She seemed to savor the breadth and distance. "When I see the Bay, now, I see you on it."

Above Clay's head the willows rustled in the light air.

"Did you know I've started working some?"

"I didn't know."

"Teaching piano in Richmond three days a week. At the arts center. And down the road in Hudgins on Wednesdays. There's a Methodist home. I play for the residents. I've offered to give lessons too, but no one has signed up yet. The people there are so old. And sad."

"I've missed hearing you play."

"I'll play for you later," she promised. She stepped down and stirred the water with her toes, and her reflected face stirred with the water under the willows in the evening light. The tadpoles darted and were still again. "There's a neighborhood cat," she went on. "It comes and watches them. I think they sink just a little deeper when it's around. I think they're smart. For baby frogs. My landlady told me the creek froze last winter. I don't know how they survived." She leaned her head onto Clay's shoulder. "Don't you like this place?"

"It's peaceful enough."

"Well?"

"Yes. I do."

"I knew you would."

Clay touched her hair, then took his hand away. "Fish'll surprise you. Like people. I guess tadpoles are fish." He looked out at the Bay. "Some fish can live in dried-up riverbeds for months. It's called estivation." He paused. "Crabs winter deep in the mud. Cold-blooded hibernators, that's how they survive a freeze."

"Not like you." Kate raised her head. Her eyes were keen, then turned soft. She took his hands, intertwining her fingers in his. "My dreams are full of you now." She said this quietly, not looking away. "They're confusing. But I see you on your river, and my blood races."

He stared back into the creek water. "I shouldn't be here," he finally murmured.

"I couldn't bear for you not to be," she answered.

"Kate."

"It's not that. I'm engaged now. And so I'm safe, as are you." She lowered her eyes. "I just wanted to tell you that. About my dreams. So you'd know. Anyway, I know I can trust you. I mean, we can trust each other."

"I wouldn't—"

"Clay," she said, interrupting him. "Don't fret. I'll help you." She heaved a sigh. "You'll only be here for the summer, anyway. Matty and I, we're both glad for your company. Your presence here. It's good for us."

He was silent. He knew he should sort this out with her. But he turned and studied the garden and the cottage behind him. "This must require a lot of work. To keep so perfect."

Kate let go of his hands. She stood. "My landlady comes sometimes and weeds and prunes the bushes. She loves to garden. But I like things natural." She threw her head back in a way she had. "Like watermen." She laughed.

They heard the screen door slam. It was Matty.

"We'll make it work. Matty and I will," she said. "I'll be your *friend*, Clay. I will."

While they started dinner, Clay went upstairs and unpacked. He had framed the faded photograph of Pappy and Sarah and him that he'd discovered in the ammunition box, and he put it on the bureau. He put his small clock radio there as well. The stereo started blasting from below. When he came downstairs, Kate had turned the volume down and put on a record of Leontyne Price singing arias from Verdi and Puccini. Over dinner, Kate wanted Clay to tell them more about the hurricane, about how it really was. He told them about the building storm and his efforts to clear *Mood Indigo* from her grounding. Kate kept asking questions about the winds. About the size and configuration of the waves. She had been reading a book on boating, she told Clay. And weather. She asked him what force he thought the wind was on the Beaufort scale. He answered, "A lot of force," and Matty laughed. Kate blurted out that she was considering graduate school. In something other than music—oceanography, maybe. This seemed to take Matty by surprise, and he frowned. He finished his glass of wine.

"You're going to set the record for changing minors and majors. I can't keep up."

"What better way to spend your working life," she went on, ignoring him, "than working to preserve this." She spread her arms wide.

"You may be being naive," Matty said.

"You always call me that."

"Things just aren't so crystal clear," he said. "Not black and white. And it's usually just about money. Competing interests over money."

"I don't mind money," she answered. "It's getting the money behind the right side. That's the key."

"Doesn't sound too naive to me," Clay offered. "But you've got a gift with the music. That's something special."

She glanced at him appreciatively.

"We should talk these things over together," Matty said.

"I didn't notice you talking over some of these new photo projects with me," Kate returned.

"Graduate school's, well, serious. Would affect our plans." His tone was more conciliatory.

She put her hand on her hips. "I'm just thinking about it. For now," she said easily. "Just thinking out loud."

Matty offered Clay a cigar after dinner, and the two of them sat on the front stoop, smoking and sipping brandy. He told Clay that he had sent the financial information about the wharf to his father. "I wouldn't expect anything, though. He's just humoring Kate, I'm afraid."

Kate joined them after she finished the dishes, and she made a point of showing Clay the narrow front view between the houses, where a patch of phosphorescence shimmered off the water across the way. The sky was full of stars.

"There's Orion's belt." She held her arm up in its direction. "My favorite."

"It's the phallus," quipped Matty to Clay.

She kicked at him, and Matty grabbed at her foot. Then he lay back and put his head in her lap and tried to name some other constellations. After a while Kate mentioned that she would be away the following Saturday night. It was her father's summer steeplechase, and she always rode in it. A party he hosted at his Hunt Club would follow. She asked Clay if he'd ever like to try something like that. Clay wasn't sure if it was an invitation.

"I wish I could," he answered. "I've never spent much time with horses, though. I suspect knowing a horse, having a true sense of it, would be something. Right now, of course, I've got to get things going with my pots. I've already lost half the season."

"Well, you wouldn't like it, anyway," Matty remarked. "I went once. As a spectator. Very formal, stuffy. Lot of pomp and bullshit. Though the horses were cool. I will say that. And I got some great camera shots." He sat up and relit his cigar, then watched admiringly as the smoke curled up in the light. "I'm staying here so I can go to the annual summer bull roast in Gloucester on Saturday night. All the local charities from around here get together, to raise money. I sent flyers around after we moved in. For freelance jobs. And the volunteer fire department hired me to do the photos for some safety posters they're making. I need to be there. You know, for business. You and Byron definitely should come to that."

Kate nodded encouragingly. "Yes, Clay. You would enjoy it."

"A bull roast. That sounds about our style. I'll ask Byron."

Shortly after that, Clay excused himself, explaining he had to get up at five. Matty told him to take his MG in the morning, that the keys were under the seat, and to just leave it at the wharf. Clay thanked him. He climbed into the comfortable guest bed, set his alarm, and turned out the light. Downstairs, Kate played the piano softly.

19

It seemed like he had just fallen asleep when he heard the click and buzz of the alarm. In the dark bathroom, he splashed water on his face and brushed his teeth quickly, trying to be quiet. He crept down the stairs in the dark, switched on a small table lamp in the kitchen, and put some water on to boil for coffee. He liked the morning silence and the sleeping darkness before the dawn.

Clay felt a hand on his shoulder. He had heard nothing, but he knew it was Kate. He turned. She was wearing her baseball cap. "My hair is such a mess in the morning," she whispered. Her face was sleepy but smiling. She had covered herself up with a large checked flannel shirt. "I want to make you something for break-fast," she went on. "It will only take a minute. And send you off with a good Virginia country ham sandwich. I bought the ham slices yesterday. I wanted to send some good luck with you this morning, your first day catching Virginia crabs."

He watched her move around the kitchen, warming the room. He took the hot food from her and ate it in silence, speaking only to thank her. She sat with him at the kitchen table, drinking coffee, until he was ready to leave. "Break a leg, Clay" was all she said, as she took him to the door.

It was already hot and dead calm, as though the water was waiting for the light. Or so it seemed to him, after sharing the quiet with her in the kitchen. As though his world was just waiting. Finding where he wanted to set the additional traps, he began to work, in his own time, without rush, and as he did, the sun rose over the flat, outstretched plain to the east like a blood orange streaking the sky.

When he pulled his first pot, the wire cage came up spewing water, eelgrass, and sea nettles and crammed with jimmies and sooks, all good-size, and a torn-up toadfish. He dumped the scrabbling crabs into the cull basket, figuring he would cull after all the pots were emptied. He checked the bait from habit, threw the pot back into the river, and worked his way down the line.

With a good workboat like the *Miss Sarah,* a single waterman could handle a day's work. But if he and Byron could get ahead, he thought, then he really could build a second boat.

Throughout the morning the hot sun overhead burned his arms and face until a slick breeze kicked up out of the south and filled the Bay with whitecaps. Inside Mobjack Bay it became choppy, slowing his work some. He had emptied the wire cages of their catch and had the large basin and several bushels full of crabs. The muscles in his arms and hands were tired, and his face hot from the sun, so he scanned the shoreline for a protected place to cull.

He motored inside a small cove outside of the mouth of Davis Creek and threw out the anchor. He sat in about eight feet of water with his rubber gloves on picking through and separating the crabs. Clay was fastidious about the culling of his crabs. Anything close he held up to the cull stick to be sure the crab, from point to point, took the measure. Even with the gloves, he occasionally caught a good pinch, though he handled them easily and talked to them while he worked.

He had not been culling for long when his concentration was broken by the sound of an outboard. He looked up and saw a Boston Whaler coming at him from the mouth of Mobjack Bay. As it came closer, he recognized its markings. It was the state marine police. Its driver motioned to him that he wanted to tie up along-side. Clay took the bowline from the officer and helped him secure his craft. The officer then climbed aboard without invitation.

"License and registration." This was all the man said.

Clay studied him a moment. He could have passed for a man-nequin in a store window displaying the clothes and accou-trements of a police officer's caricature, right up to the mirrored sunglasses. His hair was cropped short and flat in a marine crew cut. He seemed maybe thirty-five. His khaki trousers hung loose on his thin hips and legs. Clay turned without speaking and went into his cabin, then returned with his boat registration and crab-ber's license and handed them over.

The man took them and then studied each one slowly. "Your boat's registered out of state," he drawled, "but you got yourself a local license." He raised his face from the documents to Clay. "You tryin' to fool somebody?"

"Boat's from Talbot County, Maryland." Clay was calm; his voice even. "I live here now. The address is on there. It's all correct."

"Yeah?" The officer did not return the license and registration. "Well, I think I'll have a look-see around here. Where's your fire extinguisher?"

Clay showed him.

The man checked the dates and pressure. "Cushions and horn?"

Clay pulled them out. He knew everything was in order.

The officer then asked Clay to operate the exhaust fan, the oil pressure gauge, and the running lights. All worked. Finally he told Clay he wanted to look in the bilge. This required Clay to move his crab basin and all of the filled baskets, and his bait barrel, and take out four screws from the bilge plate. Clay looked at him for a long moment after the request was made. He stepped aft, though, and began moving his crabs. He moved each basket, the basin, and the barrel back toward the cabin. He took a screwdriver from his toolbox and unfastened the screws that held down the bilge plate. The officer squatted down and peered inside the bilge. Without a flashlight, he could see little.

"Boat ain't fluted right. Exhaust could build in there. Cause a fire. You're violatin' regulations." The officer took a pad and pen out of his back pocket and began to write.

"What are you talking about?" Clay heard the edge in his own voice.

The officer kept writing. When he was finished, he put the pad back in his pocket. "Supposed to have ventilation through the bilge for your exhaust."

"It is vented."

"Your bilge is full of scum. Vents is blocked. You're in violation. Get it cleaned before you come back out again. Now let's take a look at these here crabs." The officer turned his back on Clay, picked up the nearby cull stick, and started poking the crabs in the baskets.

Clay started to protest but stopped himself.

The officer put his boot on some crabs and then carefully picked out a smaller one, holding it by the back fin. "Look'ee here. I believe I caught you with a small fry." The man held in his hand a five-inch male, but one of the points on its shell had been nipped off by another crab. He held up the cull stick. With the broken point, the crab did not reach the five-inch limit. "Cheating a bit, aren't you?" The officer had a smirk on his face. He tossed the crab overboard behind him, while looking straight at Clay.

"I haven't finished culling yet. Too rough out there."

The officer took the pad and pen back out of his pocket. "If it ain't too rough to crab, it ain't too rough to cull. You're in violation." He began to write again.

"That crab was legal anyway. It had a broken point. You saw that."

The man didn't respond but finished writing out the violation. "I didn't see no broken point. Five inches is the rule." He tore off the sheet from the pad, then tore off the sheet he had previously written on. "You got a fifty-dollar ticket here for violating safety regulations. You can pay it or come to court. And if you come to court, mister, I'll be there. You got a two-hundred-dollar fine for illegal crabs. Pay it or come to court." The officer didn't hand Clay the tickets. He just tucked them, with Clay's license and registration, under the screwdriver Clay had set on the engine box. "Get your bilge pumped clean. Keep the small fry out of your boat." Then he looked directly at Clay. "Or get smart. Move someplace different. Where you won't be crowding the local boys so bad." The man then swiveled, stepped up on the gunnel, and expertly jumped into the bobbing Whaler. He turned the ignition key, loosened his painter from around the cleat on *Miss Sarah*'s side rail and pushed off. He fixed Clay again with his stare. "Don't like Mobjack Bay getting overused. Not with poachers, noway. Listen good, now. You crab this area, I will be in your shit. You best move somewheres different." Clear of the workboat, he pushed the throttle into gear. The Whaler lurched forward and up and turned away from the *Miss Sarah*, picking up speed.

Clay stood stone-still. He looked at the tickets on the engine box, ready to blow away any moment, and picked them up and read them, not believing he had been charged $250 in fines. He went into his cabin and took a flashlight from the drawer. He returned to the cockpit and squatted over the bilge, shining the light into the hold. About an inch of water sat in the bottom, hardly anything, considering the chop. He put his hand down in the bilge and ran his fingers along the wood under the water. The water was dirty, like all bilgewater, but he came up with no muck or debris. The ventilation seemed in no way impeded. He looked at the ticket

again, and then at the other one. They were real. He cursed the officer and then cursed himself.

Once tied up at the unloading dock, he sought out the old man,
Calvin. Before Clay even heaved up his crabs to sell, he told Calvin
what happened.

"Describe him again for me," Calvin said. Clay did so. "Let me
see them signatures." Calvin read over the tickets. "Sounds like
Amos Pickett's uncle, Walsh. Amos's got the *Vena Lee*. Ties her
sometimes across the way in Pepper Creek." Calvin pointed toward
the trees that separated the two inlets. "He knows the shoals there.
Has another place he keeps her up Ware Neck. Bad temper. Amos,
that is. Used to be big into oysters. Was a seeder. Bought heavy into
the spat. Got hurt with that oil spill. That and the parasites pretty
much closed his operation down. A shame. Been different since."
He paused. "Walsh, though, usually runs south of Mobjack."
Calvin squinted into the sun, then eyed Clay. "You have a run-in
with someone already?"

Clay shook his head no.

"Lay your pots atop a line of black and reds?"

"No. I stayed well clear."

"Well, I dunno. You can go an' drive to Portsmouth and protest
'em, I suppose. State marine sets there. Or wait till your court
date." He scratched his head. "Amos's gotten stranger, some say.
Likes his space. Busted up old Clem Griffin in a fight. Claimed
Clem was crowdin' him off the point. Clem moved his lays clear
up the north side after. Stay clear of him, I'd say." Calvin shrugged.
"Sorry there, son."

Clay sold him his crabs. Not enough to pay for the tickets. Then
he brought the *Miss Sarah* around to her slip and hosed her down.
He kept an eye out for Byron's pickup, as he hadn't seen it in the
parking lot. When all the gear was stowed, he went into the bar
and ordered a beer. It was around three when Byron wobbled in, a
plastic cup of whiskey in his hand.

Byron was in no condition to help. Clay asked him if he could use the truck and got the keys. Byron said he'd had it with Laura-Dez. Wanted a fresh drink.

"What happened?"

"I dunno really. We'd had a good night. Were playin' in bed. Firecrackers started blowing up around the motel. Some kids, but I started in on 'em, screamin' back and forth. Laura-Dez got to yellin' at me. I left and went down the boardwalk. Came back late, drunk. I pissed in the closet on her sister's bags. Thought it was the head. They threw me out in the morning." He rubbed his eyes with his fingers. "Fuck it, I say. Can't take a joke."

Clay drank his beer and paid for Byron to have another whiskey. Byron said he'd sleep on board when he was ready.

"What'd we catch?" Byron wanted to know as Clay was leaving.

" 'Bout eight bushels," Clay answered. He didn't mention the tickets.

Clay walked out of the bar, started the pickup, and found the highway south to Portsmouth. He looked for speed. The highway sparkled with the bits of shattered glass embedded in the asphalt. He could not outrace himself. Lost in Norfolk, he traversed neighborhoods deserted like the outskirts of a ghost city, with only an occasional witness, staring silently at him from a dilapidated front porch. He flew through these side streets, seeking the cold steel of battleships, the stark glint of an abandoned fleet. Corrosion, iron in dark rust and shadow, might cool his mind. He could not get close enough. Locked gates patrolled by bored Seabees in white hats met him at every entrance. He lost time in the endless turnarounds on the gravel roads that twisted through among the shipyards, exhausting himself. The futility of his errand became more clear the closer he came. Somewhere in the stranded city, he found a bar and ordered a drink. Then another. A hooker asked him if he wanted a date. She was young, and her face was attractive until she smiled. She wore white clamdiggers, sneakers, and a football jersey, cut off at the middle. He declined politely and left, starting the journey back. His mind drummed along with the undertow of the asphalt. Dusk seemed to come quickly. The lights on the highway rushed past like ideas in the darkness of time. Illusions that gird the modern mind. He drove without thinking until he found himself back at the house on Gwynn's Island.

"I've saved a plate for you," Kate said. "I'll warm it up." She looked fresh and young as a flower and kissed him on the cheek. "You better wash up. Matty's out late too. Down at the fire department in Gloucester."

Clay washed in the kitchen sink. The soap stung his face, burned from the wind and sun. "Look at these hands," he said, holding them out to Kate. They were red and swollen from the day and callused. She came over and took them. "Days out there'll take a toll," he said. "It's different than you think."

He sat at the table, feeling almost too tired to eat.

"What happened out there today?" she asked. She seemed to have a sense of things with him.

"Had a run-in with the state marine." He sighed. "Nothing grievous. Just one thing after another."

"What do you mean?"

"He fined me. But he shouldn't have. Everything was in order. He was delivering a message."

"From whom?"

"I don't know. Locals, probably."

"How bad?"

"Couple hundred."

She went to the refrigerator and took out a beer for him. She opened it and set it before him with his plate of food.

"You know, I'd like you to let me help you in this."

"Kate, please. You're doing too much already."

"I've not done anything, Clay. And not near what I'd like to do."

He frowned and started to eat. "I'm putting fifty in the food jar tomorrow, and if you argue, I'll leave," he said.

"Clay."

She put her hands on her hips.

"I mean it."

Kate made herself a cup of tea and sat with him. When he finished the fried chicken she had made she brought him a second helping. He told her thanks and started to eat again.

"You've built up a hunger there, Clay Wakeman." Kate had crossed her arms.

"Yes," he answered. He finished the food. He felt another surge of anger over the day, and with it a recklessness. "I have an appetite." As she reached for his plate, he grasped her arm. She didn't resist. He wanted to pull her to him.

"What?"

He let her arm drop. "Nothing. I'm just beat. Thank you for dinner."

She brought him another beer. Stepping back, she opened a kitchen drawer and took out of it some skin lotion. She dabbed some onto her palm, smoothing it around with her fingertips. Stepping behind him, she began to spread the cool cream gently onto his forehead and around his swollen eyes, working it into his face. He stiffened at first and then tried to relax. She spread it over his lips. He leaned back, feeling the gentleness and the coolness of her fingers on his skin, and shut his eyes until he heard the sound of Matty's MG in the driveway.

20

Wind chimes hung from the front porch of the cottage. They were wooden, and in the night breeze, damp from the Chesapeake, they made a muted, plaintive sound. It was Thursday, and Kate had called from Richmond, from a gas station. A hose had split in her Volvo, and she was getting it fixed. She was fine, Matty reported, but she would be late. He, Clay, and Byron had all eaten dinner together: some fried rice Clay had stirred up, with beer and buttered bread. Afterward, Byron had taken the pickup back to the bateau. Living aboard was living "freestyle," as he called it. Matty had wanted to shoot the early sunrise and had agreed to drop Clay off in the morning.

Clay had walked Byron out and then sat on the front porch. He sat rocking, listening to the soothing timbre of the wind chimes in the damp night air. His own solitude was like a blanket over him.

He was used to longing. It went where he went. He relished the work because the work filled him with a contentment that flowed naturally from it, and because it camouflaged the longing until the work was over. And then the longing returned.

He sat up when Matty opened the screen door to the porch and

TIM JUNKIN

stepped outside. Matty walked to the steps and sat down. He was holding a pipe, which he raised to his mouth, lit, and began to smoke. Neither spoke for a while. They seemed to share the sense of the night and sat together quietly wrapped in its curtain.

The embers of tobacco inside Matty's pipe glowed when he drew on it.

"If only we could read our futures in the glowing fire," he remarked.

Clay detected resignation. "You got the present and future right here, pal. You know that?"

"Perhaps. People are never satisfied with what they have, though. They want more. The active life is a greedy life." He took a silver tamper from his shirt pocket and patted down the bowl of tobacco. From a pouch in his pocket, he added more tobacco to the bowl, tamping it down as well.

"The future ain't nothing but what you decide to make it." Clay got up off the rocker and sat down next to Matty on the first step.

Matty relit the pipe, considering. "I'd have to say no to that. Least, not that you can count on. I mean there's fate. You've seen so yourself. The hurricane and all."

Clay shifted and leaned back against the banister. "Well, I guess there is a passel of surprises in store for anybody. Seems so, anyway."

"Things you don't expect," Matty continued. "They can bite you right from behind."

Clay reached for Matty's matches, took one, and used it as a toothpick. "How's the photographer's life? Really."

"About half true. Just like my pictures. Light and shadow. I like it. But it's a long road to where I want to go. And it's got some curves to it."

"What curves?"

Matty seemed to muse over the question. "I don't know. My father's pulling awfully hard to bring me into the business. He

216

doesn't understand I don't want to be just a studio photographer. You know. The art world's out there. That's where I see this leading. Of course, it's full of its own pretensions. Temptations."

"Like?"

"Lots of cuties hanging around. They seem to dig it."

On the corner of the street, a tall lamppost illuminated a small circle of the night. Clay noticed a swarm of moths and night insects flying about and into the hot light. He shook his head. "Man, you need to appreciate just what you've got going here."

Matty followed Clay's gaze to the light and the moths colliding with it. "I know," he whispered. "I know. Of course I love Kate. We'll have a good life together. A long road. But I am young. Wild oats and shit. Man, you know ..."

"I don't know dick."

"After we graduate, we'll announce the engagement. Then it'll seem more real."

"If I were you, I'd do it tomorrow, slick. Announce it, anyway."

"Both of our parents want us to graduate first." Matty nudged Clay with his foot. "So what is secret hurts no one."

Clay frowned. "I wouldn't mess up what you got. That's for sure."

"We'll set a date next spring. Get married. All so normal, predictable. I feel like a last hurrah or something."

"Maybe you've been snorting too much of that good shit."

Matty stretched his arms out. "Hell, she's gone enough. I'm safe."

"You're missing my point."

"Aw, don't worry. I'm just allowing for distraction. Life is short."

Clay turned away.

"And it's fun, man. It's really fun. How about you? You gotta get some sugar soon yourself."

"Nothing right now," Clay answered. "Trying to concentrate on making all this work."

They heard some sirens start up from way behind them.

"Fire station," Matty said. "Half the guys in town belong to it. They start their sirens for just about anything." He paused. "How's Byron making out?"

"'Bout the same."

"You remember, when he came down to visit us at school, just before he went to boot camp? Running around in that pickup with that huge knife in his fatigues?"

Clay focused on the moths hitting the streetlamp. "I remember." He sighed. "He didn't know what was coming. Any more than the rest of us, that is."

"What happened? Did he ever tell you the details?"

Clay thought for a moment. "Not really. He keeps it private. Wrote a letter to me, though, when he was over there. And he's not one for writing. Said, 'The world will never be the same for me anymore.' That was it. And then a short time later he got hurt and came home to the hospital."

Matty tried unsuccessfully to take a last draw from his pipe. Then he knocked the ash from the bowl on the side of the step. "That was all wrong over there," he said. "I can imagine. But he's seemed pretty good the last few times I've seen him."

"Well, we've had some good days this summer."

"Yeah. Well, I'm sorry."

"Yeah." Clay shifted. "But speaking of him. There's something I need to tell you."

Matty yawned. "What's that?"

"I've decided to move out, Matty. I need to."

"You just got here." Matty seemed disappointed.

"Byron shouldn't have to live on that boat. It won't work. He's got enough pressing on him." Clay spoke deliberately. "You've been generous. You and Kate. And it has been appreciated. More than I could say. But I know we need to do this."

Matty was thinking it through. "Have you told Kate?" he asked.

Clay shook his head. "I'd like to soon. If that's all right."

"When?" Matty asked.

"We have a month's rent with what we brought down. I should have enough for a security deposit by next week or so. I need to bring my car down from Maryland. I'd say another week."

"You really think living on the boat is bothering him? I mean, there is the couch."

"I'm worried it will," he said. "He wouldn't take the couch. I'm sure it's best."

"You should tell Kate soon."

"I will. If you don't mind. I'll tell her."

Matty nodded. "Sure. If you've made up your mind."

"I have."

Matty stood up. "Okay, then. I'm sure we can find you a place nearby." He stared across the street and out at the water. "Bay seems calm enough tonight."

"Tides'll start to swell soon," Clay responded. "With the moon."

"What time do you have to get out of here in the morning?" Matty asked.

Clay rose. "About five."

Matty patted him on the shoulder. "Yeah, well, we better be hitting it."

They walked inside together.

Matty ducked into the kitchen and turned out the lights. He shut the front door without locking it. "Sleep well," Matty said, turning out the light in the hall.

"You too," Clay answered.

"Five is uncivilized," Matty muttered under his breath. "A waterman's hours. But I'll be up."

The following dawn was true to the beauty of high summer in tidewater Virginia. The shores along Mobjack Bay ran with the green and gold-flecked marsh grass, rising off the mudflats, bright in the morning sun. Stands of magnolia trees lined the road in the distance. Steam rose off the river as Clay and Byron worked their pots. Flocks of red-winged blackbirds wheeled over the creeks and lowlands, flashing color upon a landscape of brightness.

They were catching crabs now, constantly refining their lay, repositioning some of the traps. Clay had told Byron about the tickets. He had cleaned the bilge with a long-handled scrub mop till you could see the paint. At least with the two of them out together, he figured, there would be a witness to any future problem.

Byron worked the controls while Clay pulled the first pot of their easternmost lay. Emptying the crabs into the basin, he caught the tentacle of a sea nettle across his face. He cursed his own carelessness, wiping his cheek with his sleeve. The poison lick just missed his eye. He paused for a moment, wincing at the sting. His eye watered, glazing over his vision. He sat there, with the pot hanging from the haul wheel for several minutes, squinting through the wash in his eye.

"Sharp as a whore's curse. Best flush it with the vinegar. Ease the sting," Byron offered.

Clay left the pot to Byron and went into the cabin. He found the vinegar bottle in the first aid drawer. He rolled up some toilet paper and used it to swab the vinegar across his cheek. He winced from the pain. When he came out, his vision was still blurry. Still, even through his watery eye, he could not miss the looming white blade of the bow of another workboat, larger than his, bearing down upon them once again. And again, it swung around at the last instant, like a speed skater twisting sideways to stop, reversing its propeller, throwing waves and spray their way. The wake shook the bateau, caused Clay to lose his balance, and jerked the crab pot loose from the haul wheel, sending it falling into the chop between them.

He walked over and stood next to Byron. Backing and churning the water with his propeller, the waterman abreast of them was the same large man, this time covered with a slick green apron, which billowed around his girth like a sail. His face was swollen and red, half hidden by a curly brown beard. The high-pitched whine of his voice was incongruent with his large figure.

"You boys is from up north, ain't you," he wheezed. He didn't wait for a reply. "Well, your pots are pushing me. I been workin' this bank and creek a good while. Crabs ain't that plentiful. I'm sayin' to you to move your pots out of this river and north Mobjack altogether. Askin' once and askin' nice. You don't want trouble, you move out. Find a different river. You steer clear. Way clear." The man stopped speaking. He spit in their direction over the gunnel of his workboat.

Byron started to speak, but Clay took his arm, and he stopped.

"What's your name?" Clay asked.

"Fuck difference it make to you. You're leavin here."

"Big river," Clay mumbled. "Room enough."

"Not around my pots. Or my creeks. I move 'em around. You're in my way." His voice was unnatural. "Be on back to where you come from, boys. 'Cause you ain't gonna poach round here."

Byron was tensed up and Clay continued to squeeze his arm. The big man stared at them, then looked around in the water. The pot buoy that had been knocked loose was floating around near the man's stern. "You been warned there, misters." He threw his boat into reverse, running over the buoy line as he backed away from the *Miss Sarah*. He seemed to squint at them as he continued backing, then threw his engine into forward, turning out and away with a heavy throttle.

They saw the buoy pop up, free from its line, cut and gouged from the boat's propeller. Its pot was lost. And each recognized the boat before reading the name on the stern as it turned away from them: the *Vena Lee*.

• • •

They didn't move any of their pots that day. Byron took some time to calm down while Clay talked to him about being smart and thoughtful. Clay got him working again, and they finished with their pots but left them where they were. Clay said they should think carefully and talk things over before deciding what to do. But belying his calm was his own anger at being bullied. And he knew Byron was on a short fuse, just looking for an excuse, for a reason to blow.

The insult was not directed just against them. It disrespected the land as well, the river. No one had rights to the river. No one, at any rate, had rights greater than any other man's. No one owned her any more than Clay did. This was basic. He and Byron would not easily retreat from this place on the water that they had found and staked out and harvested with success. He didn't plan to allow the *Vena Lee* to cheat their time.

The river was flat as they brought the *Miss Sarah* around the point and into Davis Creek, and Clay worked to calm his mind. Cat's-paws played across the surface. He would think before he acted. He would crab carefully. And be watchful. He would unload their bushels and then drive over to Pepper Creek.

They sold their catch to Calvin. After the bateau was tied and cleaned, they found Calvin rocking on the wharf deck and spoke for a while. Byron interjected a question about the *Vena Lee*.

"What you askin' for?" Calvin asked in return.

"We had a few words on the river," Clay answered. "Not real friendly."

Calvin tilted his head. "I told you before that Amos's been strange of late. Particular strange. Funny. He's closer to here than anywhere. But won't come in here to sell. I dunno. I'd say, keep your distance."

Clay listened. Byron said nothing but turned and walked into the bar.

Three times that afternoon, Clay drove himself across the spit to

Pepper Creek, looking to find and speak to Amos Pickett. There were only a few boats there, tied up against the bulkhead, but the *Vena Lee* never came in. He didn't know what to make of this. He would keep at it, though.

That evening, after dinner, in front of Matty, Clay told Kate of his decision, that he needed to move out. She started to argue but saw that Clay and Matty had already talked it over, and that Clay had made up his mind, so she stopped and turned sullen. Soon after, she went up to her room and shut the door.

21

On the river the next morning, again before first light, the air was still, and the silence broken only by the echoed bleating of distant engines moving out across Mobjack Bay, the green and red channel lights still blinking in the receding darkness.

As they rounded the eastern point of Davis Creek and pushed out past the black spar, Clay strained his eyes through the gray film of dawn and was relieved after a few minutes to see his first line of pot buoys floating in the layer of morning mist that steamed off the river.

They worked their first line in an easterly direction, toward the mouth of Mobjack Bay and New Point Comfort, the stone lighthouse rising up from the swirl, as if heralding the great, steaming Bay beyond. The traps were full of crabs, and both he and Byron, sweating in the heat, soaked their shirts through. Halfway through the line, with the sun massive in its rise above the horizon, Clay saw a small grouping of black-and-red buoys pressing against the southeastern end of his lay, though huddled in deeper water. They looked as though they had been placed to crowd him. They seemed oddly set. Deepwater crabbing was not typical for this time of year.

"See those black and reds over there?" he said to Byron, motioning toward the lighthouse.

Byron had just finished shaking some jimmies out of the lower basket of a trap. He refastened the lid and looked, squinting into the glare of the sun, shielding his brow with his palm.

"I don't get it," Clay added.

"Fucker's pinching us," Byron answered.

"I see that." Clay squinted into the sun as well. Without turning, he pointed at the pot on the rail. "Wrap it. We'll move this last bunch back to the western edge and a little south. Off the sloping channel bank."

"Clay." Byron set the wire cage down. "We got full pots right here. He's doin' the crowdin'."

Clay wiped the sweat off his face with the sleeve of his T-shirt. "Damn it, Byron, I know. But he lives here. Maybe he did plan to pot here. Let's give him some slack."

Byron unfastened the plastic top to the bait cylinder and threw the alewives into it. He closed the top and dropped the cage onto the deck. "Yeah. Well, I'm thinking this boy wants more than slack."

They worked through the first lay, and after harvesting the crabs from the most easterly traps, they rebaited and stacked them in the bateau. Gunning the inboard engine, Clay ran back to the westerly edge of his lay and, working with a sense of the depth and the bank off the channel, dropped the traps down onto the river bottom, where he believed the crabs were running. Continuing southwest, they bisected the top of Mobjack Bay and found their second string off the northwest shoal guarding the East River. These pots were full and filled the barrels with sooks and several baskets with jimmies. Clay then turned the bateau back and headed east, toward the third lay off the island. As they approached their buoys, they saw another grouping of black and reds farther out, just south of their string, bobbing close together and crowding their own crab pots. Their placement seemed, again, strange to Clay.

"We movin' these too?" Byron asked.

Clay cursed. He brought the boat adjacent to their first buoy so that Byron could hook it and bring the line into the pulley.

"I don't see any possible good in having a quarrel. This just ain't home waters for us. Empty the pot and bring it in. We'll move this group around the point."

Byron grabbed the pot as it came up streaming with sand, water, and eelgrass. He threw it down disgustedly. "This is weak. We should stand our ground."

"Byron, what are we going to do? We're alone down here, man. These people don't know us. This guy's a local. I figure we give him space. This'll blow over. We're catching crabs now. I'll find us another good shelf."

Byron shook his head. The pot was full of scrabbling crabs. He picked it up and began to angrily shake the crabs into the cull basin.

Clay grabbed a large bait fish. "It ain't worth it, Buck. Let's not let this guy bust with what we're doing. We're catching crabs." He shoved the menhaden into the bait cylinder of the pot as Byron stacked it against the gunnel, coiling the buoy warp on top of it.

"You call it, man. Whatever. But I ain't sure this guy's gonna quit."

"He'll quit. He's got no reason not to." Clay stepped behind the tiller, increased the throttle, and moved forward to another buoy, then slowed the bateau down. "We'll just stay clear of him. Mind our own business and catch crabs. Survive this season. We'll figure something out in the fall. Be back on home water next spring."

In the heat and glare, the two of them raised all of the pots in the third lay and moved them around the point and up toward Horn Harbor, looking for a breakwater to soften the strong Bay tide, where the slope and depth of the bottom might work. The water was deeper than Clay wanted, but the pots needed to be back in the river. They had to get their crabs to the wharf to sell, and he didn't want Byron to get any worse. He chose a lay in twenty-two feet at the bottom of a bank. They laid out the pots in a triangular configuration receding southeast. Working quickly, they finished in another hour. Still, it was almost three o'clock when they got back to the wharf and weighed and sold their crabs. It was a good catch, nearly a thousand pounds clear weight, including eight barrels of jimmies. They earned $180. After bait and fuel, they'd keep $150 or so.

They tied up the *Miss Sarah*. Tired and thirsty, they headed for the bar. In the middle of the parking lot, though, blocking their way as they were heading for the restaurant, was a mud-splattered pickup truck. The driver was Amos Pickett. His face was flushed. An unlit cigar was in his mouth. As they approached, he addressed them in his high rasp.

"You boys don't listen, I reckon." He took his right hand off the steering wheel and pulled the cigar out of his mouth, and then he once again spit in their direction.

Clay stopped Byron from speaking by putting his hand on his shoulder. "We saw your pots, mister," Clay said. "We got no intent to crowd your operation. We moved our lay north, around the point." Clay held his hands out, palms up. "We don't want a problem. Why don't we all start over?"

"You two birds ain't startin' shit."

Clay dropped his arms. Byron started to speak, but Clay cut him off. "Well, you pot where you want. We'll steer clear of you. Plenty of free water out there." He took Byron by the arm and started to walk around the truck.

"Maybe you don't hear too good." Amos looked away at the restaurant, then looked behind him. "Or then maybe you're misunderstanding something. I know it's one or the other, 'cause you're still here." He quieted his voice. "Your pots are crowdin' me. Your boat is stinking up my pond. And movin' a few fuckin' buoys ain't what I been talkin' about." He pointed his cigar at Clay. Byron started forward. Just then a car horn sounded from behind them, and a girl's voice shouted Byron's name, then shouted it again. Byron stopped and wheeled. Clay turned too and saw Laura-Dez leaning out of her sister's car, waving. "That best be plain enough for you," Amos growled. "I'm done talkin'." They were turning back as he put his truck in gear and pitted his tires against the gravel surface, pulling off, the gray dust spitting out behind him.

"What now?" Byron asked under his breath as Laura-Dez came running toward them.

Clay was trying to take in what was happening. "Looks like you got your hands full right here, Buck."

She interrupted them before Byron could answer, embracing Clay quickly and then turning to Byron.

"You missed me, didn't you," she said to him. "I know you did. I'm sorry about how we parted. We have to talk now. I booked us a room."

Byron put his hand to her cheek. "Kind of a bad time, now, Laura-Dez."

"Bad time? I just put my sister on the bus. And she was not so happy, Byron."

"We got ourselves a situation."

"What situation?"

Clay saw the opportunity to get Byron to a safer distance. "We aren't doing anything about it today, Buck. And tomorrow's Sunday. Go on. Give us time to think of a plan."

"Jesus. Your sister took the bus home?" Byron seemed pleased by that.

Laura-Dez cocked her head to the side. "What situation?" She held out her arms.

Byron frowned. He took her and held her, his mouth near her ear. "I'll tell you about it."

After a moment she pushed him back. "The room's just up the highway. I have the car till Sunday night."

Byron turned to face Clay. "I'm not leavin' you in the middle of this."

"You're not leaving anybody. But nothing is going to happen on Sunday."

"We might call home. Talk to Barker. See if anybody knows anything about this guy."

"Yeah. Well, we might. Looks like you might be busy there, though. Why don't we meet here Monday early for breakfast?"

"What about the bull roast?"

"Matty's going with me. Maybe he'll have some ideas."

Byron nodded. "Here. Right." He handed the keys to Clay. "I'll make some calls home. You take the truck." Laura-Dez took his hand. "We'll call to Matty's and leave the number where we are. Call if you need me. No matter the reason. Or the time. Meanwhile, I'll do some research."

"Right. Research."

22

Matty was sitting on the living room couch smoking a joint and drinking a bottle of beer when Clay got home. He was listening to the Rolling Stones singing "Sweet Virginia," and paging through an issue of *Yachting* magazine.

He raised his eyes when Clay came in, but he didn't get up. He seemed agitated. "Get a quick shower and change, man. We're late. The roast started about three. I've been saving up my appetite."

Clay had driven back down to Pepper Creek, but Amos Pickett wasn't there. He wanted to talk with Matty about what was happening, but first he went upstairs to clean up.

They drove in Matty's MG, with the top down. Matty had brought them each a beer and had saved half of the reefer. They were off the island, along a stretch of roadway bordered by woods, when he pulled over and lit the rest of the joint. Clay had been telling Matty about the problem.

"You know his kind better than I do." Matty shrugged. "Probably just a redneck bluff."

Clay looked at the trees and thick foliage around them. "I don't know. Seems serious enough. Something strange about his pot lays, though. Something off-kilter about the whole situation."

They finished the roach. Matty shifted into first gear and started moving again. They drove for a while without speaking. The road curved and then took them away from the woods and through fields of soybeans, yellowing in the sun. They passed a roadside lounge. Then woods again enclosed them.

"I mean, why does he think he's entitled? It can't be worth getting in trouble over."

Clay tilted back his beer. It tasted good. He reached his hand up high to feel the air rushing over them. "Couple of crabbers I knew up on the Miles. In Maryland. Pretty territorial. Generations working the same river. I can understand that."

"We're going to make a stop up ahead. Down Ware Neck." Matty pointed to a road sign indicating a public boat landing just as he passed it. He made a U-turn and drove back, turning down a narrow roadway.

"But this seems stretching it. Even for them." Clay glanced toward Matty. "Do you know any of the local police? I mean, is there a local guy? Or is there just county police?"

"There is at least one town cop—that I've met. Sleeps in his car mostly."

"Maybe I should say something to him. Maybe he could have somebody talk to this guy."

Matty grimaced. "The cop's worthless. Over the hill. But go ahead, if you want. I'll introduce you. His name's Pruitt. Ewell Pruitt." He frowned as he slowed behind another car. "I'm going to see my father tomorrow. For a few days. He wants to take me through his investments. I've been promising him all summer. He called. I told Kate. Be leaving early. We'll find Officer Pruitt when I get back." Matty put on his signal and then turned up a dirt lane rutted with potholes. Streaks of river reflected through the breaks in the trees. "My father said he'd discuss your wharf while I'm there. I'll push for you."

"Thanks," Clay said. But his present problems seemed more immediate. He wasn't sure that speaking to Officer Pruitt could wait a few days, over the hill or not.

At the end of the dirt lane stood a wooden structure with a truck loading platform on one side and a waterfront loading dock on the other, the cove beyond placid under the shadows of the surrounding woods.

"I'll be just a minute," Matty said.

"What?"

But Matty was out. Clay watched him knock on the door to an office. A thin man with a ponytail stepped from inside. Clay noticed the sparkle of an earring in his right ear. Looking about him quickly, the man pulled Matty in. No one else seemed to be around, though the front fender of a truck was visible off to the side of the building. Bushel baskets were stacked on the platform, dirty with scattered bits of crab shells. Clay figured the crab cooler was behind the office.

Soon Matty was back.

"Let me guess," Clay offered.

"He was pissed," Matty responded. "That you were in the car. He's paranoid. I told him you were cool. Plus he's out of blow. I couldn't believe it. He said he'd have plenty first of the week, though." Matty reached in his pocket and pulled out a small vial. He smiled. "I keep a touch in reserve. Not enough to party hard, but enough to pick us up. For later." Matty winked.

As they turned back out of the dirt parking area, Clay noticed the plywood sign he had missed before. Splintered, with sloppy hand-painted lettering, it was propped against some garbage pails. INDIGO SEAFOOD, it read.

Ten minutes later they reached the bull roast, where cars were parked in a field. Matty pulled off early and started his own row.

Music wafted from inside a red barn. Double doors opened on each side and split-rail-fenced corrals ran from each end. People were filing in through the wide doors, and Clay could see others walking out the other side and milling about in the fenced areas. A band had set up on one end of the barn and was playing a Willie Nelson song. A few people were dancing on the wooden floor.

Matty led Clay through the barn and out into the corral yard, where several horseshoe pits were set next to one another and games were in progress. Past these, a large tan canvas tent was erected. "The auctioneer's tent," Matty explained. "But over here's the food." He walked toward the steam and smoke coming from behind the tent. Two overturned and halved steel drums were filled with hot coals and covered with screens. Several large pots hissed and bubbled over, steaming soft mano clams in beer broth. Massive slabs of beef, pitchforked from a marinade barrel and tossed on the grills, sizzled next to the pots. The clams were a dollar a dozen with melted butter. Matty ordered two dozen. A keg was against the fence, and while they waited for the clams, he brought over two beers and set them on a picnic table. They ate the clams with the butter and drank the beer. They watched the cooks occasionally ladle a thick reddish brown barbecue sauce over the meat, a carver standing ready to slice a portion of whatever doneness was ordered.

"Two dollars a plate, there." One of the cooks wiped his dripping brow.

When they were done with the clams, Clay bought two plates of the beef.

After they finished, Matty went off to find dessert. The place was filling up with people. Clay watched them passing by. There seemed plenty of girls around, in pairs and groups. The air was cooling.

After what seemed a while, Matty returned with two slices of apple pie. "Sorry, man. I ran into a few people I know." Clay took his plate and started eating. "I've met people here so fast," Matty continued. "Through the photography some. And the firehouse. Word got out I take pictures." He held his hands up. "Small towns aren't so bad."

They ate the food and watched the horseshoe games, the dancers inside, and the girls in bright shirts and cowboy boots walking by.

"I've enjoyed seeing you and Byron," Matty started.

Clay glanced up briefly as he finished his pie.

"I remember you telling me about Byron when he was younger. I remember because I was struck by his odd brilliance." He sipped his beer. "You know, within his own world. Before he enlisted. I mean, he was building that cabin on his uncle's land. He was working the trotline—is that right?—in the morning and selling the crabs, and building the cabin from scratch in the afternoons. And trapping muskrats at night. Right? Skinning them, and tanning and selling the pelts?" He shook his head back and forth. "I mean, there is a certain brilliance to that."

Clay nodded in agreement. "I suppose."

"Whatever happened to the cabin?"

"His uncle wanted it. Paid him for it, though."

"Perhaps there was some kind of inevitability for Byron. You know, with his father a drinker and all. Some people suffer terrible experiences and come away intact. Some don't. But certain things are meant to be."

"Like fate, again. Or hurricanes?" Clay leaned back in his chair. "I don't believe I agree with that. Not as to him."

"Maybe not," Matty conceded. "Sometimes it seems like I'm going in a direction, though. Taken by forces that can't be controlled."

"Like a boat in a storm," Clay ventured. "Like a crabber with no crabs?" Clay picked at some crumbs.

"What do you do in a storm. In a boat?"

"Try to keep your compass. Try not to let it catch you sideways."

"Resist."

"Resist losing your steerage, your control."

"Go with the flow? Or fight back?"

"That's what Byron wants. With Amos Pickett. Stand up, and he'll back off."

Matty pushed his plate away. "Probably. Or sink your boat."

"Aren't you the jolly one."

"Tonight I'm the grim reaper." He looked at two girls passing by in blue jeans and cowboy hats. They tipped their hats as they passed, and he followed them with his eyes. "I'd like to grimly reap one of those two," he said, deadpan.

The staccato stutterings of the auctioneer started up over a microphone. They listened for a while and decided to get up. They ambled over to the tent. Inside, rows of tables offered junk of every description. The auctioneer talked so fast that Clay couldn't understand a word. Two helpers carried larger items onto a stage where the auctioneer stood. Smaller items were referred to by lot numbers off a master list.

"I'll get us a refill," Matty said, reaching for Clay's cup. "Let's get hammered."

Clay watched the auction, half curious because he had never seen one before. He watched brass beds and oak tables, oil paintings, and cheap glassware sell, each in a matter of minutes. When Matty did not return, he walked along the tables, checking out the objects for sale. He saw a pocket watch with a gold back and chain that he liked. He had always wanted a pocket watch. An old brass ship's telescope sat on one of the tables. He picked it up and put it to his eye. He could see little in the dim light of the tent, though the lenses were intact. Auctions must thrive on dim light, he thought. He replaced the telescope and then saw, sitting close to it, a thin seashell, the size of his palm and perfect in shape. On its inside surface was painted a miniature landscape—a farmhouse, not unlike the one he and Byron lived in, and a barn and pasture, and tiny cows and a flagpole with an American flag blowing in the wind. He had never seen anything quite like it. It was number 27. After three or four more items were sold, he understood number 24 was on the block. He waited and Matty did not return. He listened and watched as numbers 25 and 26 were sold, and then when 27 came up, he just reached up his hand and held it up, and the auctioneer said, "Sold!" pointing in his direction. He had bought it for eleven dollars. He paid the money to the lady at the table, took the shell, which was wrapped in a piece of tissue, and carefully put it in the pocket of his blue jean jacket. He had bought it without ever really thinking of what he was doing. He would give it to Kate. A gesture of thanks, he told himself, for her kindness. He walked out of the tent and met Matty, who was heading back in.

"Jesus, I'm sorry, Clay. I've been running into people everywhere. Here's your drink. Let's head for the party. C'mon."

"Somewhere out there," Matty said as they walked toward the barn, "lies a trap or a promise."

"I'm the one needs to be trapped," Clay said. "Trapped and treed."

"Desire can strip a man clean."

Clay looked at Matty. He had nothing to add.

"I've got questions."

"You've got everything. Except a grip."

"Who wants a grip?"

"I do," Clay answered. But Matty had walked ahead.

Inside the barn, paper streamers decked the rafters, and balloons bounced high against the roof. Near the band, a microphone was set up for the callers. An introduction had just been made, and a square dance started. Three girls began right out dancing together.

Clay and Matty found a fenced livestock stall to lean against. While watching the women dance and watching others take to the floor, they drank their beers. Clay went off by himself and took a slow tour of the crowd in the barn. He thought to begin a conversation with a slim brunet over by one of the slot machines, but the music was loud, and his mind was elsewhere. He settled back next to Matty, who hadn't moved. When the music stopped, two women approached. They came up to them from the side, and one of the women said hello. Matty hadn't seen them approach, but he turned quickly at the woman's voice. The one who had spoken was stunning. She was dark haired and olive complexioned, with a high forehead and an exotic, almost haughty air. She wore a long red-patterned cotton skirt and a blousy shirt that was tight at the waist, showing a fine figure. Her sleeves were rolled up. Her hands were on her hips. As Matty turned in surprise at her voice, she laughed and flipped her head slightly, throwing her hair back, a gesture that reminded Clay of Kate.

"Matty," she said lightly, "this is my cousin Celeste. Celeste, this is my friend Matty."

Clay thought the one who spoke looked familiar, and then it came to him.

Celeste held out her hand, and Matty shook it. "Celeste," he said, "it is a pleasure. Please meet my friend Clay Wakeman. And Clay," he went on, turning toward the girl who had spoken, "this is Rosa Satie. A client. She's a model."

"Hello, Clay," Rosa said. She spoke with clear, impeccable pronunciation, but with a hint of a European accent.

"Hello, Clay," Celeste repeated.

"My pleasure. Twice." Clay took each hand in turn.

"Celeste is visiting our family," Rosa said to Clay, as if there were a need for an explanation. "She may stay all summer. She is a student in California. Her parents are from Castille. She is learning English." She turned toward Celeste, who blushed. Celeste was thin. She reminded Clay of a sparrow.

"Rosa," Matty broke in. "Would you have a dance with me?"

The band had taken a break, but someone had started playing records. Bob Dylan sang "Lay Lady Lay." Rosa had offered Matty her hand and they were walking away. Clay considered asking Celeste also, to be polite, but sensed her discomfort and instead led her to one of the nearby tables. He tried to talk with her, but she had trouble understanding. She smiled and nodded but said little. Matty and Rosa remained on the dance floor for several songs. When they returned, Rosa had her arm linked in his.

"He's a marvelous dancer," she remarked. "He dances on air."

Rosa and Matty sat, making light conversation, and then, over Clay's protest, Rosa insisted on buying beers for everyone. She pulled Matty with her, and Matty pulled Clay. He followed them out to one of the far corrals. There, Matty took the small glass vial from his shirt. "Dessert time, Clay. Special occasion." Matty had a shortened straw. Rosa went, and then Matty. This time Clay tried to pretend to partake. Without meaning to, he inhaled some and felt the jolt. Walking back, his head was rushing like a heavy sea.

The caller started again. Matty and Rosa pulled Clay and Celeste out and made them try the Virginia reel. A large crowd was square dancing and Clay lost track of everyone. Back at the table, he found Celeste, alone. She smiled but didn't speak. Night had fallen, and outside, the lanterns glowed in the air and the summer insects whirled. After a while Matty and Rosa returned, hot and sweaty from the dance. Matty gave Clay a five-dollar bill and asked him to bring four more beers back. Clay told Matty to walk with him. It was in the line at the keg that Matty, stumbling through his words, told Clay about Rosa. That they were having a fling. "*Fling's* not the right word," he said. "She's burning into my heart. It's on fire. I'm in love with two women."

Clay walked out soon after. He was dizzy and disoriented. Matty had given him the keys, telling him he would get a ride home with Rosa. Clay found a fence post to lean against over past the barbecue pits. He took a few deep breaths. Through the smoke, he thought he saw a familiar face. Then two. He wasn't sure. The smoke was thick and their faces were shrouded. The first looked like Hugo Brigman. He was talking to the second, unmistakably the man with the ponytail and earring. They turned and moved away from him. Clay pushed off the fence post, his head spinning. He walked through the field and managed to find the car.

He drove slowly back. He passed the turnoff to Indigo Seafood and continued down the highway. He veered off toward Bavon and went down the long gravel drive to the Waterman's Hole. It was closing but sold him a last-call whiskey, which he took outside to the dock. He sat in the silence of the summer night. A light breeze cooled his face and brushed the halyard of a lone sailboat against its mast. He could hear the cicadas from the nearby woods. He watched a near-full moon rise over the creek and bay, backlighting the shadowed horizon and firing a swath across the water, to the other side of Mobjack's shining mouth. He wondered at its brightness and then at the strangeness of human behavior, and of coincidence. He stayed until the moon was well overhead and, trying to regain his sense of balance, drove back through the glistening fields of corn to Kate and Matty's house.

23

Clay slept late. When he got downstairs, Matty was already gone. He had left a note. Clay's head buzzed as he read it.

"On my way to Richmond," it read. "Sorry about last night. I needed to talk. Compulsion. Be back in a few days. Matty."

Clay showered and dressed. He drove the truck to the Highway Diner and ordered a big breakfast, which made him feel better. His plan was to find Amos Pickett. To confront the problem. Then he would make the decision. Outside, the day was hot, the sun rising in the sky over the fields. He drove to Pepper Creek, but again the *Vena Lee* wasn't there. He stopped back by the cottage to wait awhile. Kate met him at the door.

"We're going to the beach," she said. "I'm taking you. It's Sunday and I need some sun. I've had enough of grown-ups. That bad boy Matty is off again, but he's making his own way. And you deserve a day off. I'll be your chaperone." He told her he couldn't. "It's Sunday," she pleaded. "I drove back early to be here." Something in her eyes wouldn't let him say no. He showed her the painted shell he had bought for her. She took it and turned it over and over in her hand. Then she put it on the mantel, leaning it carefully against the mirror over the fireplace. "It's so delicate," she said. She saw herself in the mirror and shook her hair loose. "C'mon," she said. "The sun is calling."

Kate knew a place on the north end of Virginia Beach, away from the crowds. Clay drove the truck and she directed him there. She had a blanket, a cooler, and beach chairs, and they set up camp just above the breaker line.

"We've got enough stuff to be on safari," Clay mumbled.

"When you go, you got to go in style," she pronounced.

"We look like an Arab encampment. You must be the belly dancer."

Kate had just wiggled out of her jeans, revealing a bikini beneath. She threw the jeans in his face, then picked up a small seashell and tried to put it in her belly button. She ran down to the water, and Clay followed her. It was cold, and neither went in further than their knees. They watched the breakers fold over themselves and slide down the shore. The warm sun felt like a balm on their skin.

They had pâté out of the cooler, with French bread and a chilled Chablis Kate had brought back from Maryland. She even had canned peaches for dessert. Kate fed Clay a peach, dripping the syrup on his chest.

They washed their hands and faces in the surf and kicked spray on each other. They took a walk down the beach. Gulls and terns hovered overhead in the light breeze. Sandpipers were all along the beach, scampering ahead of the surge. Four pelicans cruised the water beyond the breakers, gliding over the surface looking for shadows underneath. Occasionally, one would swiftly rise up, as if lifted by a thermal, and then fall like a dart into the water. Kate and Clay walked back, their feet in the sea. Back on the blanket Kate lay on her stomach. Clay asked if she'd like him to spread lotion on her back and she laughed. She unfastened the back of her top. He sat next to her, his arms around his knees, watching the ocean, watching her tanned shoulders in the sun. Lying there, she told him about the steeplechase. She had competed with her father. Her horse was a three-year-old chestnut gelding, and she had done well. Her father would expect her to go fox hunting in the fall. On the last hunt, she said, the riders had fox's blood smeared on their foreheads. It bothered her more than ever before. She wasn't sure whether she wanted to hunt again. She sat up, holding her bikini top to her breasts.

"What do you think?"

Clay reflected. "I think knowing and riding a horse like you do, feeling a bond there—that's special. Being outside like that, with your father. Important to him, I'm sure." He picked up some sand and let it sift through his fingers. "I don't know. I hunt. I crab. Let it sit awhile. You'll make the right choice."

Kate fastened her top. "Yes," she said. "I guess." Then, "Did you and Matthew and Byron have fun at the roast?"

"Byron didn't come. Laura-Dez surprised him on Saturday. He's still with her."

"Oh. So it was just the two of you. Well, how about you?"

"It was nice. Crowded. Great food. Music."

"What was it that you and Matty were talking about? In the note."

Clay brushed some sand off his leg. He looked up at Kate, who was looking at him. "Oh, you know, just talk. Relationships."

"What did he say about me?"

Clay turned aside toward the horizon. "He said he loved you."

Kate hesitated. "Oh." She shook her hair out. "You know I've never been with anyone but Matthew. Matty." She hesitated. "Until you."

Clay was silent.

"Matty and I've been together since tenth grade. I know you know that. I mean, I know that's not the case with him. Not being with anyone else. Not even now. And I'm sure you also know that." She looked down the beach. "And I wouldn't want to know that from you, anyway."

After a while, Kate traced a line down his arm with her finger. "Clay?" she said. "Do you think a person can love two people at the same time? Really love them?"

With the question, he began smoothing out the sand in front of him. He took his time, as though he were preparing a tablet and about to write the answer across it. "That's a hard one," he finally responded. "Yes. Maybe. But I'm not sure it would work if you tried to act on it." He started to write something on the sand, then wiped it out.

"What?"

"Nothing."

She tilted her head. "Was Matthew's model Rosa there last night?" she asked. Then, "Never mind," she quickly said. "Never mind." Standing up, she reached for his hand. "Come on. Let's swim."

She took his hand and pulled him up. And then she was off for the water. She dove under a wave. Clay watched her in the surf. She was a pretty swimmer, with a long graceful stroke. He entered the water after her, pulling hard over the rollers, and was about to catch her when she turned and came back to him. When she reached him, she was out of breath. They were bobbing in about five feet of water, and each successive swell lifted them off their feet. She put her hands on his shoulders and let him hold her up. He held her waist with his hands. Then she was pointing at something in the water, about thirty yards off.

"What is that?" she asked.

Clay saw something thrashing in the water. He couldn't make it out at first. They both swam closer. It was struggling. "It's a bird. A big one," he said. "It looks hurt."

They both swam toward it. From its brown-gray plumage and long neck, it appeared to Clay to be a pelican, though he could not see its bill or pouch. It was entangled in something. "Can we help it?" asked Kate. "It looks bad."

"I don't know."

"Clay?"

"We'll need a blanket. Could you swim back and get it?"

Kate worked her way ashore. Clay edged his way closer to the bird. He could see its trouble now. It was caught in a fishing line that was tangled around its neck and one wing. Its bill also seemed to be caught. The bird stopped struggling. It was low in the water. It flailed just to keep its head up.

Kate returned, swimming on her back with the blanket held above her. She was breathing hard. Clay took it, asking her if she was okay and she nodded. He swam toward the bird. When he got close enough, he threw the blanket over its head and body and gathered the bundle, keeping it above the water. At first the pelican jerked, but Clay held firm, and as he kicked toward Kate, it soon gave up and was still.

She helped him get the bundle ashore, holding one side up as they swam. They walked up the beach to their towels. Kate sat down. "Hold it tight," Clay cautioned, handing it to her. They folded the blanket back from the bird's head, talking to it softly. It did not struggle. Clay took a linen napkin and wrapped its beak closed lightly, and Kate held its beak and petted its neck and whispered to the bird in a calming voice. The fishing line was cutting into its flesh. A rusty hook was embedded in its plumage at the base of one wing.

"I'll get the knife we used with lunch," Clay said. As he cut the line away, Kate stroked the animal and talked to it, watching him as he worked. He unwound the line from around the beak. On the neck, the skin was broken, but the line had not deeply embedded itself. He cut below and above it and pulled the nylon line free. Some other people, walking by, saw what was happening and stopped to watch and offer help. One woman went back to her car for some antiseptic. Clay worked methodically until he got to the buried hook. He looked at Kate and told her to hold tight. He worked it loose and then pulled it free. It came out with some blood and specks of flesh. The bird twitched but never made a sound.

"When you're done, will it be able to fly?" a little girl who had come over and was watching asked.

Clay looked up at the question. "I don't know, sweetheart," he answered. Kate's eyes asked the same thing.

"I should have been a doctor," he muttered.

"I think your bedside manner needs a little work," she whispered.

Clay took the antiseptic and poured it where the line had cut the flesh and where the hook had been caught. The last piece of line was knotted around the wing. He worked the knife inside the tight loop and cut through it.

"I wish we could take it home with us, Clay," Kate said softly. She continued to stroke its head and neck. The feathers were soft and iridescent silver brown. Its pinkish eyes seemed more alert now, and it turned its head in small, quick motions. There were furry yellow feathers atop its long, slim neck and angular head and bill.

"Talk about a double chin," Clay remarked. He probed around its body for any additional line or any sign of injury. "That's all we can do, I think. I don't feel anything broken."

Kate continued to pet the bird. She whispered to it in such a low, soft voice, Clay couldn't hear what she said. Everyone watching kept talking about how beautiful it was. Then Kate turned to Clay. "Well?" she asked.

"Yes."

Kate tried to stand, and Clay helped her, since she was holding the pelican. They walked down to the edge of the beach with the bird still wrapped in the blanket in Kate's arms. They stopped on the wet sand, just above the leading line of surf. "I know you still can," she said, kneeling down. She put the bird down, carefully unwrapped the napkin and blanket, and stepped back. The crowd had stayed up by the cooler, but all were watching. The pelican jerked once, twice, freeing its legs, and then riffled its feathers. For several seconds it stood motionless. It seemed grand, even larger than it had in the blanket. It stretched its neck, with a long rippling effect, then its wings, throwing them back as a man does his arms when he yawns. Finally, in a rush of wing and power, it burst forward and up and was airborne in an instant, climbing against the breeze, up over the breaking waves, and beyond in long sweeps.

Everyone on the beach began to cheer and clap their encouragement to the seabird. Kate was transfixed. Clay had seen her move only slightly when the bird had moved. She had risen with it, sort of pushing herself up with it, as high as she could, reaching for that lift that was needed. She was still standing on the tips of her toes.

Clay watched the pelican fly straight away over the running sea, receding in the distance until it was a dot in the sky. And he watched Kate, who was watching too. And then she walked over to him and put her arms around him, laying her head on his chest.

"Look," he said to her, pointing over the waves. She turned.

"It's coming back!" shouted the little girl.

Everyone saw it there, growing larger, coming back toward them, perhaps a hundred yards out now, flying low toward the beach, effortlessly. Once it was above the rolling surf, it began to glide, fanning its wide wings out, flat and perfect. The bird came forward toward Kate and Clay, as if in perceptible slow motion, no higher than a child could throw a stone, until it was just above them. Then, wheeling in the air with a burst of power, it turned and flew back out to sea.

They drove back with the sun falling behind an anvil of clouds. Kate sat close to Clay, her head resting on his shoulder. Clay helped her unload the beach gear in the dusk. She brought him a fresh towel and told him to take his shower first, while she started a few things in the kitchen. Then she rose up and kissed the corner of his mouth. "Thank you for today," she said, and turned away. He reached his arm over her shoulder and around her front and drew her toward him, holding her there for a moment. Then he let her go and climbed the stairs.

He heard her turn on the music. His mind was full of the light from the sea, and the images of her. He studied the photograph of Pappy and Sarah as he peeled off his clothes in his bedroom. He went out into the hall with a towel wrapped around him to turn into the bathroom. She had come up and was standing there, her shirt unbuttoned and open to him, her jeans unhooked, her hair falling around her neck. He shook his head but then found his hand in hers, and they were moving back, into his room, some- how, without saying a word, together, and her mouth and hands ran over his chest, and she knelt and buried her face in his stom- ach as she undid the towel around his waist, and he was unable to speak. She gently pushed him down on the bed and removed her shirt and was against him, gliding her jeans down off her long thighs.

They lay together and she wouldn't let him leave. She brought supper to the bed, and wine, and they ate and drank, and filled themselves with each other. They lay still, on their sides, whisper- ing in the dark, touching each other, as the moon filled the room. They never slept. An hour before dawn, Clay got up. Kate stretched out her hand, reaching for him.

"Do you love me?" she asked.

"Yes," he answered.

"Will you keep loving me?"

He took her hand. "I've loved you since the beginning. You know that. But I can't stay."

"I've loved you from the beginning too," she said.

He sat down by the bed and rested his head against her knee and told her Matty was his friend. Kate said Matty was her friend too. She told Clay to wait before deciding anything. She made him promise to come back. He started to dress, telling her he was late meeting Byron. "There's no time to pack now anyway," he said.

He tried to leave but couldn't. She was there, pale against the sheets, her hair falling over the white pillows and around her breasts. They held each other until it was almost light. He pushed his feet out of the room and down the hallway, and then he somehow got out the door and into the pickup.

24

Byron was waiting for him by the wharf, sitting half asleep against a piling, a cold stogie stub dangling from his mouth. Clay gently kicked his leg. He opened one eye.

"Early for coffee, you said?"

"Got held up."

"What?"

"How'd it go with Laura-Dez?"

Byron slowly rose. He squinted up at Clay. "Great weekend. Best we've ever been together. We went to the circus." He took the cigar out of his mouth, examined it, and threw it in the water.

Clay started. "Let's go."

"I also talked to Barker."

Clay stopped. "And?"

"He said he's gonna make a few calls. Said he'd come down if you want him. With a couple a boys." Byron grinned. "To even up the negotiatin'."

"That's all we need."

Clay began walking down the dock again. A stiff wind hit him broadside. "What is it?" Byron asked from behind him.

"I'll explain. It's Kate."

"Yeah?"

"I guess I'm in love with her."

They had reached the boat. "Who don't know that? But I ain't sayin' a word."

Clay picked up the stern line of the *Miss Sarah*. "She says she feels the same."

Byron took this in. "Where's Matty?"

"Away." Clay let the line drop. He pressed his palms over his temples. He saw her there. He could still feel her, smell her. "I want to see her already. I just left her. I'm gonna be sick."

Bending down, he unraveled the stern line from the dock cleat and pulled the bateau close. "Go on. Get in."

Byron hesitated. "We can pull these crabs up quick this morning. Get back early." He looked out. "Might be some chop though."

Clay nodded again for him to step on board and then followed, and it was then that they noticed the cabin windshield. It was shattered. A spiderweb of cracks.

"Holy shit!" said Byron.

"The cabin," said Clay. The door was knocked open. Inside, the marine radio's face was bent in, and the mike ripped off and on the floor. "And the depth finder." It was broken loose and cracked apart also.

"Goddamn. That motherfucker."

Clay gripped the stanchion. "Open up the engine box," he told Byron. They both looked in. It was clean. "See if she'll start." Clay went aft looking for more damage. He examined the freeboard and transom, cursing under his breath. Byron hit the key, and the engine started up and sounded normal. Leaning over the sides, Clay ran his hands along the lines of the boat. He checked the bilge. "No water," he said. He looked around again. "He's picking a fight, ain't he."

"Let's go find him."

"Tend our pots first, Byron." Clay cast off. "Take us out." Clay went back to the cabin, poured some water from the sink faucet into his hands, and splashed it onto his face. He dried his eyes on his sleeve. Sinking down onto the rail, he rested his head against the stanchion. He saw Byron's fist, red and clenching the tiller post as he navigated down Davis Creek.

Clay stared out across the mouth of Mobjack Bay, toward the Guinea Marshes and the smokestacks of the York River oil refineries. A crisp wind from the south was blowing the water up from the Bay, and the white manes of the waves were spilling over themselves. Across the eastern flats, out into the Bay, a freighter churned north, trailing black clouds from its two stacks. He looked in the cabin at the smashed radio and made himself a promise. Passing the black spar that marked the deeper channel, Byron made his turn. The *Miss Sarah* rolled with the breakers.

After Byron had emptied about fifteen pots or so, Clay got up and started culling. The crabs were not as plentiful as they had been before, but neither spoke of it. After the last pot was pulled, Clay slumped back down on the floorboards as Byron set the course toward New Point Comfort, running well inside the double row of black-and-white nun buoys, the wind and waves holding steady. As they approached their lay, Byron called to Clay. Things just didn't look right. Clay pulled himself up and looked over the gunnel. The buoys were bobbing in and out of sight in the waves. But there weren't enough there. Part of the lay was missing.

"Take us into it," Clay said, scanning the water. "This wind isn't that strong. The tide's not so high as to be covering our warp."

Byron took them into the middle of their pots. Clay began counting them. Twenty or more were missing. He took the tiller and asked Byron when he had first noticed the southerly spring up. Byron shrugged. Feeling the tide, he sensed it was running. He headed for the north shore. At first, as they came close to the marsh flats, they didn't see anything but spartina, driftwood, and foam catching in the stalks. Clay turned the *Miss Sarah* parallel to the marsh and was scanning the piles of blown seaweed when Byron spotted something and pointed.

"There."

Clay looked and saw a buoy floating in a tidal pool. He took the bateau in, putting her into neutral in about three feet of water. He hopped over the side and carefully waded to the buoy. Examining it, he waded back to the boat.

"It's cut," he said, throwing it to Byron. He pulled himself up and back inside. They looked at the buoy line, neatly sliced through a few inches below the knot.

"Son of a bitch."

"We're pulling the pots, Byron."

"Clay."

"We're pulling the pots, and we'll find another creek. We're protecting our operation." Byron was angry and started to speak, but Clay interrupted him. "We're pulling the pots, and then we'll settle up this score."

"You want to pull the pots, we'll pull the pots. It's the settlin' up I'm lookin' to."

They worked through the New Point Comfort lay in silence, pulling each pot, dumping the crabs in the cull basin, and then stacking the pot in the bateau. They filled the boat with the pots, stacked to a man's height. There was just room enough to maneuver. Clay said he wanted to run the pots and crabs in, move the pots to the pickup, and return for the East River lay. Byron didn't speak but turned away.

They brought the boat in. Calvin was out on the platform overseeing the buying of the crabs. He saw the stacked pots. Clay saw his eyes catch the windshield.

"We're moving our operation," Clay said. "Someone cut our buoys last night. Lost at least thirty pots."

"Jesus Christ. Who?"

"You tell us."

"Damn. I'm sorry, boys." Calvin flicked his hand at the cabin. "Got your windshield too, huh?"

Clay didn't answer. He started throwing the bushels up on the platform. Byron was already walking toward the pickup, carrying four cages.

"Any proof who? I'll call the police. If you want."

Clay raised his head. "What for? What are they going to do?"

Calvin wiped off his brow. He spit tobacco juice into the water. "I'm just sorry. That's all."

They weighed the sooks and smaller males and agreed on a price, and Calvin paid Clay for the crabs. Then Clay helped Byron move the pots.

Calvin stood there, looking embarrassed. "Shit," he said finally, shaking his head. "This ain't right. I'm calling state marine." He ducked into his shed.

"I'm not going back out with you," Byron told Clay as they carried the last group of pots to the truck. "I can't stand this runnin'. You want to, you finish. You can single-handle the bateau, anyway."

Clay was taken aback. "Byron. Hold on."

"Bullshit. You don't need my help. And I ain't goin' back out there to load our pots and run. Period." He turned and started walking.

"Where are you going?"

Byron stopped. "I want a drink."

"A drink?"

"My fuckin' life, partner. Find me in the bar when you're done."

Clay watched Byron walk away. Of all things, he didn't see this coming. He heard Calvin calling from behind him. Marine police would come by later to look things over. But he needed to move his workboat, to make room for the others coming in. Clay turned. He had to move the bateau. It would take him longer to

TIM JUNKIN

finish, that was all. He went back to the *Miss Sarah*. Calvin again said he was sorry. Clay pushed off. The wind hadn't slackened. It was in his face going out. He thought of his cut pots, sitting on the river bottom, filling with crabs, no way to find them. He thought of Kate. He breathed deep and filled his lungs with the brackish wind that blew off the wave crests. "Christ," he muttered. "Christ, what's happening?" And then he headed out to the bank off the East River.

When he came back into the creek and approached the wharf, the *Miss Sarah* filled with pots, he saw Kate in the parking lot, pacing in front of her car. She saw him and began to wave. He looked for Byron's pickup, but it was gone. As he pulled up to the loading dock, he motioned for her to wait. He sold the additional crabs he had picked up to one of Calvin's hands and then backed the *Miss Sarah* around to the slip. Kate jumped on board and helped him tie her down. Then she came to him and held him. He told her what had happened and asked her if she had seen Byron. She had not.

She helped him unload the pots from the bateau onto the edge of the parking lot. He wrapped a warp line around them to hold them against the wind. Then they checked the bar and restaurant for Byron, but he was not there. Clay had wanted to go back out and pull his last lay, north of the point, but he was worried about Byron. He had Kate drive him over to Pepper Creek. Byron's pickup was not there, either. Clay looked and saw a single work-boat, the *Vena Lee*, tied against the bulkhead. There was no one on her. Kate backed slowly out of the parking lot.

"Where to, now?" he said, half to himself.

"I'm taking you home," Kate answered. She put her hand to his cheek. "If Byron needs us, he can find us there."

254

25

Kate took him back and up into her bed. They lay in the summer heat, in the translucent, wavering light, with the sound of children playing, far off, filtering through the screened windows. Clay forgot and forgave the world, and wondered at the rapture. It made him afraid, afraid that nothing real could feel this good, that it could never last. And knowing that in all this there was Matty, and Byron somewhere, and complications he could not fathom, still, there was no end to the flood that had opened inside his heart.

She lay on top of his back and whispered to him the ways she had imagined him making love to her, so he took her again. She dried his shoulders with a towel, and then she pushed him over and dried his front. She brought him orange slices and then rested her head on his shoulder until he shut his eyes.

His dream was about Sarah. In that green light of summer. Because she had forgotten to shift, straining the old Rambler in second gear, her face wan, her heart bursting inside her, and he not knowing, there in the car, in the road, the sun washing through the leaves of the tall maples that lined the road, and then grabbing at the wheel, pushing across his young mother for the brake pedal, not understanding she was dying. Sarah reaching for him, tearing at her blouse for air, not speaking, her eyes beseeching him, afraid, and he trying to help, not knowing what to do to help, holding her, holding her tighter, the shaking, the rush of the leaves of the giant maple, a spasm of flesh, until the crash, and the silence, the stillness, and that sound of sirens so separate, so distant, and then gradually louder. Coming closer. Coming to them. A ringing he could hear. Louder and present, in the room.

Ringing . . .

He opened his eyes and tried to focus. Kate was picking up the phone and talking. She said something quietly, hung up, and came over to the bed.

"It's Byron," she said. "He's been arrested. They said it was assault. He's down at the county jail in Gloucester."

Kate drove him to Gloucester, holding his hand. Clay couldn't stop shaking his head. "Open your eyes," he said to himself. "Open your eyes."

The jail was adjacent to the county seat and courthouse. They walked through the large green double doors. "Byron Steele is in lockup," the county sheriff told them. He wore a blue uniform with a gray tie. He was older and balding and wore horn-rimmed glasses, but behind them his eyes were alert. "He cracked a man over the head with a bottle. Took stitches. Was drunk. Disorderly. Out of control. Bartender drew down on him with a twelve-gauge."

Clay was still. He had this terrible sense of familiarity.

Kate stepped forward. "How do we get him released?"

"I set a station house bond of a thousand dollars. Judge can change it, if you want to appear in court tomorrow."

"Thousand dollars." Clay shifted from one foot to the other. "Kind of heavy, ain't it?"

"He could've killed someone." The sheriff didn't smile.

"Maybe he had a reason," Clay said.

The sheriff eyed him. "I could lock you up too. Or maybe I should raise the bond. What reason?"

Clay pondered for a moment. "Nothing," he answered. "Could you give us a minute?" He took Kate's elbow and they walked out the door to the front steps.

"I could call my father," she offered. "He would give me the money. We could drive up and get it. We're four hours from Washington."

"No," Clay responded quickly. Then he rubbed his eyes with his thumb and forefinger. "I mean, thank you. But I don't want you to do that."

"What then?"

"I don't know. Let me ask him something."

They went back in. Clay asked the sheriff if he could speak plainly, and the sheriff said sure. Then he told the sheriff about him and Byron being partners, and about the hurricane and what it did to the upper Bay. He explained that he was a waterman, a crabber, and that he had a thirty-six-foot Bay-built tied up at the end of Davis Creek, and told him why they had come to Virginia. He even mentioned Vietnam. Then he asked if he could put up the title of the *Miss Sarah* as collateral for bail.

Rising from his chair, the sheriff pulled open a drawer and took from it a sheet of paper. He handed it to Clay. "List of bondsmen. You can pay them." He sat down and watched as Clay took the list. Without reading it, he held it at his side. Kate took it, glanced at it, and handed it back to the sheriff.

"We'd need cash for a bondsman. But that boat means more than money to both of them." Her words were firm, deliberate.

The sheriff put his feet on his desk and leaned back. He scratched his chin. "All right," he said finally. "If you're sure. You want to put up title to your boat, I'll take it." He took his glasses off and wiped them with the edge of his tie. "But your man don't show for court," he continued, putting his glasses back on, "you lose your boat."

"What do we need to do?"

"Bring me the title. Sign the papers."

He and Kate both thanked him.

Kate drove Clay back to the wharf where the *Miss Sarah* was tied. He boarded her and got out the ammunition box, hidden under a floorboard in the cabin locker where he always kept it, and took out the title to the bateau. He paused for a moment and looked at the chart of the spot where his father had discovered the sunken Spanish frigate. He unfolded it and stared at it, tracing the coordinates with his fingertip, wondering what was coming and when—if ever—he might be able to chase that dream. He replaced the chart, shut the box, and returned it to its hiding place. Stepping out of the cabin, he stood in the stern of the *Miss Sarah*. Kate was waiting in the car. He looked over the harbor and down the creek. Along the flats, the spartina glowed orange in the last light. He looked at the shattered windshield on the cabin and then touched the cut cord on the marine radio. Pulling the dock lines to bring her closer to the wharf, he stepped out. On the way back to the jail in Gloucester, he asked Kate what she wanted.

"I want you to stay," she said. "I want you to want me enough to stay. In my bed. With me."

"And Matty?"

"I'll tell him. He'll be home tomorrow. I just need to find the right time." She looked imploringly at Clay. "Give me a few days."

They bailed Byron out. The pickup, packed with crab pots, had been impounded, and they got it out also. Kate drove Byron back to the Waterman's Hole. Clay followed in the pickup, parking it over near their slip. They all went in together and ordered dinner. Byron's left eye was blackened. He had found Amos Pickett, he explained. Saw his truck outside the Cattail Lounge out on the highway. Pickett was with several others. Cracked him good. Said the bartender probably saved him, though. The guy's friends were moving in, and he saw Pickett draw some steel when he started to get up. "I should've waited," Byron finished. "The numbers weren't too much in my favor."

Clay grunted.

"But I wanted that son of a bitch." Byron raised up his head. "I just was hasty."

Clay could find no words. He studied the calluses on his hands. The food came and he watched Byron and Kate eat. He told Byron that he was moving the boat in the morning, after he'd picked up the remaining pots. Byron asked him where to.

"South."

"Where south?"

"Don't know. Far enough to end all this," Clay said, motioning with his hand. "And you need to stay out of any kind of trouble. We had to put up the *Miss Sarah* as bond."

Byron coughed, nearly choking. "You did what?"

"To get you out."

"Take me back to jail."

"You can't undo it; it's done."

Byron was silent. Kate reached for his hand.

"We'll get you a lawyer," she said.

"It's nothing really. You show up for your court date, I get the title back."

Byron slowly pulled his hand back. "You shouldn'a."

"Right. And you wouldn't have done it for me?"

"Hell, no. Not if you were this screwed up." Byron found a cigarette in his jeans pocket, struck a match, and lit it. He took a pull and exhaled.

"We should get some sleep, Byron. Need to head out early. Long day ahead."

"I ain't much tired."

Clay sensed he should keep Byron with him. "I need to go back to the house and pack up." He left it open ended.

Kate took Clay's arm in her hand and squeezed it gently. "What time do you all want to start out in the morning?" She chose her words carefully.

Byron shrugged.

"Early," Clay repeated.

"I'll bring you back *early*," Kate said, following his lead.

"Byron, you come with us," Clay said.

"It'll be a warm, calm summer night," Byron answered. "Might get that midsummer night breeze. Moonlit." He drew the cigarette down. "The river'll be shinin'. A good night to see things that're sometimes not so clear in the day. I for sure ain't going with you two."

Clay got up, went to the register, and paid the bill. He walked outside ahead of Kate and Byron. The full moon was rising over the inlet and over the adjacent fields abutting Davis Creek. The fields were crisscrossed with light and shadow. The water was silver and the boats in the creek rode high on their moorings, their white paint gleaming.

The other two came up behind him, and they all walked back over to Kate's car.

"We'll leave in the morning," Clay repeated, speaking to Byron. "You stay put. On the boat. No trouble. I'll take the pickup." He turned to Kate. "I don't want you getting up at four."

She started to speak and he held up his hand. "Follow me home?" she asked softly.

They said good night to Byron. Clay rode in the pickup behind Kate.

26

Inside, standing before him in the living room, Kate asked him if he wanted to undress her. They lay on the couch, tracing their futures on each other's skin. The crickets and cicadas thrust their legs to fill the silence with their rasping music.

It was well past midnight when the ringing of the phone once again rattled the peace. Clay answered it and heard Byron's excited voice on the other end.

"Clay, you ain't goin' to believe what I found." Byron spoke in a rush.

"What's that." Clay was short.

"I went out. Feelin' itchy, I guess. Thought I'd raise our last pots. Save us time in the morning. So bright out here. Like day."

"Can't it wait?" Clay interrupted.

"It's drugs, man. Big time. Coke. Bags of the shit."

Clay shifted the phone.

"That's what those bogus buoys were about. Get it?"

"Whoa, Byron. Get what?"

Byron took a breath. "Okay. I'm out there driftin'. Watchin' the moon. No lights. But I'm against the bank. Blendin' in, I guess, hard to see. I've loaded up our pots, there on deck, when I spot this ocean trawler coming at the mouth of Mobjack from out of the Bay. And it's where it don't belong. Goin' slow, watchin' the channel like. And it goes up to where those black and reds were clustered—over the channel edge, where you said it was too deep, remember?— and drops several new pots right there and picks up some old ones."

Clay listened, a knot forming in his throat.

"But you know what, Clay? No lights on the fucker. No lights."

"Byron, what about the dope?" Clay spoke in a whisper.

"So after it heads back out to the Bay, I wait awhile and go to check it out. I pull 'em. Two or three don't have nothin' in 'em. But then I hit the jackpot. The buoys are attached to pots, all right. But the pots ain't got crabs in 'em, partner. And no alewives neither."

Clay listened, looking at Kate, who was sitting up on the couch now, the blanket falling from her shoulders and bunched around her waist.

"I got those fuckers' dope, Clay. It's payback time."

Clay swallowed hard. Then he heard a key in the front door. As he and Kate stared, transfixed, it opened, and Matty stepped inside. He saw them, of course—Clay standing naked, with the phone in his hand, Kate pulling up the blanket. Matty paused, his face changing form before them. He put down his bag, his eyes turning from Kate to Clay. Then he shouted and started for Clay. Kate stepped to intercept him.

Clay spoke quickly to Byron. "Don't move, Byron," he pleaded. "Don't move an inch. I'll be there quick." He got the phone hung up just as Matty got to him, Kate trying to hold Matty and talk to him. Clay sidestepped Matty's charge and let him fall forward across a side table, his momentum carrying him down with Kate clutching his arm. Clay grabbed his pants, shirt, and shoes and looked at the two of them. Matty's face was bloodless and contorted with a look of disbelief. Kate knelt, holding her blanket against her, trying to talk to him.

"I'm sorry," Clay whispered. He hesitated. "I don't know how to start." He looked at the open door. "I've got to go. Byron's in trouble. It's serious." He turned and headed toward the door. "Christ," he said again, looking back.

Clay ran for the pickup, hobbling on his pants. He backed out of the drive and started for the wharf, pulling on the rest of his clothes as he drove, steering partly with his knees. He got his shirt and dock shoes on and realized he was going over seventy. He slowed some. He couldn't get visions of Kate, and of Matty, sprawled, out of his mind. But a danger of a whole different kind was closing in on him, and he knew that it would be unforgiving and that he needed to think clearly. Fields of corn flashed by under the moonlight, but the trip to the boat seemed far. Rounding the curve at the end of Planters Landing Road, he came into the narrow bottleneck that led only to the wharf. Byron was there, in the parking area, pacing. Clay braked to a halt and jumped out.

"C'mon," Byron said, taking Clay by the arm. Clay could smell the bourbon.

Byron hurried him along as they walked to the *Miss Sarah,* which was tied alongside the crab dock on two cleats. They jumped aboard. Byron lifted a blanket; under it sat two crab pots, each containing packages wrapped tightly in layers of plastic wrap and crisscrossed with tape, each package about the size of a one-pound bag of sugar. There were six in each pot. Byron had opened one of the cages and taken out one of the packages. He had worked a hole in the corner of it with a screwdriver. He picked it up and shook a small amount of white powder into Clay's hand.

"Taste it. It's coke."

Clay dabbed at it with the tip of his tongue. It offered the bitter, jolting sensation of cocaine. Clay raised his head up and cursed. "This is big trouble."

Byron shook his head. "We ain't takin' it back out to the river."
Clay was silent.

"Hey, partner. You know, we could go north. Figure out a way to sell it?" Byron shrugged.

"How much you had?"

Byron sniffed. "Just a taste. I'm fine. It's pure. Lethal. Once cut, it will increase to ten times the powder." He paused. "Hell, this right here's probably worth enough to buy back Pecks from the bank and then some."

Clay wiped his hand off on his jeans. He looked at the plastic packages, so heavily wrapped. Then he let his gaze sweep down the creek and out over the gleaming bay. He thought about Pecks, and about Kate and how he could be so close. He looked back at Byron. Then he shook his head. "We've got to get to a phone and call the police."

Byron sagged, sitting on the rail, holding the package tight against him.

"You're not thinking, Byron." Clay spoke quietly and firmly. "These guys'll chase it. Wherever it goes. This is heavy shit."

"Could ask Mac Longley to help us. He's still runnin' it. It'd bring a pile a money."

"My guess is Mac Longley's a part of this."

"Longley? Come on, Clay. That's a stretch, ain't it?"

"How did Longley know I talked to Brigman about working for him?"

"I don't know. So?"

"I think I saw Brigman at the bull roast."

"Here?"

"He was talking to Matty's coke source. Guy with a ponytail and earring. Deals out of a crab loading dock. Get this: the business is called Indigo Seafood."

"Indigo Seafood? Get out. No shit?" Byron shuddered.

"You said yourself it was a network."

"Longley said it, not me." But Byron wasn't convinced. He held the package close. "We could still keep it. Sell it ourselves."

"Money's not what we've been after, Byron. Least not first off."

"They won't know who's got it. Not for sure."

"Of course they will. Take 'em two seconds. Why you think they wanted us out of here so bad?"

Byron shook his head, like he didn't want to hear.

"Amos Pickett's bad business, Byron. And he and the whole lot will be after us. Wherever we go. If I'm right, and Brigman's with him, they'll have people up and down the shore. We don't know the extent of it, but it's there. Christ. The chances of us dealing with them and survivin' are about zero." He spoke slowly, choosing his words. "And even if we could handle 'em, then we'd have to turn into a Mac Longley, or worse. Selling dope. Being drug dealers. I'm not ready for that. I don't think you are, either."

Byron heard him, though it was still hard to let go. "What if we can't even prove whose it is? To the cops, I mean."

Clay pulled the dock lines, bringing the bateau against the wharf. "The police'll get it. They'll believe us. And no one will have any reason to be coming after us. And even so. Losing this"—he motioned at the bags—"this here's enough to hurt them plenty." He climbed out of the bateau. "C'mon. We'll use the phone outside the restaurant. I've got a dime."

Byron still resisted. "I ain't sure mixin' this up with the cops is the right move for us."

"We need to make the call," Clay said. "Together. We need to decide this. We aren't drug dealers."

Byron sat still. Neither said anything. They just watched each other. Then Byron said, "I suppose we ain't. Drug dealers, I mean."

"No sir."

"Just somethin' else."

"I don't know about that."

"What?"

"I see us more than 'just something else.'"

"What?"

"I'm not sure. Just more, that's all."

Byron stood up.

Clay continued. "Nothing just average about being a waterman. Living independent. Feeding folks. I'd say that's more than 'just something else.'"

"And partners."

"That too. Though your partner is someone who himself is falling right now."

Byron caught the break in Clay's voice. In his bruised eyes. "Hold on," he said. He put the package down and climbed out of the *Miss Sarah*. "I'm coming. Let's make the call."

Halfway across the parking lot, Clay heard the sound of a car engine. He recognized the headlights of Kate's Volvo coming up the gravel drive. They waited, watching it pull into the parking area. She got out and ran over to Clay, who was walking toward her.

"Clay," she gasped. "Oh, Clay." She threw her arms around him. "I'm so sorry about what happened." She stepped back to look at his face and grabbed Byron's hands. "Byron, what's going on here?"

"Where is Matty?" Clay said.

Kate shut her eyes. "Oh, Clay, I'm sorry." She opened them and looked at him. "He had a fight with his father and came back early. I couldn't tell him. Not yet. I didn't know what to say. I told him I thought Byron was in trouble and that I'd be right back. I promised him. I should only stay a minute."

Clay kicked at some gravel. "You better go on, then."

"But what's going on here? Please tell me." She seemed about to cry.

Clay started to try to explain. But then he heard another engine and looked down toward the road. This time it was a truck he saw coming. Up from the Pepper Creek turnoff. A pickup. In the moonlight he could see the silhouettes of at least two men in the back, standing as the truck moved across the flats. They had rifles or shotguns pointed in the air. He knew it was Pickett's truck. There was no way past them.

"In the bateau!" he shouted at Byron, taking Kate's arm and running her back with him to the *Miss Sarah*. "They've got guns."

Byron saw the truck and was running behind them. Kate kept turning and asking what was happening. They got her on board and followed behind her. "Hold on," Clay told her. In seconds he had the engine started and Byron had the lines off. Byron pushed against the piling, and Clay backed the bateau up quickly, to give him enough room to turn, and then shoved her into forward and gunned the engine. He watched behind him, over the bateau's stern, as the pickup came up the lane and into the parking lot, spewing dust and gravel behind it. Two men jumped out of the back, and two others from the front. Running toward the dock, one raised his gun. Clay saw the man had a ponytail. He grabbed Kate and pushed her down, but then he heard somebody yell to put the gun up. "Out of range!" the man shouted.

Clay saw them talking. One of the men remained on the dock with what Clay figured must be a shotgun. The others got back in the truck. The headlights from the pickup swung out and away from the parking lot. At the end of the drive the truck turned toward Pepper Creek. Byron stepped close. Clay had eased her back to midthrottle. The creek was too narrow and shallow off the channel to risk going faster. He knew, though, that in a matter of minutes, the larger and faster *Vena Lee* would be pushing out of the mouth of Pepper Creek. She could get into Mobjack Bay as fast as he could. She wouldn't be far behind him.

"They must've come right after me," Byron said.

"Figures they wouldn't let this stuff sit in the river for long."

"You could swim her ashore here," Byron offered. "I'll make 'em chase me clear to Easton."

Clay studied the marsh along the shoreline. "Too risky, Buck. In this light. With guns and a truck. They'll be hunting for us. Truck'll probably follow us down the creek. We'd probably get stuck. Up to our knees. And even so there's nowhere to hide or run to. If they spotted us, we'd be done."

He looked forward and saw that Kate, sitting on the washboard, was shaking. Clay asked Byron to take the tiller and, once past the red markers, to head straight for the black spar blinking a three-second green and then to the southwest mark off the lighthouse. He went over and put his arm around Kate. He took her inside the cabin and talked to her, trying to calm her. He started to tell her what had happened.

She interrupted him: "Why don't we just swim for it?"

Clay thought he heard something and wheeled and looked across the flats, west toward Pepper Creek. He couldn't see Pickett's workboat yet. But the lights from the truck were running back toward them, down the creek road.

"They got a pickup, guns, radios, and it's dark. And they're looking for us. I don't like the odds if we jump. They'll hunt us down. They have to. We know too much now."

"What?"

"It's over drugs. It's a drug operation. Cocaine."

"Oh, my God." Kate wiped her eyes with the sleeve of her shirt.

She already knew about Amos Pickett and the cut pots and the damage to the boat. Clay tried to tell her the rest calmly. He walked her aft and showed her the drugs. "Smart operation, really," he said. "Avoids customs or deck searches. Ocean trawler smuggles the stuff in crab pots. Inside U.S. waters, another boat gets in sight, they throw the pots in the ocean. Note their location. Foolproof."

Kate reached down and touched one of the packages. She lifted it, feeling its weight. "This is a lot, isn't it?" she said.

Clay nodded as she set the package down. "Once in the Bay, the trawler drops them up here and Pickett picks 'em up. He's a crabber. Who would suspect? Moves it to a seafood wholesaler. Brigman, I think. Indigo Seafood. Christ."

Kate looked startled. "Brigman? From the sailboat?"

Clay let out a deep breath. "I think. Probably moves it in seafood trucks. Or cars. Or his yacht. That would be good cover too."

Kate seemed to be trying to take all this in.

"That's why he wants the seafood operation at Pecks, I suspect. A Maryland base. And it's an all-cash business."

"My God, Clay."

"I know."

"What's going to happen?"

Clay took her shoulders. "Get you safe, first of all. And then get me and Byron out of this. Get to the police."

She shut her eyes, took a breath, and opened them. "And then?" She spoke quietly, looking at him.

Clay started to speak, but Kate put her hand over his mouth. "Don't say anything now." She took her hand away, studying his face. "Just know I meant every word I said to you," she said. "Everything I told you is true."

Clay knew he heard something this time and turned. He saw the reflection of a spotlight back over the marsh spit and knew it was them and knew they were coming. He listened harder and heard the motor, faint in the distance. Before he reached the island and the opening to the Bay, before he found a cut or swash to hide in, Pickett would be behind him and would have him in sight.

Clay turned back and reached over and touched her damp cheek. As he did so, he felt the gradual veer of the hull as they neared the eastern shoal guarding Davis Creek and Byron began angling toward the stone lighthouse in the mouth of Mobjack out beyond. As they slowly turned, Clay saw the spotlight already out of Pepper Creek to the west behind them. Pickett's boat was less than a mile away. He nodded to Byron, who levered the throttle down. He looked back at Kate and saw the tears holding in the corners of her eyes and her fighting them back. He brushed each one with his thumb and kissed her lightly, then rose back up and looked.

"I'll get us out of this, Kate." He looked back at the spotlight. "This problem here. One way or another. Then we'll work on these other things."

He led her back to the controls, the engine straining as the *Miss Sarah* sliced through the waters of Mobjack Bay, heading east for the mouth. Taking the tiller, Clay looked at the clear sky and took the measure of the bright night. He had easily seen the shining white of the boats moored along the creek and now saw the water shimmering out in the Bay. Even the marsh flats alongshore reflected the moonlight. The darkness wasn't deep enough to shroud them, even without running lights. The stars were faint, but Clay found the Dipper's handle off the horizon to the west. Four or five hours left till dawn. The moon would not set first. Shadowed against the sandbanks, the floating spartina revealed an ebb tide that would bottom sometime after sunrise. He considered these things against where they were as he listened to the second engine drumming. It was coming. And he knew there was no meeting it and surviving.

Pickett's boat ran without lights but periodically shone its spot in their direction. Clay asked Byron to check their fuel. One tank was half empty; the other full. That was good news. He studied their pursuer. He had sized up the boat before. He knew it was fast, slightly faster even than the bateau. It would take a while, though. Pickett would be surprised at the speed of the *Miss Sarah*. But the *Vena Lee* would creep closer. A good hour—maybe an hour and a half, Clay gauged. That's what it would take for them to catch him, to get within a shotgun's range. Somehow he had to keep from being overtaken, at least until Byron and Kate were safe. Or if only he could make it to home waters. Then he knew he could lose them.

They ran the mouth of Mobjack Bay, the blinking red southwest marker approaching close on their port side, the black-and-white nuns way off to their right, the silence of the great estuary around them broken by the hammering engines of the two workboats, one leading the other, and by the sound of the wash off their hulls and of the waves breaking in their wakes. An osprey, startled at the intrusion, left her nest atop the red buoy and circled, screaming, overhead, her shadow large under the moonlight on the water. She came around three times before settling back behind them on her nest. Clay heard her again moments later, upset by the boat behind them. She circled and cried out until finally quieting down in the receding distance of Mobjack Bay. They pushed on. The drum of the bateau's cylinders filled the air as she pushed with all of her power, and behind her the more distant hum echoed over the water. Ahead the pulsing moon glowed over a vast silver plain, the blinking green and red lights marking the horizons in the distance, clear and true, markers of the deeper, safer waters. Clay took note of the slight breeze and kept constant watch of the steadily gaining *Vena Lee.*

He asked Byron to open the engine box. Byron knew what he was thinking and found some twine. Opening the lid to the engine box, he tied the carburetor throttle back as tight as possible to maximize the engine's power.

"Byron," Clay said.

"I'm sorry about this, Clay."

"Yeah. Well, what's done is done. Forget it. I should've figured it out before. Hell. Who was to know?"

"How would anybody know?"

"You keep a hand check on the engine. Every ten minutes or so. Make sure she isn't running too hot."

"I will."

"You got any heavy weights in that tackle box of yours?"

"A few."

"Weigh those buoys on the crab pots down. I want them as low in the water and hard to spot as we can make 'em."

Clay turned to Kate. "Look in the drawers up in the cabin—dark pens, markers, anything like that."

She hesitated, uncertain. Then she went forward and started searching.

Clay thought for a moment and opened the stern hatch. Inside the toolbox he found some black electrical tape. He called to Kate to come back. "Wind the tape around those buoys Byron is weighing down. Make 'em look black." She didn't ask why, just began to work. Clay wanted to get out where the swells from the south might help, but not too far, and then slow them down with the buoys. The shoreline was his best hope, he thought. The shallows. He drew less water. He'd run for it then.

"Byron."

"Yeah, Clay."

"When you're done, unravel each buoy line. When the time comes, I want all the pots over at once."

"You're gonna tangle her up?"

"She'll probably cut right through most of 'em. Maybe one or two'll slow her down. Or maybe they'll think it's their dope and hunt for it. Course, her propeller may get fouled."

When Pickett got close, Clay intended to throw the buoys, then to swing back toward shore to set up below the long shoal protruding from Windmill Point. He hoped to lose his pursuers by heading north, across the shallow bar where they couldn't follow. But he was uncertain, disadvantaged without a working depth finder. If that plan failed he'd need more than one trick to keep them at a distance. Pickett's fuel might run out first, but Clay knew he couldn't count on that. If he could just figure out a way to gain a sufficient lead, he'd cross the Bay, run for the shoals around Smith Island, above the Maryland line, and Deal and the Hooper Islands beyond, maybe even the Little Choptank, where he knew the waters. If he couldn't lose the *Vena Lee,* he'd need to get Kate and Byron off and safe. And himself as well. But he wanted to save his boat too. In Maryland waters along the Eastern Shore, he thought he'd have a better chance. At top speed the *Miss Sarah* ran about fifteen knots. Smith Island was forty-plus miles away, across the wide Bay—with the wind and tide, at least three hours. Deal Island was an hour more.

Out in the Bay proper, the swells rose from the south, pushing the bateau's stern and helping them along. He kept a steady course, and the bateau ran down the crests and held her bow high as she overtook the waves below her. She was lighter and could make better use of the waves and tide than the *Vena Lee* could. On the open water, he set a northerly course. They all sat together, listening and watching—watching the luminous Bay around them, the milky-dark sky above them, the blinking green and red lights in the distance, hearing the drumbeat of the engines, their hunters behind them, their hunters getting closer mile by mile, their spotlight flashing intermittently.

Clay held their course steady so his pursuers would do the same. They were getting discernibly closer now. It wouldn't be long.

He held her steady and used the power of the waves behind and underneath him. Ahead, still a speck in the distance but sparkling bright, he recognized the lights from a tanker coming down from Baltimore.

After a while more, he decided it was time. The *Vena Lee* was close enough, almost too close. Every few minutes they would turn on the spot and isolate the bateau's wake in its beam, then scan the water and turn it off. Clay waited until the spotlight finished searching the water the next time, then put Kate on the tiller and pointed out the course setting, and he and Byron heaved the pots over the stern and port and starboard sides. They threw over thirty or so, tightly bunched, hoping the lines would snag in the propeller of Pickett's boat. At least, Clay thought, she'll have to slow and navigate through them. The weighted buoys, most darkened with the black tape, settled low in the water and were not easy to see.

He retook the tiller and gunned the throttle, watching the dark water behind him. The white hull of the *Vena Lee* was now perhaps a hundred yards away, the outside range for a shotgun. Soon he heard shouting and cursing. At the bottom of a trough, he turned westerly, heading back toward the shore.

The *Vena Lee* had stopped. He could hear more shouting, the sounds receding behind him. Her spot went on, and a man stood on her bow, partially blocking the light, apparently looking out for what was in the water. After a while her engine started up again. She was moving slowly, not sure where to find safe going. Clay was certain she wasn't fouled. But he had regained the lead he needed to run for the shore.

He asked Byron to get the chart and a flashlight. "Use the light against the stern on the floorboard." He looked at Kate and then took her into the cabin. "Take the wheel and run us at two hundred ninety degrees."

She took the steering wheel as he showed her the heading on the fluorescent compass and how to keep to her course.

Clay returned to the stern. On their knees behind the transom, Clay and Byron studied the chart together.

"We're crossing the mouth of the Piankatank, I figure," Clay said. "I'm thinking about trying to cut the shoal off Windmill Point. We got to draw a foot less than that cannon. Maybe we can lose them there."

"Maybe. But that guy's no fool with his boat. An' that's miles of shoal. You know these charts can be off. Course, maybe you can feel her through. I can drop the plumb. No help going by that, though." He pointed at the chart. "Not for tryin' what you got in mind."

Clay knew the truth in what Byron was saying. It was dangerous. But it might work. He wanted Kate safe. He wanted them all
safe too much. "I know," he answered. "I want to try it, though. I
think we can lose them. If we don't . . ." He paused. "I just don't
know these waters that well. I don't know where there's firm bottom to walk. And he's sure to have people following onshore over
here. Or trying to." He raised his eyes to the eastern sky over the
rail. "This doesn't work, I'd like to sneak out and head for Tangier
Sound. But we'd never make it without more of a lead. Still, if we
could just get that far, if we could beat him across that broad
stretch of Bay . . ."

"What?"

Clay had stopped.

"What?"

"Byron."

"Yes."

"One way or another I'll need your help here." Clay figured
Byron sensed what was coming, since he didn't answer. "We're
friends?"

Byron turned the light off. "Well, you're sure my friend. I
wouldn't blame you if I ain't yours any longer."

"I need you to do something for me. No questions."

"What."

"I need your word on it."

"Clay. What?"

"Your promise."

Byron got off his knees and sat back against the coaming.

"If we don't lose them crossing the bar—and like you said,
that's tricky enough—then I'm going to find someplace safe and
put you and Kate out."

Byron tried to interrupt, but Clay stopped him with his hand.

"No. No talk. If we can lose them or build a decent lead by
trimming the point, we'll turn northeast and cross over. Other-

wise, I'll have to drop you somewhere on this side. My hope is to cross, and head for Tangier Sound. Even if they tried to follow, from a distance, they might run out of fuel first. Or we might find help. A pleasure yacht or something. If we cut across and they're still behind us, I'll put you and Kate out over there. Closer to home. I'm thinking just off Wenona. Off the Deal Island shoal, in three feet of water or so. That's what it'll be when we get there. But it's about a two-hundred-yard walk, or wade. But if we have to do it, there or over here—wherever—you get her ashore safe. That's what I ask. That's what I want from you. Then call Barker and the state marine. If we make Wenona, they'll be close by. Hell, call the Coast Guard too. Get some reinforcements. I'll be running north."

"Let me take the boat."

"No."

"Why?"

"I know that area. Better than you. Better'n them. If we can make the marsh, I can outfigure 'em." He paused again. "Maybe I can lose them. Or at least ground the boat where we can find it later. I thought it over. I've got the better chance. My mind's solid on this."

"Why across the Bay? Why not above the Rappahannock? Or Potomac?"

"I don't know these waters, Byron. And who knows how many guys they might have following us onshore. I figure we're taking 'em up the western shore now. If we cut across, any of Pickett's men following won't have time to get back down and over the bridge tunnel. That's just a precaution, of course. They may have men on both sides."

Byron sat there looking at Clay. He didn't say anything for a while. Then he put his head between his knees. "I'm really sorry," he said.

"Hey. They were after us, Buck. This was coming down. You called it. One way or another. Only one who didn't know was me."

"The funny thing is, now I don't feel so afraid." Byron looked calmly at Clay. "Not at all. I'm ready to fight. Do whatever." He shut his eyes. After a few moments, he said, "I never finished tellin' you what happened. Over there. There was more."

"No. You didn't."

Both of them tensed as the engine behind them fired up to high acceleration again. Clay raised his head up. Their pursuers were well behind. He saw that Kate was holding their course well and sat back down

"I will. When this is over. I want to tell you." Byron reached into his back pocket. He took out a pack of smokes and a pint of Calvert whiskey, mostly gone.

Clay frowned, then shook his head.

"They can see us anyway." Byron turned the lighter in his hand. "What difference does it make?" Byron's tone betrayed the answer. "Right." He returned the lighter to his pocket and crumpled up the pack and threw it in a corner. "Funny how you always think there will be time—time to get things right with people, to tell them what you mean." He squinted at the whiskey in the bottle, took off the top, and turned it upside down over the rail, then threw it into one of the empty wicker baskets.

"We'll have time, Byron."

Byron looked at the night sky, then smiled. "Shit. It's only been six months. Fuckin' excitin' enough, ain't it?"

"Yeah, ain't it." Clay grabbed the gunnel and pulled himself up. "You know, if we cross the Bay, we're gonna run right over our buried treasure. Our wreck."

Byron stood up as well and looked across the water. "She's safe enough, I figure. Least till we can return. Better jacked. Then we'll raise her. That will be a story there. Raisin' buried treasure from the Bay."

"That, it will."

"We find that treasure, we'll be fat."

Clay chuckled. "Yeah. Fat city."

"Okay. What's the plan again?"

"Yeah. The plan."

27

Clay had moved back under the canopy top. "Okay. We're running for the bar off Windmill Point," he said to Byron. "We'll test the depths. Try to lose them there, where the bar gets too shallow for them to follow." He looked over the charcoal water. "We have to make this work. We have to lose them. Or at least put considerable distance between us. Then we'll aim east, across toward Tangier and Crisfield. If they still try to follow, I'll put you off and lead them up to Fishing Bay. If I can make the Hooper Strait, I might shake them there. They won't know that water, there."

"Lotta ifs."

"If I can't get that far, I'll slide off and let the *Miss Sarah* run on. By then, the Coast Guard ought to be close. Long as you don't forget to call 'em."

Byron snorted. "I'll try to remember."

"Yeah. Well, let's lose them right here," Clay said. He set his face toward the shore. "For now try to find that flare gun in the cabin," he added. "I might need it later. And make me a gas cocktail. Use your empty whiskey bottle. I knew your drinking would come in handy. Rag at the top. You know. Siphon the gas. And give me your lighter."

Byron handed it to him. "Thought you were slidin' off."

"I am. But just in case."

"No hero shit, Clay."

"No."

"For real."

"For real."

"Yeah."

Clay checked the heat of the straining engine with his hand. It was hot but running steady. He went to Kate and had her release the wheel and led her back to the tiller post and controls at midship.

"How are we doing?" Kate asked. She leaned up against him.

"You've done perfect," he told her. "We've got some breathing room. Just keep an eye behind us. Anything changes, tell me quick."

"I'm scared," she said.

Clay held his hand out.

She took his hand, looking back behind them. "Will your plan work?"

"It should," he answered. "Just keep a good watch."

Clay had been pointing the workboat toward the shore below Windmill Point, the northern spit jutting down off the Virginia coastline and marking the entrance to the wide mouth of the Rappahannock. The *Vena Lee* followed every change of course. Off Windmill Point, a mile-long shoal extended out toward the channel. The chart showed much of it at three feet. It was across this shallow water Clay hoped he could skim the *Miss Sarah,* but the closer he got, the more worried he was about the accuracy of the depths on the chart. And, he realized, Pickett might know the shoal better than he did. And Pickett had a working depth finder.

The lights from the distant shoreline appeared as a maze of indecipherable sparks on the edge of the wide, watery black plain. Clay tried to read them to know where he was. The boat was now running crosswise to the waves, which rolled the bateau for a while, though the rollers diminished as they got closer to shore. The wind stayed calm. Studying the shoreline and channel markers and then the chart, Clay realized he couldn't pinpoint his position as closely as he had expected. If the *Miss Sarah* hit bottom first, they would be caught. He asked Byron to begin the depth soundings with the plumb line. At the place where he thought he was, judging from the blinking buoys around them and his course and speed, the chart read five feet. Byron got four from his plumb. He took other soundings. They were all different from the ones on the chart. Clay knew his position. Not with total precision, but close enough. The chart was off. The bottom was too uncertain. The water was too shallow already, and they weren't yet on the shoal. To continue was to move forward blindly. He decided he couldn't risk it. But they were already far up, no longer in a position to cut across deep water in a northeast course. There was no choice but to turn back out, more easterly, toward Tangier Island. Since Clay had sacrificed his pots, Pickett had narrowed the distance between them. And he'd make up more of the gap with this turn. Clay knew if he ran straight for Tangier Island without any advantage he'd be caught. He swerved the *Miss Sarah* back out. With the change in course, Byron came up to stand next to him. He checked the shoreline and the chart and timed out loud the four-second green off their port side, knowing what was going on. He lay the chart down, saying nothing. He went and retrieved the flare gun from the cabin. Then he started making the gasoline bomb with the empty whiskey bottle.

Heading east, back into the Bay, Pickett closer now, Clay studied the southern horizon, peering into the darkness, focusing on each light that shone across the wide expanse. He asked Byron to get the binoculars from the cabin locker. Through the lenses he could see little against the Bay's huge darkness. But he could see the timed reds and greens blinking on the channel buoys, as well as the running lights of other ships or boats. And the lights dotting the shoreline—he should have used these earlier, he thought. He watched, and waited, and watched. He was in dire trouble. The chase was closing as the *Miss Sarah* pounded out her rhythm, out toward the open Bay. He considered turning back, toward shore, and running the *Miss Sarah* right onto the shoal, and taking his chances with Byron and Kate swimming or wading. But Pickett might intercept him first. And with his depth finder, Pickett might get close enough on the uneven shoal to pick them off.

Then he thought he saw what he needed. An unusual configuration of running lights was way to the southeast, moving north. He concentrated on the movement of the lights for a while, watching through the binoculars. Then he adjusted course, slightly more to the north, handing the binoculars to Byron. Anxiously he glanced back at the boat behind them.

"They're going to catch us, aren't they?" Kate whispered.

Byron found what Clay had been studying.

"What is it?" Kate asked.

Byron handed her the binoculars and frowned. "Timin' that'd be right touchy."

"It's a big tug," Clay answered. "Pulling a barge up north. It's moving fast. It must be an oceangoing tug and the barge must be empty."

"Oh," she said. "They could help us?"

Byron put his hand on her shoulder. "Those tugs won't stop for nobody. Can't. Those barges don't have breaks."

"What, then?"

"You really thinkin' what I think you are?" Byron whispered.

"It's already happening in my mind."

"Can we intercept it in time?"

"If I judge it right. Dangerous, though."

Byron chewed his lip. "Well, this ain't exactly a safety zone we're in now."

"Please tell me," Kate asked again.

"It's a tugboat," Byron said. "With a long cable towing a barge or scow behind it."

"Yes?"

Then Clay spoke: "Byron, keep your eye on the tug. Kate, keep your eye on that boat behind us. Call out its every move. That tug you see is moving fast. Eight or nine knots, I'd say. The cable's a quarter mile long, maybe more. Tug needs that distance for the barge to slow down and stop. And to separate the barge from the tug's wake and backward propeller wash. Anyway, I aim to keep Pickett behind me and to cut in front of that tug. Close. Real close. Too close for Pickett to make it. If it works, he'll have to run along-side the tug and cable, or turn back behind it. We won't lose him, but we'll put more space between us. Probably double our lead. Give us what we need to round Tangier light. I can pick up more distance there, as well as off Smith Island. I know those shallows."

Kate nodded, taking in what he was saying. "Will it work?"

"Might work."

"The man's in his zone," Byron muttered under his breath. "It'll work."

Clay stayed on the tiller, keeping track of the steady progress of the tug and the water and waves. He felt the wind and tide, and sensed the distance, and gauged with his deeper instinct the time and point of conjunction, and pushed forward, angling, adjusting course with imperceptible pressures of his hand, moving north now more than east. He had less than thirty minutes, he believed, before Pickett would have him in range. Less than thirty minutes to intersect and cross in front of the tug, which would crush the *Miss Sarah* into pieces if he came too close. He pushed on.

Byron watched the tug with the binoculars, reporting her progress in a steady stream of talk. They rode the waves, and time seemed to pass quickly. They could see the Tangier light directly off their bow, though it was still far away. The moon moved with them overhead. But Clay's attention remained on the tug, its lights becoming brighter as it drew closer, its turbine now clanging eerily in the distance, mixing with the other sounds of the night. It would keep to the center of the deep channel, he was sure, and he knew where the channel veered. He plotted the tug's course in his mind and marked the place where he would meet it. Kate reported periodically that Pickett was gaining but remained directly astern. Clay knew that Pickett was gaining, but he also knew that Pickett had no way to stop this from working. If he could time it right. That was what mattered.

He ran northeasterly until the lights of the tugboat were bright and the outline of its smokestacks rose against the sky to starboard. He came abreast of it and knew its wake would be huge if the *Vena Lee* got behind it. The barge had running lights that showed its presence, seemingly so far behind the tug that pulled it. They looked like Christmas lights moving on the water. A novice would never know the cable was there, in the dark, low on the water, until it was too late. But that was too much to hope for with Pickett.

Byron and Kate sat mesmerized as Clay took them closer to the path of the oncoming tugboat, the giant powerhouse looming just off their starboard bow, its engine's roar now blotting out all other sounds, churning on a collision course with them, the black-bladed hull cutting like a monstrous chisel through the inky water, sending out a seething white wake of spume and spray. Clay ran with his lights off, doing nothing to cause the tug to change course. But behind them, realizing Clay's maneuver, Pickett was flashing the spotlight, running with his lights on, and sounding his horn—which was all but drowned out by the boom of the approaching turbine—hoping to cause the tug to fall off and give him a chance to get across its path as well. But the tug never flinched, moving inexorably forward as they watched, and Clay took the *Miss Sarah* across its path not three boat lengths from its iron-girded bow. It rose above them sharp like an ax blade and bore down on them without pause or mercy. Clay prayed that his bateau would hold steady, and she did and was in and across the tug's path and running past while he angled easterly to escape its wake. The tugboat sliced by and just behind them close enough to almost touch, and its wake hit the stern like a wave rolling in off a reef, lifting the bateau high and sending her bow crashing down and then up, then sending water cascading over the stern rail and onto her floor. Clay steadied her while Byron vented a whoop of relief, nearly drowned out by the turbine, and Kate clung to Clay as he watched the *Vena Lee* bouncing in the wake on the other side of the cable, unable, at least for the moment, to follow them.

With his lead regained, Clay set a course northeasterly, inside the Tangier light toward waters he knew, and where he knew it was too shallow for Pickett to follow. Pickett would have to circumnavigate the island's shoal, losing more distance. Once Clay cleared the point, he would head north and skirt the shallows off Smith Island, again where Pickett wouldn't follow. Clay was confident he could now maintain his lead past Crisfield and up off the southwestern edge of Deal Island, where he could slip Kate and Byron off at the shoal and they could wade or crawl to land near the town of Wenona. He watched Pickett's boat maneuvering to go behind the barge. The *Vena Lee* was momentarily moving south and falling farther away.

Kate had her hand on Clay's shoulder. She was watching his face as he turned away from his pursuers, studying the waters ahead. "What are you thinking?" she asked.

Clay motioned to Byron, who took the tiller. "I'm thinking what I want is to get you to a safe place. I'm also thinking about Matty."

"I was thinking of him too." She let her hand drop, brushing down his arm. "He told me why he fought with his father." She eased slightly closer, concern filling her eyes. "I'm sorry, Clay. They fought over your wharf."

"Ah, Kate. Jesus."

"Clay, it's not your fault." She pressed her forehead against him and kissed his shoulder. "He's probably worried, though. Right now."

"At least he doesn't know enough about this whole thing with Pickett to be really worried. Or, unfortunately, to call the police. He may still be sitting in your cottage waiting for you."

"Or looking for me."

"You can tell him I'm sorry. When all this is over."

Kate searched his face. "That's something we can tell him together."

She reached to touch him again, and he pulled her against him and felt her warmth. He held her and then sat with her on the washboard, his arm tight around her, and none of the three spoke as they continued running east.

When they neared the southern spit of Tangier Island, Clay retook the helm, and studying the landmarks and remembering the distances and depths, he ran a straight course inside the light, transecting the long shoal where the chart showed only three to four feet of water. He slowed enough for Byron to drop the plumb several times, and the line consistently measured three and a half feet.

"I think you got her," Byron finally said.

Clay whispered a prayer as they continued through and then cleared the shallows. All the time he kept an eye on Pickett, who stayed near the channel, looping outside and around the shoal and light, falling farther behind.

Once in deeper water, Clay pointed north and they ran up Tangier Sound. After a while he asked Byron to retrieve the rain slicker from the front locker, and Byron went forward.

"What's up your sleeve, now, Clay Wakeman?" Kate whispered. She kissed his cheek.

"Get us all safe, is all."

He heard Byron coming back and turned and took the olive rain pants from him and held them out to Kate.

"Put these on."

She hesitated. "Why? What for?"

"They'll protect your legs."

Kate didn't move.

"Up ahead there's another shoal, comes out from the edge of Deal Island. You and Byron are going to slip over the side into about three feet of water and get to shore. The boat behind will keep following me."

She stepped away. "No. That's crazy. We're not leaving you."

"You have to go to call the police. I'll either outrun them till the police show up, or I'll slip over the side, same as you, just up the Bay some."

Raising her arm, Kate pointed to the distant lights of Crisfield. "Why not just take the boat over there, into that town? We've got a good head start now. We could run to the police. Or hide."

"Pickett's got a radio on board, Kate. It's a public airway, and he's got to be careful, but he might have men onshore in that truck, with guns. Maybe more than one truck. He's known for quite a while we were heading for the eastern side. If we pull into Crisfield harbor and his men are waiting for us, we're all done. There's no way out by water but how you go in. And even if his men aren't there, I'm not sure anyone'd be around to help us. Not at this time of night. We'd only have a few minutes, and Pickett'd be on us. This way, I know we'll all make it."

"Byron," she pleaded. "Talk to him."

Clay's eyes turned and held those of his friend.

"He'll be all right, Kate." Byron's voice was firm. "He's got the Bay slidin' in him. He's way ahead of those fellas out here on that. I don't want to leave him either. But he's right."

Motioning for Byron to take the tiller, Clay took the rain jacket from him and led Kate forward. He held her close against his chest and whispered to her that he loved her and that she needed to trust him now, that there was no time to lose. He told her that he'd catch up with her soon and they would figure all of this out somehow. Then he was quiet and they just held each other. When she nodded, she had tears in her eyes. He helped her put on the rain gear and tied the pants tight, and then he kissed her, her face wet and salty.

"You don't really need the pants," Clay told her. "But they'll protect you if there are nettles. The bottom might be soft but together you'll make it. Just keep your body low in the water and crab-crawl together the first hundred yards or so. Stay together. Stay within touching distance. Don't look back, as your face might reflect the light. Don't talk. Let Byron lead you."

He opened the engine box and scooped some dirt and grease off the compartment side with his fingers. He held Kate's face with one hand and smeared the dark mixture on her cheeks and forehead. He nodded to Byron, who put some on his face as well.

"Looks good on you, Byron," Clay said. "Definitely an improvement."

Along Smith Island, Clay steered as close as he dared to the eastern flats, and Pickett again was forced to give a wider berth to the shallows, losing some of the distance he had made up since entering Tangier Sound. Clay held Kate's hand as they cut through the current, back into deeper water, climbing north. They could hear the James Island horn. The lights of Crisfield, to the east, cast a halo in the night sky over the marshy land, and the green and red beacons, pulsing in the dark, out ahead across the water, tracing the channels to safe harbor, seemed to be part of a mysterious pattern, so pure and colored with promise, if only one could find the code. They watched transfixed as the lights passed by them, and soon they were crossing between the mouth of the Big Annemessex River and Kedges Straits. Behind them the *Vena Lee* was running once again without lights. The *Miss Sarah* ran hard, with her wake falling off, the sea air freshening, until Clay saw in the darkness the looming stand of pines that defined the tip of Deal Island.

He continued on until he was adjacent to the ground off Wenona.

"Throw over a plumb line," Clay told Byron.

As Byron dropped the plumb line over the side, they watched several geese rise from the dark background of the island into the sky.

"Four feet," Byron reported.

Clay turned slightly northwest. He pointed. "That's where you're going. There's a boat landing and a dirt road, and some farmhouses along the way. It's a short walk into Wenona. Find a house and call for help." He eased back on the throttle. "Throw it again," he asked Byron.

"Three feet."

"Byron, give 'em everybody—Brigman, Longley, the works."

"You'll be there with me, Clay. Right?"

"Right behind you."

"Least this way Brigman won't get Pecks."

"No, he won't," Clay whispered.

Clay throttled back and put the engine into neutral. Still holding Kate's hand, he led her over to the starboard stern. He raised his hand with hers and brushed her cheek. Then Byron came up and took her arm. The two men faced each other. They didn't speak. Clay motioned for them to go and helped Kate follow Byron as they slipped over the rail and slid into the waist-deep water. "Take care of each other," he whispered to them as the *Miss Sarah* coasted away.

He watched them begin to move landward, and then he turned harder toward the west and increased his speed again. Waiting until their heads had faded into the darkness over the water, he picked up the flashlight and flashed it as he pushed farther west to give his pursuers a clear picture of his position. They would adjust course to keep straight behind him, he knew, taking them farther away from the swimmers. Peering behind him, he saw that Pickett, once again, was closing the distance.

He checked his fuel. The one tank was gone and the other low. The engine was hot. He placed the flare gun next to him and positioned the bottle explosive upright behind a rail shelf next to the tiller. They provided little comfort. Neither would be of much use against guns, he knew. He needed to lose Pickett or get off.

He ran northwest past the marshy shore off Bloodsworth Island, setting a course through Hooper Strait, but he sensed the straining engine was beginning to tire. The moon had set and yet the sky refused to darken. Dawn was not far off. His vague hope that he might make home waters was impossible, he realized, and had been all along. Opening the port hatch, he located a light line. He figured he would head out, up through Hooper Strait, and maybe find some watermen coming out from the Hooper Islands. If not, he would tie the tiller off tight, aiming the bateau for the marsh, slide over the side off the western shoal, and swim for the town of Hoopersville. The bar was wide and shallow. If Pickett didn't see him, he could swim to the bar and crawl to shore and find his way to safety. It was the right plan, he concluded. He pushed forward, thinking that Byron and Kate were probably ashore now and on their way to call for help.

But Pickett was closer, and he was shining his spot. Not just shining it, but blinking it at him. Clay looked around. Why was he blinking the spot on and off at him? He turned and watched it. He looked away, but it kept on, and he looked back. And then it came to him. It was code. They were sending the pattern of short and long flashes of light used by marine vessels to communicate. Morse code. With rising fear he finally began to read and translate and to decipher the message.

W-E-H-A-V-E-M-A-T-T, he made out. WE HAVE MATT. He sensed the rest as he figured it out: STOP NOW OR WE KILL.

He felt the sickness as it came up from his belly. He tasted it. He found his flashlight. His mind retraced the events. Matty must have followed Kate to the marina. And they had taken him in their pickup on their way to the boat. He saw his own hand on the flashlight. It was shaking. He took deep breaths to calm himself. He looked around. He could get off and swim. They'd follow the boat. He snapped his head back. He needed to get closer to shore, he knew, closer to the shoal, to the sandbar off Hoopersville. He turned slightly north and began to flash a message back. He did it slowly, inexpertly, intentionally confusing the lights, buying time. Tried it again. Confused it.

Short flash, long flash, short flash. That was the first letter, R. He went on. REPEAT MESSAGE, he finally sent. REPEAT. OVER.

They repeated the message. He tried again to send a confusing signal, the *Miss Sarah* running hard. He garbled it, then started it again. He was closer to the shoal now.

They interrupted him with another series of flashes. He deciphered the message as it came. TIME UP. STOP OR WE KILL.

Clay turned his running lights on as an answer and quickly threw over the plumb line. Four and a half feet. He ran for another minute. Four feet. Then, cutting the engine, he let the *Miss Sarah* glide forward. He grabbed the cleaning knife from the tackle box and ripped open a white flotation cushion, stuffing it into one of Pickett's crab pots. It would absorb the water at the tear and become heavy. Closer now, across the bar, the land point of Hoopersville was visible in the swirling predawn mist. A breach of light flared above the eastern horizon. The sun would soon surface. Positioning himself behind the engine box, with the flare gun and gas-filled bottle within reach, he watched the *Vena Lee* approach. He held up a package of the cocaine with one hand, the rest of his body protected by the rail and engine box. The larger boat cut back her engine. She idled forward and turned parallel to him. The man with the ponytail stood on the bow, aiming a shotgun at Clay.

Another sat on the cabin roof, with a large pistol, held in both hands, pointed in his direction. A man in the stern was holding Matty, a shotgun barrel stuck under his chin. Pickett was at the tiller. The cabin windows were dark, but Clay could see the outline of two figures inside it.

"Game's over," Pickett snarled. "You're good, I'll hand you, but the game is over."

"I'll work a trade," Clay quickly shouted. "Otherwise the dope goes overboard now. We're all drifting. You'll never find it."

"No trade. Where are the others?" Pickett shouted.

"In the cabin, where I told them to stay," Clay answered. "We're armed too," he added.

"Tell them to show themselves."

"No, sir." Clay's voice was firm. "Trade or don't trade. Your choice. Dope's going overboard." Clay waited. "I mean it. Now!" he shouted.

"Hold on," Pickett answered.

The cabin door opened. Mac Longley walked out, shutting the door behind him. He seemed nervous.

"Take it easy, Clay. Just calm down." He held his hands out, palms toward Clay, skittish. "Think about where you are, here. People I work for have given you every chance. They'll give you one more. Just turn it over."

"Longley, goddamn you."

"Come on, Clay. I'm here to help you. It was me finally figured you'd know Morse code."

Clay shook his head. "Why are you here, Longley? What are you doing down here? Aren't you out of your league?"

"Superbig shipment, Clay. Biggest ever. Everybody's in on it."

"Shut up about that," Pickett told him.

Longley wiped his face. He looked scared.

"Let Matty swim over here, Mac. He's not part of this."

"Listen, Clay. The man here gave you every warning. Every

chance to move, or leave. You not only didn't leave, you stole his shit. What wasn't yours. Still, you do what they say, things'll work out. Understand? Otherwise this is way over my head, man."

No one spoke.

"All right," Pickett wheezed again. "Enough. You've said enough. Where's the rest of the dope, mister?"

"In my hands and laying at my feet," Clay shouted. "It will all be in the water in seconds if Matty isn't let go."

Clay saw Pickett hesitate, undecided. He glanced toward the shadowed figure remaining in the cabin.

"Put Matty in the water." Clay didn't want to give them any more time to consider. "Let him swim over to this boat. Once he gets here, I'll drop your crab pot, full with your packages, over the side and back off. You can retrieve it. We'll forget this ever happened."

Clay saw the man in the cabin flick his hand. A moment later they had pushed Matty in the water. "Swim, you," one of them yelled at him.

"Any more tricks, he dies. Then you die," Pickett wheezed. "We're done playin'."

Keeping his head down, Clay crawled over to the nearside rail, holding one of the packages above him. Rising up slightly, he started speaking to Matty, encouraging him to swim. As he got closer, swimming the breaststroke and coughing out water, Clay told him to swim around to the back side. Matty seemed to ignore him, and Clay told him again. "Swim around the stern, Matty, to the far side, or I won't let you up, goddamnit."

Matty heard and worked his way around the stern, Clay following him by scuttling along inside the bateau, staying low, beneath the top of the gunnel. On the far side, Matty grabbed flailingly at the rail. The oversize engine box blocked them from the view of the men on the *Vena Lee*. Clay stopped Matty from trying to climb on board, pushing him back and trying to calm him. Pointing toward the land and the lights, he handed Matty a life preserver. "Matty, you swim that way, now. You're on a shoal. A wide one. Another fifty yards, you'll be in three feet of water and they can't follow you. Stay low and swim. Once you touch bottom, stay low in the water and crawl. You'll get to land. There's a town there."

Matty's face was pallid, with bruises on one cheek and around his forehead. He was coughing and scared. "Where's Kate?" he asked.

"She's safe," Clay whispered. "With Byron. They escaped. Now you go. Swim."

He hesitated. "Why?"

Clay paused. He didn't know just how far the question went. There wasn't time to answer. He wasn't sure if he had an answer. "Go," Clay implored. "Swim now. I'll be in and coming right after you. Trust me."

"Trust you?" But Matty's eyes registered. They were frightened but steady, boring into Clay's eyes, and acknowledged his help. Matty turned and started swimming away, hidden by the *Miss Sarah* from the sight of the men in the other boat.

"Where is he, goddamnit," Pickett yelled. "Show yourself."

Clay stood up, most of his body still protected by the engine box. "He can't get in the boat. He's hurt. He's holding on the side. He's too heavy to lift."

"What a shame. Well, now you best throw us the crab pot, mister."

Clay gambled for time. "Why don't you tell Brigman to come on out and say hello?"

"Throw the dope over," Pickett repeated.

"Tell him to come out and join the party."

Pickett leered at Clay. "I'd heard you were smart. But guess not. You talk too much."

"The man's a coward, Pickett. He won't face me."

The cabin door opened. It was Brigman who stepped out. The

men on the boat all turned to look at him. He crossed his arms, then uncrossed them and pointed at Clay. "You shouldn't have fucked with this, Clay." His voice was like ice and carried over the water. "You're a goddamn thief. Throw what's mine over now. Otherwise I'll tell them to shoot."

"If I throw it, then what?" Clay answered.

Brigman stared him down. "I won't repeat myself, boy."

Clay considered. "Take your guns off me, first."

Brigman hesitated.

"I mean it. I'll waste this stuff so fast."

Brigman nodded to Pickett, who motioned for his men to lower their guns. They did so, except for the one on the roof.

Clay pointed to him. Slowly he relaxed, placing the pistol down at his side.

Clay took a breath. Then nodded. "Okay," he answered. "Okay. Hold on." Remaining behind the engine box, he acted as though he were opening the crab pot and putting in the white packages. He took his time and watched Matty, who was moving gradually away. Clay finally stood up, holding just the top portion of the pot above the engine box. "I'll start my motor now and drop this overboard. Then I'll back away."

"No," Brigman commanded. "No motor. Just throw it out here. We'll hook it in."

Clay raised one hand. "Whatever," he said. Using the buoy and warp line as a sling, he heaved the pot with the ripped white preserver in it out between the two boats. Pickett backed up and then came forward close to the buoy. From the side of the *Vena Lee*, one of the men extended a boat hook out over the water to retrieve the float. As the man pulled it in, Clay eased lower behind the engine box, praying for Matty to swim, to go. Clay looked back and saw him make the bar and on his knees in the shallows. Brigman, Pickett, and his men were focused on the buoy in the water. One of them grabbed the buoy and they had the line and were pulling up the pot, all watching it break the surface. It came over the side as Clay reached for the flare gun. He wheeled and fired it at them just as they reached the wire pot and saw the preserver inside, and then he dropped to the deck as pistol bullets and shot splintered across the rail and engine box. His flare had broken through the window and ignited their cabin. He could see and hear the flames. Lying behind the engine box, he reloaded his second and last flare. Splinters were flying around him as the guns pumped a fusillade along his deck. He lit the rag on the gas-filled bottle. Throw it and dive in the water, he told himself. He reached his left hand up over the engine box and fired the second flare blindly. The guns ceased momentarily, and he reared back and heaved the lit bottle at the *Vena Lee,* but in his follow-through, a searing heat tore into his abdomen and he heard the echo of the pistol and then the explosion of the gas bomb. The impact knocked him back on the deck, and the pain was there now, below, and at first he wasn't sure, but he felt with his fingers and knew. He heard more shots and shouting and commotion with the fire, and he felt the wet around his belly flowing over him and onto the deck like warm grease. Then, in the distance, he heard sirens on the water. The men in the boat near him heard them also and were cursing, and he heard their engine engage and the acceleration as they moved off. He lay and reached his hand up and with all his strength pulled his head over the rail to look for Matty. He saw him, far off, wading across the bar headed for land, and then Clay let himself collapse back on the deck. Pulling his shirt off took him forever with the grinding pain below. He tried to tie the shirt around his middle to stop the bleeding, but the blood seeped around and through the cloth. Listening, he heard the sirens out in the Bay coming closer.

He felt the drift of his boat and sensed that the tide was taking him out into deeper water, pulling him south. Above him the gray dawn transformed itself moment by moment as he gazed into blue morning. A dull ache flowed over the pain he had felt, and he was tired, his eyelids heavy. He struggled to hold them open to see, lying on the wooden deck, adrift, and feeling the rocking of deeper water as his *Miss Sarah* moved along in the strong current. Trying to keep his eyes open, he thought of Matty, saw his face horrified back at the cottage and then white and frightened in the water. He was sorry. But he also knew that he hadn't had the power within him to stop loving Kate and that saying no to it had not been a possibility for him. Overhead he heard a cry and opened his eyes, which had shut, and saw gulls whirling, their feathery white bodies luminous in the dawn. He listened to them crying.

Clay shifted and tried to think and supposed the tide was carrying him out above Smith Island. He smiled inwardly at the thought that he was drifting somewhere near the place on his father's chart marking the wreck. Maybe even floating right above it, his Pappy's dream, and his as well, in the water just below him. He could almost see it there. And he thought he could see his own shocked boy's face in that living room so long ago. His face, Matty's. He listened to the creak and drift of his boat. It was the waves now, and the breeze above, and the lapping water on the wooden boat, and the gulls. Then, in the distance, he heard another siren. Coming closer. They were coming for him, his Pappy at the helm. He would be saved. He would set things right, begin anew, ply the river, a waterman, like his father. A waterman on the river. A decent life. A fresh start. In a clean, abundant Bay. And so with the sirens coming and these thoughts washing over him, he felt his own heart pumping and his blood running and the motion of the boat in the current, all with the same rhythm. In the blue air above the mix of river and ocean, the gulls were crying. Whirling in the ether of a new dawn above him. White gulls over the blue Bay.

He remembers the sound of their footsteps on the mud and grass and weeds. There was the lapping of the river and the occasional brush of swamp grass in the wind. But mostly there was the darkness and the mist and the quiet. The mist and quiet. The mist above all . . .

He was excited . . .

Acknowledgments

Special and particular thanks to my editor, Shannon Ravenel, for her sense of this book, her instincts, and her enormous assistance. I am grateful, also, to my agents, Robbie Anna Hare and Ron Goldfarb, for their belief and constant support. To Stephen Goodwin, who became an early reader and source of encouragement, I am most appreciative, and to Louise Wheatley for her initial review. I thank Lowry Hudgins for his tour of Mobjack Bay, Rachel Careau for her fine copyediting, and, with great esteem, all the people at Algonquin Books.

To those friends—present and lost—who have inspired and nurtured the seeds of this story I will always remain indebted. And, likewise, to Kristin, Isabel, and William Junkin for providing the ballast I needed and so much more.